ASCENDERS SKYPUNCH

Book Two

ASCENDERS
SKYPUNCH
BOOK TWO

C.L. GABER

This book is a work of fiction. Any references to historical events, real people or real locales are used fictitiously. Other names, characters, places and incidents are products of the author's imagination, and any resemblance to actual events or locales or persons, living or dead, is entirely coincidental.

Interior Formatted by

E.M. TIPPETTS BOOK DESIGNS

emtippettsbookdesigns.com

BOOKS BY C. L. GABER

Jex Malone

Ascenders Series

Ascenders

Ascenders: Skypunch (Book Two)

Coming Soon: *Ascenders: Omorrow* (Book Three)

Coming Soon: *The Claires* (An Ascenders Novella)

To Ron—You always bring the love and light. LYM.

There are two great days in a person's life.
The day we were born.
And the day we discover why.

—William Barclay

You can't shut off the risk and pain
Without losin' the love that remains.
We're all riders on this train.

—Bruce Springsteen

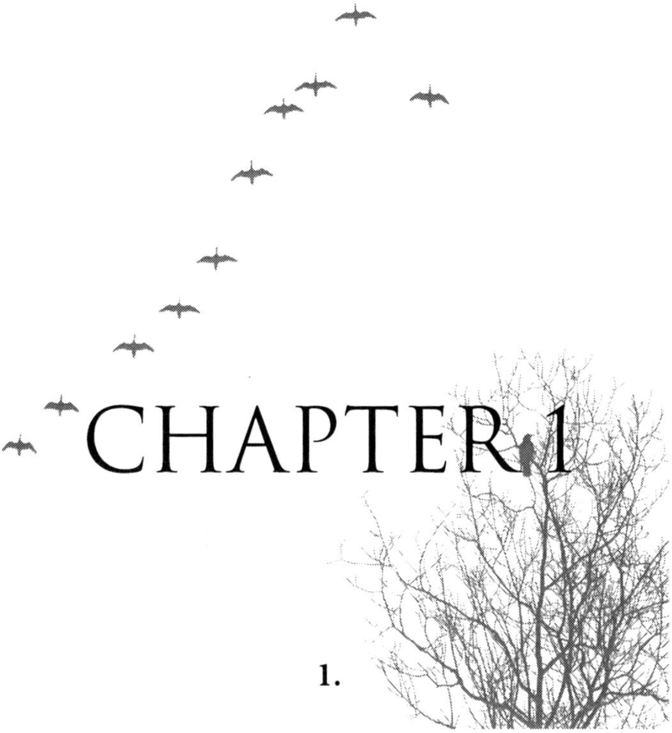

CHAPTER 1

1.

I have never been much of a back-talker.

Occasionally when I did let my mouth run on full tilt, my mother would send me to bed without dinner while it was still light outside, even on those endless summer days that refused to slide gracefully into the first murky blots of night sky.

All alone, I would sit and count the seconds until dawn when I could resume my normal nothing specialness. That was the worst of it, but what did I know back when I was alive?

Before I ascended.

Being dead at seventeen is a lot like being sent to bed before it's dark outside. You're not sure what you're missing, but you're sure that you're missing something.

My name is Walker Callaghan. Nice to meet you—but you'll never meet me. It happened a little over three months ago when my crushed body took a header out of the back window of my mother's little blue Honda. Like those tiny August hummingbirds, I took flight—then landed with a thud, headfirst, limbs mangled in a ditch, glistening with fresh, freakish September snowfall.

Hey, I don't want you to get out a crying towel. It's not your fault.

By the way, my so-called afterlife isn't half-bad. I faced it without saying a word. No back talk.

Why not pitch a fit?

The truth is simple. Since I've been gone—*expired, dead, finito, over and out, a flatliner, gone, baby, gone*—I've never felt more alive.

2.

For those of you who fear death, it's also simple.

Just say to yourself, "Okay, here it is—the thing I have always feared."

You can't ditch it or duck it, so meet it head on. Get to know it. Fill in the blanks. How big is it? How strong is it? How many parts does it have? How many arms, tentacles, and secret limbs reaching out? Then you just jump into the pain, howl, and get on with it.

I got on with it.

This is what I've learned (so far) being dead: Life is a blur and then afterward . . . it all comes into focus. In death, I found love. On strangely warm winter nights in the Midst, as we call it, when Daniel Reid's lips are on mine, honestly, I can't imagine being anywhere else.

I don't mean to get emotional on you, but such is the plight of a ghost in love.

I was only two days dead when I met him, a fellow death dweller, and my heart burst open for the first time. It was immortally etched in my mind: A broad-shouldered rebel in a black leather jacket blasted into my first class of afterlife high school. He was rugged, with a tiny scar that ran the length of his top lip and several light-green tattoos sneaking out of tight sleeves.

"Pay attention, Callaghan. You might learn something," he said with freezing calm, running a hand through jet-black hair that was shorter on the sides than the top. It looked recklessly hand-combed off a masculine, square face that was marked by about a day's growth of facial stubble—you could barely see it, but the shadow was there and it made him look older, and darker.

And dangerous. In all the right ways.

He told me you can't die twice.

What he showed me is that you can . . . die again and again. In your heart.

3.

Months later, Daniel and I have just returned from a little field trip we took back to the living realm, which is utterly forbidden here. We did this despite the dire and desperate warnings of everyone in charge including our beloved principal at the Academy, Dr. Marvin King. He warned us that we must never even think about going back to life, let alone engage in actual long-distance realm traveling. "There are severe consequences to your immortal soul," Dr. King warned us.

Frankly, it sounded like a load of BS.

At our age, immortality could wait.

We had no choice but to realm-jump back to where we once

belonged to find Daniel's youngest brother Bobby, an earthbound spirit, trapped at the sight of his death. He didn't arrive here with the rest of the Reid family children who punched out in a plane crash. A lost baby bird, Bobby Reid was begging to be found.

We were *all* home now. Safe.

I made it back first, my shaking right hand pushing through the portal and firmly holding a much, much smaller one that belonged to a six-year-old hellion. For a horrifying hour, I didn't think Daniel had made it back to this realm and was stuck on the living side with demons so fierce they could extinguish everything that *was* and *is* you.

"Callaghan, you're the only one who could break me into a million pieces," he grunted when I finally saw him, all two-hundred-twenty-pound, six-foot-two, lean, mean, tat-covered, precarious, authority-defying, beautiful, whole molecules that made up Daniel Reid.

He simply stepped out from behind a tall oak tree in torn jeans, a mud-caked black tee, and his shit-kicking black boots. I would never be sure exactly how he fought off so many devils that were out for their predawn hunt. I figured it was dogged determination mixed with an alarming attitude and a hint of stupid luck. Wasn't that always the win? With platinum-grade willpower, Daniel had muscled his way back to this side.

But there is no resting in peace for us. Falling in love is the most terrifying and electrifying thing you can do in this or any other realm. Here, like everywhere, there are no guarantees on how long you will stay. The eternal mystery isn't solved in death.

It remains.

CHAPTER 2

1.

Our neighborhood in the Midst looked like any other charming, suburban slice of small-town America. There were blood-orange terra-cotta pots at the end of the blacktop driveways and the chalky pots housed ruby-red geraniums that defied the winter chill. Flags of different nationalities and sports teams hung with pride from posts on the brightly painted garages used as canvases for art students.

It was dinnertime on Christmas Day and I wondered if Bertha and Izayah, our friends from school who were babysitting Daniel's siblings, made any kind of dinner. I was so hungry that those geraniums looked mighty tasty, but I refrained. Here, no one touched your stuff. It was civilized. It was the home you dream about when you're alive.

I had other visions of loveliness.

In my split-second daydream, Bertha was basting a juicy

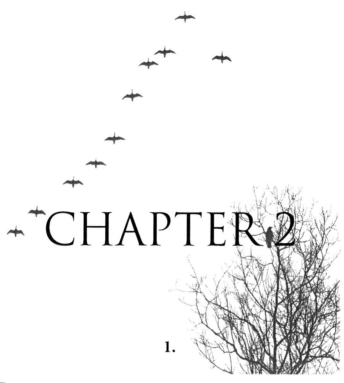

turkey and using the drippings to make gravy while Andy and Jenna smashed up some sweet potatoes for a pie. It had only been about an hour since I had dropped Bobby off in the loving arms of his family before I had trance-walked alone to the Academy thinking Daniel was lost forever.

And now that he was back, and we were walking home together, small hand in protective one, the best Christmas present of all would be a night with the family. It didn't matter if there was buttermilk biscuits and pumpkin pie fresh out of the oven. I didn't care if Izayah cut down a tall evergreen from the nearby woods and dragged it into our living room. I banished any thoughts of the Reids having sparkling ornaments or a graceful, thoughtful angel for the top of the tree—which seemed like an odd concept now. Were there actually angel ornaments in *this* of all places?

Daniel lifted me off the ground and swooped me up into his strong arms as our street, Burning Tree Court, came into full view. His mouth was soft and warm when it touched mine. His face was harsh plains while his eyes were silver-gray like an early morning sky before the sun began to bleed its presence. He held my weight as if he was picking up a child, and I circled my hands around his rock-solid neck.

Daniel's intense gaze lingered on my face as he carried me past an apple tree, blooming with fat, white, spring flowers. My long, stick-straight brown hair caught on a breeze that made the tree rain down sugary-scented petals, creating a flower blizzard. The petals floated into a front yard onto tender green grass that was peeking through a thin blanket of snow. (Even old-man Harry Volkman at Action News back in Chicago couldn't figure out *this* ecosystem.)

Jeff and Mark, fraternal twins on our street and victims of a defective ski lift at age sixteen, had wound about a thousand Christmas lights around a plum tree and it was a wonder it didn't catch on fire—although a few flames (or an inferno) couldn't hurt any of us. A Christmas tree blinked merrily in their bay window while a fat, blow-up Santa sat proudly on the front porch wearing a T-shirt flaunting a dancing, rose-crowned skeleton. Rumor was that a visiting teacher, Jerry G, would be making the rounds with some music students for a little caroling tonight. It gave new meaning to the grateful dead.

Not too many people on our block had cars here because we walked everywhere. The families who arrived (or died) together had actual houses. The rest of the student body lived up the hill at the Academy where the dorm rooms were lush and inviting with ginormous fireplaces, king-sized beds, and comforters that were a *hundred thousand* thread count—made in places unknown. Kindly Miss Maude Travis, a Mary Poppins for the ages, proved to be the best and kindest dorm mother and orientation advisor. She also made a mean cup of chamomile tea during an emotional crisis.

In a complete switch of fate, Daniel and I were the parents now, taking care of *the kids*—his younger brothers and sisters: Peter, fifteen; Jenna, thirteen; Andy, eleven; and now six-year-old Bobby, too. I didn't plan on having a family at age seventeen, but life, not to mention death, didn't run according to my agenda.

When I was alive, I thought about mundane things like senior year, my editorship of the school newspaper, getting into the college of my choice, and being asked to prom. I was well beyond the prom now, and satisfied with what I had found on the other side.

By the time we made it to our driveway, the people I loved fiercely now were out on the porch waiting for any kind of news.

First, they spotted the tall force of nature that was their biggest brother hoisting me down the street and they went absolutely apeshit. Pete stuck his neck up to the sky and let out a long, happy, super-loud wolf howl as he barreled toward us, followed by Andy and Jenna who were streaming projectile tears as they raced at top speed, and tackled Daniel to the snowy ground. Somehow he had managed to seat me in a snow pile before allowing them to take him down to ground zero, the girls rolling over his chest like two thin, but unbreakable twigs.

Formerly MIA Bobby did what any six-year-old would do under the circumstances. He sat on his brother's head and threatened that he would turn on his own personal fart machine. I smiled and then laughed loudly as our dog, Jake, made good on that threat and then rolled in the mud. "He's the best, grossest, dirtiest dog in the history of the world," Bobby said with glee. "He can even out-fart *me*!"

It was the best, grossest, dirtiest welcome-back in history.

2.

It turns out our celebration was just beginning. The next round featured a former inmate at the Institute for Troubled Teens, aka ITT, a grim afterlife penitentiary for wayward teens. Fierce and loyal, Bertha stuck her sweet, round face out of our screen door and all three hundred and fifty pounds of her shook like she was staging her own personal earthquake. "Jesus, Mary, and Joseph," she began to cry. "Christmas miracle. Thank you to the father, the son, and every single ghost in between them."

Next came the waterworks because she never thought she would see Daniel and me again. She was wearing the cutest red Santa apron I had ever seen in my life, proving that there was a Forever 21 in the afterlife. Now that we were back, she could focus on what really mattered to her.

"I got it all on the table and it's gettin' cold," Bertha said matter-of-factly, blowing her nose in her sleeve. "Got the turkey, sweet potatoes, biscuits, collards. I'm not much of a hockey goalie, but I'm one hell of a cook. C'mon, everybody. C'mon, Walk-*her*," she said. Bertha had been an inner-city Harlem girl who started at ITT as a minor-league girl gang member in need of some redemption. The Higher Authority, our governing board in the afterlife, wisely decided that a girl with no chances in life should be given a second chance in death. She ended up paroled and sent to the Academy, which was lucky for me because now I counted her as one of my best friends.

"Come on, Danny Boy. I don't know whethers to feed you or bandage you. I don't even want to knows what that green stuff is on your jeans. Izzy stop acting like the fool that I know you are! Run to their room and get Daniel some new pants. Everybody, it's Christmas and we're not getting any younger," she ordered.

Handsome Izayah poked his head out from around her. He was Daniel's wingman on our championship hockey team, the Academy Aces.

"I never thought I'd see you two idiots again," Izayah said to us, rounding Bertha, and jumping down the two wooden stairs to toss me over his shoulder like a sack of potatoes. Laughing as I swung through the air, I struggled to get down, but he was a six-foot-four wall of steel with the looks of a much younger Denzel Washington, but less of a life expectancy after fighting childhood leukemia. He died at seventeen at eighty-two pounds. Now, he was whole again—and very rambunctious.

Our arrival was cause for a celebration and Daniel lifted a grinning Bobby into the air and let out a loud howl that had the little boy wiggling with delight.

"Going back to life means one thing. I'm starving," Daniel said.

"I'm not eating my collar," Bobby whispered, pointing to

Bertha. "She said that she cooked us collars. And she needs to hug me less. She keeps squishing me. I'm gonna barf, Danny."

"Not collar—collards. And you need some meat on your baby bones," Bertha said as she ushered us inside. "I've never seen such a skinny bunch of dead bones. At ITT, those kids licked the plates—and that was the foulest grub in any realm. This meal is gor—"

"Gourmet," I jumped in knowing her education ended at the sixth grade. Bertha's life had been shuffled more times than a worn deck of playing cards.

"Come on, Julia Child," I said to her, knowing she knew that name because nutty Julia was actually our latest Home Economics teacher. Yes, Jules was a still little loopy—or drunk on cooking sherry—with that high-pitched voice and annoyingly positive attitude, not to mention her obsession with foul-smelling French cheeses, but everyone simply adored her. I wasn't sure how much Bertha had learned from her, but the signs were good from the smells sneaking out from the kitchen.

"Let's eat. Realm jumping has made me starved," I said.

"I have hungry tums! I've had nothing since we raided Walker's mom's fridge . . . you know, back in that other place. And she eats really healthy. Apples. Salad. Gross," Bobby interrupted, sticking a finger down his throat.

"You actually saw Walker's now *living* mother," said an unbelieving Izayah. "In the flesh. Living flesh?"

"We saw a *whole lot* I want to forget," Daniel said. "But we'll save that for a later time."

"Demons. Monsters. Ghosts. Souls exploding. *Ka-boom*! Eff me," Bobby said in a matter-of-fact voice, finishing it up quickly with a question before anyone could admonish him for the foul language he picked up during his years of being a stuck little ghost. "'Zactly where is the grub?"

"Who *exactly* did you hang out with at that airport in the living realm?" Daniel queried, mentioning Lake Forest Airport where we found the little boy lingering.

"You know, gangster guys, mobsters, a guy who played a bad guy on TV named Jimmy, my friends Cappy and Dilly, some guy who said to call him Uncle Buck," Bobby rattled off. "He said a lot of swears and had bad BO." Then he changed the subject. "Is there gonna be presents after dinner? I haven't had a real Christmas in forever. Does Santa come here? Can I have a bike? A hot tub?"

"Maybe Santa could replenish our stock of medieval weapons," Daniel said under his breath.

Izayah's eyes went wide. "Later," Daniel reminded him.

"Big mama," Bobby yelled to Bertha, and for a moment I held my breath. But her smile revealed that she loved the nickname.

"Yeah, baby string bean?" she said.

"Can I have pie with whipped cream?" Bobby asked in his scratchy, little-kid squeak. He was a spunky tyke in jeans and a red hoodie that was half-torn from our escape. His face was also still partially streaked in dirt mixed with green water from the Chicago River. Later, I'd make him take a long, long bath and then we would tuck him in.

As usual, food was the great distraction.

"I got pumpkin pie. Pecan. Chocolate. Cherry. And apple. I was so damn nervous. Cooking de-jangles my nerves," Bertha said. "And with Walker and Daniel gone, my nerves were on maximum jingle jangle."

"What are we waiting for? Big mama says eat up. Hot damn!" Bobby yelled, sneaking under her armpit to run into the house.

"Hot damn!" I repeated.

My head lifted and he had me on lock—Daniel stared at me from the front lawn that was covered in muddy patches of snow. Then he closed his eyes for just a moment in what could only be crazy, stupid relief. I took one slow, deep breath. The lilac bushes were in full bloom and filling the air with an intoxicating smell of renewal.

But instead of feeling a warm rush, a terrible chill raced around my veins. *What were the consequences of our little field trip?* Glancing down the street and past the tall evergreens, I could see the Academy, our majestic school looming large on the highest hill, an arrogant mansion jutting higher than the eye could see and slicing into the starless evening sky.

Did they know what we did?

And what would they do about it?

3.

The inside of our little white house was warm, fragrant, and smelled like my favorite holiday. The people I thought I'd never see again were joyous—like big, bad Izayah who wrapped an arm around Bertha and announced, "I'm real hungry, baby B." Bertha was so pleased that her entire being seemed to glow. I could tell that for the first time in a long time, Bertha felt as if she finally belonged to something real—something that wasn't going to reject her without any warning. She was one of us now.

Meanwhile, Izayah Spencer bellowed one of his deep, trademark laughs that sounded like the old singer Barry White was reborn. Izayah was seventeen, but sounded much older. He wore little round glasses that made him look like some ultrasmart hunk who belonged at Harvard. He had fierceness behind those specs, which made him one of the best air hockey players at the Academy. Despite his jock status, he was the kind of guy who looked past Bertha's weight to give her a genuine flirt. Even I wondered about his intentions.

Now over two hundred unstoppable pounds of pure muscle and broad shoulders, he was what our guidance counselor Miss Elizabeth dubbed a wild bull. Translation: Indestructible.

"I never see you *not* hungry," Bertha said, minutes later watching all of us fill our plates with herb-rubbed turkey, big mounds of fluffy sweet potatoes and sunshine-colored corn-bread stuffing. Daniel grabbed one of the drumsticks, savagely biting into it as Izayah took the other, which was a deal breaker for young Bobby who had been dreaming of a drumstick for far too long.

He began to pout.

"No fair," Bobby cried. "I'm the one who's been standing in a field for *like* forever. I'm real, real hungry."

"What did you do for all that time?" his sister Andy inquired, almost stopping midsentence when Bobby involuntarily shuddered.

"Hiding, mostly," he said, biting into the barbarian-sized drumstick Daniel had moved quietly onto his plate. No one asked him about it again that night and the conversation returned to the food (delicious), the company (amazing), and the joy of Christmas (even better now when we knew what could be lost).

Daniel sat by my side, gently rubbing his index finger on my knee under the table and smiling in a way that made it hard to look anywhere but at him. When he stood up to refill platters, he didn't care who noticed when he bent down to kiss the tip of my nose.

"Can you two get a room? Oh yeah, you have one. In this house," smart-aleck Pete said as he looked at us. I knew that at his age, he was more intrigued than grossed out.

"Watch yourself," Daniel bit out.

"Do I have a room?" Bobby said with a trembling lip.

I knew the answer.

"Your room has been waiting for years," Andy said, ruffing up his hair. "We drew Snoopy on the wall, but not Woodstock because we know you don't like birds or the color yellow. And we ended up with some of your toys. Your Legos arrived before you did."

Any strife between the older brothers was short-lived. Daniel lobbed a buttermilk biscuit at Pete like he was holding a baseball and throwing his trademark pitch. Pete didn't move a muscle or even look in the direction of the flaked baked glory. Lightning fast, he simply lifted his left hand and caught it as if his palm was a baseball glove and he had eyes everywhere.

"Shit," Daniel said in an admiring voice. "I don't know how you *do* that. And ever since you were a kid, too."

Daniel whipped three more biscuits at him, and each time Pete's hand was faster than the ball. He didn't even move his eyes or his head to keep track of what was being whipped. He just caught it. It was a fascinating carnival act.

"You can never get anything past him," Daniel said, laughing while Pete buttered all four rolls and ate them one after the other. He was at that age where he was a walking garbage disposal. "You are joining the hockey team this year," Daniel informed him.

"No thanks. Not for me. I might join the chess team," Pete replied, a junior-Daniel who was thinner and less muscular, but with the same flash of dark hair and cloudy-day silver eyes.

"Wonder if the debate team needs someone?" Pete pondered aloud. Despite the fact that, at fifteen, Pete was finally growing into his body, he made it perfectly clear that being a jock was the last thing on his personal development list.

Without allowing Pete to see what he was doing, Daniel had something under the table. A nanosecond later, he lifted his arm and whipped a balled-up cotton napkin at Pete, who yawned before lifting his hand to catch it.

"Damn," Daniel said.

"Damn it all to hell," Bobby repeated—and then some.

"That's enough," his two big brothers reprimanded in unison.

Reluctantly, I left them to follow Bertha into the kitchen to prepare for dessert. I had barely opened the fridge before she cornered me in the cold air and I bumped right into the three pecan pies on the second shelf. My butt was certainly laced with whipped cream now, but her planted feet weren't moving an inch.

"So, Walk-*her*," she said. "Tell me . . . no don't tell me. No, tell me. What was it like? You know. To go back? To the living part? Is it the same? Can people see you? Feel you? Do they still have McRibs?"

Looking at her eager, fleshy face with the crevice-like dimples, I struggled to find the words. But I tried. "It was like going back to your old school or your old house. It looked so much smaller. It *felt* so much smaller. And the strangest part was that I knew I didn't belong there anymore," I said. "It was almost as if I had never lived there. The living years seemed more like a dream."

As I handed Bertha two pies and closed the refrigerator door, I could see Daniel in the dining room trying to describe it to his sisters and Izayah. "It was funny," Daniel told them while Bobby rolled around the floor with Jake. "Leaving here was like being away from home. Going back there was like being on vacation where the place looked really good, but you didn't really live there anymore."

As the other kids joined Bobby and Jake on the floor, Izayah and Daniel moved toward the kitchen speaking in hushed tones. As they reached the doorway, I could make out what they were saying. Daniel told Izayah, "Dr. King followed us there."

"Get the hell out of here," Izayah said. "He ascended to the next level—at least that's what they're saying at school—and they had this big celebration on the front yard."

"It's bullshit. He's eternally screwed, if he even exists at all," Daniel replied, shaking his head. "He's trapped there and I have to get him back. The last thing he did was save my sorry ass. I won't leave him there. . . . One way or the other, I have to be sure because if there's even a chance . . ."

"Oh, here we go again. No way are you trying that stunt again! I'll rat you out myself," Izayah muttered harshly before whispering, "And what do you mean if he still exists?"

As Bertha whipped fresh cream from scratch, I stared out the window into the dark night.

I could see shadows nearing the back door of the house and what sounded like the distinct stomp of heavy workman's boots. I could hear them pounding up the three little wooden back stairs that led to the lime-green door. Flashlights were streaming through the little window in the dense wood and they momentarily blinded me. Suddenly, there was a thud and a loud crash that sounded like the door cracking into splinters. A pair of thick, black boots kicked open what remained and hard hands shoved me face-first against the pantry door, which creaked a little in protest, but held rock firm as my features pressed into the wooden slates.

I didn't cry out.

"We got 'er boss," said a craggy-faced man speaking into a walkie-talkie as he stood in our kitchen. Grabbing me by the hair, he yanked my face around until all I could see was the amber light from his flashlight and his beady cop eyes.

"Are you Walker Callaghan?" he demanded, pressing his fleshy face an inch from mine. His hot, poisoned breath stole my own. In slow motion, I began to nod.

"Walker Callaghan, you're under arrest for crimes against eternity," he said. "The Godfather at ITT is waiting for you. For sentencing."

"But wait," I begged. "I can explain . . ."

"Walk-*her*, Walk-*her*," Bertha said, shaking me hard as I still stood at that window. "What's a matter with you, girl? It's like you're dreaming, but you're wide awake."

Whirling around, I saw that Bertha and I were the only two people in the kitchen. There were no cops. No arrest. No foul smell. My mind was on some sort of warp-speed overdrive and set in the impending-doom gear. Desperate to snap out of it, I took a deep breath and tried to focus. *Nothing bad was happening. Nothing bad would happen.*

"I think you needs some rest," Bertha said, grabbing her bowl of whipped cream and guiding me back to the dining room, where, once again, everyone was gathered at the table. "Of course, rest comes after cherry pie."

All I could do was nod because I was numb. And all of my arm hairs were still standing up, stick straight.

4.

At midnight, after the presents were unwrapped and everyone raided the fridge for the third time, the house slept. Two revelers were still awake. Suddenly, I felt nervous and my hands were actually shaking as I stood in the bedroom that I shared with the man who brought me to this small room the day my mother disappeared. There was a reason I never moved out and he was working on getting undressed a few feet away from me right now.

My mind was on some sort of warp-speed overdrive again as my heart raced. *What's wrong with you, moron? You've been sleeping next to him for months now. This isn't a first date. You know his every nuance from the taste of his full bottom lip to the way his muscular arms feel when they wrap all the way around you holding you tight for the entire night. You know the smell of his peppery skin, the sound of his throaty, low sighs, and the sweaty nightmares that make him shake at three in the morning. You know how he feels when . . .*

"So, don't move, Callaghan, okay?" Daniel said, looking around the bedroom for something while calling me by my last name, which he almost always did. For some reason, his voice suddenly sounded deeper and somewhat mysterious.

"No problemo," I said, watching him rummage around in the closet now. You could have hidden a body in there. That's how messy it was with both of us cramming everything into it.

"Shit!" he said, stubbing his foot, although it didn't really register pain. Just old habits dying hard.

"Don't hurt yourself," I said, knowing it wasn't possible in the physical sense.

Finally, he emerged from the depths of our walk-in mess of a closet clutching two fat purple candles.

He proceeded to light them and I couldn't hold my smile any longer while sliding a band out of my now almost butt-length dark hair, which hadn't been cut in ages. I was never slick. Never would be. I tried to shake out the hair in a way that looked sexy. Some of it got caught in my teeth. The rest of me was in a white tank top and my favorite I-heart-Chicago shorts.

With one hand, he tore off his shirt. All that remained was very low-slung black sweat pants.

We had only been together like this once. The rest of the time I slept here we were simply sleeping together in the same bed with an emphasis on the slumber part.

I turned off the light and suddenly the room was illuminated with hope and shadows.

And then I walked over to him, until the heat of his body mixed with mine on a sigh. He cupped my face in his big warm hands and waited until I lifted my eyes. Then I got lost in the joy.

There was no doubt about it. I was in love with him. On

the bed, with his body moving and then fitting over mine, his lips wandered down my neck. When he got back up to my ear he stopped nibbling and softly said, "I can hardly remember not knowing you . . . wanting you . . . needing you . . . breathing you."

When I woke up in the middle of that night and opened my eyes, he was lying wide-awake and watching me with a look so tender and overflowing with kindness that my heart detonated in my throat.

I snuggled closer to him, winding my fingers through his, and rested my heart against his chest.

"Let's just stay here forever," he said in that husky voice.

"We can't be afterlife dropouts."

"Do we need a degree where we're headed?" he asked.

All I needed was an oath that we'd end up there together. But there was no such guarantee. We were separate entities who could remain in this realm for the next five minutes or five years or five hundred for all I knew. There were only questions and now.

He took my other hand and kissed it, safely placing it onto his pillow where he could lay his face on its palm.

I began, tracing my free finger across his bottom lip, which was only a start. The rest of him was magnificent—a carved and crafted wonder of sinewy muscle, solid bone, and taut skin that was a road map to all things wonderful.

"It should be enough that my girlfriend has an amazing brain and major guts. But you also have that great arse," he said, laughing while I silenced a gasp. No one commented on my arse when I was alive.

Daniel sobered. "Walker, there's a lot I want to say to you."

I wanted to hear what he had to say, but my emotions were running so high that I knew I needed to coast for now. "You talk too much," I said, lifting my head and then pressing my lips to his. I felt his mouth curve as I rolled on top of him, fanning my fingers wide across his expansive chest.

"Callaghan, you're killing me . . ." he said, kissing me back as if his very existence depended upon it.

When he flipped me over as if my body was made of negative matter, my hands tumbled off the narrow bed and I felt like I was flying.

We didn't sleep that night.

Who in their right minds would have?

CHAPTER 3

1.

Somehow the blackness of night bled out into a foggy, colorless morning and we dressed for school in order to keep up the routine. Never before had the idea of sitting through class felt as good. For some reason there was no Christmas vacation here, which meant there were kids to feed and lunches to pack. Normality at its finest.

It was all so ordinary, but something felt strange about it. We had been back for over twelve hours and nothing had happened. No calls. No visits from school authorities. No warnings. No texts saying to report to the principal's office because you went back to life and now you would pay the ultimate price. *What if last night was our last night at this house?* I forced myself to stop.

Stop. Breathe. Repeat.

The truth was we didn't have a principal anymore thanks to our actions and his reaction, which was to follow us into doom.

Could we get away with going back just this once—and get away with it again to find Dr. King? Maybe the Higher Authority would believe that little Bobby Reid just somehow finally arrived (a few years late) to be with his brothers and sisters. People arrived every single day. People left. Maybe they didn't miss us at all day yesterday when we were realm hopping. *Maybe.*

There was really no time to think about it. We had a small and demanding child in our little family and someone had to make sure that he was clean, brushed, washed, dressed in actual leaving-the-house clothes, and vaguely presentable.

I ran a brush through Bobby's unruly dark hair and tried to smell his breath to detect any rancidness. Since this was a place for dead teenagers, I wondered what they would do with a little boy who absolutely could not be separated from his family again. Then Daniel spoke to his youngest brother as if he knew what I was thinking.

"It's going to be great, little man," Daniel told Bobby, carrying him to the breakfast table by hoisting him under his arm like a beach ball. "There is an elementary school at the Academy. For the tagalongs."

"Don't little kids usually wind up somewhere else?" I asked, making ham and cheese on rye for Jenna and Andy because they detested cafeteria food.

"The kids can stay to keep families who arrive together intact, which was how it was supposed to be for us," Daniel said, running his hand through hair that was sticking up everywhere. It was bedhead at its finest.

"You're my plus one," he added, looking up at me with a lusty smile while eating a half-burned Pop-Tart.

"Our little buddy just arrived late," I said, watching Bobby dive almost headfirst into his Frosted Flakes with gusto while

Daniel walked to the sink to make him a peanut-butter-and-jelly sandwich for lunch, minus the crusts.

"Don't wanna go to school," Bobby moaned, while trying to sneak half of his breakfast to Jake. "And I want pizza for lunch. Want hot dogs, too. And cotton candy."

"Barbecue the dog if you want hot dogs, little bro," Daniel suggested and Bobby laughed, Frosted Flakes spilling out of his mouth onto the floor. The dog was elated.

"Oh Danny, you are so not funny," the kid shot back, scooting off his chair to chase Jake around the kitchen table. Soon, Andy, Jenna, and Peter were fighting over the last two frozen waffles.

"All right, campers, let's try to get there *today*. Get your shoes on," Daniel said, pointing to a hill of mismatched shoes by the back door.

I had to stop and stare at him for a second while something big dawned on me. This was how you created a family. You connected one little dot at a time until the solid lines formed.

Daniel snuck up behind me and put his hands on my waist. "I know you're worried, but one minute at a time, baby," he said. Leaning closer into him, I nodded my head as my eyes began to tingle.

"One minute at a time," I repeated.

2.

By 8:40 a.m., the front steps of the Academy were overflowing with bewildered new arrivals. Was there any other kind?

Miss Maude Travis, admissions guru extraordinaire, grasped her well-worn wooden clipboard and heaved a heavy sigh. In her standard dark wool skirt and unraveling cardigan, she always carried a heavy load and I noted that the silver clip on her board was threatening to explode. Our months ran parallel with the living realm and it was winter, which meant accident season thanks to slick roads, space heaters, and the insanity of hauling one's body off a mountain with tiny planks strapped to your feet. Some preferred to call it skiing.

My school friend Tosh, a willowy prima ballerina who died of anorexia, morphed from the shadows of the oldest elm tree where she was devouring half of a chocolate doughnut. Gliding toward me, her way of walking, Tosh leaned in to whisper the specifics of this morning's new arrivals.

"What was their catastrophe?" I murmured, breaking off the end of her doughnut and scarfing it down. I followed her pointer finger to see that she had the inside skinny when it came to a group of fifteen- or sixteen-year-olds who were wandering around aimlessly on the expansive front lawn. It wasn't walking dead time, but they were quite a bit dazed and a lot confused.

"Horrid accident. Mass drowning," Tosh rattled off, shaking her head in a way that said no judgment, but she was, of course, judging. *How did they drown as a group?*

"Imported beer, plus minors, plus joyriding equals they drove somebody's daddy's SUV through a fence and then hit the gas instead of the brakes. They managed to flip the thing into some megarich family's swimming pool. It was the shallow end of a drained pool with just a foot of water in it from melted ice," Tosh whispered.

"The crazy thing is no one died from the impact of the car crash. They drowned in that little bit of water. *All of them.* It was hardly enough water to fill up a kiddie pool in your backyard. But it was enough to do the job," she explained.

I counted three, four, maybe five newbies that appeared to

be just as lost as I was on my first day when kindly Miss Travis welcomed me to the Academy with my mom nervously at my side. Those were the heady early days when Mom, presumed dead, lived here with me and was a head-turn away. I constantly had to remind myself: *She didn't choose to return to life; Life chose her.*

"Dears, if you'll just follow me," Miss Travis said in her infamous, high-pitched voice that didn't quite hypnotize these not-so-deep-sea drivers. These were rich kids, and it was clear that they were used to bossing around their elders. You had to give it to Miss Travis for trying.

"We already have your files and your permanent records. No need to worry about the paperwork. It arrived minutes after your unfortunate *incident*," she chirped.

"Hey, Geritol! No one cares about school records. Here's the sizzle reel: I really need to call my dad about the car—or what's left of it," said a tall, beefy jock who was clearly foggy about why he was suddenly standing in front of a gigantic mansion.

"Am I in freaking Michigan? Did I go on a ski trip during break?" he asked. "I don't do cabin or cocoa. Where the hell am I?"

There were so many questions. Always.

"I didn't have time to call Geico. Somebody has gotta call the lizard," he blurted. "Is the car totaled?"

Miss Travis just smiled in that protective, all-knowing way.

Lizard or no lizard, Mr. No-Neck Former Football Star began to rattle off his version of current events. "It wasn't my fault. We really weren't partying that hard. I think I hit a fence and the car flipped three times before it went into the neighbor's pool." Pause. "Why would anyone put a pool there?"

"Shut up, Zeke," said a leggy blonde girl standing next to him, nervously twirling her stick-straight princess hair between two fingers. She wore new jeans cut at the knees and a plain blue wool sweater, which looked like an Academy- issued arrival shirt.

Clearly, this was a girl who should have been in a cheerleader's outfit because she could have given our Demanda, the head rah-rah queen at the Academy, a run for her pom-poms.

Immediately, I decided to rename her: Legs. It seemed that Legs also had a pressing concern. "I don't want to say anything about last night without first talking to our family lawyer, Bernard," she said. "Bernard does commercials, you know. 1-800-LAWYRUP."

"Like you need a lawyer," said No Neck.

"Like you have anything to say *about anything* after crashing the car," Legs retorted, adding, "Has anyone seen my cell? By the way, where are we? Is this some fancy rehab? I already did rehab and I'm fine. Do we have to take a Breathalyzer? I really need to call Bernard."

"Miss, you don't need a lawyer here," Miss Travis repeated.

"Excuse me, but you *always* need a lawyer, lady," the girl argued.

I smiled at Miss Travis who refused to sweat a minute of her daily routine—and she saw this behavior every single day. She didn't return the smile. Who could blame her?

Legs, who wasn't as clueless as she seemed, interrupted my mental gymnastics. She took one look at Tosh and me before hissing, "What are you two nosy bitches looking at?"

In that moment, I was sure Demanda would soon have a new BFF.

"Kindred spirits," I told Tosh. "Her and Demanda."

Tosh stifled a laugh, which caused Legs to mutter under her breath, "Lesbians."

Just a few months ago, I was the clueless one who thought we had moved to a new school in an unknown town. My million-dollar question after we arrived was: Why couldn't I e-mail my friends back home? Now, it all sounded so preposterous. What was I going to write? *Hi guys, having a splendid time dead. See you . . . in about eighty years. Enjoy graduation. Use sunscreen.*

For me, this school was a major upgrade from our lower-middle-class life of living at my Aunt Ginny's house after my father died of cancer when I was a little girl. By contrast, the Academy was a splendid European-style mansion with grand towers and pointed turrets that jetted past the thick clouds and pierced the sky. Inside the main parlor, there were creamy walls, dark wood floors, and endless winding staircases past priceless works of art on curved walls. They were masterpieces that seemed to disappear from the living side. They were here for safekeeping.

This school welcomed teachers who chose to come here to pass on their vast life knowledge. It followed that the faculty here included the famous or infamous. It was fun to do a quick round of "Who's Who" with them and fill in their last names, which were eye-poppers for sure.

The Higher Authority, however, wasn't thrilled when Amy started teaching music here last month without an invitation. Like in life, she just showed up. The school ironically turned the twenty-seven-year-old (forever) icon into a health and wellness instructor. The girls in her class, however, spent endless hours asking her how to create the perfect beehive and winged-out eyeliner. When it came to actually teaching wellness, Amy simply laughed and sang an a capella, throaty-voiced, "No, no, no."

Here, we didn't take tests or work on our SATs. Say good-bye to worrying about being accepted into the college of our former choices. We were told to study only what we were truly interested in. This was learning for the pure sake of gathering true knowledge for the next level—whatever that might be.

The truth of this place wasn't self-evident on the first day because first days usually suck.

"I said, I lost my wallet with my driver's license. Do you want me to stand at the DMV forever to get a new license? That's a fate worse than death!" complained one of the new arrivals, a skinny, pimply girl in sky-high pumps and microscopic booty shorts.

A quick glance to the left and I saw Harold, our intrepid gate guard, muscling some older-looking dark-haired boy with long, slicked-back hair. "Son, there's no room for you here," he said in his deep voice that was all business now. "Your records say ITT. Simon says, 'Don't bring guns to school.'"

Harold wasn't his usual pie-loving, jovial self today, but a strapping force with much larger muscles that I ever saw when he was at the gate or driving us around. In his gate-guard attire, he looked like someone's grandfather. But now, wearing black pants and a matching turtleneck and with a newly shaved head, he was formidable.

"Screw you, pops," the kid said, spitting into Harold's face. It didn't take long before something I have never seen before, an ITT SUV, pulled up. Without much muscling, Harold slammed the kid into the car and gave a thumbs-up for the SUV to take off.

"A glitch," Harold said to a perplexed Miss Travis who nodded and then returned to her regularly scheduled program of getting the drowning victims into their first classes. "Harold is ex-CIA," whispered Tosh, who added before I asked, "When I first got here I spent a lot of time in the counselor's office talking about my eating problems. I know *everything*. We should have a sleepover sometime here at school and I'll tell you."

"You got a deal," I said, momentarily distracted when I looked over at Daniel who was busy talking with Izayah just like any other day here before first period. As the first warning bell rang, I saw Iz and Daniel take off just like nothing had ever happened. Then my attention was diverted.

"I don't think we're *com-mun-icating*. We must find my wallet. Hello! I have an Amex with no limit," Legs cried to an increasingly unsympathetic Miss Travis. It was too soon to tell this girl that she was dead and everything here was free anyway, so you never needed money or a credit card again.

"Your dad has your Amex," said Miss Travis. "And you don't need to worry about your credit limit ever again. We don't do credit cards here."

Legs looked mortified.

"Are you on drugs?" she finally responded.

"Drugs don't work here either, my dear," said Miss Travis who chose that moment of nonhysteria to take command of this crazy new group.

"New arrivals need to report to the front parlor for tea and schedules. More will be explained. Enjoy your time," she said.

Tosh and I smiled at each other while mouthing the words, "*Dead freshmen.*"

3.

I was being summoned.

"Everyone's supposed to go to the auditorium first period. Victims of the Titanic are talking about the sinking of the ship. Attendance is mandatory," Tosh reminded me, explaining a school-honored tradition I had yet to take part of at the Academy: an assembly.

"I always wondered how James Cameron sunk that big ol' boat," Bertha said, moving surprisingly fast to join us. She looked fabulous today in a new winter-white skirt, plum shirt, and her long, curly hair up in a high bun. She was a talker, and I loved to listen to her ramble.

"Do you think they'll let us try on that big blue necklace? You know, from the movie. *That* was some rock!" Bertha said, slapping my back so hard at her own joke that I fell forward a few steps.

"I don't think this is about accessorizing," Tosh said in an amused voice, her birdlike hands flying through the air. She was always moving. "These people hit the iceberg and today's history assignment is to go listen to them talk about surviving an epic disaster. Didn't you get the text?"

Our destination was the Great Assembly Hall. It was located just beyond what we called the Wildly Winding River with its white, rushing waterfalls. They served as training ground for the Academy's award winning high-dive team. Early morning practice today had, of course, been cancelled.

The entire student body was headed out of the Academy and I felt safe blending effortlessly into the sea of thousands of students as we made our way through the grand main hallway, zigging past the Van Goghs and the Picassos.

Bam!

My habit of passing through quickly without looking reared its ugly head when I ran smack into my music appreciation teacher, Kurt, a guy who used to have this band. He was one of my favorites here and I knew the feeling was mutual, which made me a little giddy like a groupie.

A funny, warm-hearted coffee drinker who was never seen without his guitar, Kurt was known for stopping to talk to you about the meaning of it all and why life was just one long, run-on lyric.

"Hey, Kurt. Merry post-Christmas," I said with a warm smile, as I was crowd-bumped into his soft flannel shirt. "I'm so sorry," I began. But instead of smiling back at me to ease my embarrassment, he put his head down. And without as much as one word, he walked away.

"Didn't Santa visit? Did Courtney?" I whispered to Bertha

who just shrugged and sighed as she stared happily at the back of his faded 501s. Kurt was at the top of her laundry list of teacher crushes.

Ignoring his snub, we soldiered on, ducking outside again and cutting through one of the lush rose gardens, a perfumed wonderland overrun with feminine, pink flowers that could fill the palm of your hands.

As luck would have it, straight ahead was our gym teacher, Walter, a guy I knew counted me as one of his favorite students. We were both from Chicago and loved a good hot dog with green relish, or piccalilli as the locals called it.

"Hey, Walter, how was your Christmas? Did Santa deliver a new jersey?" I shouted to the man in navy-blue nylon workout pants and a Bears T-shirt.

As if he hit some imaginary brakes, Walter stopped on a dime, stared into my eyes for a second, and then pointed his Nikes in the exact opposite direction.

"No one wants to get back to the grind today," Tosh said and I didn't argue. It was so unlike two of my favorite teachers to be in such a foul mood.

Maybe they missed their families back in life. Or maybe they resented the fact that there was no time off here. Or maybe still, it was just an extreme case of the holiday blues from the loneliness that invades during the so-called happiest time of the year.

I didn't have time to feel snubbed because there was bossy, but brilliant, Miss Elizabeth in the prettiest silk lilac dress you had ever seen on an afterlife high school guidance counselor. Her movie-star pale smile glowed, her black hair gleamed, and her tapered fingers were each covered in enormous, priceless gemstones given to her by some past lover or husband. I think she preferred the first to the latter.

"Good to see you, Miss Elizabeth. Merry Christmas," I called out, stopping to talk to her even though she made it clear that she didn't support my living arrangements with Daniel.

There was no way that I was going to accept another rush job, but I had no choice. I saw her focus on Demanda, including sashaying around me with a gigantic smile and arms outstretched. Legs was trailing behind Demanda looking befuddled and beautiful at the same time. As for the most stunning one of all, Miss Elizabeth didn't say a word to me, but simply swept one patent leather heel to the side to embrace my least-favorite cheerleader.

She had walked around me as if I was afterlife roadkill.

Tosh, Bertha, and I trudged on as my mind raced. *They must know. But if they did, I wouldn't be allowed to roam the halls as if it was just another normal school day. So,* did *they know? What about that dumb luck now?*

When we finally reached the hall's main courtyard, even my two best friends looked utterly disgusted.

"Really?" Tosh said. "I hate crowds."

At the Academy, the campus was so vast that it was easy to forget there were tens of thousands in this student body. I had never seen them ALL convened together this way in what looked like the world's largest rock concert or political rally. Everyone was here. I even spotted the newbies led by Miss Travis. And Harold was here, still wearing that unfamiliar bad-ass nonuniform.

I waded into the courtyard, which was filled with wooden benches for lounging, although no one was sitting today. The sheer capacity of the crowd moved everyone along like some sort of ocean wave. It was a pity because it would have been nice just to sit and enjoy nature, including the rows of tall pines decorated with silver tinsel for the holidays.

This sanctuary adjacent to the massive theater-like structure was buzzing with student conversations and bewildered mutterings about why or how an assembly came together so fast after the holidays. Stopping to pull one of the delicate white flowers off a jasmine branch, I gingerly placed it behind my ear, which was so girlie of me. Daniel brought out that side of me and I started to smile when I felt a large hand touch the middle of my back.

He would lean in to smell the flower, and then give me a quick kiss. Now this was a great way to start the day. . . .

Instead, he muscled me from one side, slamming into me with all his body weight. His friend wrapped a hand in my long hair and ripped it as hard as possible, like a hunter taking down prey with his bare hands.

My head snapping back, I easily crumpled to the frozen ground, landing hard on my palms and knees. I could feel a pair of hands behind me reach out and grab at my right ankle, fingers squeezing tightly like he was trying to break the bone. The sheer force threw me off balance as I wobbled recklessly to my side. He took one meaty hand and slapped something cold and tight around my leg just below the calf. It was metal and he yanked on it with such extreme force that it felt like a deep bite from a bloodthirsty creature sinking its sharp, jagged teeth into fresh meat.

The metal was now red-hot and burning as it burrowed even deeper like some sort of flesh-eating disease. The sickening smell of cooking flesh filled my nostrils as the device melted off the top layers of skin, still searching for some sort of internal landing pad.

It wanted bone.

Reaching its mark, it implanted itself with a dull thud that made my stomach lurch and my breakfast rise to my throat. I wanted to throw up, which was odd because you couldn't get sick here. You couldn't feel pain here; you couldn't bleed.

But I felt sick to my stomach.

I felt pain that made my nerve endings burn like fire.

In the blur of what happened next, I saw the impossible: a small pool of my own blood on the pristine white pavement.

When I tried to reach down to touch the fire in my right leg, the biggest of the men kicked me in the stomach so hard that I crumpled belly-first, my face slamming into the ground. Biting hard into my inner lip, the impact was so seismic that my teeth actually rattled as my mind screamed for mercy. My heart, overtaxed and overwrought, was hammering an escape route out of my chest.

Metallic-tasting blood leaked out of my mouth and raced down my chin.

For a moment, everything went quiet. When I regained my senses, one of the foul men blew his rancid breath into my face as he squatted down to look at me, clearly enjoying himself.

"Get your skinny ass up," he ordered, tangling his hands in my hair again like he meant to rip me to my feet.

Then came five words that I knew were fated.

"Walker Callaghan, you're under arrest."

4.

They knew.

My mind flashed to Daniel's face resting so peacefully in our bed that morning. *Why couldn't we rewind—and run?* I tried to move my head to see if he was being arrested in the courtyard, but one of my captors threw a black hood over my head before cuffing my hands behind my back. Then he put some sort of metal chain between my upper limbs so he could haul me around like an animal.

Run, Daniel!

Run, baby, run!

The chains around me rattled in a shrill chorus that sounded a lot like the droning clatter of a child practicing an impossible musical instrument. Almost on instinct, I could hear the other students began to take giant steps back and away from me as if my horrible fate was somehow contagious.

If there was an off switch when it came to existence, it felt like someone had flipped mine down.

5.

Though I didn't know it at that moment, Daniel did run. Hard. Fast.

After body slamming the first whale of a guard who chased him up the back staircase of the Academy, Daniel broke into a fierce sprint that resulted in a whirlwind race through the teacher's lounge, past his first-period English class, and then he cut a sharp left down another staircase and through the cafeteria.

He lost them in the wood shop, although rough-and-tumble Chuck, our shop teacher, wasn't around that morning to unlock the tool shed where he might have hidden.

Daniel was quick and agile from all of those years playing soccer, but it was a hopeless race through avenues of futility. The Higher Authority had dispatched five elite guards to hunt and trap him. A few of them had been members of Scotland Yard back in the day and one was a CIA henchman who worked the Middle East during the Saddam reign.

On the twenty-yard line of the Academy's football field, Daniel was tackled and shackled with the same pain-inducing bracelet melding into his flesh. The CIA guy put a black hood over his head and hung extra-thick chains from his arms and legs. "We got a runner and a big one—a strapping young man," he said into something implanted into his wrist. "Those Hussein boys pulled the same crap and you know what happened to them."

"It was my idea!" Daniel repeated, over and over again. "I kidnapped the girl and forced her to go with me. Let the girl go. Do anything you want with me!"

It was futile because the guards weren't judge and jury; they were simply here to act as trappers. "Daniel Reid, you're under arrest," said a Scotland Yarder, yanking those chains hard.

"What are the charges?" Daniel demanded as they placed a metal ring around his neck. He dropped to his knees. Hard.

"You're under arrest for crimes against eternity," the guard stated, closing the noose tighter before he shouted, "You're not paralyzed. At least, not yet. So get the f— up and move!"

CHAPTER 4

1.

In the end, the subject of the assembly was never the survivors of the Titanic. It was for two others who were sinking fast. Quite obviously, the Higher Authority knew what we did from the moment we left this place. They just didn't want to interrupt anyone else's Christmas with the inevitable repercussions.

For a hot moment, I thought that the simple act of explaining what we had done might actually work in a place where peace and fair play were prized. But the guards were like most guards anywhere. They didn't care about words or reasons because they were robotic authority figures given great responsibility and guns. They manhandled first, talked later. One of the larger bullies in a blue uniform the color of the night sky led me by the tight, thick chain that clamped my arms together.

The true mortification was being yanked through the courtyard as public enemy number one . . . or two. I wasn't sure where I ranked next to Daniel. Even worse was when my legs buckled after one of the guards used his sturdy, government-issued black boots to savagely kick open the metal doors of the assembly hall.

It didn't take long for the bright yellow rays of sunlight to go away and the bleak artificial light to fill my eyes. Even with my vision partially blurred by the black hood, and the auditorium lights turned down low, I could see the endless faces. The entire student body of the Academy had been summoned to today's hazing. To ensure my humiliation, a guard chose this moment to yank off my hood.

Glancing around the guards to my right, I could see poor Tosh in convulsive tears as an almost hysterical Bertha held on to her tightly. But it was Andy who screamed when the doors were kicked open again and Daniel was paraded down the center aisle, led by a guard who held a thick, black chain attached to a yoke around his prisoner's neck. Pete had to physically hold Andy in place while Izayah kept his own firm hand on Pete who was yelling, "This is bullshit! Total bullshit!"

Of course, it was Jenna who shouted the loudest, "It isn't fair! It isn't fair! They were saving my brother!" Out of the corner of my eye, I saw Miss Travis grab her in a tight hug and walk the young girl backward out a side door.

Shoving me up the stairs of the auditorium stage while my feet struggled to keep up, my guard yanked me hard like I was a stupid barnyard animal who was resisting the idea of being broken. I fell up each of the imposing black steps, scraping my knees on the corners of wood, and was mercilessly jerked forward until the guard forced me into a kneeling position center stage. I could see three bulky guards now shoving Daniel up the stairs. Of course, he resisted, kicking out hard and putting his entire body weight into the fight. In the end, it was an exercise in insanity.

Daniel was deposited right next to me and fell with a loud thud onto the floorboards in a way I was sure would make his knees go right through the stage. Our placement guaranteed that we were only inches away from each other, but too far. I strained my fingers. He jerked his shoulder, but we couldn't bridge the gap. I felt his breath on the side of my face. A few long-held tears slipped out and landed close enough to his hand for him to reach out and collect them.

2.

No trumpet sounded. No drumbeat registered to start the proceedings.

Someone obviously hit the "on" switch and a giant spotlight illuminated the stage and caused a visual whiteout. When my eyes cleared again, I focused on my lurching stomach praying that it wouldn't betray me in front of the entire student body.

I could see Daniel desperately trying to turn so he could look into my face. That was also futile. All I could see as I stared straight ahead was a long black conference table that had been placed on the stage. My vantage point gave me an excellent view of several pairs of dress pants that were pressed to perfection. I counted about ten pairs of them and two skirts. I did the math and added up twenty-four spit-shine, fancy shoes attached to feet that were either still or tapping impatiently.

Focus on your reporter instincts. You were going to work for the New York Times *one day. All you needed was the facts.*

There was one pair of heels attached to panty hose supporting the kind of shapely gams that my dad's steelworker friends might have admired. They would have called her a Monroe. And she was the worst—tapping furiously as if she was sending out some sort of ADHD Morse code.

Despite the body count of the room, you could hear the air conditioner kick in and the loud clanking of a school janitor pushing a bucket and mop to clean up after a few kids, hippies by nature, who fought authority today by throwing wads of paper, coffee cups, books, and various other things at the stage. One yelled, "Power to the people—even the dead people!" and was promptly removed. The distinct thudding of a man's dress shoes interrupted the commotion, as the owner of these black, spotless leather uppers tapped across the stage with strident purpose.

As plain as day, I heard the click. It sounded like a shot.

This man didn't walk directly to the microphone set up for him, but instead made a beeline over to a small table to manipulate what looked like an old-fashioned reel-to-reel tape recording device. With determined zeal, he turned it on.

"As some of you know, I like to record all of my proceedings," he stated.

Ridiculous thoughts entered my mind. *Was it legal for him to tape us without our consent? Did legal even matter anymore? Did we have any rights? Could I ask for an attorney?*

"To clarify, when the president, I mean, new principal of the Academy chooses to keep a vocal record, it's never illegal," the man attached to the leather uppers announced as he walked to the podium. *What the hell? He would begin the proceedings with a disclaimer?*

"Students, teachers, esteemed members of the Higher Authority, I regret that we have to meet this way on this day, especially after such a lovely Christmas holiday," he began in deep tone laced with a hint of a rural California twang. You couldn't forget that voice. It belonged to a man who, in life, once served as the governor of California, before moving on to a higher office. I knew of this man. Young and old, dead or alive, we all knew him. Which was unfortunate.

"This is a tragic day at the Academy, but one that you will always remember," he continued to speechify. "I've been given no choice but to summon an emergency session of the Higher Authority who, incidentally, were on extended vacation elsewhere and have honored us with their presence here today. I'm so very sorry for this *inconvenience.* Tragically, I was forced to cut their time off short because a heinous crime of the highest order has been committed by two Academy students."

A buzz from the crowd morphed into a dull roar.

"Silence!" he bellowed, hushing the crowd.

Then he began again. "As I was saying, I had no choice but to summon—"

But he wasn't allowed to finish. A voice from the bleachers interrupted him in a way that sounded like a sharp crack to the face. The tone was smooth, calm, sure, and young. It came from a student who made his way to the very top of the bleachers where he was wildly waving his hands overhead. There was no mistaking him.

"Who the hell are you?" shouted Izayah who didn't suffer fools easily—and obviously wasn't a history buff.

"Remove him and bring him to my office," our self-proclaimed new principal bellowed into the mic as two beefy morons in uniform shoved aside rows of defiant students who refused to part. The student body was no match for specially trained guards who tore Izayah down from the stands. From the corner of my eye, I could see our strong and loyal friend being led away by three men, which was what it took to overpower him.

"Children. I hate children. And teenagers are the worst species of children," the man with the mic said—but not into the mic. He had carefully turned it off, but I could still hear him muttering low under his breath. When he turned the mic back on, he banished his formerly fake pleasant voice.

"If you must know who I am," said the infuriated speaker, now leaning into the podium like he had some sort of back ailment. "I am your new principal. Call me Principal Dick."

Under my breath, I said, "You've got to be shitting me."

"Did you say something, Miss Callaghan?" Principal Dick boomed.

"No, Principal *Dick*," I said in a sure voice with an emphasis on the last word.

I said it loudly and clearly. Because, really, what was the point of hiding behind good manners now? I was pleased when the entire auditorium broke into loud, spontaneous laughter, high fives, and cheers.

Thus, my new life as a back-talker began.

3.

"Silence! I command you!" our new principal roared.

I remained more than a little bit proud of myself because I refused to feel this thick layer of shame that they were slathering all over us. We rescued a lost boy. If these higher-ups didn't like it, well, I didn't really give a shit.

"He sounds pissed," I whispered to Daniel.

In life, the polite Walker Callaghan would have "yes sirred" and "no sirred" her way out of this mess. The dead Walker Callaghan would take a stand for what was so obviously right that any fool or new principal should be able to see it for what it was worth.

Looking down at us now with complete contempt, our new

principal said in a chilling tone, "I sound . . . what did you say? Pissed as in 'pissed off'? How eloquent of you, Miss Callaghan. We know for a fact that English isn't your major."

"Actually, it is," I blurted. "But how tricky of you . . . to pretend not to know."

Once again, the student body cheered their approval.

It was obvious that Principal Dick didn't suffer insolent teenagers. He walked closer to me, shoving my head down with his small, manicured hands until my chin rested on top of his glossy black shoes and I could smell the fresh, waxy polish.

"Don't get the impression that you raised my anger," he went on. "You see, one can only be angry with those he respects."

Lowering his hand again, he gave my head a second, much harder shove. My chin bounced against the stage floor like one of those little balls your mother buys you for fifty cents from a supermarket machine. I heard gasps, winces—and Demanda's shrilly laughter. "Do it again, Dickie," she shouted, but her bravado didn't last long.

"You will be seen—and not heard!" bellowed one of the guards who lifted her out of her seat and carried her out of the auditorium despite her screams and cries.

My mind was racing.

How did the Academy appoint someone who was supposedly "not a crook" as the esteemed new principal and the chief governing force of this realm?

Obviously, the man who made my face kiss wood wasn't resting in peace anymore. To use his own words, students (and he didn't have good luck with our kind after that "unfortunate" Kent State incident) now had Dick to kick around again.

The hereafter had a funny sense of humor.

4.

As for me, I knew that my afterlife was about to change in the same way my actual life pivoted hard when I least expected it.

"Let these two be a cautionary tale," said one of the members of the Higher Authority who looked and sounded very familiar. Someone called him Carl.

"You were warned by Dr. King that one must never attempt to go back to the living realm. You were cautioned to never even ponder it," said the female toe-tapper who had silenced her nervous leg in order to appear threatening and serious. I knew her from the evening news.

Principal Dick couldn't resist commanding the stage. "The rest of you were brought here today to witness the true and lasting repercussions of defying a sacred rule."

"There was a little boy. An earthbound spirit. Waiting for years to see his family," I shouted.

"Enough!" Principal Dick commanded, without ever raising his head that almost permanently drooped down. "You broke our most solemn rule—and there is no reason under heaven or earth that can be entertained here. I submit that this was the highest crime you could commit in our realm and you committed it for your own personal satisfaction and without regard to eternal consequences. You might as well have stayed on the living side to experience extinguishment," he said. "If I could extinguish you myself, I would."

Two words pulsed through my brain: What and now. My mother always told me that if you erred on the side of what was good and right then the truth would win in the end. Daniel wasn't the best speaker, so I would speak for both of us and explain how we had to find a young soul and absolve my mother.

"Esteemed ladies and gentlemen, you have heard the facts," Principal Dick told the board. And then he added, without a hint of remorse, "By the power vested in me by the Higher Authority, I hereby condemn you, Walker Callaghan, and you, Daniel Reid to both serve eternal sentences at ITT. So be it!" he boomed.

"Wait!" I cried as my captor guards viciously yanked my sleeping legs to an upright position.

The room went silent. "No one read us our rights. I demand at attorney," I said in a breathless rush as my knees ached and then folded while I struggled to stay upright.

"To be clear, you have no rights anymore. All you have now is the right to try to breathe," Principal Dick said. "You have the right to exist—if you can call it that at ITT."

I could hear Daniel fighting with his chains.

"An eternal law has been broken. Do you believe that each individual should determine what laws are good and what laws are bad and what laws he or she should obey?" our new principal ranted on. "Should you only obey the laws that you like and disobey the laws that do not strike your fancy? That creates total anarchy in a civilized population. In death, as in life, there will be civility." I heard a click. The mic was off again.

My world went silent.

An eternal sentence at ITT.

Never free.

Never to greet fresh air.

Never to smell the rain.

Never to touch Daniel again.

Never.

I closed my eyes and tried to go back to Christmas just the night before with the kids playing around the tree and Daniel and

I sitting with our legs draped over each other on the couch. The memory came, but just as quickly it was dashed by the vision of this man on stage saying the words, "You both will serve an eternal sentence at ITT. So be it."

"Student body stay seated," Dick now boomed. I opened my eyes. He made a hand motion toward us and muttered under his breath to the guards, "Take them through the front again. Let the new disciplinary policies of this school begin today. Let the student body know that unlike in the days of lazy, incompetent, moronic Dr. King, there is no whining or talking your way out of disobedience. There is only acceptance and absolute adherence to school policy."

Someone shut off the spotlights and only thin flashlights were shined on us as we were yanked off stage and to the ground floor of the assembly. Brave students took out their cell phones, hit a button, and tried to guide our way. It was standing room only below, and our captors took us wading through the crowed where I felt hands reach out to touch us; some recoiled away.

Perhaps fate was contagious. And if so, we were now eternal lepers.

5.

We were purged from the Academy in record time. After the humiliation of the public spectacle, we were at our first stop to nothingness. It was a little white van parked in the service entrance next to the auditorium.

"Get your ass in the back," one of the guards barked, shoving me up and then whacking Daniel hard in the center of his expansive back when he tried to reach out for a little payback.

I didn't cry when they lifted me, ramming me into the rear of a vehicle that in the living realm might be used to catch dogs. Inside, it smelled foul from others who had been there—adrenalin and sweat, mixed with pure fear. Sitting on the hard metal bench with my arms cuffed behind me, I felt that strange bracelet they attached to my ankle begin to vibrate harder. The feeling made my teeth rattle and a cold sweat break out on the back of my neck.

For the first time in a long time, I felt something that was like a long-lost enemy.

Intense pain.

The reset button was gone. So was the adrenalin of being on that stage in front of all of our fellow students, which masked the pain. Now in this isolation, I began to hurt. Everywhere.

Pain and shock mingled to make me tremble, although I tried to mask it from Daniel whose sharp eyes never left mine.

From the little window inside the van, I could see the student body, who were all in good standing like we were once upon a time ago. They were filing out of the hall and probably on their way back to class, shell-shocked but free.

The others were obviously told to leave the auditorium so they could watch us while we were transported. Principal Dick was all about the show.

If any of our classmates were even entertaining the slightest thought of going back to life, well, I was sure that they were certainly rethinking it now.

We *were* the ultimate cautionary tale.

CHAPTER 5

1.

ITT loomed large, shoved into the side of a mountain as if some gigantic clawed monster had slammed the multistoried building right into the rock. The mammoth penitentiary was suspended in a way that made it look like one strong wind or the impulse of a very large finger could just flick the whole thing away as if it never existed. But it did exist; and it was our new home. It would be part of us; and we would be part of it. In many ways, an individual sentenced to ITT was equally embedded into the side of all that granite.

You didn't live there. You were stored there.

The institution was born out of necessity. It turns out that not everyone gets a one-way, first-class ticket to some form of a heavenly resting place or pleasant in-between limbo to grow and mature. Certain people of the teenage persuasion were thrust into a very definite and quite familiar hell. Of course, it was a hell of their own making—or so the Higher Authority deemed it, as they personally reviewed each case and sent the "student" to the appropriate afterlife facility.

If you screwed up in life, you were screwed in death.

We screwed up in death, and now we were just screwed.

It surprised me that Harold was at the wheel, but he was absolutely silent as we made our way past the Academy grounds, snaking along the backstreets, cutting through the woods at a breakneck speed so that each tall pine tree looked like a greenish-brown blur. For one crazed moment, I thought that Harold had a great escape plan under his bomber jacket sleeve. *He would drive us into the deepest woods to a secret hideaway where we would lie low for a long time, but we'd be together braving it out.*

Harold shocked me when he maneuvered expertly until he reached the bottom of the mountain and the front entrance of ITT, and I knew there was turning back. I could hear that sickening noise of grinding metal as the steel arm barrier was lifted by ITT guards to allow us to approach. The sound of the gates reminded me of the time I lost a spoon down the garbage disposal and the metal eating metal made the hairs on my arms stand on end.

In the back of the van, we were shackled, but close enough where I could take the tips of Daniel's strong fingers and squeeze them hard. He didn't say much, but stared silently at me with eyes so sorrowful now that it took everything in me not to burst into body-shaking sobs.

Guilt is a powerful drug, and I couldn't allow him to overdose on it.

"Walker," Daniel finally whispered in a thick tone that betrayed his inner resolve. "You listen to me. Listen real good. You follow the rules. You do what they tell you. Don't resist. Don't react."

No longer able to hold back the tears, I nodded. Because I couldn't speak.

"Walker, I'm so sorry, baby," he said. And when his voice cracked, I wept even harder. He was looking at me with so much love that it took my breath away. "I'm so sorry, baby. This was all my—"

"It was my pleasure." I cut him off in the strong voice I had found at my own father's funeral when I was five. I meant it. I used that voice for all the years I told my mom it was okay that we were struggling. Coping, I knew. I was a master at how to flip the switch and damn up the tears.

"I would do it again," I said. "I'd do it right now."

"Thank you," he said in a clogged, husky voice. Despite the shackle on his neck, he strained his head to look upward. Anything not to let tears slip.

"No, thank *you*," I said.

Then it dawned on me. *I'd probably never see him again. The mountain was big. It would swallow us and then digest us in different pieces of rock. I would never look into those eyes again. I would never touch his hand. I would never hear his voice.*

The dam burst and my tears now rushed.

"Walker, no more tears. You have to be steel here or they'll eat you alive," Daniel said in a voice that was hard and determined.

"I'm the daughter of a steelworker," I replied in that same tone. "I have steel in my blood."

2.

Harold drove the van forward, stopping sharply at the entrance elevator that would take us into the bowels of pain and purgatory. I knew that this wasn't the only entrance into ITT, but it was the main one used for all receivables including sacks of potatoes, fresh laundry, and new recruits.

When Harold opened the back door, I wanted to fall into his arms, but I didn't. He wouldn't be allowed to catch me—or maybe he wouldn't want to try anymore. The look in his eyes was cold. I had disappointed him on an epic level. That much I knew, yet he was still a gentleman.

Gingerly, Harold helped me out of the van as best he could despite all the chains. Pretending that he was untangling what was tangled, he whispered into my ear, "Walker Callaghan, don't you fight these people, little girl. You need to keep quiet. Keep your head down. Be as careful as you can be. And hang on to hope. When all else fails."

I never had a grandfather—until I met Harold.

But now, like everyone else in my afterlife, it seemed as if he was gone as quickly as he had arrived.

What was left was our sentence. To that end, we weren't met on that platform by the warden, dubbed the GF (or Godfather), the fat slob SOB of a blowhard we had met during our previous visits here.

There was only a bald and beefy admissions officer with a neck the size of the state of Georgia who was pacing in front of ITT's loading elevator, swinging a clipboard from his meaty fingers and stuffing the last of what looked like a turkey club with extra mayo into his doughy face. A few stray lettuce pieces escaped, hit his shiny shoes, and then seemed to evaporate as he ground them into the dirt. It was a clear sign that nothing got out of here whole.

He proceeded to lick some remnant mayo off his fingers, then wiped the rest of it on his black ITT guard's shirt, which had seen better days.

His name tag read: Jimbo.

"Walker Callaghan. Daniel Reid. Welcome to de show," Jimbo

announced like he was checking us in for some gala party in the hood. For a moment, I imagined that we were being ushered into a movie premiere. *Yes, we were here. Where was our swag bag? Oh, there's the paparazzi. Was that Brad and Angelina?* Then reality set back in.

Another guard had keys that unlocked us from our handcuffs and chains and then I heard him mention something about cooperating. Yanking me forward by my numb shoulders seemed like fun for him and I could see Daniel's face contort in rage, but there was nothing he could do.

I began to shiver as light, freezing rain rolled through my tangled dark hair and onto my almost-numb cheekbones. Jimbo just shook his head as I wiped the rain out of my already misty eyes.

"Girly," he said. "I'd advise you to toughen up. No use crying over the last rainy day you'll ever see."

"Steel," Daniel whispered after another bigger guard yanked him forward by the choke hold around his neck, which was not removed.

"You give me any trouble and I won't give it a second thought, asshole," the bigger guard, with a cigarette dangling from his mouth, hissed at Daniel as he touched a gun that was firmly attached to a leather holster resting on his hip pocket. I wasn't exactly sure what a gunshot could do to us now that there was no reset. You couldn't die again. But you could hurt. And you could be maimed.

When Daniel clenched his fists, the big guard pointed at his ankle bracelet. Then he took his large billy club and slammed it hard into Daniel's midsection. Caught by surprise, Daniel doubled over in a coughing fit while the guard chuckled and wheezed equally hard from all his cigs. "Not having the reset anymore—what a bitch, big boy," he said.

"Ya'll think you're tough when you walk in here," Jimbo added.

"Give it a month and you won't be nothing no more. This place has a way of breaking you down—and fast."

Righting himself as quickly as possible, Daniel stood up tall next to me. In fact, his body seemed hard like granite. I knew he would break in private when I couldn't see it. But not now.

My body began to tremble when I heard the heavy metal elevator coming down in a giant whoosh of air. As the doors opened, I felt as if the sky was being ripped away from us along with the clouds, the trees, and the fresh air. My new world would be made of black concrete and steel with large, imposing guards at every turn. A feeling of bleakness I hadn't experienced since I lost my mother here washed over me.

"Time for you law-breaking lovebirds to say sayonara. I might even cry now. Boo hoody hoo," Jimbo mocked. "Ya wanna give him the big smoochie good-bye before your personal escorts arrive?" He was taunting us, but I didn't care. I reached out to grab Daniel's hand, but the man I had been living with for all of these months simply pulled away and my hand fell flat to my side. It reminded me of the first day we met in music class. When I advanced again, he took a finger and gave me a slight shove back.

"Sorry, Callaghan, that you were stupid enough to go with me. What happens from now on is your problem. You're on our own," Daniel said.

I knew he was showing them that he didn't care because they would certainly use that against us. That would be the easiest, most gruesome form of torture.

"What do we got here? Romeo and Julie having a spat?" Jimbo mocked, as the sky turned the light mist into bands of fat and steady raindrops that bounced off the cruel guard's glossy bald head.

"Hockey boy Reid, you're ours now. We'll take it from here, Jim," a shout came from behind us. We turned as a Neanderthal, walking with his equally large friend, yelled into the rain again in a way that made his spit mix with what Mother Nature was tossing down on us. "Welcome to the jungle as they said in 'Nam. The GF has special plans for you. He wants you processed and then shot way down below to the Hole for a few weeks. We call it the Cooler. And it's really chilly there," he laughed.

I willed myself not to react when my mind was screaming, "No!"

"We do that to all the tough guys. It's the easiest way to break you—and we never met one of you that we couldn't break," he said.

I remembered the immortal words of my soon-to-be neighbor Eddie Wargo: "Few escape the Hole with all of their marbles still shootin' right."

The Hole at ITT was a small underground tube buried several hundred feet in the earth, a grave of sorts where you didn't speak with anyone for the duration of your stay. It was pitch black and there weren't any modern conveniences like a sink or toilet. Small amounts of food and water were sent down every few days through special service pipes for the most basic survival.

"If that ain't enough to mess you up but permanently, I don't know what is," his friend smirked, puffing on a Marlboro and blowing the smoke at Daniel as he took possession of his neck chain. "Next time you see your little boyfriend, missy," he said to me. "His already limited brain will be turned to mealy mush."

Before they led him away, I raised one fist up a few inches and I knew that Daniel not only saw, but knew what it meant. Just two days ago when my father and his buddies were beating off the demons, the last sight we had of them was on Addison Street in Chicago. They were three ghosts raising their steelworker hammers sky-high in victory.

I slowly lowered my hand as I saw a look in Daniel's gray eyes that was absolutely foreign to me.

It was raw fear.

Before I could blink he was gone, and I was alone in every way that mattered. Standing on the entrance platform, amid the fresh arrival of carrots and pinto beans, facing the cold, institutional walls ahead of me, I stopped myself from convulsively shaking or screaming on the top of my lungs. Molten steel didn't shake when someone tried to reshape it.

It hardened.

3.

"Time for your processing," the guard who had removed my chains bit out as the elevator doors opened once again and we stepped in. My afterlife faded to black, except for one dim bulb inside the car to oblivion. "You're in for the ride of your life. Wait until you meet the dean of women prisoners. You might have heard of her."

He pressed the button for level one and the doors closed behind us. "She goes by Lizbeth now. Started out as a cutter, still a cutter. Not much of a name change, if you ask me," he said with a chuckle. "Whacked-out broad doing a thousand years here for penance. Personally, I like to call her Lizard and then back away. She doesn't like familiarity—or family for that matter. But you must know the story."

The elevator doors in front of us opened wide. He yanked me by the arm down a long, dark hallway past little arrows that read: PRISONER PROCESSING. STAY TO THE LEFT.

Then he stopped because we couldn't go any further.

Her office was the last one down a twisting corridor. The guard knocked three times on her door and then shoved me inside. He pushed me hard, so he didn't have to get any closer. His last words from the hallway were simple.

"Don't lose your head, kid," he said with a vicious chuckle.

4.

She was waiting.

A tall, well-built woman with sparse black hair pulled back into a prim bun, her onyx eyes were close-set and her nostrils flared like they were two wide tunnels with direct access to brain matter.

A whisper of an old woman's grayish-pink top lip rested on a nervously bitten and frequently chewed bottom one, and neither hinted at a smile. She was dressed in all black, but the freaky part was that Lizbeth, dean of women prisoners, didn't wear the standard-issue ITT guard uniform of unflattering pants and a crisp, black, collared shirt.

She was clad in a flowing Victorian dress that reached the floor, her arms completely blanketed in yards of sooty-colored lace, and her throat obscured by a collar that reached upward to her chin. A white cameo pin rested on the neck of her turn-of-the-century fashion statement, and a small gold heart locket dangled against her chest. It was open to reveal two blurred black-and-white photos.

I couldn't decide what to stare at harder, the small nameplate on her desk that read DEAN BORDEN or the two faces in that locket. One was a middle-aged, wealthy-looking man. She knew where my eyes had settled. "My father, Andrew. *Mur . . . der . . . ed,*" she said in a voice so scratchy and old that it sounded as if she was on her last words. The other photo was a woman who couldn't have been her mother because there was absolutely no family resemblance. Lizbeth was dark and brooding; the woman was blonde and fair. "My stepmother," she said in a tone that offered no feeling, and certainly no remorse.

"Terrible, terrible news, so said I," Lizbeth told me, gliding out from behind a desk that was cluttered with files. Two candles flickered, the only light in the room. In one of her craggy, old hands were several papers with my name on top of them. In her other hand was something silver that caught the dancing light. In that stifling hot, dark office, I could see that she was holding a small silver ax by its bloodied wooden handle.

"Terrible, terrible news," she repeated almost as if she were in a trance. "I said to our maid, 'Maggie, come quick! Father's dead. Somebody came in and killed him,'" she recollected, as if she was telling a jury. As she spoke, she began to tap the ax repeatedly against the desk in a steady drumlike motion that seemed to get louder by the moment. Now striking the blade against the wood, she smiled each time the sharp edge got momentarily stuck in the porous pine. Frustration bordering on rage set in when the blade remained lodged. Her face contorted viciously as she ripped it out hard and then plunged it in even harder.

"My father, struck ten times. No, eleven times, so said I," Lizbeth told me in her wispy, singsong voice as she moved closer. My eyes never leaving the glint of that ax blade, I could feel my heart begin to drum so hard in my chest that I thought it might rip open my flesh. I couldn't move away because the office was a prison cell of sorts. There was absolutely nowhere to go.

Focus. Stay calm. Steel.

My eyes went wide when she found a new victim. Lizbeth began to slice her left hand with the freed ax blade and a strange calm returned to her face when her own blood began to freely rain down in small plops to the floor. She took delight playing with the thick liquid snaking through her fingers and smiled to reveal several holes in rotted, blackened teeth.

That stupid, childish song raced through my mind: *"Lizzie Borden took an ax, and gave her mother forty whacks. When she saw what she had done, she gave her father forty-one."*

How much more ironic could it get that I had chosen to do a sophomore-year report on her that got me an A minus. I knew that her victims' heads were removed during a pretrial autopsy and the skulls were brought to the trial and used as evidence. Borden even fainted when she saw them, which helped the jury to acquit her along with the fact that they never found her murdering ax. Later, the heads of her victims were buried at the foot of each grave.

Present-day Lizbeth had a strange way of moving that was almost floating, and it made chills race up my spine. "Waaaalker," she said. "Put your hands on my desk." With a long, spindly finger, she pointed to the hacked-up pine desk in the middle of the room. In that moment, one of the candles burned out.

"Wh . . . what?" I whispered.

"The desk," she said. "Put your hands on the desk. Lean forward. Put your head down, too. You need your rest, dear."

"I . . . I want to stay standing," I said. "I'm not tired."

"Oh, Walker," Lizbeth said, smiling with her rotted gums. "Go to the desk. Head down. I insist, dear. And I'm in charge now."

I knew that the guard was gone. It was just Lizbeth and I, and her veinless hand solidly holding that ax. Silently, she became enraged, floated behind me and pushed until I smacked my head hard onto the pine wood. I saw stars, but forced myself immediately to stand straight up. She backed away for a moment and then kicked me hard behind my kneecaps. As a reflex, I fell forward onto the desk again. I could smell the freshly hacked wood, and could see several blood splotches embedded in the crevices.

"Keep your head down, dear. Sleep," she advised.

My head now throbbing, I couldn't lift it. I could hear her long dress brushing the floor as she moved even closer again. That heavy silk taffeta continued to make a hard swishing sound as Lizbeth closed the gap.

Out of the corner of my eye, I could see her lifting that ax.

At that moment, I whipped around hard until we were eye to eye. The only thing I could move was part of my face, so I head butted her as hard as possible, which made her scream out and then fall back. I could hear the ax fall and the blade made a shrill ringing noise when it hit the cold linoleum floor. At that moment, Lizzie laughed in a way that made bile rise in my throat.

Reaching for the papers with her bony hands, she checked a box that I could see clearly. It read: RESISTANCE.

"Now we know how to process you, Walker." She said as she stood up. "Those who do not fight back go immediately to their cells. Those who decide to fight must participate in the Outing."

"Bring it on, you freaky bitch," I said, rubbing my right temple because it throbbed.

Lizbeth took that moment to lean so close to me that I could smell her ancient breath. I kept one eye on the ax that was still on the floor. "Walker, if you ever resist again, they will bring you back to me," she said, her eyes glazed as she stared into space.

"They never found my bloody dress," she whispered. "Burned it in the stove. Burned the ax handle. Oh, the blood."

"Nineteen whacks," she said with glee. "If I see you again, you will get twenty."

5.

I was so happy to get the hell out of there that I didn't really think about what could happen next. My guard had returned, collected me, and proceeded to drag me down another narrow hallway where I was placed in the supposedly capable hands of a tall, shapely woman. Her eyes were so bloodshot that almost all of the white had been obscured with crimson.

She had wild, blonde frizzy hair and made no secret of her drinking habit as she took a small swig from a highball glass filled to the brim with an amber liquid over large cubes of ice that clinked in a way that made me jump.

"Stress disorder, baby?" she said to me, lifting her glass as if making a toast.

It was obvious that my guard didn't want to stay here any longer than absolutely necessary, either, so he spit out the facts. "Walker Callaghan, the little bitch who went back," he told her.

"Back as in . . ." she began.

"Back as in back. Wake up! Do I have to draw you a picture?" the guard said in a clipped tone as he dumped some forms in her hands.

"Try reading, Aileen—if you can," he said in a mocking voice.

"You know the rest: Life sentence. D Block. No-frills package."

"I will treat her extraordinarily," the woman slurred.

"Have another drink, Aileen," said the guard, shaking his head.

"I think I will," said the second most infamous female serial killer on record. For some strange reason, I wasn't afraid of her because I knew that she was infamous for killing *men*, although the former prostitute said that all of her killings were (naturally and *extraordinarily*) committed in self-defense.

Before he left, the guard tossed my chain to Aileen as if I was some surly dog he was passing off. As a good-bye present, he shoved me hard from behind and the pain seared when I bashed stomach-first into her desk. I had no choice, but to crumple to the floor, chains clanking, head pounding, and chin bleeding.

"Get your sorry ass up," Aileen barked. "You'll have plenty of time later to get on your knees and pray that you never heard of this place. What the hell were you thinking going back? No one's worth it to go back for, even that slab of prime beef they just transported to the Hole, if you ask me. How could you be so damn stupid to trust a man?"

She manhandled me into another nondescript room run by a large Hispanic female guard with two cheerleader ponytails sticking straight up off the top of her head. She said something to me in Spanish that I didn't understand. There were other new recruits in there, too—hundreds of them—and all around the same age, although I saw a skinny girl as old as eighteen and a shaking boy as young as thirteen. Some stood; others sat on the floor with their heads hanging down. I knew we were waiting.

But for what?

Then he entered. And every guard shut up and stood at attention.

The GF ambled in and took it from there. He was a disgusting man whose rolls of fat hung over his low-slung, stain-covered polyester pants. The sweat didn't just pour off him from the extra girth, but made him smell like milk left on the counter for days. I lowered my head enough, hoping he didn't remember me from our last encounter when I came to do our mock school project.

The GF promised he would make me disappear if he ever saw me again. And now he had that chance on a minute-by-minute basis.

"Good morning. I am the GF, as my young captives like to call me. I'm not pleased to meet you and I'm sure you're not pleased to meet me," he said, wheezing until he made it to a wooden podium that he leaned over. It was a miracle that it didn't just snap like a toothpick.

"I am the warden of these parts—and I have a few pronouncements."

In any regular school, the principal would take the next moments to talk about the football team and clubs. This wasn't anything regular.

"To put it simple and easy: You're mine now. You are wards of ITT. You have no freedoms. You have no choices. You have no desires, no will, no wants, no hopes, no dreams, no chances," the GF said in a carefully controlled drawl. "You are here to be stored like old furniture in a shed. If I had my way, you'd all be put into a drugged stupor, but some might find that inhumane."

"We are nothing if not humane up here," the GF added and laughed hard as if what he said was the biggest joke of all. "Boys and girls, your only options are to breathe, eat, shit, sleep and then do it all over again, day after day, for the rest of the time you are given. Your time will be determined by one person: me. Your every breath—determined by me. Your portion of food and drink—graciously provided by me. Your fears and terrors—joyfully provided by me. Every day will be the same—unless you're sent to see me. And you better hope to hell that I'm having a good day. But I'll tell you now. I don't have many good days here in this craphouse."

"One more thing," he spit out. "Please try to break out. You will be hunted—and terminated. No one finds that inhumane. Personally, I find the hunting and killing of teenagers to be a fine pastime, like playing Candy Crush or shooting deer. There's nothing I like so much as a good hunt."

He wasn't finished because this was obviously a man who liked to hear himself talk.

"I am your boss, your father, your mother, your wife, your husband, your mentor and your worst tormenter," he whispered harshly in a way that made it sound like he was engraving the words into your skin.

He chose to walk now, and padded his girth past me. I let out a breath I had been holding, but held it again when he turned with the speed and agility of big cat sizing up tonight's prey.

At the top of his upper lip, I thought I detected a smile. "Well, well, well . . . they always come back to me. Can't get enough of me . . . now can you?" the GF said, moving his face inches from mine. "I'm everything you know now. Don't make me do something . . . distasteful. But maybe I'll do it anyway." His eyes bore into mine, and then he turned on his heels and headed for a small door. Before he could squeeze himself through the threshold, he yelled over his shoulder, "Take them to the showers! They all stink and I don't want to frighten the bedbugs."

What followed was Shawshank time.

There was the humiliating freezing cold shower with Aileen watching and enjoying. Afterward, my entire body was sprayed with some sort of white disinfecting powder that burned my nose and eyes. For both of these acts, my chains were taken off, which was good, but it wasn't so good when my street clothes were thrown down an incinerator to be burned. I was handed the standard-issue, gray ITT jumpsuit that made me look like some sort of felon Evel Knievel. I didn't resist. What was the point?

Back in Aileen's office, I saw her looking at my spanking-new ITT file, her brow lifting when she discovered Lizbeth's big X in the category that rated my difficultness.

"Sucks to be you, sugar cheeks," Aileen drawled.

"You're sending me to the Hole?" I asked. At least, I'd be closer to Daniel, although I was afraid to the core of being confined that way. Claustrophobia had never been my friend, but Aileen soothed my fears.

"Nah. You're a camper," Aileen said. "You get to experience the Outing."

"I don't do camping," I stated.

"Baby doll, here is the deal. I like you, maybe too much already," she said, coming closer to run a smooth hand down my cheek. "So, my little fellow rebel, I'm going to show you some respect and give you a sneak preview. You're going to spend night one outdoors on the top mountain ledge. Think of it as another little exercise we have here. And don't think of escaping because it's not possible. Take one foot off that ledge and it's a two-hundred-foot drop to the next roof," she said. "By midnight, the temperatures will be far below zero. And that's not your only problem."

"I have a problem?" I repeated. "So far, the orientation has been nothing but positive."

She chortled with snotty laughter that caused her to blow her nose into a nearby paper towel. And then she came in closer to explain the rest of it while running a long press-on nail down the other side of my face. "You'll have a candle and a thin blanket. Best to move around. A lot. We do have a high fence, so the critters can't get at you—at least not most of them. We did have one kid eaten by one of the mountain lions because lions are jumpers, but that was just one kid. What's one less kid to store? We've found several campers frozen to death. Remember, you don't have the reset anymore. Frostbite is nasty and if you go beyond frostbite, you're blood will actually freeze you in place. We found a girl frozen exactly like that. She was just sitting there, crisscross applesauce, with her hands raised in the praying position. Like a human popsicle."

"What happened to her?" I hated to ask.

"Thawed and we cut off her frostbit parts that would never work again. Lizbeth is good at chopping off the worthless pieces. Legs. Arms. Tongues. She loves it."

Then she added with a smile, "Happy camping, candy girl."

6.

It was at least ten below zero by midnight with winds sustaining thirty miles an hour. Being a native Chicagoan, I knew Mother Nature and I knew her well. I knew how she could whip her vengeance off Lake Michigan making you believe you *could* actually freeze in place. But no one ever froze while waiting for the city bus.

This was different.

The ITT prison ledge was primal—a narrow, jagged piece of rock made of carved slate and dirt and without a trace of anything living. Even the plants didn't dare try to poke through here. Above me was a flat, steep mountain wall jutting thousands of feet high into the sky. Below, a thousand feet of mountain plunged to ground level past the ITT building itself. Escape was a pipe dream. In fact, to place me here, the sadistic guards put a harness around my middle and lowered me from up above. Once my feet hit rock, I was told to unbuckle and they yanked the thing away.

I wasn't exactly dressed for camping without a coat, gloves, or a hat. My only defense from Mother was my thin, gray cotton jumpsuit and a wisp of a black prison-issued blanket the thickness of a piece of notebook paper.

Kneeling on the rocky floor with the black blanket over my head, I pulled my legs up against me until I couldn't feel them anymore. Then I remembered a movie I saw about a girl who lived in Hawaii. She was my age and spent lazy afternoons floating in the ocean on a raft, gently kicking her feet in those deep blue ocean waters to propel her journey.

Without a rational thought left in my head, I jetted my frozen legs outside of the blanket. And then I slowly began to kick, imagining I was swimming in warm, gentle waves with Daniel on a balmy day. We were on a large raft, me lying on his chest, and my legs were dangling in the tropical waters kicking gently so we could move to an even better location.

I did this on the rock until physical exhaustion set in and my feet were ice blocks.

At some point, I must have passed out from the bullying cold because I woke on my back staring up at a starless sky. The blanket was next to me and two black crows were perched on my frozen legs, but my eye movement indicated that I wasn't quite dinner material for them—at least not yet. I knew I couldn't die twice, but I could suffer pain and bodily damage including amputation. Losing a limb from Lizzy's blade sounded horrifying, but even raw fear couldn't motivate me to move. My eyes began to droop and then shut as my mind floated back into the Hawaii trance.

That's when I heard his voice. It was familiar, caring, and deep.

"Get up, grunt," he said in a soft, low tone. "On your feet. Immediately."

Something was tickling the side of my face and I saw it clearly—or did I? Maybe this was just a hallucination. He had my lucky green rabbit's foot and rubbed it gently on the side of my face. When I blinked hard and shook my head, my eyes focused. Nothing was there.

I sat up.

"Wake up, beautiful," he said.

The man I saw had broad shoulders, long blond hair that was slicked back off his face, and a square jaw that had been a target a few times in bar fights.

"I got you," Cass said. "Wake up and listen to me. If you want to make it."

I had met him only two days ago, at the end of our journey home. I only knew his first name and that he attended DeVry University. He was a mortal, human, living person and we visited his room in order to find the portal home. A not-so-geeky computer student, he looked more like a guy who should be riding ocean waves on some sunny beach in California than a tech student spending the holidays with his studies.

He wouldn't give us information unless I kissed him, which naturally I didn't want to do. But there was no choice because there was no time. He was lonely; his help came with a price.

Daniel wanted to kill him for turning his face at the last minute. Instead of a peck, my lips landed on his. Cass was psychic. He saw all of us, including Dr. King, and he helped us evade the demons.

The rest was history, although it wasn't the kind of history I ever wanted to repeat.

"Sugar," Cass said. "You need to wake up and listen to me. You're in trouble."

"This isn't real. No even remotely close to real," I muttered to myself, sinking back down until my face grazed the rock. "I can't move. I can't get up. My legs don't work now."

"Get the hell up now!" Cass barked. "Before I went to DeVry, I was in the Marines. I know every cold-weather survival trick in the book. You don't have fire and shelter, so you're oh for two there. But you do have to move or you'll spend the rest of eternity without a leg or arms."

"*You* were a marine?" I said in my stupor, lying back down with my blanket as a pillow. I was so numb that I couldn't even feel the cold anymore. It all felt like nothing.

"So why aren't you in the Marines anymore—wouldn't get the haircut?" I mumbled, curled now in the fetal position.

"Angel, no one in your platoon thinks you have all your marbles after you get drunk one night and announce that you're psychic. They call you *psycho* and grant you a dishonorable discharge. Now, get the hell up!"

He yelled it so loudly into my ear that I couldn't even enjoy drifting off into the void.

"Shut up. You're not here," I said to nothing.

For the next twenty minutes, he tickled my face with the rabbit's foot. He was so annoying that, finally, I used my shaking arms and the mountain wall to pull myself to my feet, but my legs—my poor frozen legs—wouldn't cooperate. Just like bendy straws, they bowed and then crumbled. Once again, I did a face plant with the rock.

"Again!" Cass barked. "Put your hand on the wall. Pull yourself up!"

I did it slower this time. My legs shook and my left leg didn't register even a hint of a feeling. With my hands, I hoisted myself vertical.

"Gently, shake one leg at a time like you're slowly using that leg to sweep a front porch and then brush yourself off. That's an order. Dirt makes you colder. It blocks ventilation," he said.

"I don't take orders," I grumbled.

"Fine, kick the shit out of me later, sugar. That might even be fun," he said. "For now, start with your feet. You need to move every single body part. Wiggle your toes. Stand tippy toe on them after you feel something. If it hurts, then scream. Then stand on your heels. Exert enough energy to move, but not enough to sweat. Sweating is your worst enemy. The water will lower your body temperature. Just do it!" he barked.

"I can't," I cried, as what felt like hot fire seared up both legs.

"If you do it, I'll tell you about your mother."

My heart stopped.

He said it in a low, controlled voice. His words hit me like a bomb.

"What do you know about my mother?"

"I know she lives in Greektown in Chicago. I know that she's in physical therapy at a rehab center. I know she left her apartment to take a walk around the block six hours and ten minutes ago. I know that because I went to check on her. In person. Why? I don't know. You can thank me later," he stated. "I know all about you, Walker Callaghan. You intrigue me. Now move your ass!"

"Tell me something about my mother that you couldn't know from reading the papers," I demanded, moving my feet, my ankles, and then lifting my bent knees up to my chest.

"She needs a new white cardigan. Lots of ravels in the one she wears," Cass said, adding, "Where's Boy Wonder? Execution-squad victim yet?"

"Never mind him," I shouted, moving faster now in some sort of spastic dance.

"Not too much moving," Cass said. "Slow, controlled motion. No sweating. We don't want to deal with hypothermia."

And so it went on with Cass telling me when to move and when to stop. When I refused, he dangled another tidbit about my mother's daily routine like a hunk of cheese taunting a hungry mouse. "Some wacko old lady named Minny visited her," he said. "She pulled up in some crazy-looking bright-green VW."

"Aunt Ginny?" I croaked into the night wind. She had that car since she was eighteen.

"She smelled like . . . and I don't mean to be rude, but what do you call a combo of that mouthwash . . . yeah, Listerine . . . mixed with the fine smell of kitty litter?" Cass asked.

"Aunt Ginny," I sighed.

After an hour of these tidbits, I believed him. But I still wanted him gone. That's when he gave me the rules.

"You can dismiss me. You can tell me you never want me to visit you again. That's your right—and I have to honor it. Call it a spiritual code of honor," Cass said. "That's how it works between my type and your type. Tell me to get the hell away forever, and I have to comply. The thing is, I wouldn't get rid of me for good if I were you, Walker. For one thing, I'm a lot more interesting than your candy-ass boyfriend."

"Piss off," I shouted into the wind.

"That's not good-bye, so I'll take it as a positive," Cass said. "And for another thing, I'm your special TV channel for information about your mother," he taunted. "Unless you don't want to hear about her ever again."

"And you're doing this because . . . ?" I asked, lowering my voice now. "You're this hard up for a date on a Friday night? They ran out of hot babes in the living realm?"

"Feisty when you're cold. I like it," Cass said. "Now, let's put some of that rage to good use. Get out of your head and into your body. Your body is stronger than you know—especially now, in your current state of being. Do five jumping jacks and tell me about this rabbit's foot. Who gave it to you? I bet it wasn't the rabbit."

"My father gave it to me. I would never hurt an animal," I bit out.

Then it dawned on me.

"Is that how you reached me? My rabbit's foot?" I demanded.

"Smart and beautiful. A hard combo to find in any realm," Cass said. "Yes, it helps if I have something that meant something to the person I'm trying to reach. Sorry I ripped you off. Lifted it right out of your pocket when you were in my room. But I can't send it back now can I? FedEx doesn't deliver where you are."

"Go to hell."

"Someday," he replied. "For now, jump up and down three

times and tell me about your dad. Steelworker, right? I overheard your mama talking to Ginny about him. Gotta love Aunt Ginny. But back to Dad. He was hardheaded like you, I'm sure. A real know-it-all when you're really just a know-some-of-it-all."

"Stop minding my business," I screamed into the night. "Don't you have a life to live?"

"Wiggle your right hand, sugar. In fact, flip me the bird," Cass demanded and I did as I was told. With both hands.

"Get down on the ground and give me five crunches. Your ribs are turning a little blue and I'm worried about your internals."

"Leave my internals out of it," I yelled.

"Stop flirting with me," Cass said.

Around three in the morning, Cass confessed that he loved *Dancing with the Stars*. I sneered as he cha-cha-ed across his dorm room at DeVry. From that moment until dawn, he made me dance every single dance I remembered from that show . . . and then dance them again. I have always been a horrible dancer with two left feet and absolutely no rhythm.

But I was a good mover.

And that made me a great camper.

After the sun came up and I was pulled off the mountain, an ITT nurse looked at my bluish feet and decided that I would keep them because actual frostbite hadn't set in—at least not to the point where amputation would be required. My hands were given the same prognosis.

I don't know how I survived that night. Maybe it was sheer willpower or knowing that Daniel was somewhere very near, buried deep in the ground trying to take his next breath in the pitch-black darkness. If he could make it until morning, so would I. That's how I survived—in spite of Cass who never left me.

His best survival technique: Annoyance.

CHAPTER 6

1.

After a much too intrusive wellness exam in the infirmary the entire next day, where I can sadly report Florence Nightingale did not appear, I was immediately taken to my new forever home: D Block. My new house featured side-by-side, eight-by-eight glass boxes where the worst of the worst teenage criminals were housed for all eternity.

On the A, B, and C floors at ITT, the cells were stacked upward as far as the eye could see, like children's building blocks. Those in D Block were "special" and there was only one long row of glass boxes. What lurked inside required "observation" from specially trained guards with zero tolerance for specially incarcerated adolescents.

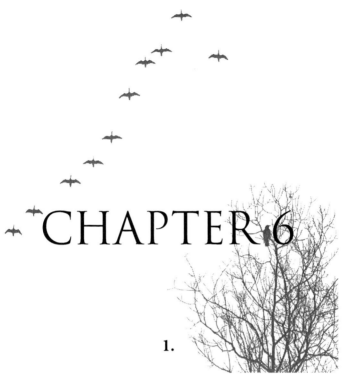

A guard with crater-sized pits in his face took me "home" to Cell 18. First, there was the walk through the "hood" to meet my new neighbors. A baby-faced murderer flipped me the bird while two gangbangers, housed side by side, chose to start licking the glass like it was the most delicious Popsicle. One girl, described as a "very bad babysitter" took a finger and faux slit her throat. A dimple-faced drug kingpin laughed like a lunatic, but I couldn't hear him. Unsatisfied, he hurled his body hard against the glass three times until he landed flat on his back on the floor. Almost every single one of them, male and female, made eye contact because I was fresh meat, their favorite meal.

I also found that there wasn't much ceremony to being locked away forever. Pit Face swiped three different key cards over some complicated, computerized lock system, an upgrade of what you might find at some fancy, five-star hotel. Instead of glass, each cell had an electric force field in front of it that was "managed" by devices that protected the guards, but nearly melted off prisoners' flesh if they tried to take even one step out of their cells without express permission.

What I saw inside my own cell shocked me.

"There's nothing in here," I said to the guard as we stepped into my new surroundings.

No bed. No desk. No chair. Just a translucent sink and toilet.

I spied a sliver of soap as my only amenity.

"What about a blanket?" I demanded. Didn't I still have basic human rights for food and shelter?

"Girlie, you gotta earn those things and it might take you a year, but no matter. All you got is time. Lotta lotta time," Pit Face smirked, handing me what looked like exactly five squares of toilet paper.

"Use 'em wisely—and use 'em again and again," he said, laughing loudly at his own bad joke.

"I have to earn freaking toilet paper?" I responded, standing there completely astonished and devastated.

"You earn everything here. You know that cakewalk that most

of you call a teenage life. Sweet face, your life of leisure . . . it's *o-v-e-r*," he said, spelling it out. "Every single thing you need will be determined by someone else. You have no choice but to live with it. Lights out or I'll bust the bulbs," he yelled before activating my electrified cell entryway, but I couldn't comply. I didn't have a lamp. I only had my five squares and my sliver.

And just like that, the world went black.

It was dark to the point that when I held my hand up high, it was obliterated by the void. The force field that contained me was soundproof, but there were two rows of small air holes along the top and bottom of each glass wall dividing the cells. I could slightly hear other prisoners—and the sound effects were nonstop.

Focus Walker. You're locked in. They're locked out. What about the glass? Can they break it? Can I?

It didn't take long for the broken kids on Cellblock D to start their evening moans and screams. "Wanna go home!" one moaned, starting a chorus of woe. "Mom!" yelled another. "Save me. I'm sorry!" Those who yelled the loudest heard their force field abruptly turn off. Then came the screams. The guards beat them into submission until silence reigned again at ITT.

This was the nightly routine.

"Hello," said a meek voice into the silence. "Helloooooooo?"

You couldn't miss the little-boy tone. It belonged to my next-door neighbor over in Cell 17.

"Say something," he whispered, and then spoke for me. "Something!" he answered with a muffled giggle. "Scientifically, it's the opposite of nothing . . . . Hello?"

His excitement was palpable.

2.

How could I have missed him when I arrived in Cell 18? Of course, I knew who was in Cell 17 because I had recently visited him. I knew only too well, but it just didn't register in the moment.

A.E., as he liked to be called, was always bright and eager like a fresh puppy. He was a fourteen-year-old genius boy who redefined skinny. He had a Dennis the Menace do, a fresh sprinkling of zits, and a smile that ignited his entire extra-long jaw that would have someday fit his face.

In the blackness of ITT, I heard him shuffling around. My eyes hadn't totally adjusted to the darkness yet, but I could sense he was trying to stare at me. "Hey, Walker Callaghan," he whispered. "Come on, Walker. I saw you come in even if you didn't see me. But now you have to talk to me. You have to tell me. You know. You promised."

At first, I pretended not to hear him and sat on the hard floor of my cell. When my legs began to fall asleep, I tried the prone position of staring up at the glass ceiling with the fabulous view of the leaking drainage pipes that made it bone-aching cold and damp.

When my bones began to throb down to the marrow, I got frustrated and stood up. "How do I get out of here?" I yelled to no one in particular.

"Shut up! The guards will come again," screamed a low voice several cells away. When things became quiet again, the little boy's voice filled my head.

"It's A.E. here. Where is my report?" he demanded. He was a kid who wanted what he wanted—now.

"A.E., I don't have anything to write on," I said, tears springing to my eyes. I didn't even have a pencil and would probably never see paper again. Suddenly, it was the little things that were big things. Daniel had absolutely nothing. Not even fresh air. Clearing my throat, I added, "Why don't you run down to the local computer store and get me a new laptop so I can get on that report right away."

"Okeydokey," he said in a cheery voice. "But I don't think there is an Apple store here. Plus, no moola for a computer. So, it can be like a speech. Start talking."

Was this kid insane? Did he really think I cared about his needs?

"First, I need to know . . . how do you survive in here?" I whispered, the tears flowing now, as I allowed myself to collapse to the hard floor again with my face buried under my hands.

"Never sleep," he whispered. "And never cry."

I heard his small voice coming from the lower left side of the floor. He wouldn't be silenced now and jabbered on and on. His words were clear and contained the promise of actually conversing with another life form. I knew it was crazy, but for some reason, I found myself sliding on my back, over to the glass wall we shared. Again, I didn't say a word.

He did.

"Where is my report," he demanded, speaking into the six tiny air holes between our cells.

"You've got to be shitting me," I responded in a low voice. "'Where is your freaking report?' That's all you can say?"

"You went back. You're here, so you got caught. No one is going to throw a party, but still . . ." A.E. reasoned as he sulked at the same time. "You promised if I helped you find the portal then you'd write a really good report and give it to me. You promised to type it, Walker. Double-spaced. Just sayin'. A promise is a promise."

I had just been arrested, stripped, showered, and left to freeze overnight on a mountain ledge. Then I was examined and put in this pit of a glass cell with five squares of toilet paper as my only worldly possessions. What was I supposed to carry his report in? "Kid, your report is in my luggage. I'm sure the bellman will be delivering all my stuff soon. Watch for my bags. Just slip the guy a fiver and you can go through my stuff and find your freakin' report," I said.

"Rude," he said with a hurt sniff.

For the next few minutes he was silent, but the quiet was even worse. A.E. would not be dimmed. Now that my eyes had adjusted, I saw him do cartwheels in his cell and then he stood on his head for what I estimated to be a good six minutes. It was like watching some sort of prisoner version of *Limbo's Got Talent.*

Great. I would have to spend eternity next door to the most annoying kid-brother figure in history. For an encore, he blew spitballs at the opposite glass wall. One by one, they stuck then fell. ITT had a way of making anything buckle. Except for A.E.

"I can do the splits."

"Knock yourself out, Cirque du Soleil," I said.

"What was it like?" he asked after he had unsplit himself. "Just tell me. Please. It makes me feel like I'm alive again. Tell me one thing. One word. What was it like?" he begged. "Was it hot? Was it cold? Did you get to eat anything good? Did you see anyone you knew?"

"Shit-ass scary. That's what it was like. You got three words. Now, leave me alone."

Of course, he didn't and he wouldn't, which is the way that most friendships actually form in life or here. One person resists and the other convinces them that they should try it on for a while. Once even the thinnest foundation is poured, you keep building until something solid remains.

Daniel and I poured that foundation with A.E. before we went back. We had come to ITT to get his help and he told us where to find the portal back. He had also warned us to bring ancient weapons with us, as those were the only things that worked against the demon forces back in the living realm—and he was right again.

In many respects, he saved our dead asses.

My anger faded when I realized a hard truth. A.E. saved me once. Maybe he would again. For now, we only had each other.

As days turned into a week or so, I tried not to let my mind wander to Daniel. But sometimes I'd wake up in a sweat, screaming his name, and A.E. would whisper up to the air holes, "Sis, breathe. Just breathe. And please be quiet or they will beat you. They beat you for anything in here." I shuddered to imagine anyone putting a finger on this kid who was so skinny he could snap in two.

I stifled my screams and my tears and life fell into an uneasy routine.

Over the next few weeks, A.E. proved to be a decent next-door neighbor. He put one of his many *Archie* comics that he'd earned up to the glass, so I could read something. And he always looked away when I used my toilet or "showered" if you could call it that. Mostly, I just drip-dried after washing off at my sink. Each week, when I was given a fresh, clean uniform, A.E. would press his face into his bed, so I could change.

At fourteen years old, he clearly found any sort of public nudity to be absolutely mortifying.

Modesty wasn't really a problem here.

Our cells faced a jagged, brown stone fortress of a wall that was the side of the mountain. Few guards ever walked in front of us except at mealtime when a small tray was slid through a slot in a narrow strip of glass wall that bordered the electrified field. Cell 19 was empty, so there were no privacy issues for me there.

One morning, I woke up worried sick after dreaming about Daniel and my head hurt. My back felt as if it was broken after sleeping on that hard glass floor and I was barely able to move.

"I could read you the comics. Get closer to the air holes," A.E. offered in his chipper morning voice.

"That'd be great, A.E." Just moving a little made it feel like tiny knives were twisting inside my muscles.

"Albert," he interrupted. "It makes me sound older. Like fifteen. It also calms my anxieties."

"Okay, Alfonso."

"No, it's Albert."

"Yeah, right, Albino. You got anxieties in here? Why? Think of it as a vacation."

"Studies show that high school students now have the same anxiety levels as insane asylum patients in the nineteen fifties," he quoted. Where he was quoting from, I wasn't sure, but my money was on the idea that he was right.

"Start reading, Archibald."

So I sat there on the floor all day with my muscles contracting as he read. It was one of the most beautiful acts of kindness ever bestowed on me because in those hours, I could transport myself out of ITT to the land of Betty and Veronica and no one could chain me.

And it was that evening I told him everything about our trip back to life. By the time I finished, it was dark again and his eager-beaver mouth was silent.

It's hard to speak when your jaw is firmly planted on the floor.

3.

Meals were actually the worst of it. Some no-name guard with a cigarette hanging from his lips, ashes dangling precariously close to the food, was a one-man "room service" staff. He pushed a metal tray through a locked slot in front of your cell, and some of the time it got stuck and it was up to you to pull as much of the food through as possible.

Most of the time the meal was either slightly molding, rock-hard white bread laced with one thin slice of mystery meat, or greasy beans with a few pieces of pork gristle in them. It tasted like mushy salt and there wasn't enough of it. I pretended the pork fat, the stuff they probably threw away at the Academy, was slightly pink filet mignon. The other meal of choice for breakfast and dinner (there was no lunch) was a small bowl of cold oatmeal with a slice of fake, vomit-scented cheese on top.

"They had the same menu at San Quentin," A.E. told me.

He knew a little about everything, which amounted to a lot.

One day, breakfast came with an old copy of the ITT school paper. *Words! Glorious printed words!* I wanted to devour them, not caring that the actual words were about the mundane life at ITT including news of their "red-hot hockey season" that was already in progress. My eyes were as hungry as my stomach and I read the same words over and over again. It was all about beating the Academy. "I'm seeking vengeance for last season's pitiful loss. Ruin 'em. Disembowel them!" the GF was quoted.

The next day, my dinner was accompanied by something ever more bizarre: a warm can of Coke Zero. I guzzled it down like it was the kind of fine champagne that movie stars ordered for five hundred dollars a pop.

These odd offerings continued. A Snickers bar was pushed

through the slot and I wanted to give it to a bug-eyed A.E., who loved candy. Unfortunately, I couldn't get it to him and in a moment of weakness ate it in three big caramel-and-chocolate-infused bites. The next day it was a bag of chips (Heaven!) and after I pitifully begged the no-neck guard, he begrudgingly slid them into A.E.'s meal slot. I knew what the kid would do—and he didn't disappoint me. Separating each chip as if it were made out of spun glass, he gingerly counted his spoils.

"Twenty-three beautiful, crispy, perfectly greasy potato slices," he boasted.

Every hour or so, he allowed himself exactly one chip, eating it in several microscopic small bites to make it last longer. When he crunched his last, he turned away to not-so-silently cry.

Finally, after seven days of treats, I received a simple note with my hamburger and greasy fries. It was addressed to inmate D-18 and simply read: MY OFFICE. 6 A.M. TOMORROW. Confused, I looked at A.E. who was leaning hard into the clear wall to read it, too.

"Whose office?" I asked. A.E. just smiled and pointed up. Staring at the ceiling of my cell, I looked at nothing but clear glass, drainage pipes, and rugged mountain. I shrugged and he laughed like only a fourteen-year-old boy can. "No, silly," he said. "Read the top of the paper."

The insignia was from our warden.

4.

At 5:45 a.m. the following morning, a nameless guard entered my glass cage, cuffed my hands behind me, and gave me a slight shove toward my safely open cell doorway. After walking the gangplank of D Block and taking the main, heavily guarded elevator down to the second level, we arrived at a small gray waiting room outside the GF's office. The guard uncuffed me, and then left without saying a word.

There was nowhere to sit except for a hard, faded black-and-blue-checkered couch that looked as if it had already served back-to-back life sentences. Some of the squares were rubbed out from wear and others sported blood and other stains of a bodily fluid variety.

Absent was the pleasant secretary type who flanked Dr. King's office at the Academy. I'll never forget that on my first day there. I was similarly summoned to the highest authority figure's lair, but that time an assistant met my mother and me with cookies and hot tea.

This was obviously . . . *different.*

A skinny guard with a pointed chin, long hooked nose, and black, beady eyes flanked the GF's outer office. He sat with his feet propped up on a desk and twirled his standard-issue .38 revolver. He also wore a big, black billy club that ran the length of his sticklike legs—just in case. Of what, I didn't know. A prison riot seemed unlikely, but possible, I guess. Then again, maybe I had seen too many movies.

The guard was watching a rerun of *The Sopranos*, a show I loved when I was in the living realm. Squinting to make up the distance, I could see that this was the episode where Tony's mother died. *Good episode. Next comes the part where all the guys say they're sorry although they're not so sorry because Tony's mom had put a hit out on him. Everyone knew it. . . .*

"Girlie! I said, girlie!'" the rat-faced guard snapped in a nasally voice like he had the world's worst cold. "On your feet! That couch doesn't say, 'Prisoner resting area' now does it?" he wheezed. "And no monkey business, girlie, or I'll take care of you myself."

I stood.

I thought about Daniel and tears sprung to my eyes. *Where are you, Daniel? I know you're here, somewhere. I feel you.*

I stood and clenched my fists because I was absolutely powerless. Finding Daniel wasn't an option because even moving a few inches without express permission was forbidden. I wouldn't mind every push, punch, and punishment in store for me if I found him. I knew that guards like Rat Face, here, knew how to inflict pain. They lived for it.

"So, why am I here?" I demanded.

"Girlie, what am I? The evening news?" he wheezed. In the background, I could hear Tony Soprano putting out a hit on someone. In my mind's eye, I imagined that Tony could put a hit on this guard who resembled basic gutter vermin crossed with Barney Fife.

Yes, I was powerless, but that still didn't explain why I was outside the prison warden's office after eating a lovely breakfast that included two cold waffles and a day-old mug of French vanilla coffee. I shuddered to think what the GF wanted from me.

"He will see you now," said Rat Face in an ominous tone. "Move!"

5.

I found the most powerful man at ITT with his big, fat fingers buried in a double slab of Kansas City ribs from Barry's Barbecue, a place that didn't skimp on sauce. It was 6:15 in the morning and the misty light of a rainy day filled the room. Breakfast time—thick red stuff rolled off of the GF's cheeks, dripping onto his enormous wooden desk. With no obvious thought of hygiene, the GF wiped his messy hands on a large bath towel that served as his personal napkin. It looked like he had just used it to mop up a bloody murder scene.

"Miss Callaghan," he said in an almost elegant voice. "I hope you're finding your accommodations here to be suitable. It's not a penthouse at the Four Seasons, but we do what we can."

"Sit," Rat Face commanded, first tapping his billy club on a chair in front of the warden's desk, and then poking it lightly into my ribs. I didn't sit down.

"That's enough, Eugene. There's no need for actual harassment," the GF said. "Go out there and round up a Diet Seven Up and the big bag of Famous Amos."

"Always drink diet colas. Force of habit," GF said to me, patting his ample girth and sneering as his bottom lip curled into what was a half smile. "That was a joke, Miss Callaghan," he added. "I do expect you to laugh. Or we can revisit the idea of actual harassment."

I gave him my best cold smile. My eyes were dead. *Why was I here? Why was I being summoned?*

"Why are *you* here?" I was bold enough to blurt out. My reporter's instincts knew that it would throw him. It wasn't the question he was expecting.

"You could say I'm here because the angel gig doesn't always work out," he bit out.

"Was that ever really an option?" I said in my boldest voice.

What did I have to lose now? My mother was gone; Daniel was lost to me. I was standing in an office with a bear of a man in his undershirt, old suspenders, and greenish-gray pants like the ones my grandfather George used to wear. Sweat poured off the GF making him smell like the public bathrooms at the beach on a hot,

hot day. One part mold. The other part rot. He seemed to perspire even more mulling over what I just asked.

"Sit down, Miss Callaghan. I have a proposition for you that you might find interesting," he said. "And generally I hate small talk, so let's just get on with it."

With no choice, I slowly sat while he grabbed my two armrests, leaned in hard, and towered over me. Small sweat drops hit my face, my arms, and my legs.

"First things first. I can't call you Walker. To me, the name Walker means Chuck Norris. You know, the Texas Ranger. So, I'll just call you Literature. Yes, I like it. Literature."

My face was as blank as a white sheet of typing paper.

"I don't see you as the mopping floors type, Literature. But it is time to find something for you to do in here. An idle mind is the . . . well, it's not a good idea."

I stared into his lifeless brown eyes.

"I'm embarking on two massive projects," he continued, searching my face for some sort of excitement. *Yes, he wanted me to think what he was about to tell me was thrilling. If he loved it, I was supposed to love it. It was forced enthusiasm at its best. You could ask Heath. I wasn't that good an actress.* "First, I'm going to win back that hockey trophy if it's the last thing I ever do. I can't tell you why it's so important to me—but it is. Secondly, when I was asked to prepare a speech that I'm delivering tonight at the Friar's Club, it got me thinking about an even more important project."

I was gazing down at my fingernails so he grabbed my chin in his beefy hand and forced me to look into his eyes again.

"As you might imagine, I lived quite a colorful life," he said, chuckling. He sobered when his eyes dipped lower.

As I recoiled, he pushed off the chair, which sent the furniture and me flying backward across the room. When my head bashed into a wall and my neck snapped back, he didn't flinch or stop talking. I saw stars and wondered if I could even manage to stay sitting. I wanted to slide to the floor.

The GF threw me his used barbecue towel. "Personally, I don't care if you're beaten *and* broken. I don't care what the guards do with you—or to you. I won't care if you are locked in a glass box so deep into this mountain that no one even remembers you exist anymore. Prison is like real estate. It's all about location, location, location."

I dabbed the blood that dripped from my temple and down my neck. There was no choice, but to listen to him.

"As I was saying, and it would behoove you to listen, I grew up poor. Real poor. In New Jersey. Never knew my Daddy. Ma worked down in Atlantic City inside the hotels, dancing, mingling, if you know what I mean, until she got too old. Kicked me out when I was eleven. You could say I was a self-made man whose living room was the streets. Ran card games under the Boardwalk. Got shot the first time when I was fifteen, but we'll save the good parts for later."

He was intent on me actually listening to him, so I nodded.

"And that was just the beginning. My life story comprises the sum total of what I need you to do for me. But, of course, you have a choice. Write my memoir, Literature—or go to the Hole and think about doing it until you break."

I just stared at him dumbfounded.

"You're my ghost writer," he said, laughing at his own miserable joke. "Ghost. Writer. Do you get it?"

I got it. And I could see it clearly. Hours and days and weeks and months in this office. With him looking at me the way he was looking now. My skin was crawling and the open window actually seemed like an option. For either of us.

In my misery came just one second of clarity.

"If I do it, what do I get out of it?" I brazenly asked him. "I don't exactly need another can of warm Mountain Dew."

He took a few lumbering steps closer to me again. This time, he grabbed the neck of my prison-issued shirt and pulled me to my feet. When, with one hand, he lifted my feet off the floor until they were dangling, my will almost snapped. But I still looked him square in the face, especially now that our eyes were level with each other.

"Your pay is simple," he bit out. "You will get a bed to sleep in. You will be issued a blanket so you won't freeze. You will get a whole roll of toilet paper for when you need to . . . well, wouldn't want your dainty skin to get a rash now would we?"

He ran a fat finger up from my chest to my face, and I willed myself not to flinch when he lingered on my bottom lip.

"You will earn a desk and a lamp, plus a typewriter and paper to work after hours—and don't even think about upgrading to a computer; we do this the old-fashioned way. You will also get time out of the cage. Out of D Block. You'll get the luxury of spending time in here with me. Interviewing me. Writing my book. We will grow excitingly close as we share secrets with one another. And, in return, I keep visitors away from your cell at night. *All visitors.* Including certain janitors who have you on their wish list, as do several inmates with the last name Wargo. And if I like what you write, that list of no visitors will also include myself."

He said that last part long and slow. Of course, I understood. Prison wasn't exactly a safe place for a girl my age.

"You're a very attractive girl, Walker, and you would fall under my personal arm of protection when it came to that kind of thing—and no one would dare disappoint me," he said in a low voice. "It's not often that we get such a lovely, smart, and clean girl here like yourself," he added, smoothing a few strands of my hair off my face. "That's better. Your face is lovely." My stomach lurched.

"What I desire is only one thing," I said, boldly and loudly, ignoring his advances.

I continued to dangle.

"I don't have a hearing problem," he said. "Just say it. I might even find some generosity deep within my soul. You give to me . . . and I give to you."

"Daniel Reid out of the Hole—today," I said, leaning forward slightly as a challenge. He still held me up as all my blood was rushing to my feet.

"A girl with balls. I like it," he said in a considering voice. "But that's not on the menu, Literature. Tough Guy stays put. We'll know in a few more weeks if his marbles are scrambled or not."

"*A few weeks*!" I said in an astonished voice as my hands began to shake. "He was only supposed to be in the hole for a few days and now it's weeks?"

A scary silence set in.

"Your decision?" he demanded. "Say no and your boy will never leave the Hole."

I lifted my head, which had sunken deep into my chest, and nodded in agreement. It was the slowest nod I had ever produced in my entire life or death. Moving my head in micro inches, I felt part of my soul literally slipping away. What he wanted was what I held dear to me. What was left.

My writing and Daniel. *He would own both now.*

"We will start tomorrow at promptly 6:00 a.m. Give Eugene your breakfast order," he said. "I suggest eggs and bacon."

"And for your cooperation, Literature, and because you have some real balls for a girl, I guarantee you one thing to really make it interesting . . . because I love to make it interesting. I've been here since February of nineteen twenty-nine or thirty . . . I forget. No matter. So I gotta keep it interesting."

My eyes focused on him for the last time that day.

"Your little boyfriend will get food and water today. He hasn't had much of that in a long time. See? I have a heart under all this soul. One more thing: Get a good night's sleep. Tell that sniveling brat next door to shut up, or I'll move him. Can't have my writer coming in here exhausted tomorrow," said the now chipper GF.

But he wasn't finished.

He flicked his finger and dropped me to the ground. I landed knees first in a bleeding heap. "Each day you write, your boy will eat and get water. On days when you choose not to write, he will starve and go thirsty," the GF bit out. "If I don't like what you write, he will be beaten. So, you better write real good. You could say that his fate is in your nimble typing fingers."

As Rat Face dragged me away, the last thing I smelled was my heartless captor opening the box of deep-dish pizza that had been set on his desk. After devouring what was left of me, it was time for his next snack.

6.

You can close your eyes to the things you don't want to see. But you can't close your heart to the things you don't want to feel. I was having the best dream of falling hard, face-first, through one of the waterfalls near here with Daniel's strong arms and legs wrapped around me . . . when Aileen shook me.

"Honey bee, I'm your early morning wake-up call. Apparently, you have some permanent day pass to go to the Zoo," she said.

The Zoo? Was she going to feed me to the tigers for her own personal amusement?

"Yeah, the Zoo. That's what I call the GF's office because it's always filled with you animals," she said with a smirk, resting her hands on hips that were shoved into jeans at least a size too small.

"He has a lot of animals working for him including that repulsive rat Eugene, and Eddie. Eddie's a raptor. But I like you. With your long legs. I'll call you the giraffe," she snorted.

Then she tossed me a heap of cotton that was tied with a rope in the middle.

"Here's a clean outfit. The GF doesn't like his zoo animals to smell," she retorted as I unfolded what looked like regular Levis and a black, low-cut tee. I wore a medium and this shirt was a small.

"So what animal is the GF?" I asked,

"He's a mountain lion. Downs his prey in one bite. Get dressed," she said.

I turned my back to her and quickly changed clothes. Dangling my chains from her fingers, she gave me a pitying look, but didn't move to cuff me. Obviously, it was a trust issue and she skipped the chains as I followed her meekly to the elevator.

When we reached the administration floor, once again, I looked through actual windows that gave me a glimpse of the outside and I walked as slowly as possible to take it in. Funny what you miss when you're no longer allowed an existence. Through those dirty prison windows, I saw puffy, low clouds with yellow drenches of sunlight pouring through them. The pureness of the natural light made my lungs back up. Had weeks gone by or was it months? It was all becoming a blur.

Then my mind cleared.

It was a Tuesday. It was probably February. It was cold. I had to write today.

Rat Face nodded as we walked through the waiting area and, luckily, the main office was empty. Apparently, the GF was somewhere else doing God only knows what.

About a half an hour later, I was sitting at an archaic black 1950s-style typewriter in the corner of the GF's office when, suddenly, another prisoner waltzed in with news. He had obviously been doing his rounds, spying on students in A Block, and found a few who had apparently been plotting a rebellion. He blurted it out without noticing his boss wasn't there. Finally, when his brain kicked in, I met Eddie Wargo's lusty gaze with a frosty one of my own.

"You're a narc?" I stated.

I heard Aileen's voice in my head. *Eddie is a raptor.*

When I stood up, he took his hands and shoved me hard into the wall. Ducking to the right, he body checked me and there was no doubt which zoo mammal was stronger. We hadn't had an encounter since I decked him when Bobby and I were racing out of ITT. Eddie obviously wanted a little payback.

"Not so tough now without the big guy protecting you, huh? GF will get tired of you. Then you won't be protected no more and no one will care what happens to you. Of course, I'll care when I come visit you late at night," he promised.

GF chose that moment to walk in and he shook his head.

"Eddie, stop flirting," he said, booting him out the door. "Literature, get back to work."

CHAPTER 7

1.

A month passed and I did my work, day after day after day, carefully timing my once-a-week inquiry to the GF.

"What about Daniel Reid?" I asked.

"He resisted again," GF said. "We actually took him out of the Hole to the hockey stadium. Hog tied him in the middle of the rink and had my guards shoot pucks at him. Do you know how fast a hockey puck travels?"

I shuddered.

"Ninety miles an hour," the GF smirked, coming around his desk to hand me a few pages he had edited. "What I didn't plan on was your boy keeping a few of the pucks by sneaking them down his pants and then shoving one down a guard's throat. The man has no tonsils now. So, your boy's still in the Hole."

"Sadist," I couldn't help muttering under my breath.

"Miss Callaghan, I'm hurt by the judgmental things you say," said the GF, moving closer.

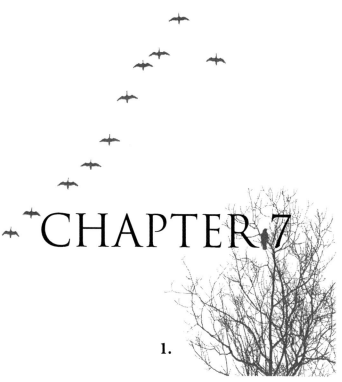

"Imagine the things I hold back," I retorted and braced for his punishment. If Daniel could withstand the pain then so could I. I could feel the GF's breath and then his hand when he cracked me across the face, but then I was saved by a red light flashing on his phone. Turning away from me, he ordered, "I want to see the chapter four revisions in the next hour—or neither of you will eat tonight. You or Lover Boy."

The fact that Daniel could resist gave me hope, despite the sting in my cheek. His brain was still on max.

2.

The blackness of each night was the worst of it, although occasionally a visitor snuck through—the type that the GF couldn't get rid of for me. Cass was tuning into my dreams, and most of the time I dismissed him. But one night he came to me, before I had drifted off, holding what looked like a piece of 8x10 paper. On it was a picture he took of *my mother*. She was walking by Lake Michigan with only a cane. Her hair was swept back and her face had color again

She was getting better.

"Thank you," I told him in a depressed voice. "I mean it. Really. Thank you, Cass."

"No problem, sugar," he said into my left ear. "How are you feeling?"

"Can you send my mother a message?"

"Not now," he said, adding, "but I can stay with you unless you want me to go. Do you really want me to go? It's your choice."

"Yes, go for now," I said because his mere presence made me

feel as if I was being unfaithful to Daniel, which wasn't possible.

"Sleep well, Walker," he replied, honoring my wishes. Maybe it was my imagination, but it felt as if someone or something pressed warm lips to my ear in a kiss.

My days were occupied by writing down the stories the GF told me about his days of murder and mayhem in the great state of New Jersey. He vividly described the night when he shot up a hotel where Benny the Hat himself was having a steak and lobster dinner at a place known as the Shrimp Box. Benny was, of course, known for his love of charred beef, his black fedora, and killing anyone in his way.

"It was your classic drive-by near the shore in Asbury Park. We shot that place up with thousands of slugs—and the place ain't that big," he bragged. "Benny, the local mob boss of Jersey and a coward, was cowering in the corner when my brother Stevie came out in a khaki Army shirt and brown overalls. Stevie had a Thompson submachine gun with a hundred-round drum. He hid in the doorway and emptied a storm of bullets into the place, wrecked the shrimp fryer in back, but nothing hit that bastard Benny." He laughed hard and added. "So after he was out of slugs, Stevie strolled back to the car and we went to breakfast at Grandma's."

"Your grandmother's house?" I inquired for purposes of accuracy.

"No, Grandma's as in Timmy One Foot's basement hideaway. Timmy had no numbers on his house and he made great Swiss cheese omelets," he said.

Noticing me wince, the GF licked his lips. "Not a fan of dairy?" he inquired and I looked down and kept typing.

"That's why I've been here for at least eighty years and counting. Lots of penance to do, Literature. But with penance done right comes perks. Believe it or not, I'm one of the most powerful men here now. A real decision-maker. Each year, I'm entitled to more and more perk-o-lators, as I call them. I'm not one of the Higher Authority, but I am one of their advisors—and I enjoy expanded powers—especially when it comes to anything having to do with ITT."

"Don't write that last part down," he added. "They don't want people to know there are advisors," he instructed. "Advisors are always ghosts, so to speak."

For a minute, I stopped typing. An even bigger pause was required when Rat Face tapped on the door.

"Where do you want it?" he said in his wheezy voice. "I could deliver it to your office or maybe we's run it through the laundry. Needs some serious cleaning. Or I could kick the shit out of it and deliver it outside your window where they let the dogs take their dumps."

"Bring it in—now," GF barked, giving me a "wait a minute" finger. I stared down at the typewriter, waiting for my next marching orders.

"Here it is," Rat Face said, and I heard him shove something massive onto the office floor where it landed with a thud.

As Rat Face left the room, I finally stared at what he had left behind.

Daniel was out of the Hole.

He looked like a mountain man with over two months worth of beard now and long, schizophrenic hair falling forward into his steely eyes. His face was thinner, cheeks hollowed, and skin yellowed from the lack of food and the conditions. Obviously, he had found some way to move in those tight conditions because, in a gray jumpsuit, Daniel's body seemed even more sinewy, his broad shoulders and muscles barely contained in the snug prison garb. The strong lines on his arms looked like a well-defined map. He must have spent the time working out, probably doing sit-ups and push-ups, using his own body as the weight.

He looked animalistic to me. Wild. Ready to strike. I could see a new, thick, dark scar that now ran along his jawline. I could also see the red, swollen welts up and down his arms and legs from those hard hockey pucks that they must have continued to torture him with.

His eyes were hard, focused, hungry, and furious.

They also registered momentary shock at the sight of me.

He wasn't wearing any chains, except for the collar around his neck, which surprised me. Our eyes met and locked. But Daniel recovered quickly from the jolt of our reunion. He turned his face a microfraction on second thought. He refused to make eye contact with me again, measuring if it would be safe and knowing it wouldn't. I'm sure he could smell my nerves.

I was paralyzed at my little makeshift desk in the corner of the room. And then I couldn't stand up quickly enough, which meant the loose pages of manuscript went flying like large sheets of confetti.

"My book! She's not done writing my book!" the GF screamed, entering the fury zone. He wasn't sure what to do first—punish me or grab the pages that could easily fly out the open window into the spring winds.

"Stay," GF boomed in my direction. Then with his neck veins bulging, he lumbered to his feet as quickly as he could move, which was blindingly fast for a man of his size. He used his greasy fingers to grab as many pages as possible as they flew around the room like a mini tornado.

For a minute, it looked like Daniel was stepping forward to help him retrieve the work.

With great purpose, Daniel took three strides toward my desk.

Lightening fast, he took my face in his bloodied hands. Quickly, I ran my hand over his scar. He lifted my right hand and brushed his warm lips to it.

"Stand back, you son of a . . . !" the GF yelled, dumping the pages onto his desk, securing them with a paperweight rock and pivoting hard to rip Daniel away. Always the agile soccer player, Daniel easily evaded the older man's fumbling grab, leaning his top half way back, Matrix style, which caused the GF to miss and then fall face-first over a pile of books I had stacked on the floor.

He fell hard enough for the tile floor to rumble. Like a beached whale, the GF tried to roll to his side, his arms and legs scrambling. His face was deep crimson from humiliation and red-hot anger.

"The only reason you're here . . . is for a chance . . . to make the right choice!" the GF bellowed, his words forced as he reached for my desk to right himself. He was too big, and the desk legs crumbled, which caused my typewriter to come crashing to the ground.

Daniel did the only thing he could do under the circumstances. While the GF tried to pull himself to his feet again, the man who had survived over two months in the Hole tenderly grabbed the back of my head with his large, loving hands and swiftly drew me in for a deep kiss that made my brain roar.

"You will regret this!" the GF screamed, hitting a button on his belt. Rat Face and two guards were instantly in the room, helping the mountain of a man to his feet. "Take him away. Thirty more days in the Hole! I hope it was worth it!" the GF barked, but first he took one of those meaty fists and punched Daniel hard in the mouth.

"No!" I screamed as his dark hair and pale flesh snapped backward.

Because Daniel didn't cry out, the GF took a small hunting knife out of his side pocket. The two guards flanked Daniel, and

Rat Face slammed cuffs on him. The GF approached and ran the blade over Daniel's bottom lip, making a deep slice. Blood spurted onto his chiseled chest.

"Don't hurt him!" I sobbed, lunging toward Daniel until the GF flung me backward with a mindless swoop of his club-like arm. I heard his knife fall to the floor.

"It was," Daniel said, spitting a spray of blood into the GF's face. "Worth it, if you're still wondering."

The GF buried a fist into Daniel's midsection. My screams didn't register, nor my tears.

As for Daniel, he was smiling and bleeding as the guards began to push him out of the room by shoving him hard in his back with billy clubs. When that didn't work, they hit him in the gut again, but he refused to register the pain. I was the one who felt it.

"I want to see ten new pages by the time *Jeopardy* is on," the GF barked, as my eyes glanced down. "I mean it! This better be prize-winning crap on those pages!"

The knife.

Where was it? I heard it drop. Maybe if I could hide it? I began to reach down. Slowly. Surely.

Just like that, he was in my face.

"You think I forgot about my knife," the GF hissed. "Pick it up for me, Miss Callaghan. I dare you not to. Pick up the damn knife."

I had no choice, but to comply. But what I found on the floor was even more interesting than the weapon. Crouching down low, I was at a unique vantage point to see the GF's lower half. The knife was near his feet, and as I reached for it, I saw that he had a slight scar and a minor bulge—by his anklebone.

In that moment, I knew. *He didn't enjoy the reset.*

He could be hurt.

Maybe it was his criminal past. Or perhaps the Higher Authority thought the ankle device would come in handy at a later date if the GF fled these parts unknown or defied them. The fact remained: The GF was not invincible.

My journalistic mind roared back into gear. *Information is power.*

Baring my best poker face, I rose and handed him the weapon. He slowly closed it in his palm and then suddenly advanced, pressing me with his stomach girth closer and closer to the open window until my upper body was leaning halfway out. With a fistful of my hair in his hand and the rest grabbed by the wind, he pulled me forward, so I wouldn't fall. Then he rested the knife blade against my lips as the brisk spring wind bit into my face.

"Have a taste of your lover's blood," he said, smearing my mouth with Daniel. "Next time, it will be your blood, too. Or maybe it will be mine. Fate's a bitch—and so are you."

My flesh burning, I twisted away because he allowed it. Somehow my typewriter didn't break from the entire ruckus, so I calmly set it down on a small end table, sat in front of it, and began to type with shaking hands—slowly at first and then faster after a few moments.

My mind remained uncaged and wild. My lips still tasted Daniel—and the man seething across from me knew my thoughts weren't on him.

He could own me, but not all of me.

The line had been drawn. For now I would let him think that he was ahead, knowing that perception was often the most dangerous weapon of all.

3.

That night, A.E. tried to offer me some comfort, but his honesty got in the way of his compassion.

"Listen, Walker, it's a miracle the big guy has made it this long," he said.

"I'm listening, Albert," I said from my pancake-thin mattress, setting down the one book the GF thought might inspire me while writing his memoirs: Mario Puzo's *The Godfather*. "What do you want to tell me? But make it quick—Don Corleone is about to deliver that chopped-off horse head, which is disgusting if you ask me."

"I just wanted to tell you that things don't look too good for your boy."

"I know, another month in the Hole," I said, closing my eyes hard so I saw little stars instead of Daniel trapped like some kind of tortured mole under the earth's core. "I tried to appeal to the GF, but he won't—"

"No, it's bigger," A.E. interrupted in a nervous, twitchy voice. "That kind of solitude in a confined space messes with the mind. It shuts down the brain. The longest I've ever heard of anyone surviving the Cooler is two months. Your boy is doing his third round. It's March, you know. Doesn't look good."

"Doesn't look good for what?"

"He has probably already lost it, mentally speaking," A.E. began, "or maybe he has gone deep into himself, which is just as bad. Seen it a few times. Guys do that kind of time in the Cooler and they never talk again. They can't think straight. Their marbles are scrambled in a way that can never be unscrambled again. They are like walking, breathing zombies."

"Enough, A.E.," I said. "I don't want to talk tonight. Besides, I saw him today. His marbles were absolutely freaking fine."

His silence unnerved me. Then A.E. spoke softly.

"No one has lasted a third round. Ever," he said with such sorrow that I knew he hated to tell me. "Just thought that you should know. It's the third round that does it."

In the silence that followed, a question lingered. It was such a big one that I had to start the conversation again.

"So what happens in here if your marbles are scrambled . . . permanently," I asked.

A.E. didn't answer for a long time. Then, in a small voice that was a mixture of terror and dread, he finally said to me, "If it's really bad, they send you away from here. To the other school."

"What other school?" I asked, remembering bits and pieces I heard about other schools in this realm, although I hadn't really dared or had time to look beyond the Academy and ITT.

"Frederick Reardon," A.E. said in a whisper.

"Never heard of him," I insisted.

"The **F**rederick **R**eardon **E**stablishment of **A**cademics and **K**inetics," he said, overenunciating the first letter of each word. "Kids around here call it by the initials."

I remembered hearing those initials mentioned before.

"F-R-E-A-K," I spelled out.

"Freak U," A.E. said, the twitchy voice getting more frantic by the moment.

"Why would they send someone whose marbles were scrambled there?" I had to ask. "What could he study there if his mind wasn't working?"

"*He* wouldn't study anything," A.E. said. "*They* would study him."

"Tell me."

"They welcome odd specimens up there. The PC way of saying it is 'curiosities.' In fact, that's what the place is all about in the first place," he said. "Freak U. When you don't belong *anywhere* else—when you're the freak of nature."

"I'm done talking," I said.

"I just wanted you to know," said a sorrowful A.E.

"Not another word," I whispered.

4.

Each day, I continued going to the GF's office listening to the trials and tribulations of his life of crime during his living years. "And then we blew that bastard's head off because he didn't pay by Friday and you know how I feel about deadlines," GF said one day, adding, "After that, I went over to his house and shot his dog. By the way, do you want the ribs for lunch or the barbecued chicken? I'm sending for takeout."

"How about hot dogs?" I posed.

The GF smirked. "When I don't want to bury you, I enjoy you, Miss Callaghan," he said. "Keep typing." But I was done for the moment.

"Can you send him my food? If he eats, then I relax and write better. I'll send you extra pages tonight, I promise," I bargained. "I'm on chapter twelve. We only have four or five chapters left."

We never mentioned Daniel by name. When I thought about it, I had the uncomfortable feeling that the GF was *jealous* of him.

The GF narrowed his eyes to think about it for a moment. "I guess when you go over the bend, you still have an appetite," he said. "I don't care if he eats the dirt or a rack of Kansas City's finest. You think he wants fries with that?"

"Ribs are good. They're hearty. Fries. Rolls. Soda," I rattled off as I continued to type. "Send it all."

"Literature," said the GF licking his chops. "You do realize this is pointless? Got a straitjacket waiting for Daniel at Frederick Reardon. I already did the paperwork that admits him to the discovery ward. He won't last the rest of this month. No one has even heard him speak this week."

He wasn't speaking.

"Send him the food," I insisted, still typing away.

"Then you don't eat today," the GF bargained.

"Send him the food," I said, locking eyes with him. Then I stopped typing and pushed my chair away from the desk.

"Don't test me," hissed the GF. "There are many ways to punish someone who tests me."

I handed him a page of writing. All I had typed was the word "the" about four hundred times and that one word covered the entire page. It only took a moment for the GF to look at it and then furiously ball up the paper and throw it back in my face. It took everything inside me not to move.

"I don't feel well," I said without blinking. "And if I collapse because of nervous anxiety, we'll fall behind on your book. And an almost finished book isn't a book at all. It's just a bunch of words and pages."

The air molecules in the room seemed to vibrate with his rage.

The GF refused to break our staring contest, but he did place one of his fat fingers on his intercom and told Rat Face, "Two KC dinners. Extras all around. Send one down to the Hole—and order whatever you want for yourself. Miss Callaghan will have nothing."

"What's that, boss?" Rat Face inquired through the PA. I could hear the strains of *Seinfeld* in the background.

"She lives on love," sneered the GF, who whipped his massive head in my direction again and yelled, "Fun is over. Get ready to take notes about my time in San Quentin, which was a palace compared to this shit hole. And I better see a lot of different words on the next page or you'll be moving downstairs, too. When my book is done, I won't have much use for you either. I'm sure Frederick Reardon would have a field day with your headstrong personality disorder."

5.

On those dark prison nights, A.E. would play a game, pretending that the evening's beans were a gourmet delicacy. "Smell this gorgeous meat stew, Walker. I believe mine is filet," he said as we both hunkered down on the floor to eat our cup of mush. We ate down there in order to pretend that we were at a fancy restaurant and our "order" had just arrived.

"Do we want warm French bread and creamy butter with it?" I joked, knowing that all we had was one stale piece of white bread and no butter.

"I'll stick with my flaky croissant," A.E. insisted. "I can feel it melting in my mouth with tart strawberry jam so thick on top I put it on with a spoon."

One night when the beans were cold and rock hard, I slammed the plate on the floor and asked A.E., "How do you stand it? You wake up smiling. You joke around. How do you do it?"

"I'm getting out of here one day and returning back to life—at least for a visit. In fact, I plan on visiting regularly."

"And you really believe that?" I mocked him. "You've been at ITT for I don't even know how long and you believe that you're going to be some regular realm traveler with enough realm traveling points to spend a few extra weeks on a beach in Honolulu?"

"I do. I believe it to the marrow in my bones," A.E. said with firm conviction. "Our belief is our reality. If you stop believing then you're really dead."

"You're a unique one," I finally told A.E., shoving those last hard beans down my throat, so I wouldn't pass out from lack of food.

"A limited edition," A.E. said with a hearty laugh, sticking out his tongue to reveal a smiley face he made out of beans that were glued to his teeth. You had to hand it to this kid. Even with nothing, he made it something.

But our rare moment of levity was interrupted by Eddie Wargo's ugly mug suddenly appearing outside my cell. I remembered the GF's words about how he was always looking for a prison girlfriend and the hair on my arms stood straight up. The smug look on Eddie didn't help matters either.

Before I could find the right swear word to express my disgust, I saw Eddie step back. In fact, Eddie didn't say anything else because he was just the front man for a posse that was making its way slowly, but surely, down the dark corridor. I knew this wasn't about me and relief flooded every molecule of my being. Fear was replaced with curiosity. Without getting up from my perch on the floor, I could see three burly guards dragging someone along with them, the gray ITT jumpsuit giving away the fact that we had a new arrival on Cellblock D.

Was this another killer? Rapist? Human trafficker? Who was going to live next to me in Cell 19 for eternity?

I couldn't see his face, which was mired in shadows. Was it some psycho? Pusher? Molester? At least A.E. was as respectful as possible when it came to my almost nonexistent privacy.

The prisoner's head was bent down and flopped low like his neck muscles didn't have the strength to hold up his head anymore.

His long legs sagged behind him like two useless tree trunks, buckling at the knee, which was why the guards were pulling him along the cold tile like some sort of hideous, lifeless side of beef.

"Toss him in there, boss" Eddie called out, his finger still pressing my intercom, as he moved aside to allow one of the guards to punch the code that made Cell 19's force field deactivate.

That's when I saw his face.

It was bloodied. It was mangled. It was caked in layers upon layers of old settled mud.

He didn't even glance my way or any way. His faraway, trancelike gaze was directed inside like a light had been shut off to the outside world.

They tossed Daniel into the cell like they were throwing away an extra heavy bag of garbage. And then they left him in a heap on the floor, raw wounds that were deep gashes exposed on the back of his legs. Limbs contorted under him like they were now boneless and useless. He didn't move. Not an inch.

Just like my own on "opening day," his cell had no bed, no blanket, and no desk. All he owned was what was left of his body, a mind that was probably the consistency of Jell-O, and those five small squares of toilet paper.

Prove them wrong. Get up. Look up!

Eddie Wargo also wanted Daniel to move. With his shit-clomping prison-issued boots, he gave the mass of flesh on the floor a lethal gut kick that was designed to snap ribs. What chilled me to the core was that Daniel didn't even wince or try to defend himself. He just lay there . . . and took it.

He curled up on the glass bottom of his cell in some self-protecting fetal position, his ear kissing the floor. Slowly like he was savoring the moment, Eddie moved his leg back and kicked hard connecting to the side of Daniel's face. A mist of spit and dark-red blood sprayed like angry rain. Daniel's head snapped back, only to stay that way, as if it was dangling by threads. A thicker trickle of blood snaked across the clear floor.

Then Eddie directed his slit-like eyes to me. "I heard you liked girls. There's a pussy on the floor," he hissed. But he wasn't finished. With a broad grin, he slid a crumpled piece of paper through my meal slot.

Keeping my eyes on Daniel, I reluctantly crawled to the front of my cell and ripped the wrinkled, food-stained paper from the slot. In my panic, I uncurled it with lightening speed only to find my hundreds of the *the*'s written in rows. Over the repeated words that I had typed, the GF had taken a thick black marker and written one word: END.

Scrambling to my feet after Eddie and the guards left, I raced over to the cell wall closest to Daniel and spoke his name loudly so he was sure to hear me. My hands were shaking and my heart was a bullet train. At the sound of my voice, he still didn't move. Not an inch. His head remained cocked back, mouth open.

My mind was shooting off rockets of fear. "If you can, please give me some sign that you're in there," I begged, cursing myself for being so selfish.

Yet, the Daniel I knew would move heaven and earth to bend a finger, but this man did nothing. I couldn't even tell if he was still breathing while blood continued to trickle out of his right temple.

"Ok, ok, ok," I said, my heart racing. "Sleep."

There was no response.

"A.E.'s next door. Remember him? Well, he asked how we met and I was going to tell him."

For two hours, I told the entire story—the long, excruciatingly slow version. Daniel remained lifeless.

Late, late that night, I could only repeat what my mother would say to me when I was a little girl and sick with the flu. She would tuck me into bed, read a story, close the book, and then tell me the same few words before I drifted off.

Pressing my whole body against the glass, I banished any quiver in my voice and said, "You are the blue in my skies and the sweet in my dreams."

Nothing.

He was there. But he wasn't . . .

6.

Somehow, I must have fallen asleep on the floor and when I woke with a start, I opened my eyes to nothing. Darting my head left toward Cell 19, I blinked hard and fast to focus on . . . an empty glass box. The silence contained within felt like hard rock music cranked up to ten.

There was no Daniel. Scrambling to my feet, my head moved so fast that whiplash should have set in. There was a void in the middle of that cell punctuated by a little puddle of dried blood and a bigger circle of sweat and bodily fluids.

Frantically, my eyes darted to the front of his glass box. And I knew. In the middle of the night, they came again and took him away forever to Freak U. A human science project. It was the END the GF had tormented me with the night before. The ultimate payback.

A guttural moan drifted from my stomach, up through the back of my throat, piercing the lump that had formed. I wasn't sure I could go on in here and my mind went to a place where a heinous plan began to form. I could stop writing the book. And I would surely end up in the Hole. And I could never survive even a week of it.

Would he hate me if I allowed myself to free fall?

"Daniel," I cried.

I dropped to my knees and let my forehead fall to the floor into my open hands.

"Don't cry, baby."

My head shot up. The thick, rumbling voice came from the far dark corner of Cell 19 where Daniel was crouching low on the other side of the toilet and holding himself up by the translucent sink.

"I have a bitch of a headache, so don't argue with me. But first, this is important. I didn't shove you in that lake. You fell in."

"Idiot," I said in a thick voice as the tears started to roll. Closing my eyes in gratitude, I whispered, "You let me drown."

"You know that's not true. And now you need to know something else," Daniel said. I couldn't see his eyes in the dark, but I knew exactly what they looked like—no question about it. "You need to know that we're getting the hell out of here, baby" he promised savagely. "I'll dig us out of here with my bare hands if it comes to it."

And I believed him.

7.

Storms came that day with streaks and I heard them boom overhead, but could only imagine the bursts of lightening ripping across the bruised sky.

At 5:45 a.m., Aileen came with fresh clothing. Lustily, she eyed

Daniel who looked at me while I changed. "What a sexy bastard," said the infamous serial killer. "I like 'em beefy with a side of attitude. You want some deodorant and a date?"

From his perch in the middle of the glass floor, Daniel was mildly amused. "I want a hot shower and a real bed," he said.

"I'm more than available for all of the above," Aileen said, ignoring my pointed look. One thing about Aileen was that she was primal in her needs. When she opened Daniel's cell door to toss him a whole roll of toilet paper and some antibiotic ointment, she put a shushing finger to her lips and cooed, "When I watch you shower later this week, we'll consider that payment in full."

She was a breeze compared to what Daniel had just endured.

When I came back that evening, after writing duty, what I gathered from Daniel who "didn't want to talk about it ever" was that he survived the Hole thanks to meals that came twice a day to him. They weren't large, but they sustained him. "The rest of it was thanks to a yoga class I took in high school to help me play better soccer," he said, his eyes warmly caressing my face. "I focused on my breathing. Made it sound like ocean waves. It's called Ujjayi breath. Breathe in through your nose and out through your mouth. It requires focus, which keeps your mind much sharper than even regular existence. And in my spare time, I must have done about five hundred thousand sit-ups and push-ups."

It rained constantly that whole week, and I wished Daniel could enjoy it. On one of the days, the GF gave me the treat of going with him outside to greet new prisoners. When the GF was busy with the riffraff, I took off my shoes so I could feel the warm, spring water on my feet. Breathing the freedom, all I could smell were the drowned weeds at the mountainside giving off that pungent moldy scent of rotting greens.

I remembered my mother telling me about her honeymoon with my father in the Florida Keys and how they played in the warm rain. They would take their shoes off and walk where the street dipped into the gutter, allowing the sky-heated water to flow between their happy toes.

The warm April rain on my toes outside of ITT felt just as sweet.

In the evenings over those next several weeks, we were a fraternity of sorts. It was all about Daniel, A.E., and I talking about everything and nothing at the same time.

Late at night, Daniel and I would curl up next to each other as best as we could, despite the wall of glass that separated us. Daniel would wait until the wee hours to say sexy things to me, but I always hushed him . . . after a few minutes.

"So here's what I'm doing with my hands," Daniel mouthed.

"We have a PG-thirteen over there," I whispered, knowing A.E. had fallen asleep on his floor near my wall . . . or did he? The kid didn't miss a thing. But it's not like he hadn't heard worse in here. "So what were you doing with your hands?" I whispered. "Remind me." It felt good to focus despite the screams coming from down the cellblock.

It was A.E. who ended the night by saying, "Well, I know what I'm doing with my hands. Putting them square over my ears."

One night after dinner, Daniel and I curled up by the wall to talk about our eventual escape from this nightmare. During our breakout talk, A.E. joined in when there was an opening. "You can't dig out of here or get lost and run. They have this place on ultimate lockdown. Plus, you'll be hunted and punished. Remember, you don't have the reset anymore," he warned. "Walker, you don't know what it's like to be shot or scalded or cut. You can't die again, but you can feel pain. Bad, bad pain. Pain that will make you wish you could be extinguished by one of those demon things."

"So, no one has *ever* escaped?" Daniel demanded. Obviously, he wasn't afraid of pain after three stints in the Hole, but I knew he worried about how much I could endure, if anything at all. When I was alive, I couldn't even stand a tooth cleaning. My dentist had a running joke: "Here comes Walker. Get out the numbing shots, so we can brush her teeth."

"The Wargos tried it one time by tying those XXXL shirts of theirs into a rope. They snuck up to the mountain ledge with Eddie's keys and a half-baked plan to scale down the mountain. They almost froze and Daryl got bitten by a cougar. He would have been dinner for that cat, but the GF sent Rat up there to fetch them," A. E. informed us. "You know that ankle bracelet they put on you? It not only takes away the reset, but it's also the universe's most potent GPS. They will find you. And what happens then is worse than the Hole."

"What could be worse?" snapped Daniel.

"What could be worse is *him*," A.E. said in a scared tone, pointing out of his cell into the distance toward the janitor's closet. "What's worse is they find you and give you to him. Remember

John? The friendly janitor, portal keeper, and serial killer? He lives down the hall."

"And then what?" I demanded.

"All I know, Walker, is that when someone is given to John, they never come back—in any way, in any form," A.E. answered. "It's like they've been fed to a garbage disposal. Ground up. Gone. I knew Simon from the Academy. He came here on a school project. Mouthed off to the GF. Gone-gone."

8.

To entertain ourselves, we shared our life stories as if they were scenes from the movies. One weekend day when the hours didn't move, it dawned on me. I had never quizzed A.E. about his trip back to the living realm. The fact that he was proud of it, like he was wearing an eternal realm traveler merit badge, meant he would probably *want* to talk about it.

"So, kid, what happened after you got there?" I boldly asked, the reporter in me kicking in again. "Spill it."

"It's a long story."

"Really? What else is on the agenda? Afternoon tea with the Obamas?" I retorted.

"It was such a cinch," he suddenly blurted out. "I mean, I knew there must be a portal around these parts. In any realm, there is always a portal. In the living realm, portals are everywhere. Why do you think certain people just disappear never to be seen again? Portals. Only a fool doesn't walk through a door that's so easily opened."

Looking into my hazel eyes, A.E. sounded like a little boy confessing as he began his story.

The dorm rooms at the Academy were especially hot that summer. I had a box of popsicles in my minifridge and a big fan pumping hard when, looky-loo, there was Dr. Marvin King just standing in my open door. He had this sixth sense of knowing when I was really missing my mom and dad back home. There I was, sweating and crying a little. And there he was in his dark-blue suit, smiling and standing without a bead of sweat on his forehead. Always cool. Always concerned. You didn't have to call for him. He was there because he sensed my pain.

He also told me the truth. "Son, you won't see your mother and father for a long, long time," Dr. King said.

I guess you need people who tell you what you don't want to hear—as much as you need them to tell you what you do need to hear.

This was our little routine. He'd wander by my dorm room a few times a week and stand there, pondering and thinking. I don't think he ever knew what in the heck to do with me. Sometimes, he'd stand there for over an hour, just telling me about life as a principal in Detroit. I told him about my favorite show, Criminal Minds. *It felt like talking to my Dad about nothing and everything.*

One day, a big smile crossed Dr. King's face and he told me that if I was that interested in the criminal element then maybe I should do something real about it rather than just watch some worthless cancelled TV show with bad actors—his words, not mine.

"Son, why don't you go study what interests you at ITT? It's one thing to watch it on TV, but you might discover something important by being around those who have strayed from the rules," Dr. King said. He knew that all I did was think about how to get back to my family, and told me time and again that it could never happen, so he was always looking for ways to distract me. Sports weren't really an

option, if you know what I mean. Look at me.

Go study at ITT? I was scared. Poop-in-your-pants scared. But I was mad-dog curious.

Then one night, it came to me. I missed my family so much, and I couldn't find a portal back to the living realm at the Academy despite years of endlessly searching. It didn't take a genius to figure that if there was a way back, they would put it in the hardest-to-get-to place in this realm. It had to be at ITT because the place is so guarded. And every escape route or portal needs something or someone to block you. The universe just works that way. There are no easy exits.

Dr. King's offer sealed my fate.

"Sir, I want to go there," I told our principal, who quickly got started on the paperwork. This was before that Simon kid from the Academy disappeared and during a time when the GF and Dr. King were enjoying one of their rare truces. A few days later, Dr. King yanked me out of art class with a big smile on his face. He had pulled some strings. I was going.

It was about sixty-five degrees and thunderstorming when I arrived at ITT. I was immediately sent to A Block to interview a few of the lower-ranking prisoners who didn't give a flip about a prepster like me. Then I guess the guards thought they would pull a real good prank. They took me up. Way up. One of them said, "Kid, you came here to talk about the criminal element. Let's give you something to flap your jaw about when you get back to Happy Land." So we went.

To D Block.

To scare the crap out of me.

What happened next wasn't pretty. I think I barfed up an entire summer of food right then and there. When I saw the row of single cells and some crazy leapt at the glass, I began to heave. And I kept going for several disgusting minutes. I had eaten a big Academy breakfast of bacon and eggs and pancakes, so it was a huge, disgusting mess. What did they expect? My stomach was flipping over and over again and it wasn't just because of the bad element here. I could sense it. It was the portal. I knew I was close. I've always had very keen instincts.

The guards looked at each other like I had just thrown up nuclear waste. One said, "I ain't cleaning that stuff up. I'm union." Another said, "I'll lose my lunch. Go find that nasty janitor." They left me standing at the front of D Block by myself with all this barf in big puddles on the floor. That's when I saw the janitor's closet. It was right there. Lazy-ass guards. I figured I'd just go in there myself and find that pink sawdust stuff to clean up my mess before anyone could make too much fun of me or tell Dr. King that I was a stupid barfing geek.

So I went into the closet, but couldn't find the sawdust. Then I walked through another door that was open a crack. My entire body began to vibrate. I saw all the clown stuff. I don't know why I touched the wall with the clown drawing. Something just drew me to it as if someone inside of it was whispering to come closer. The wall felt nice and warm and I was so cold. The wall spoke to me. It asked me touch to it.

When the mouth opened, I walked through it. Any kid would have done the same thing.

I didn't mean to go back. I was summoned.

I walked through and landed in a clump on the sidewalk a few blocks from my house in the suburbs. Oh, glory! It was just as I remembered it—with green lawns and grass so thick your toes got trapped. There were barking dogs and white picket fences. All of a sudden, I looked up and knew exactly what to do. My heart was doing cartwheels because I was by the Feeney's house and I knew how to walk home by myself. Did it a million times when I was alive. Hoofing it down my street felt like eating a hundred hot fudge sundaes. It smelled the same—like chlorine, rose bushes, and burnt hot dogs. Mrs. Kirkland was watering her flowers and Mr. P was sunning himself on his driveway and reading his gossip rags.

I said, "Hi, Mrs. K. Hi, Mr. P," but they never even looked up. It was like I was invisible—because I was. Then I saw Maise, the cool bulldog owned by Mr. and Mrs. Long. Maise was all they had left since their son, Cal, who was only seventeen, had drowned racing his little speedboat in Moosehead Lake the summer before I died. Suddenly, I was real sad because that bulldog was only a pup when I left town. And now her muzzle was snow-white and her hips wobbly. But I guess they wouldn't face putting her down, despite the way her body swayed in two different directions when she tried to take a step.

She was Cal's dog.

I reached out to pet her, but Maise limped away as fast as she could which caused Mrs. Long to call out, "Take it easy, girl. You don't want to get overheated. Your heart can't take it. My heart can't take it."

So, Maise dragged her back legs away, which hurt deep inside, because she was such a good dog and I remembered when she ran like the wind. I wanted to tell her that it would eventually be all right, but I couldn't take time to sit with her that day. I had to see my family, and there was nothing better than just walking through our red front door that my mother painted during her fêng shui obsession. Literally, I walked right through the wood, which felt sticky and thick. But I made it through. And inside . . . oh, oh, oh, it was so normal and so beautiful that I had to stop and sit on the bottom stair of our winding staircase. I couldn't stop crying. Everybody was there. My mom. My dad. And my little sister—but she wasn't so little anymore. Now she was older than me. They were right there in the dining room over to the left, passing a platter of pork chops—my favorite—at the old, oval wood table that my grandma had left behind.

Dad was passing the peas to my sister and said, "Eat your veggies, Taylor, or your bones will dry up and you'll snap in two." I started to laugh. Dad with his dried-bone warnings. He's an inventor and knows science and even medicine. Still, his bone theory was his way to push the carrots and those disgusting Brussels sprouts.

My chair was still at the table and it was empty. That made me want to cry again, but I bit my bottom lip until I tasted blood, which was odd. Then it dawned on me that the reset was gone. But I didn't care. I'd rather feel the pain here than be gone again.

All that mattered was that this was such a happy moment, so I walked over and slid into my chair. Like any other day.

I sat. With them. When I reached out and snagged the smallest chop, my mom looked really confused. She told my sister not to hoard the food and eat all the chops. Taylor swore that she didn't take more than one, but nobody believed her.

"Then where are the bones?" Taylor demanded, and my father couldn't even answer that one. "Just eat your peas," he insisted. As if peas made everything A-OK.

I licked those bones clean. My mom puts on a lot of garlic and some spicy green stuff on all her meat. I can taste it right now by just thinking about it. No one can cook like my mom—or ever will.

Wellza, after dessert—lemon cake with white frosting that I kept digging my finger into and licking—we started watching the very first-ever Star Wars *in the new den that I guess they built after I left.*

In the old days, I'd always grab a big white pillow off the couch and lay on the floor. It was cool that someone had placed a brand-new pillow in my spot the floor and it was so white I could tell that no one used it. Before I curled up into it, I walked up to my mom and wrapped my arms around her in a hug. That's when I saw it. A flicker on her face. Something felt old, maybe familiar. Maybe she wasn't sure, but she knew something.

Then she did the impossible.

Mom wrapped her arms around herself like she was cold and then closed her eyes. It was eighty-five degrees that day and humid.

Her eyes were still closed. She shivered. There was no way she was even a bit chilly. When her eyes opened, I saw one tiny tear. Without anyone noticing, she shook her head once, maybe twice, and then bent down, picked up my pillow and hugged it to her chest for a second before fluffing it and putting it exactly back into place.

"Really, Mom, how long are you going to keep doing that?" Taylor demanded.

"Taylor," scolded my father. In that dried bones voice.

I sat on the floor next to my sister as the movie continued. Twice I reached out and gave her hair a tiny tug. For old time's sake. Swatting at the hair like she was annoyed, she didn't say a word. Mom was on the couch, and dad in his recliner. It was just like any normal night . . . until the demons blew in. They slid through the screen door that led to the patio. Seeping through the tiny boxes that made up the actual screen.

They were disgusting versions of me. Gross ones. Some had big teeth and huge heads. At first, they sat next to me on the floor pretending like they wanted to be friends, but I knew they were bad. Real bad.

I also knew that my Dad kept a gun. He did ever since our house was robbed when I was young. It was in the safe in the den, so I pounded hard and ran in there and when I furiously tried to turn the combination lock, my hand went right through the safe and the lockbox inside of it. With all my might, I pulled that gun out.

The demons followed and one leapt forward and tried to bite me, so with a sure hand, just like I did with my BB gun, I shot him! I hit him right in the chest, but he just laughed, so I shot him again. Nothing. It was so scary that I dropped the gun on the rug. The crazy thing is my family heard something. Maybe not the shots. But something. Then I saw my parents run into the den to find their gun on the floor. They screamed at Taylor who said she had no idea how it got there. But I didn't have time for a family debate. I had to run with everything left in me.

With my feet almost flying, I raced into the kitchen to find a different weapon because, remember, I didn't have anything with me. All I could see was my grandma's old carving knife that was still in the sink soaking from cutting the chops. It had been in our family for generations. So I grabbed it and stabbed two of them right in the heart.

I'm not that good a stabber. It was lucky that they ran right at me, got stabbed, and then . . . exploded! The last one was harder. He kept coming at me and I dropped the knife. Before I knew it, he was chasing me with it. And I started to run even harder.

Now, I'm just a boy who weighs no more than ninety pounds. That night, I pounded hard with all my might through my back door and into my yard, where I led the monster to the family firewood pile. My dad was always letting me practice with his ax, but I was never very good at it. Or so I thought. In that moment for some reason, I could have chopped down a forest.

After that last demon burst, I had a true friend by my side. Bulldog Maise was right next to me, licking me and jumping all over me. It was like she was a young puppy again, which made me do a hard double take. She even looked brand-new with tall, sure, sturdy hips and glossy brown fur around her muzzle—and man, was she fast. She kept nipping at my hand until I followed her. Both of us started pumping our feet hard, and I didn't know where she was taking me.

Maise knew where. She was taking me to the nearest portal.

We ran like we were jet-propelled to the rain gutter at the end of our street. It's funny because when I was alive, I looked at that thing about a million times and rode my bike over it about two million times. I never knew it was a portal, but like I said . . . portals are everywhere.

Maise, who had passed from a heart attack not long after I arrived, slipped down the rain gutter paws first, sliding on her stomach, and I followed her, scraping my stomach on the dry pavement until I was free-falling into a dark void.

And then we landed in a field. Somewhere.

She was such a good dog. The last I saw of her, Maise had jumped high into Cal's strong, waiting arms and he was hugging her so hard and yelling, "My girl! I knew I'd see you again!" He gave me a quick wave and said, "Real good to see you, Albert. Thanks for bringing my girl to me. Enjoy your time."

"But I didn't bring her," I yelled to him as he walked away. "She brought me to you." Cal smiled and pointed me in the right direction. I started walking, but I looked back once or twice. Cal and Maise were rolling in the grass.

Cal and that dog were everything to each other. Now they're together again. Somewhere else. Not here.

Enjoying their time.

"Would I do it again? I'd do it right now. I'd do it over and over again. The next morning, Dr. King was back in my doorjamb looking sad and I was arrested and sent right here, to ITT. No trial. No nothing. I don't blame Dr. King. People who give you their best can also give you their worst."

"Lights out," one of the guards yelled. The three of us complied. In silence.

9.

That midnight, I had an unscheduled awakening.

"Wanna go for a ride, pretty girl?" he said.

I sat straight up on my thin, hard mattress that slid on the translucent block that was my bed frame.

The first thing I saw was the car, which was unmistakable. The blue Honda had a new windshield. The dents were pounded out.

What a bitch. The car survived.

He showed me the car and then allowed his gaze to pan down Clark Street in Chicago on a sunny summer morning. Then he moved in for a close-up, so I could get a better view of current events in the living realm.

"Cass, I don't know what I would do without you," said *my mother.*

There she was in a green sundress that was obviously one of her sewing projects, with a new little white sweater over her shoulders. There was Cass helping her like the world's ultimate gentleman by guiding her elbow as she limped down the street with her cane. Gingerly, he guided her into the passenger seat. "I didn't want money for the accident, but it sure has come in handy," Mom said. "It allowed me to hire a helper. It brought you to me."

My mouth flew open. He wasn't just working her. He was working *for* her.

It was official. He was part of her world.

"Mrs. C," Cass said, reaching around to make sure my mother was belted in the car. Obviously, twisting and bending still hurt her back. "You're the one who saved me. I really needed a job. Plus, you're always feeding me, which wasn't part of the job description."

"Cassy, I'll make you some homemade mac-and-cheese later," Mom promised.

What the hell. My mom liked him? Anything more and he would become the son she never had.

"Just let me drive. You rest your back." Cass smiled at my mother and then moved his head away fractionally to remove himself from her immediate field of vision. I knew this was for me when he grinned into nothingness. "You're such a handsome young man," Mom said. "I wish you could have met . . ." Her voice trailed off.

Mom's long red-brown hair gleamed in the sunlight, and I could see that she had freshly cut bangs. She looked far younger than someone approaching forty. It made me happy to see that she still carried the same little vintage beige purse that my dad bought her about hundred years ago at a local flea market.

Almost as a second thought, Cass remembered her cane leaning up against the Honda and popped out to put it in the trunk. His lips didn't move when he said to me, "Sugar, I thought you'd like to actually see how she is doing. Hearing is one thing. Seeing is proof. By the way, you look cute with your hair all mussed up."

Then he winked. Anyone walking by on the street watching a man wink at the clouds would have thought he was . . . just another crazy Chicagoan.

Back in the car, mom was rifling through her purse, looking for something when her wallet decided to take a dive to the floor. Grimacing like it hurt her back to even think about bending that low, Cass, now in the driver's seat, dipped low and said, "I'll get it, Mrs. C. Don't exert. We got a big day coming up. Doc appointment. Then some grocery shopping. And then I'm going to take you surfing in Lake Michigan. A little disco dancing. You gotta have some fun."

"Oh, Cass," sighed my mom. "You make me laugh."

What happened next horrified me. Mom was suddenly producing pictures from her wallet. "There's my Walker. Sorry that

I keep doing this, but you would have loved her," Mom told him, showing him my senior class picture from Kennedy High.

"She's a gorgeous girl. And smart," Cass said, looking over the steering wheel now onto the horizon. *I saw him nod.*

"How do you know she was smart?" Mom sniffed.

"She's your daughter," Cass replied, looking down, but I could see the grin on his face was spreading wider. He was . . . enjoying himself. And I wanted to kill him for it.

"I just . . . I don't . . . I have," Mom began to ramble. Then her voice broke.

"Tell me," Cass said to her in a soft voice. The grin faded. "I know how it is. I lost some family members a long time ago, but the feeling never goes away. Tell me everything about Walker. It will make you feel better."

"Cass, I miss her every single minute of every single day," she said. "It's like I lost part of myself."

Oh, Mom. I began to cry silently while I willed that the earth would swallow Cass whole.

"I feel like I know you . . . and Walker," Cass said in an even voice, his long blond hair, pulled into a man bun, shining in the hot sun. The rest of him looked large and sleek in white basketball shorts and a vintage Beatles T-shirt. Really? Did he need black Ray-Bans, too?

"We have one more stop today. I know this sounds insane," Mom began. "But I have another appointment."

"Just tell me where," Cass offered with a helpful smile. "Who's the lucky recipient of a visit from you, Mrs. C?"

"It's over on Halsted Street. The place is called Angel Mediums," Mom said. "Please don't judge me. I just need to know about my daughter. I need to talk to a woman named Natasha. If you would have asked me in the past, I would have told you that psychics are just a load of baloney."

Cass nodded and then shot me a look in the driver's side mirror. "Some people like baloney. Some love it," he said, firing up the ignition. "It's an acquired taste. But not all baloney is true baloney, if you know what I mean. There are a lot of con artists out there when it comes to this stuff."

The movie abruptly ended.

"No!" I began to scream in my mind. "No! No! No! I want to see more." Then I jolted up and began to pace.

Daniel scrambled to the air holes. "You okay, baby?" he whispered.

"No, I'm not okay," I said. "I have to tell you something—something you're not going to like. But I need to tell you right now. I didn't tell you before because . . . we have enough on our plate. But I can't keep this to myself any longer."

And so I told him about Cass and the visits.

Because keeping it from him would constitute cheating—and I was no cheater.

"That freaking bastard does this on a regular basis?" he bit out, pacing around his cell now.

"Three times so far," I said. "I don't know how he does it—or why. But I'm his emotional hostage. I dismissed him the first two times. But now he's upped the ante. He's offering me an afterlife cable station called Mom TV. If I want to know about my mom, I can't dismiss him. And he's working for my mom, so he's around her all the time."

Daniel kicked the glass. Twice. Then he was silent for a long time. "I don't like it," he said in a lethal voice. "But I don't know what I can do about it. I can't ask you to exile your mother."

"I don't know what I can do about it either. All I know is I'll tell you about it, every single time," I promised. Then I added, "It's not about him. It's about her."

"You can pass on a message to your emotional kidnapper," he finally said in a low, deliberate voice. "There will come a day when

I'll let him know how much I hate cable TV."

We decided to let it lie there, and the rest of the night passed without any middle-of-the-night late, late shows from the living realm. As dawn broke, the only thing I felt was hungry and dejected. Daniel was still seriously pissed off and the Angel Medium was probably the only winner here as she had collected my mom's hard-earned cash.

I did have to admit that Cass, however, was the real thing.

He pierced the wall.

CHAPTER 8

1.

June.

I was mindlessly typing away in the GF's office when, outside in the waiting room, I heard the clanking of chains. The GF had these little intimidation meetings on a regular basis and clearly he enjoyed them. I was used to them, which is why I didn't bother looking up. The other reason I didn't take my eyes off the page I was typing was that I didn't want to look into the mug of another terrified kid.

On this sunny Tuesday morning, the GF asked me to do something that he rarely required. "We're going to take a short break. I'd like you to leave the room," he suddenly announced, which made me quickly exhale. I'd gladly leave his presence, but it was still strange.

The man liked an audience.

When I didn't immediately move, he ditched the manners and

barked, "Get the hell out until I call for you, pretty please with sugar on top. When you come back, arrive with a large Coke over ice. Now, move your cute ass." Sometimes, it's better to say nothing and move away.

In the waiting room with Rat Face, I saw why I was dismissed.

Two burly guards had firm grasps on the chains they pulled from Daniel's feet and neck. They yanked their prisoner along as the worst of the worst, Eddie Wargo, led the way.

"Boss, we lassooed this douche, like you asked," said Eddie, looking at me and then licking his lips in an ultraglossy way that made me want to vomit. Glancing at Daniel, I kept myself in check in more ways than one. I wouldn't allow him to get too near, fearing he'd end up back in the Hole. And I couldn't let Eddie get to him either because any kind of fistfight would never be Eddie's fault.

Daniel's grim face told the whole story.

"Little girl didn't want to come, but I told him, 'Like you have a choice!'" Eddie bellowed, laughing at his own joke as he helped shove Daniel into a hard wooden chair inside the inner office. The GF wandered into the waiting room and joined in the laughter, telling him, "Good job, Edward. Now, I want you to take a seat. Outside."

Eddie was stumped. Even his few brain cells told him that this wasn't good.

"Um, boss, whad I do?" Eddie spit out, but the GF remained silent, which wiped that superior smirk right off of Eddie's meaty, pimpled face.

Cool, calm, and collected, Walker. No emotions.

Clutching my typed papers to my chest, I gave Daniel my steel look and he returned the favor.

"Close the door after everyone is inside, Literature," the GF demanded, leading the way back into his inner sanctum.

2.

In the waiting room, I could have walked to the ends of the earth pacing on the thin rug, which didn't seem to annoy Rat Face who was happily into his sixth episode of *The Sopranos* for the day. "It's the one where Tony takes Meadow to college and chokes out an informant," he told me without ever looking in my direction. I could have been doing naked cartwheels and he wouldn't have noticed.

The one who might have enjoyed that was Eddie, who had left quickly when the lunch bell chimed.

No one noticed that I didn't close the door of the GF's office tightly, knowing that the air conditioning blast from the vent above would pry it open even more. The sliver of opening allowed for various words to drift out and I paced close enough to the door to gather as much information as possible.

From the inside, I heard the GF saying, "You WILL do this! I've wanted this for DECADES! I get what I want!" Daniel's chains rattled and I heard several loud slaps. I felt each one rip into my own skin.

Then I heard Eddie, who had come in the back entrance of the inner office with GF's lunch, yelling from inside, "You can't do this to me. It's mine. I won't do it. I won't!" The GF bellowed back about Eddie being the ultimate loser. "I'm the only reason you've lasted this long. You won't get away with disappointing me," the GF screamed and his words were punctuated with the sound of bone on skin. The slaps were an appetizer; the GF was going to use them as punching bags.

In the mix, Daniel shouted back, "Go f—" The rest of the syllables drifted off.

Then the GF again, yelling, "I'll send both of you to the Hole. The girl, too. Even better. I'll send her down for six months. She won't make it. You know that. Then I'll send her to Fredrick Reardon to be dissected! This isn't a negotiation! That's the problem with your generation. You think everything is a negotiation!" the GF boomed.

"Screw you," I heard Daniel reply.

When Rat Face pushed back from his desk, my heart almost pounded out of my chest. He grabbed me by the arm and yanked me backward, but this time it was for my own good. Eddie blasted through the door silently and didn't stop walking until we couldn't see him anymore.

Daniel was still in there, and the last words I heard were the GF saying something like ". . . worth your while. I have the key."

And with those words, Daniel was ejected from the GF's lair. Moving slowly with his right cheek flaming red, he refused to look at me as the other guards bodily dragged him through the outer office. I prayed he was going back to his cell.

"Literature."

"Yeah. Yes, I mean."

"Chapter fifteen! Where's my drink?" the GF barked at me. "If I hear any back talk from any of you today, I'll bring out the locusts. I'm a fate controller. I can do it!"

Apparently, he was also a plague controller.

Back at my desk, my fingers flew, but my mind moved even faster. *Why was Daniel summoned here? What did the GF want him to do? And why was he so adamant about not doing it? And how many hours would it be until I could go back to my cell to ask him about it? Would Daniel even be there for me to ask?*

3.

When Aileen escorted me down that long D Block walkway back to Cell 18 that evening, I wanted to run, but I kept myself in check, even waving to the lunatic in Cell 7 who had rubbed off her eyebrows. My heart lifted when A.E. popped his head up from his Civil War book and gave me his spastic, hopeful wave. The kid waved like you were on a boat about to dock after a five-year absence. Then my heart thudded when I saw Daniel pounding around the cage. *He was there.* When I came into view, he allowed the worry to melt from his face.

"Hey, handsome," Aileen said. "Must suck to be you. Your girlfriend so near, but yet so far. If I know one thing, it's men and their needs."

"You're too much for me," Daniel retorted, flashing a hollow smile. The last thing we wanted to do was piss off Aileen who might even allow a few minutes of actual skin-to-skin time someday.

"A girl can dream," she winked and slowly walked away.

From inside my cell, I did my trademark greeting which was to press my hand against the glass sidewall. Daniel pressed his hand to the spot on the other side. Closing my eyes for a second, I imagined how it really felt from the hundreds of times in freedom when I held his real hand. *But he was here.* If I had learned one lesson in here, it was simple. Happiness is in your heart—and not in the circumstances.

I couldn't take it any longer.

"Tell."

"Not going there." He stalked around his cell.

"You've got to be kidding me."

"Do I look like I'm joking?"

His eyes were steely like he meant business. But so did I.

"Oh, we're going there," I insisted, my hands on my hips and staring at him. I'm sure they could hear me on C Block.

He had seen that determined look in my eyes in happier times.

"Shit. Okay. Callaghan, it comes down to this," he finally said. "The GF really wants to win his damn hockey championship this year. He's obsessed. Apparently, there hasn't been a clean win for ITT—whatever that means—for more than ten years. Either I play hockey for ITT to help 'give him his trophy' or I can spend the rest of my sane days down in the Hole. Those are the choices—the only choices."

"This is about hockey?" I gasped. "Who cares about hockey!"

"The GF does. He lives, eats, breathes winning," Daniel explained. "Because as much as he hated Dr. King, he hates Principal Dick more, for reasons he wouldn't get into now. His head turned bright red and nearly exploded off his stump of a neck when he even mentioned good old Dick."

"So, finally, we have something in common with the GF," I muttered.

"Starting Saturday, I play. Against Frederick Reardon. The so-called Freaks," Daniel said, which sent A.E. into a tailspin. "Boy wonder over there has been filling me in on a few particulars."

A.E. began to actually skip around his cell singing at the top of his lungs, "*They're creepy and they're kooky, mysterious and spooky. They're all together ooky, the Reardon family.*"

"It's just another school up here. Big deal," I said, knowing that it would bother him to try and win a precious hockey championship for the prison school, the very institution that he helped defeat last season as captain of the Academy Aces.

"Only A Block goes to the games," A.E. whispered to me through the holes. "The rest of us just wait for the grand announcement of who won and who lost. It's one of the few things they actually announce here. Like I care about hockey."

"You look like you could play . . ." I began, and finally I said, "Chess. Yeah, that's it. Chess."

"Monopoly," A.E. chimed in, laughing. "Two hundred bucks for passing Go!"

"The game of Life," I interjected, wondering if that was actually a *really* bad joke.

All of us, including the champion brooder, had to laugh. In the darkness, there wasn't always light. But there was irony.

4.

Bleak didn't begin to describe Daniel's mood the next night after a day of practicing with his new teammates, which included all three of the infamous Wargo brothers from Booneville, Alabama: Our least-favorite prison intern, big-mouthed Eddie, and his half-wit brothers, drooling sociopath Daryl and baby-faced murderer Billy.

Unlike his days playing for the Academy, Daniel was taken in cuffs and shackles to the actual gymnasium for a practice session and was eventually unleashed like a dog given only temporary freedom. It pained him to put on a black ITT jersey and gear and carry the matching hockey stick. Trying to keep a low profile, he hovered by the equipment room, but it didn't work.

The minute Eddie walked out onto the rink in his full hockey gear and a menacing sneer, he took one look at Daniel and then flew over to their coach "The Rocket" Richard (pronounced Ree-chard), a formerly famous and absolutely surly NHL player. Eddie was afraid of Rocket, but his rage blurred his never-that-solid reasoning.

"Why do we need that jackass?" Eddie demanded, pointing his hockey stick in Daniel's direction. By default, this Wargo was the team captain—until now.

Rocket didn't mince words. "We're using him because he has 'transferred' to ITT and now we're going to take advantage of it." Poking his large finger into Eddie's chest so hard that the teenager recoiled backward, Rocket warned, "Listen to me, Wart-go. My ass is on the line here. You treat him like everyone else—or I'll get involved in it, which is something no one wants. Now, give me fifty laps around the rink."

When Richard walked away, Eddie answered in the best way he knew how with the loudest, smelliest, most disgusting burp ever heard within those walls. "Yeah," he whispered loud enough for Daniel to hear. "I'll treat him like he deserves to be treated."

It was only beginning. Trying to prove who was still the alpha here, Eddie signaled for his two brothers to flank him as the trio skated up to where Daniel was quietly shooting pucks into the goal. Seeing that wall of Wargo coming up to him, Daniel continued to shoot while maintaining his standoffish, aloof attitude. They circled closer . . . and closer.

"The first Wargo who makes the next move," Daniel warned, "will be the first Wargo in agony."

As Daniel skated wide around Eddie, the eldest Wargo purposely sped up to invade his air space. Bumping him hard in his chest, Daniel rocketed back on the pillow of pure blubber. Instead of punching Eddie in the face, Daniel slammed Eddie down on the air that mimicked ice and shot Eddie into the goal.

"Mother Effer!" Eddie shouted, his shoes tangled in the net and his rather large behind wedged in deep.

Soon, Daniel found himself surrounded by the two younger

Wargos who circled in a pack like the feral animals that they were in life. Young Billy reached out to push Daniel over, but he was ready for it and stayed upright long enough to grab his tormentor by the jersey and send him rocketing up to the ceiling. Daryl backed away and joined his little brother. Never one to be forgotten, Eddie recovered, sailed up to the left, and soon was in Daniel's face again. Before he could pull anything, an extremely peeved Coach Richard skated close enough to grab the two younger Wargos as they floated back to the ground.

"Open your eyes, Billy and Daryl. Can't you morons block?" the coach taunted.

Eddie decided to let the Rocket focus on his siblings while he jetted up behind Daniel and checked him into the boards. As both of their bodies crashed into the hard, fiberglass wall in a tangled mess, Eddie bit out, "What the hell are you really doing here, Reid?"

"I'm on the damn team," Daniel barked, shoving him so hard in the chest that Eddie's head, bent low, crashed into a wall and cracked one of the boards in two.

"You're an Academy a-hole," Eddie taunted, head-butting Daniel who recoiled backward. When he righted himself again, Daniel sunk his right fist deep into Eddie's lower rib section and heard bones cracking. Even with all the extra layers on Eddie, Daniel was sure that Eddie really felt it. "That was for the kick in the head," he growled. "And for every single time you've even thought about my girlfriend."

"So, all in all, it was really a great practice. Go team," Daniel said with a wince while he nursed his wounds that night and drew up a few plays on a note pad. His first game was on Saturday, which was just three days away. For some strange reason Daniel seemed consumed by it. "Why not just blow it?" I asked him, shrugging. "Show up. Just stand there. My way of playing hockey."

"Not an option, baby."

"You can't or won't?" I asked.

"Both," he said. Sometimes Daniel put up walls that were made out of stone.

5.

That Saturday, he returned to his cell at dusk after the game with the Freak school. I couldn't wait for the details, but Daniel was in a dark mood and silently sat on his floor eating his steak and potatoes without speaking. It turns out that hockey players had the finest cuisines of all including ice cream that he wanted to share, but the guards forbid it.

As the evening wore on, he relaxed and gave me a few particulars about the third school in the realm. He had seen some of them before, but I hadn't during my abbreviated hockey season. And I was fascinated when he told me about an entire row of young bearded guys with neon-blue and purple hair who sat in the always-overheated stadium covering their legs with thick black blankets.

"Students with disabilities?" I asked.

Daniel ran a hand through his black hair that was slick from his makeshift sink shower.

"Odd-type legs," he said.

"Don't stop now," I begged.

"From the knees down, it looked like their legs were fused into just one leg until you reached their ankles where they separate again. At that point, their feet were flared out in different directions like . . . it sounds nuts . . . like a fin," he said.

"Like . . . mermaids. But, they're dudes?" A.E. asked, beside himself with joy because this was high-level interesting to a kid his age. "Human, walking, talking, breathing merdudes with hippie hair. I love it!"

"But they could stand. And walk in small baby steps. I've seen them a few times now . . . for lack of a better word . . . waddle over to the concessions booth," Daniel said.

We heard how Daniel started out playing defense while the Wargos were on the frontline. The score was 0-0 for the longest time and then Freaks-1, ITT-0, thanks to the fact that Eddie refused to give the puck to Daniel who could have easily scored.

Rocket was beside himself screaming, "Give him the puck, you fool" about a thousand times at the top of his well-used lungs. Eddie continued his fancy footwork, which resulted in a lot of bad plays.

"That's crap!" Rocket screamed. "Screw you, Eddie! Go warm up the bench." Then Rocket pointed to Daniel and said, "You play center." With Eddie tomato-red-faced and ready to self-combust, Daniel took the job and scored two quick goals in under a minute. ITT won, 2-1 over the Freaks.

The GF was so thrilled that he ordered pizza for all of A Block.

And the Rocket warned Eddie that if he had one more crap game, he'd be off the team.

"Don't worry, baby, I'm getting back to the Freaks," Daniel said.

"With most of them, it's not obvious," he continued. "They have so-called emotional or skill oddities. So who the hell knows? Plus, I'm exhausted. Tonight, my body is going to force me to sleep. I'll see you on the other side in a dream."

I heard Daniel snoring and cozied closer to the air holes I

shared with A.E. "You know what they say about having eyes in the back of your head?" A.E. whispered. "One actually does."

"Tell me one more before we go to sleep," I yawned.

"So, there is a guy they call Chronos," A.E. said in the delighted voice of someone telling a really juicy secret.

"It's about time and age with him," he said. "His nickname stands for chronological, and it means that he looks at you and for a few minutes he can age you, or someone you're looking at, upward or backward."

I was confused.

"Ever wondered what your three-year-old face looked like or how Daniel would have appeared at age ninety? Well, he will show you by actually morphing you into that age for only you to see in your own mind. It only lasts for just a minute until it wears off," A.E. said, shivering again.

"But why would he do it?"

"He messes with your mind, like some sort of paranormal fortune teller," A.E. whispered. "Your past is obvious, although you probably don't remember all of it. He shows you what you couldn't possibly remember, and it's usually the bad stuff. The real bad stuff that you've blocked for some reason."

"And the future?" I pondered.

"Even worse," A.E. divulged. "He can show you two or three versions of yourself, or anyone else, at different stages in life . . . or, for us, afterlife. It's up to you to decide what's probably true. It's like that game, Two Truths and a Lie."

It was becoming clear that this teenage boy was a walking, talking head trip.

"He might show you your future self with Daniel or someone else. What do you want to believe? What will haunt you? Are you an optimist or a pessimist?" A. E. rattled off.

"He's a terrorist that plants an image in your mind and you

walk around terrified of your own future," I responded.

"Exactly," A.E. confirmed. "Think about it. Don't you think you'd live differently now, so to speak, if you thought you'd be in the Hole next week? Or shot? Or released? Or gone—as in never seen or heard from again? What would you do about today, if you had a few clues about tomorrow? But all of his clues aren't necessarily true. His mind messes with your mind."

Many more nights passed after that first game, and as the season wound to a close, either Daniel or A.E. would enlighten me with some other Freak's story.

The soft winds of midsummer were here, and there was only one hockey game left. The big game.

CHAPTER 9

1.

Six a.m. Game day.

I've always been an early riser, so I watched Daniel scarf down his breakfast, his metal tray piled high with thick slabs of bacon, a mountain of sunshine-colored scrambled eggs and a big bagel. Instead of a tin of some lukewarm water from the tap, he was given a gallon of bottled, fresh water. There was even butter, jam, and all the trimmings.

Daniel thought I was sleeping and there was no real way we could share, so I watched as he shoveled it into his mouth. His hockey jersey and pants, now the onyx black ITT colors, were also freshly pressed from the prison laundry.

Today was the league championship between ITT and the Academy.

Daniel finished breakfast and dressed quietly. When he saw

me watching, he pressed his hand to the glass. He smiled at me and I returned the sweetness. Then he motioned me to come closer. "Baby," he said. "You should sleep in. You finished the GF's book, didn't you?"

I nodded.

"You look so beautiful in the morning. When I was in the Hole, all I thought about was watching you sleep on the pillow next to me. Your face. The little crinkle on the top of your nose. Those big hazel eyes. The way they cloud over when I kiss you awake. The way you feel when I touch you."

He moved his face as close to mine as possible.

"I love you, Walker," he said. "Don't you ever forget it."

The last I saw of him, I held up a hand and he kissed my fingertips through the glass before placing his big hand over mine.

I closed my eyes.

2.

7:20 a.m.

I had Aileen in my face and she looked like a lady of the night who just figured out that it was morning. She wore a low-cut, red silk halter-top that left little to the imagination, and slick-skinned black leather biker pants. Her eye shadow was bright blue and she must have put at least ten coats of mascara on her lashes. Her porcelain cheeks were stained hot pink.

She was also in possession of a universal unlocking key, which she dangled in my face like it was a diamond watch. "Wake up, Sleeping Beauty. You got one busy day ahead of you, girlfriend."

"I really did finish the GF's book yesterday," I mumbled. "Give me a break. I just want to sleep all day."

"Girlie, you got that final chapter. He said to give it to me," Aileen said with a laugh, although I'm not so sure what was funny. "You give—you get."

"What do I get? A box of Twinkies?" I said, reaching under my bed and handing her the final chapter of the GF's memoirs.

"Let's get you presentable, Walker. You're going to the big game, sweet cakes."

"I'm what?" I blurted out. "No one from D Block goes to the game."

"If the GF says you go to the game, you go to the game. Got a new outfit for you, too," she said, heaving something resembling clean laundry in my direction. "Hurry up. It would be nice if we could wash your hair."

The outfit was the regulation gray prison pants accompanied by a plain black, somewhat formfitting, long-sleeved shirt remarkably missing any ITT lettering.

Aileen looked at me with bored eyes. Dressing in front of her leering gaze was the least of it, although I felt ridiculous as I slumped over to show the least skin possible. Afterward, she snuck me into the B Block shower, turned away, and allowed me to wash my hair and even blow dry it. Afterward, she shackled me up, we skipped the breakfast routine, and she accompanied my rumbling stomach and me to the loading dock outside, where both of us waited in the blissful fresh air. An ancient white van pulled up and sputtered to a stop in front of us.

I longed for the luxury and sweet smile of Harold.

"Don't try any funny stuff," Aileen said, shoving me inside. For a second, I thought about running, but to where? With no options, I took the high step into the vehicle and Aileen followed. She actually looked happy when the driver rolled down one of the windows before we took off. With the warm late-July wind in our hair, Aileen closed her eyes for a minute. "Anything to be out of there. Even for a few hours," she said. "Smell the pine trees, baby. Suck it in."

"I hear you," I said, inhaling deeply. "You know, you're not as hard on me as you could be."

"Just say thank you."

"Thank you, Aileen."

"You're a survivor. Reminds me . . . of me," Aileen said. "But I have better hair."

She shook out what looked like a long, blonde wig. And I had to laugh as my long dark hair danced outside the window. "I guess blondes do have more fun," I retorted.

I couldn't help but remember the last time I was headed to a hockey game when things were so vastly different. It was the day of my first big game as fill-in goalie for the Academy Aces and the boy I loved was captain of the team. We were there to win the championship game, and my mom was in the stands rooting us on, amused by my newfound afterschool activity because she knew I insisted, "I don't do sports." By the end of that day, Mom was gone and back in the living realm and my life had twisted on a dime again.

Flash-forward and now I was dwelling in an eternal penitentiary with no hope of any sort of parole. Daniel was playing for the devil and I was obviously being given a front-row seat to watch him give away everything he believed in.

I've said it before. Life isn't a bitch—death is.

3.

The music in the air hockey auditorium was blaring at a decibel usually reserved for rock concerts. I heard the last strains of Aerosmith's "Walk This Way" followed by the somewhat ironic "That's Life" by Sinatra.

Once again, I was stepping into the strangest hockey venue in the universe, but I wasn't alone. In the distance, I could see my old "fruit appreciation" teacher, Steve, sharing some popcorn and cotton candy with Kurt and Jerry. Miss Elizabeth was in the stands, too, reapplying fresh lipstick.

Unlike any hockey stadium in the living realm, once you passed through a small reception-like hallway and entered the actual arena, you levitated a good six feet off the ground. Burly ushers had to literally grab you by the arms and glide with you to your seat. Once seated, a protective harness dropped over your chest like on a roller coaster ride. They had to make sure you didn't just float up and up to the ceiling.

When playing human air hockey, the players didn't need skates to slide across the sleek air, which we called "ice" because it was smooth, slick, and extremely slippery, although there was nothing icy about it.

Aileen had an usher, but I didn't—she held on tight to a chain attached to a harness around my waist. Pushing me into my seat, Aileen gave my leg shackles a forceful yank to make sure they were still on lock. Then she tightened my handcuffs until I felt little tingles race around my fingers. "Don't need you going all AWOL missing," she said, snapping her gum loudly before taunting me in her smartass voice. Our moment of bonding was over. "I heard how you like to disappear," she said.

Given absolutely no choice in the matter, I sat in the small section that was mostly comprised of A Block ITT students who had done minimal crimes and were well on their way to parole. None of the A Blockers were cuffed and shackled, which made me quite the object of gossip from the moment I sat down. I could hear the whispers.

"They have a D Block girl in row ten. I heard she offed her entire family and half her school."

"No, I heard she poisoned her parents."

"No, I was told by a very reliable source that she knew Saddam Hussein."

High school. It never changes.

The wispy blonde next to me broke the ice by introducing herself, but not only by name. She decided to make a first impression with her crime.

"Computer hacker. Stole some SAT scores. I have low self-confidence. Oh, and my name is Miracle Teresa Hernandez. A Block," she said, offering her birdlike fingers for me to shake. Then her face burned bright red. Of course, I couldn't shake, so she looked down, reached out, and shook index fingers with me.

The friend next to her was much larger in frame with wild, red, frizzing hair and a crooked smile like she hadn't seen a dentist in a long, long time. She wore my same standard ITT outfit, which wasn't exactly a high-fashion statement.

"I'm celebrity breaking and entering. Broke into all the good houses. But strictly A-list. Channing Tatum. Julia Roberts. Kardashians—if you can still call them A-list."

"Razzy," she said, introducing herself. "For Razzle Dazzle. You can call me Raz, but please not Roz, which I detest."

When I just nodded and didn't speak, frizzy red Razzy bit out, "Cat got your tongue?" Then she noticed Aileen next to me, holding my waist harness, and her tough-girl act faded. For a minute even Raz looked like an innocent, doe-eyed girl who took a few wrong turns. "What. Did. You. Do?" she whispered, moving a little bit away from me like my crime was contagious.

"D Block. Realm traveler. Enough said," I retorted as Raz's eyes went extra wide.

As expected, the girls looked at each other knowingly, sealing my fate. We would never be besties. "Maybe we could hang later," I offered with a satisfied smile. *Why not have a little fun with them?*

It wasn't the site of Daniel in that heinous black ITT jersey that made me stare. Yes, I saw him, but my eyes were instantly diverted when I landed upon a sight that brought me to hot, rolling tears. Across the auditorium and filtering into the Academy's section was Bertha being led to her seat by not one, but three ushers. Then I saw Daniel's sisters Andy and Jenna traipsing in behind her, each clutching their favorite midday snack, a giant cloud-like puff of pink cotton candy. Little Bobby, as cute as ever, was bouncing along shotgun, a DQ Blizzard in one hand and a fat, doughy pretzel in the other.

Look at Jenna with her gleaming raven hair in a new short bob. Andy looks so much older in a black skirt and tights. Someone should have told Bobby that his Captain America sweatshirt on was inside out.

For some reason Pete wasn't there and I wondered why. The kid was never that into sports, and maybe he was protesting his brother playing for the rival school.

Most of my family had arrived and they looked sweeter to me than all of those treats.

You know how they say life goes on without you.

Apparently, death goes on, too.

4.

After double-checking my harness and shackles once again, Aileen excused herself impolitely with a burp and headed to the refreshment stand. Immediately, I did a quick skim of the stands across from me. Bertha was the first one to scan the crowd as if she was a CIA agent on a top-secret mission. She was a master at detail work, and her concentration couldn't be diverted. It didn't take long before I could see her pointing directly at me because Bertha also had that urban laser stare. She could find you even if you worked real hard at staying hidden. Her natural track and hunt skills worked for her as a foster child on the streets and then later when she was the goalie on the ITT team.

In her scope and on lock, I saw Bertha shuck off those ushers to wave hard to me. She was wearing a pretty pink sweater, black skirt, and a rainbow-colored infinity scarf. Closing my eyes for a moment, I imagined one of those warm, tight, motherly Bertha hugs enveloping my entire being until I couldn't even breathe.

Andy and Jenna glanced across the room and also waved wildly in that same way as if their arms were going to fly off their lithe teenage bodies. Now, I was the one scanning for little Bobby who seemed to have disappeared, but what else was new? The kid was stealth, unless you knew where to look. Out of the corner of my eye, I could see the slippery six-year-old slithering low through the legs of the ushers as he made a quick break from the pack. There was a reason why Bobby eluded demons all those years in the living realm. The kid knew how to go rouge.

He was slowly making his way around the entire arena, asking Academy students to hold him down as he floated beyond them like some sort of mini drone set on slow motion. Of course, the students obliged because this was better than sending an inflated beach ball through the crowd. Even from my vantage point, I could see Bobby grabbing the metal molding of the chairs so he wouldn't levitate up.

The kid managed to make it all the way over to the ITT stands, which was strictly forbidden, and was now grabbing the lower bars of my seat despite all my chains and shackles. It was the best sight in the whole world.

"Walkie! This is bullshit!" he cried in a breathless voice, reaching up to hug me hard. I held him tightly in my arms and managed to hug him back even harder despite his foul language.

"We miss you so much. Where's Danny? When are you coming home? Why are you still in jail? I've been taking care of Jake. He's fine. Kinda dirty from rolling in mud. But fine. Is he allowed to eat potato chips?" He rattled off the questions and information like any other breathless kid with a lot on his young mind. "Hey, Walkie, gimme me the key and I'll get you free," he said, ever the savvy warrior who knew when it was time to stage your exit.

"Baby, I don't have the key," I answered.

"Where's Danny? Let's break you guys out of that shit-hole," he said.

"Your brother's not here . . . he's over there." I pointed to the rink where I could see Daniel warming up in his ITT uniform before he went back into the tunnel to wait for the team introductions. His black ITT jersey said it all.

His kid brother saw it, too.

"Horseshit!" Bobby said, his little jaw trembling.

"Language," I semi-scolded, but he was right. It was horseshit.

"He's playing for the bad guys? Danny's one of the bad guys now?" Bobby said, his chin quivering, glistening tears ready to roll onto his inside-out sweatshirt.

"They're making him do it, baby. He had no choice. Where we live now, they force you to do things like how I force you to eat your peas and carrots," I said and he listened in a way that was almost reverent. "There's a big difference between being one of the bad guys and being forced to do something you don't believe in."

There wasn't time to say anything else to him because security was quickly descending upon us. Almost as if Bobby was a bug ready for crushing, they converged on us, quickly and wordlessly plucking the little boy away to return him to the Academy's side.

Flailing his arms hard and trying to connect his kicks to where it counted, Bobby didn't go easily. "I'm coming back, Walkie. Ticktack, no take backs," he called out and I could have sworn I saw his trademark mischievous wink. I had to smile because those guards had no idea what they had just done or who they were dealing with.

It didn't take long before those same guards were childless again and I could see their heads whipping around frantically. Moments later, I spied that little spiked haircut pop up again near the tunnel where, momentarily, the ITT players would race out for their first introduction. If I knew anything about this boy, I knew that he wouldn't rest until he saw his big brother.

Bobby crouched down and held tight to the lower portion of tunnel wall. I could hear harsh voices coming from the bowels of the tunnel where Bobby had become an actual fly on the wall. The kid and I locked eyes for several seconds, zeroing in on our newfound understanding that had been formed while fighting side by side in the living realm.

"Good luck, kid," I mouthed to no one in particular.

In the waning moments before the first puck was dropped and the bell sounded, Bobby stayed extremely low as he snaked back over to me, his little belly almost scraping the ground while dragging himself back to the ITT stands.

He actually made it all the way back to my seat without being seen.

Out of breath, he hugged my legs, so I leaned my head down to talk before they could rip him away. Nothing could have prepared me for what he said next.

He said it fast. "I heard Danny talking to some big, ugly man about getting free," he told me, words tumbling out in a breathless rush. "He said if Danny wins, he gets out of ITT! The fat guy said it's a done deal."

Through the pounding in my ears, I could hear Bobby yell, "Danny's coming home!" He said nothing else as the guards carried him away.

Now I knew why he said good-bye to me the way he did this morning. *Daniel was playing for his freedom.*

"Win," I prayed. Moments later, it was inevitable that I thought about the aftermath and my own selfish interests: I'd still be at ITT.

Eternally alone.

A horrible wash of happiness and sadness mixed in my heart.

"Win," I whispered in my most determined voice because there was no other choice. I wanted him to win more than I ever wanted anything. If one of us could get out of this hellhole, it was the ultimate triumph.

"Not because I like you or anything," Aileen interrupted, and I stared at her numbly. She was back—tossing a crinkling bag of all-American Cracker Jacks into my lap. "And you better fork over the prize," she insisted. "I just love those wash-off tats."

When I didn't answer, she looked genuinely hurt. "What? You don't like Cracker Jacks?" she demanded in a shocked voice.

5.

Five minutes from game time and Daniel was fast spinning across the rink where he levitated a good six feet off the ground as he whacked the puck with a new viciousness. I couldn't take my eyes off of him as he eased his six-foot-two body around the rink, dark hair flying back like he was caught in a windstorm. I forced myself to memorize everything knowing this might be the last time I ever saw him. The GF wasn't likely to grant D-18 any visitors.

I resisted every urge inside of me not to cry as my dear friend Izayah did a fast glide out of the Academy's tunnel flanked by new teammates including a goalie who already had a large, molar-protecting mask securely planted on his or her face. There was my beautiful, not-so-fragile friend, Tosh, the ballerina-twirling secret weapon. They waved at their own stands while the ever-polite ITT students chimed a deep chorus of boos.

"Well, that's sportsmanship," I said mindlessly to Aileen who just laughed while stuffing her acne-scarred face with cheese nachos.

A loud boo erupted from the Academy's side as the three Wargos slid into the spotlight followed by Bonnie Phillips, but without her brother, Clyde. Gossip-bag Aileen leaned in to whisper, "There was nothing anyone could do with Clyde. He went Down, as they say. Way Down."

I nodded and waited for the inevitable.

My eyes drifted to the Academy's side and I could see their new goalie going through the pregame paces. The person who replaced me was tall, thin, and well practiced. No nerves here. He or she kept the mask on and took their post in the net, wisely warming up a few inner-thigh muscles by crouching low like a cat and then sliding slowly from side to side.

On the ITT side, someone new had replaced Bertha guarding the ITT net and he was a massive male, almost as big as she was. In fact, he was so big that it seemed the puck wouldn't have a sliver of room to pass him.

"He trained with ISIS until they beheaded him for calling home," Raz couldn't resist telling me. "In fact, he's one of the most vicious prisoners here."

The three Wargo brothers skated in unison to the center of the rink. Bonnie joined them followed by Daniel who looked rough and ready.

Oh my God. This was really happening.

"You should have resisted!" Coach Walter yelled out to Daniel and it was clear that his once-star player was now the enemy. "Stay the course!" Walter shouted to his team. "Daniel Reid is no longer with us. He's a felon now. Get over it! Play to win!" My heart was breaking for Daniel who considered Walter a role model.

It's so easy to switch sides. All it takes is that first step in the other direction.

In the center rink, I could see Daniel standing face-to-face with his best friend, Izayah, but now they were just two countries divided by loyalties and missions.

"WTF, man?" Izayah ranted. "Are you out of your freaking mind playing for them?" When Daniel just stared at him with absolutely no emotion, Izayah reached out with the palm of his wide hands and smashed it hard into his opponent's chest. He shoved Daniel back several inches, which should have brought on the first fight of the night. But Daniel thought better of it and remained emotionless. "You've gone to the dark side, man," Izayah yelled.

Daniel gave him a steady look. "Drop the puck already," he said to the ref without ever taking his eyes off his former classmate. It didn't take long for a bell to ring, and Daniel to get his wish.

Daniel hit the puck with a satisfying whack. Never pausing, he raced to get it back as quickly as possible from Wargos. *Focus. Don't take your eye off the prize.*

Now the puck was being passed between the two youngest Wargos, Daryl and Billy. They swiped it back and forth, but were no match for Tosh who shot up while doing some sort of circular ballet move that confounded them. Tosh hit the puck with a satisfying smack as she moved it closer to our goal. It shocked me when Daniel bumped her left side with all his might, which sent her flying into the wall where her head ricocheted off the reinforced glass. Tosh was his friend. But the stakes were his freedom.

Out of the corner of my eye, I noticed the GF gleefully standing next to the new Academy leader, stone-faced Principal Dick who looked as if he would rather be anywhere than at some inane high school sporting event.

Turning back to the game, the puck seemed to have a mind of its own, careening every which way after Daniel slapped it, and then Izayah slapped it the other way. The Wargos had their own plan and Billy and Daryl cut off Izayah, slamming him into the boards.

Eddie took it upon himself to steal the puck from the Academy and jettison it down to their goal. Stretching as far back as possible with his solid, hammock-sized arms, he slapped the puck, hitting it with a mighty thwack. Like a bullet shot from an expert marksman, the puck shot straight for its target.

A quick lift of a right arm and the goalie made a swift glove catch.

No score.

On the rebound, Tosh grabbed the puck, slapping it to Izayah who moved it back down the rink. Daniel slid toward the puck and collided with Izayah. Both of them went careening into the boards, arms and legs tangled to the point that when the punches began to fly, few even connected. It was enough of a commotion for the teams to get distracted, which meant Tosh took the puck and did the impossible.

She scored.

Rocket Richard went ballistic. "What's the matter with you, idiots!" he screamed.

The game continued with multiple body checks, but no goals. As the clocked ticked down to thirty seconds left in the first period, it was Daniel with the puck, racing down the rink and passing it to his teammate Bonnie, a slick little hustler who waited a moment then sent it careening back his way. Slapping it with all of his might, Daniel sent the puck airborne. Facing forward, the Academy goalie lifted one large glove in the air and caught it.

"No score," called out our faithful announcer, Dick Clark, as the buzzer rang. "At the end of period one, the score stands Academy, one, ITT, zero. Please stay seated if you're in the stands. If you need to use the washrooms, buzz your usher to help float you over to the closest facility."

6.

My mind didn't know the meaning of calm.

What if they win?

What if they don't win?

Daniel had to score. Twice.

He had to do what we promised before we went back to the living realm.

Make. It. Count.

A few minutes into the second period and ITT was having serious defensive struggles that looked like the sport equivalent of the Cold War setting in.

For what seemed like an eternity, Tosh and Izayah owned that puck until Daniel managed to steal it and fly down the ice to the Academy's goal. Then passing up and back with a resentful Eddie, his attempts at a goal were blocked by the moronic Daryl who wanted the glory, dug in for the puck, and then lost it to an Academy player.

"This game looks like it will mark another winning season for the Academy even with the star power of Daniel Reid playing for ITT," Dick announced. "End of second period. Score still one for the Academy, zero for ITT."

In a furious flourish, the GF left the stands to march into the ITT locker room and I could only imagine the kind of "pep talk" he would be giving his players. Maybe there were threats of time spent in the Hole . . . or worse.

7.

The shrill sound of the buzzer made me jump a bit in my seat, although my harness held me down. I saw Daniel race out of the tunnel, and then stop and stare up at our stands. His eyes didn't register shock at the sight of me. And they did not soften. If I didn't know him like I did, his intense stare would have frightened me.

Walter skated out with his players doing his own version of

an award-winning pep talk. He was yelling, but that was Walter, one of the all-time great motivators. "One more period, Aces. One more period and we make it a nice, even decade of hockey championships. Don't you dare let Sweetness down! Party tonight on the hill. My pad. A big celebration."

From my days as goalie for the Academy, I knew the drill. Walter almost certainly told his players to just keep the puck away from ITT, run out the clock, and then enjoy the spoils of your win. That's exactly what Tosh and Izayah were doing as they leisurely slid the puck between the two of them, quickly enough not to lose it to the Wargos or Daniel, but in a savvy way where the clock kept winding down.

Only five minutes were left. Score 1-0.

Izayah didn't take kindly to Daniel trying to steal the puck and responded by shoving his best friend to what should have been the ground. Daniel threw a hard, frustrated punch to Iz's jaw and then found his own right cheek pummeled as a return on his investment.

"That's two minutes in the penalty box for the both of yous," yelled the ref who had a strong, clear New York accent. Time pushed forward until I could barely sit still.

One minute left—and then this game and Daniel's freedom were over.

Once sprung from their respective boxes, it was Daniel who roared up to steal the puck from Izayah before he was able to catch a pass. With the speed of an Olympian, Daniel rocketed with that puck across the entire length of the air, then whacked it with all his might, and watched it shoot mercilessly toward the Academy's net.

The boos were deafening when ITT scored their first goal.

Forty-five seconds left.

It was almost impossible to win at this point.

Thirty seconds left.

At least the game would now go into overtime because they were tied 1-1.

Twenty.

Nineteen.

Eddie Wargo now had control of the puck and Daniel raced with him down toward the Academy's goal. *Shoot, Eddie, shoot,* I prayed. Close to the goal, Eddie couldn't get a clear shot, so he passed to his brother Billy, who was at a terrible angle, so he passed it back to Eddie.

It hit Eddie's stick in the worst possible way and Tosh grabbed it for the Academy, but Daniel was too fast for her. Like a thief in the night, he stole that puck back and slapped it high and hard, which I knew was futile. If nothing else, the new Academy goalie was a master at catching high ones. It was such an easy catch.

Daniel even allowed his head to flop down as I stood on my feet screaming, "Please!"

The Academy's goalie lifted an arm just short of the puck, allowing it to sail right in and drop into the precious net space.

"I've never seen anything like it!" Dick shouted. "With only twelve seconds left on the clock, ITT has won their first hockey championship in a decade!"

What happened next made me catch my breath. Almost in slow motion, the new goalie pulled up his mask. The face underneath it was unmistakable.

It was Peter Reid.

Pete never missed. He didn't even have to look. He was the best catcher in the universe. But tonight he missed. He had to know.

Bobby got to him.

He missed on purpose.

As the two Reids locked eyes, a hint of a smile played on Pete's handsome face.

Cigarette dangling from her oversized lips, Aileen took a key out of her back biker-pants pocket and bent down to unlock my leg shackles.

"Thanks for letting me walk easy to the van," I whispered, knowing I would walk slowly so I could remember forever Daniel running out of this place as a free man. Still without saying a word, and now balancing her smoke between her clenched teeth, Eileen unlocked the handcuffs that were cutting into my wrist. With a last twist of her key, she removed the harness from my waist. In a quick fluid motion, she waved what looked like a magnetized key card over my embedded ankle bracelet, and it promptly dislodged from my skin and fell to the concrete ground below the stands.

I felt dizzy and sick to my stomach.

"That feeling will pass in a minute. Just walk it off. By the way, you're free, dollface," Eileen announced in a bland voice as if she was rattling off a grocery list.

I stared at her as the dizziness passed.

"Your little boyfriend played for lifetime immunity from ITT and somehow won. The next part I don't understand. He gave his immunity to you," she said. "What a package. Self-sacrificing and hot. Where'd you meet him?"

No! No! No! My mind began to scream. *He couldn't do this. He had a family. He had a home.*

"No!" I cried loudly. "I don't want the immunity. Give it back to him. Give it back. I won't take it!"

"Immunity is yours and it has been decided. Damn, I've never seen the GF do this for anyone. He really wanted that hockey win. Enjoy your freaking time or whatever those losers at your kiss-ass school say to each other," Aileen said. "Corrupt you at the next level, sweet cheeks."

"I demand that you take me back to ITT! Take me back!" I screamed, every fiber of my being going into some sort of convulsive reflex meltdown. "I want to go back to ITT . . . now! Cell eighteen, D Block!"

When I gave her the direct order, she just shrugged. "You don't have a cell there anymore. Some gangbanger has already filled it. I hear she's from Compton. Female with an Uzi, a bad temper, and a nasty skin condition," Aileen said.

Bored with this conversation, Aileen lit a new cigarette, and walked away, raising her hand in a backward good-bye.

With hard, purposeful strides, Daniel skated to the middle of the rink and had me on lock. He pointed hard to the sign that read: EXIT. I could leave now of my own free will. I could go through all the exits I wanted to if that was my choice. Choices were mine—his were now forever over.

"No! No fair!" Bobby screamed when his biggest brother lifted his hands to allow an ITT guard to shackle them. In front of the crowd, the same guards ripped off his ITT jersey and pants. Standing naked now, except for his underwear, he was instructed to put his legs into a gray prison jumpsuit. Daniel didn't resist. He complied. My feet were flying. Pushing past people in their harnesses, I made my way to the rail that separated the crowd from the playing field. Leaning over as far as I could, I screamed to Daniel, "Take it back! You have to take it back!"

As they shackled his legs, I could see him smiling up at me with glistening eyes. When I pushed hard and tried to step into the rink, large security guards stopped me. "It's only for the players," one shouted, so I ducked low and tumbled onto the levitating air, yelling, "I am a player."

Sliding on the slickness, I raced up to Daniel where I threw my arms around him and, despite the chains, he drew me into the type of enveloping hug I hadn't felt for so long. We fit like puzzle pieces, hip to hip, chin to chest. His skin felt so warm and I tried to breathe in his smell as his heart pounded against my breastbone.

Then he was pulled away and my knees buckled.

"Go home, baby," he shouted, moving away from me on his

way to the tunnel. "It's done. It's perfect. I can rest easy now. I did what needed to be done. For once, the GF kept his promise."

I frantically shook my head as he began to disappear.

"I'm happy," he shouted. "I love you. Go home, baby. Make it count. Make each day count."

And then he was gone.

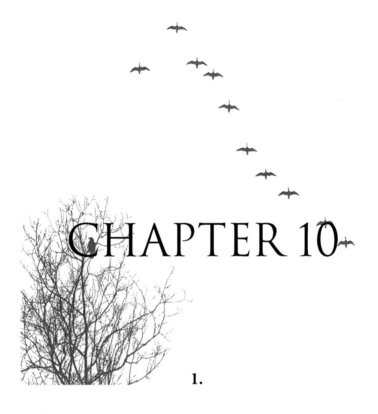

CHAPTER 10

1.

My legs were shaking convulsively as I made my way out of that auditorium. Mine were bashing into each other with such force—flesh and bone in some sort of wild drum solo—that I didn't think I could even walk home on my own volition.

Steadying myself against the outside of the building, I stood there in my ITT uniform in the hot summer sun. The park across the street was brimming with teenagers and I heard diving board springs cry and then a splash from the public pool. This is what it meant to breathe actual freedom. It felt foreign to me after all of those months in lockup, so I took another breath, savoring it as if it were thick cream after a steady diet of thin water.

In the distance, I saw him. I wasn't sure if he was just in my imagination or I willed him to pull up.

Harold had magically arrived with the trademark Academy

Bentley, which he parked in the no-parking lane, and I knew this was my ride. Harold almost always obeyed the rules because regulations were important to him. But this was a special occasion, and he didn't mind bending them a bit to park in a red zone.

For the first time ever, he actually took it upon himself to gingerly lift me up and carry me into the car. At one point, he loosened his grip to fumble with the car door and I slid, as if boneless, to the hard concrete below. My face kissed the ground in a move that should have hurt, but it didn't. No blood. No pain. My ankle bracelet had been removed and the reset was back.

Pain was no longer my friend.

"Sorry, Walker," he said. "I don't know what to do or say."

Those were the most honest words ever spoken. And so damn hard to ever admit.

I knew I wasn't thinking clearly, and I'm not even sure what kind of gibberish I said to Harold, when he lifted me again like I was made of spun glass and settled my body into the baby-soft black Corinthian leather. "I hate this damn place," I started ranting, clearly in some sort of postmortem shock. "It's just pain and loss. Loss and pain."

The last time I saw my mother here was at this auditorium, and it would be the last time and place I'd see Daniel. I knew the GF was smiling. Keeping Daniel inside was a neat way to make my time on the outside its own prison.

"Miss Walker," Harold said in his gravelly voice. "Where to? Where do you want me to drive you?"

All I could do is roll into a ball on the backseat. Grabbing my knees with my arms, I held myself and wept for all the new nevers that would fill my new existence without Daniel.

2.

In the end, I did the only thing I could under the circumstances. I did what we all do. I went home.

I went home to the house I shared with the Reid family—who had become *my* family the day their brother carried me through the front door when my mother left this place.

The Reids never locked their front door. I knew that much.

Feeling stronger now, I stepped out of the car on legs made of putty and waved Harold off. Then I took the slow trek up their front walk, past the little violet peonies Jenna must have planted. I sidestepped the Big Wheel on the front porch and almost buckled again when the dog tackled me. For a moment, it struck me in a profound way.

Things do go on without you. Meals are eaten, dogs are walked, and flowers are planted. Even here.

I didn't have to knock.

The Reids saw me coming and did a full family rush. "I'm sorry. I'm so sorry. I don't know what to say," I wept.

After they hugged me, the girls brought me upstairs where I showered and vowed to burn that prison uniform. Back in my own faded jean shorts and comfy bright-yellow T-shirt, which felt like heaven, I returned to the living room and felt the collective rage pulsing through the four walls as each Reid took turns pacing and plotting. The kids were furious that this get-out-of-jail-not-so-free card wasn't a two-for deal and their white-hot anger fueled their future plans.

"We'll break him out of ITT. We'll ride up there on Danny's

bike with guns," Bobby cried. "Big guns. Boom! Mow 'em down, Al said. Bury 'em in concrete like Hoffa!"

"Slow down," I told him. "Breathe, little man."

But at age six, the kid was unstoppable. "Death blows with Tommy Guns like Al used to tell me. He's a nice man, but kinda weird. Told me over and over, 'Always do your taxes, kid,' whatever that means."

"Hey Walker, long time no see," said a sheepish Pete, also back in street clothes, and meandering downstairs to join the rest. Leaning against the arch that separated the small living room from the kitchen, he looked round the room in his eternally embarrassed way.

Pete started coughing to cover up how truly shy he was around girls. He was just as handsome as his brother, but he had cropped ink-black hair and nerdy glasses to cover those steel gray eyes. I knew he had crushes on girls at school including my friend Tosh—an older woman at eighteen—but the last thing he would ever do was admit it.

"I just wanted to say that what happened out there . . . on the ice, I mean, air, " Pete stammered. "I mean, the way it went down . . . you know, I know he wanted it that way. He wanted you to be free. He wouldn't do it any other way. He told me to tell you not to be too mad at him, too. For what it's worth, he said to tell you, 'This is what makes me happy.'"

"Did he say anything else," I said in a quiet voice, knowing that each word was precious now.

"That's, um, it," Pete concluded with a hard swallow and a careful look back down at his worn boots shoved under faded jeans.

I swallowed hard, so I wouldn't lose it. In a strange way, I felt like I was their mother now and I knew I had to keep it together.

No blinking. No weeping. There was time, endless time, for the rest of it. Later. In private.

"I don't know what to do now," I told them, trying hard to chase the quiver in my voice away. Jenna noticed it and quietly moved closer to hold my hand. Her palm felt surprisingly strong and sure.

It occurred to me that Pete had no idea that his brother had even made this deal until the end of the game. I could only imagine how horrible it would have been for him if the Academy won and his brother would have been denied his one chance. "I told Petey what to do. Snuck into the locker room for a pee and told everything," Bobby boasted.

My mind flashed to the GF and his cunning manipulations. He set this one up in the most exciting way for himself, playing the cards close to the vest and allowing fate to intervene. If I hadn't finished the book, I might have never been allowed to go to the game. Then it hit me. Daniel had asked me several times in the last few weeks how the book was going. He kept insisting I finish it. I thought he didn't want me spending my days with the GF. Now, I knew. Daniel made this deal from the start. After the GF made him an offer he truly couldn't refuse, Daniel put a stipulation on it. My freedom for him playing. The GF knew he would win every game. What a cruel bastard the GF was. He amused himself by treating people like chess pieces.

"So, let's start from the day you left. Here's what you missed," Pete interjected, trying to lighten the mood for a moment. "Fun exciting things have sort of, but not really, happened here. Oh, and before I forget, the dishwasher doesn't really work anymore." He stopped, stared up at me for a split-second, and then continued. "And then there's that tiny matter of the carpeting upstairs, but I'm told that with the right cleaner all that red stuff should come out."

"Oh, and there's one more thing," Pete added after a short

pause. Digging into the pockets of those faded Levis, he fished out something that caught the overhead light.

From a distance, it looked like the kind of pendulum that a hypnotist might use to tell you that you were getting sleepy, very sleepy. When I looked closer, I could see that it was a delicate gold chain with an engraved medallion hanging from it.

Pete was always particularly uncomfortable talking to me about private family matters, but now it seemed that he had no option. By no choice of his own, he was the man of the house now.

"It fell off Daniel when they arrested him, but I found it in the dirt. At school. It's old. It belonged to our mother. Actually, it belonged to her grandfather Ethan. Daniel doesn't always wear it because that's girly, but he did on the day you went back to school after bringing Bobby back. He thought it would bring the two of you luck. Guess that theory didn't work. But still, I want you to have it. He would have wanted it."

Would have. Since when did we start talking about Daniel in past tense?

Pete knew. I knew. He was gone. The grief was so thick that it felt like I was breathing wet sand.

Numbly, I nodded when he pressed the necklace into my hand.

"Our mom always loved horses. So did her family, even though they were too poor to ever own one. We owned a lot of horses with my dad. Mom would ride and race them around our grounds in Lake Forest. She said she never felt more alive than when she was on a horse. Now . . . uh, you can keep it." Pete shuffled his feet around to manage his embarrassment. "You don't have to wear it. You don't have to do anything. You know. Just be here with us. If you want. We hope you want."

I looked down wondering if I should give this family heirloom to Jenna or Andy. When I looked up at them, they knew it, and began to shake their heads in a "no."

The tarnished medallion was shaped like a horse with its legs folded under a mane flying backward. It was as if someone had captured this beautiful creature on a full-speed run as it created its own hurricane-force wind.

Even frozen in gold, it felt alive.

On second glance, I could see that the piece was so old that the eyes and nose on the horse had been worn away. The featureless face made it even more haunting.

"Thanks, Pete," I said, slipping the necklace over my head and then feeling the horse fall until it landed over my heart.

"This means a lot," I said. "I want to wear it. For your brother."

For that last ounce of good luck that might still be in it. Especially since I didn't have my lucky rabbit's foot anymore.

I was so lost in my thoughts that I didn't hear the silence.

Then it dawned on me: Kids were never this silent, which forced me to look up.

The Reids stood almost frozen in time.

Click.

Daniel shut the front door behind him.

Then he took a few steps forward until he was inside.

He was home.

3.

He took one look at his mother's necklace around my neck and in a thick, gravelly voice said, "Looks good on you, sweet baby."

Almost as if he wanted to stop time, he tore his eyes away from me for a moment to count heads. One long look at his brothers and sisters settled his mind because they were all there. Standing there in his gray ITT jumpsuit, taking us all in, I could see that his handsome, world-weary face was covered in days of mountain-man stubble and freshly dried blood from the game. A pained, forced smile said more than words ever could.

I actually pinched the inner flesh of my arm and felt it. *This wasn't a dream. This was real.*

The kids had other thoughts post door-slam. In fact, they were suddenly transformed. Pete high-fived his brother and the girls wept over him. Bobby went for a direct, full-body muscle hit to his brother's kneecaps. Finally, Daniel reached out with a strong arm, grabbed my yellow tee, and yanked me into his arms in a way that was hard and forceful, which almost caused the shirt to rip, but sealed our family reunion. The world, our world, had clicked back into place.

It was one loud click.

"How?" I whispered, and the words got stuck in my throat. He crushed his lips to mine, skin to skin, and it felt like the first day of every summer I had ever experienced. When he pulled back, then did it again, I could have sworn I spent the last several months underwater and now was taking my first breath. I never wanted to exhale.

"I'm out. For now. The Higher Authority was backstage at the game. They need me to do something for them," he whispered as the kids disappeared to give us some privacy. "I don't have all the details except that you're officially paroled. And I'm out for the time being."

"What do you mean?" I begged.

"I'll tell you later. Let the kids think it's all good because they need some good," he said.

Tears rolled because I was never good at stopping them and I knew my face was bright red now.

"Shhhh, baby," he whispered into my ear. "This is all that

matters. Right here. Right now. It's more than we had yesterday."

We didn't talk about any more particulars because the kids returned and glued themselves to us. Even when I went to the bathroom, Jenna camped outside the door.

When the kids asked what happened, Daniel said, "I guess winning for the GF meant a lot for him and he let me go." I could see Pete and Jenna didn't believe it, but Andy and Bobby were too happy to question it.

Even after eating loads of snacks while catching up that afternoon, at dinner we chowed down on vast quantities of boxed mac-and-cheese, followed by enough Rocky Road to deplete the realm's resources. I washed the dishes and everyone watched back-to-back reruns of *Friends* because there was nothing else that felt as normal as watching Monica and Ross stage a love-hate fest. Then Bobby had a belching contest with Jenna. All was right with our world.

Finally, Daniel and I settled a bouncing-off-the-walls little Bobby into bed and then retired to our room. It should have felt awkward, but there was no room for embarrassment when he gingerly lifted me off the ground and fell with me to the bed. He cushioned my head in those large biceps like I was made of mist that could slip through his fingers.

There wasn't an inch of his body that I didn't try to heal and he lingered over every inch of me in a way that made me feel cherished and protected. The reset was back for Daniel, too. When I kissed his ankle, I could see that where his device had rested, his skin was pink and healed.

We could only feel joy, which is why Daniel found pleasure at four in the morning by tracing shapes on my stomach. When the night sky revealed its first hints of retreat, he told me it was time to fill me in on his miraculous return home.

In less than an hour, I would learn why Daniel wasn't really a free man. Just like in life, you can't be free when there are conditions.

4.

Under the milky predawn sky with an infinite stretch of road in front of us, we drove like the road would never end. Jumping on the back of the Harley, I wrapped my arms around Daniel, not because I needed the warmth—I needed the connection.

"What month is it?" Daniel asked, leaning down to kiss my hands bandied across his chest.

"It's summer," I replied. "Almost August. Just drive."

Daniel gunned it, but skipped the woods to head off on a quiet two-lane street that led to a small spot of beach that I had never seen before in this ecological question mark. Peaked sand dunes and straw-green tufts of grass greeted us and led to a sandy path that stopped at what looked like the shore of an ocean, although I couldn't be sure. The horizon was much too murky to see anything beyond a few feet of gently rolling waves.

No one was there. Several faded red wool blankets, all vacant, rested on the sand and I wondered who or what placed them there. I saw a sign that read: BEACH RENTAL—FREE.

On one of those blankets, Daniel cradled me in his chest and I leaned into his strength. When he kissed me, my breath clogged in my lungs. A tiny sand crab ran across my leg and I closed my eyes to listen to gently lapping waves that were soothing and affirming. I allowed myself a minute to imagine that we were just a normal couple spending the day mindlessly sunning ourselves.

That minute abruptly ended when Daniel told me about the terms of his parole.

He explained it in the simplest terms. In a nutshell, after I was granted my freedom, he was shackled and brought to a training room in the back of the stadium. There were three men in dark suits in the room, including the bastard otherwise known as the Academy's Principal Dick: "Mr. Reid, first let us commend you on that lovely display of . . . how shall we say it . . . self-sacrifice? It almost brought a tear to my eye, but I'm not the kind of man for sentiment. I'm more a man of practicalities and needs. And I'm wondering if you might be the one to fulfill a most pressing concern."

Daniel reclined under a sky the color of vanilla. At least he could relax. I had already stood up to pace, kicking grains of sand in the calm air that had more than a hint of fog in it. A thick gauze of ground-bound clouds circled my body, reaching out and embracing me as it enticed me to go toward the thicker mist near the water.

Reaching into his pocket while I raised my eyebrows, Daniel sat up and pulled out a crumpled half sheet of standard white typing paper. I could see from the short distance that what was on it was a photocopy of something very yellow and very old. The handwriting was in giant loops, as this was written back in the day when men actually practiced the ancient art form known as cursive writing.

Silently, I read it and then I gazed up at Daniel's face. Then I reread the words out loud to him in a most reverent voice. "The discoveries of man are not always what's best for mankind. History's shadows keep the secrets and the humble shall serve as guards. For they are the ones who have been entrusted with The Hiding."

Shivers ran up and down my arms.

"Here's all that I know, baby. Something has been buried in history. It's in the living realm. The Higher Authority wants it.

They need someone to get it for them—and I've been there, done that, and found a kid. I'm going back—as their personal delivery service," he said.

"But," I began, my mind reeling.

He jumped up and kissed my forehead. "They need someone who knows how to travel," he hedged. "Before you ask . . . that's why me."

"They can go screw themselves if they want you to go back there . . ." I began.

"I'm going. If I get what they want then I'm permanently free—like you. If I fail, then I go back to ITT for eternity. It's pretty clear-cut. It's business," he said in a quiet voice. "And the worst part of it is, I'm not going alone. But we can talk more about that later because you're not going. That has already been promised. I am going with a team from here."

"You can't," I began.

"Two things are nonnegotiable. You're not part of this and I want to swim," he yelled, as he leapt to his feet.

"Wait," I cried because for a minute he was lost in the fog.

"I can't wait," he yelled, running backward now. "I'm not sure if I have the time to wait. But I am sure that I have the morning and the beach. And I'd rather have five minutes with you in this sand than eternity elsewhere."

He stretched out his arms and held out his open hands.

Knowing my response like it was his own, he kicked off his boots and stripped off his clothes. Before I could say anything, he put two fingers to his lips, blew me a kiss, and took off. What else could I do, but swallow my fears and rage, and strip down to a bra and panties to follow him as he jettisoned into the foamy surf. Under fat, white clouds, we swam hard, matching each other stroke for stroke in water that tasted salty sweet.

We weren't cold, but we sure were wet. And when Daniel

picked me up and tossed me in even deeper, I vowed payback. He was too big to topple, but it was fun to try. A gleam entered his eyes.

"Hold your breath—or don't," he said.

"Why?"

"I might want to administer CPR," he teased as I raced up and grabbed him by the shoulders to dunk him. "A dreamer with attitude and visions of grandeur," he said, lifting me gently and then sending me flying into the warm summer air.

For the first time in months, I saw him smile where his eyes crinkled at the corners. He didn't look like a man on borrowed time, but someone who was content with whatever happened.

Surrender. I stretched my arms out in the water and held open my two hands like he had done on the beach. He grabbed one and we swam hard underwater toward the faraway horizon. The closer we got, the further it appeared.

I could have sworn I saw land in this direction or maybe it was a cloud. "Maybe we could just swim away," I lifted my head above water and suggested. The eel-like man next to me just grabbed my hand and pulled me fast and hard under the water.

Eventually, we turned around and swam back to shore, collapsing in the drenched sand. In that moment, I knew I would no longer be a prisoner of anything, including circumstances. Two things were nonnegotiable. I wasn't ever going back to ITT. And neither was Daniel.

When I looked up, I saw the first sliver of morning sunlight. It was tomorrow.

CHAPTER 11

1.

The glittering early morning bounced off the water and turned it golden as we reluctantly walked away. It was almost eight a.m. and we couldn't stay even though the water seemed to whisper to me, *"Don't go. Just jump back in. Where it's safe."*

We rode home on the Harley and found that the kids had already left for school. The evidence was the whirlwind of plates and half-eaten breakfasts spread across the kitchen like a food tornado had gone through when no one was looking. Not knowing what we should do—school or not—I was leaning toward a free day. The idea of the ex-felons coming back to class was unappealing at best. I wasn't sure if I was ready to explain "doing time" to Tosh and Gracie, who probably never did anything worse in their lives than jaywalk.

But my thoughts of a lazy day alone in the house with Daniel were interrupted by a firm knock on the door. Praying it wasn't

Miss Elizabeth with some gentle counseling, I took a deep breath and turned the knob. It wasn't the violet-eyed starlet. It was Abby, one of the Welcome Wagon ladies who delivered instructions to my mom and me on our first days here.

"Hi doll, you look skinny. I heard that you went on an extended vacation to that horrid place we need not ever mention," Abby said, adjusting her too-tight leggings while her earbuds dangled. "Poor little lamb. I'm bringing over a tuna noodle casserole tonight. Do you like hamburger helper?"

As usual, she made no eye contact and dug through a deep tote bag with big yellow flowers on it. "Slow morning for newbies since it's the dog days of summer. I expect there will be more pool accidents and motorcycle daredevils, but not today. That's why I'm also on mail service."

Handing me an envelope, she smiled and said, "Keep it real. I always do."

With those words, she took her calloused hand and placed it on my cheek.

"You need a good meal, Walker. I promised Maddy that I'd look after you," she said. "Your mama is salt of the earth. She's my kind."

"She told you this before she left?" I asked.

"You should come over someday and we'll talk about it," Abby answered.

With those words, she smiled and then waved while she bounded down the three front porch stairs. Something caught in my throat: *People were kind. When you least expected it.*

Then I looked down. In my hand, I held an envelope that read: Mr. Daniel Reid. The senders stamp was unmistakable in dark blue with gold trimmings: The Higher Authority.

"Thank you," I called after Abby and she stopped in her tracks. For a moment, I thought she was going to tell me something earth shattering about my mom, which would have been the only news I had heard in a long while. Since I had dismissed him one night when he just wanted to "talk" without my mother there, Cass had never appeared again.

Sharply, Abby turned toward me.

"Silly me," she said, jogging up the stairs with her hand on her heart. "I forgot something. I'd lose my mind if I didn't have those sticky notes."

In her hand was another envelope.

It was from the Higher Authority and it read: MISS WALKER CALLAGHAN.

2.

Livid was an understatement. Daniel picked up a coffee cup on the counter and threw it hard across the room until it was raining shards. Quickly, so the dog or various children didn't cut themselves, I bent down to pick up the pieces while he kicked a ball across the room at a speed that was lethal.

"That bastard swore that you wouldn't be a part of this bullshit!" Daniel shouted, taking vicious strides between the kitchen and the living room.

Sitting down at the kitchen table, I had no choice but to open the envelope and read what was inside. It read: MISS WALKER CALLAGHAN, YOU ARE REQUIRED TO MEET WITH THE HIGHER AUTHORITY AT 4:00 P.M. TODAY. A MAP HAS BEEN PROVIDED. BE PROMPT. FAILURE TO ATTEND THIS MEETING WILL RESULT IN IMMEDIATE PLACEMENT BACK AT ITT.

Without asking, I opened Daniel's letter and it was much the same, but also a bit different. On the bottom was a handwritten note from Principal Dick.

It read: *Adjustments were required.*

3.

At 3:30 that afternoon, Daniel kicked the Harley into action again and we sped at a hundred and fifty miles per hour in the opposite direction of Main Street on a route we never took for no real reason except it was mostly steep roads angled up with no straight path into the woods. Zigging and zagging, Daniel jettisoned us on so many hairpin turns around large trees that I had to close my eyes.

This time, my grip on Daniel was rage for our situation. His silence showed his contempt for the Higher Authority's wishes. Given no choice, Daniel kept going until the path stopped sharply and he hit the brakes so hard that I slammed into his back. "Sorry, baby," he said, squeezing my hands. "Detour."

And then I saw it. There was a simple metal chain across what looked like a well-worn dirt path. It was marked clearly on the map as a road of sorts. A road with no name.

The bike whined to life again, and he continued on, driving right through the chain that broke easy thanks to the powerful cycle. The road was narrow and twisting now like it didn't want survivors. Several times, I got my hair full of pine needles, as the trees were that close to a path that wasn't paved and mostly dirt and rock.

While I clung to his back, Daniel pushed the Harley as it chugged reluctantly to the top of the road where suddenly the ground leveled out. A man in a dark-blue suit and black aviator glasses darted in front of us with one hand up as our own personal stop sign. I could see him looking down into a book that sported our photos.

The man spoke into his wrist, "Callaghan and Reid."

Pause.

"Yes, they came alone, but we can do a sweep."

I looked at Daniel.

"I can be sure," the man said, approaching us.

"Step forward," he instructed in a terse voice and we obeyed. He took a tiny device and waved it over the front of each of us. His device made two rapid beeping noises.

"Aura check," said the suit. "ID positive."

A voice came out of his sleeve that sounded robotic. "Permission granted to enter," it said.

Daniel wasn't even allowed to park, and we were instructed to get off the bike, which was then handed to another blue suit who jumped on to drive it . . . to where?

The entire show was so fascinating that I didn't have a moment to look up. But finally, I gasped at what stood before us.

It was a fortress made almost entirely of green-hued glass, supported in front by what must have been hundred-foot pillars that were completely translucent. Despite the architecture, it wasn't clear what lurked inside. It was the kind of glass where those inside could probably see you, but you couldn't see them.

By now, we were staring ahead at what looked like a mammoth twenty-foot-high glass door. We didn't have to knock. A butler in his midsixties and wearing a black tuxedo was already sliding open the slab of glass, which protested with every inch as if it wasn't opened very often.

I knew that there was nothing I could say to the Higher Authority that would prevent Daniel from going back to the living realm to do their bidding. This was so much bigger than either of us. Why I was here remained a big question mark. But Daniel's fate was sealed. It was one thing to go back to find Daniel's brother *by choice.* But it was quite another to risk everything to do someone else's bidding. Of course, young men and young women had been doing just that since the beginning of time.

It was called war.

4.

In many ways, it was the Camp David of the afterlife. From my years studying United States history, I half expected to see Ronald Reagan and Eisenhower curled up with good books on various dark leather couches.

So far, there weren't sightings of either as we took our first cautious steps inside.

There was a grand foyer, which was a mixture of dark and light that included mahogany wood floors and a babbling Chinese water vase that had been turned into a large circular fountain. I knew that it was good luck to have water at the entrance of anything and perhaps that would bode well for us.

We walked past stone pillars the color of a rusted car fender. They were spiked into the dark wooden floors that stopped at a sweeping all-glass staircase ascending countless stories into the sky. The entire back wall of the house was made of enormous panels of glass that made it seem as if you were floating in the wispy clouds that served as the artwork on invisible walls.

I didn't have vertigo, but climbing those glass stairs made me feel dizzy and as if I was walking on water.

Upstairs in a massive living room, we could see an almost

360-degree view of the realm we called home, although the Academy looked like a mere dot on the horizon. When I looked far down below, I saw a secluded courtyard overrun by vibrant pink bougainvillea plants that lined a winding path feeding into the dark, lush forest.

My eyes drifted back to a large piece of furniture in the great room. It was a grand conference table for fifty or sixty people made out of an ashen white oak with branches supporting its expansive wooden top. Principal Dick stood before this monstrosity, looking like he ruled the world as he admired a large earth-colored pottery bowl in the center of his long pulpit. Obviously, he knew we had arrived, but would take his time acknowledging us, which meant we had no choice but to stand at the opposite side of the table and quietly stare at him.

It was the perfect way to establish his authority. He would feign extreme interest in a bowl; we would stand and squirm.

Finally, he spoke.

"It's called a hibachi," he said, pointing to the pottery. "It has ashes of the dead inside of it. Warlords and emperors would warm their hands over it before they went into battle. The ashes inside of it are four hundred or five hundred years old. It's an authentic piece."

I couldn't resist starting the day's activities out in the only way possible. He was, of course, the man who publically humiliated us before sending us off to prison.

"And did it work for you when you were president? When you had to resign?" I asked. "I guess the warlords couldn't help you then, so you might want to clean the thing out."

His laser gaze was intended to slice through me.

"Life isn't meant to be easy, Miss Callaghan," he said. "It's as hard being on top as it is on the bottom."

He said those last words while looking at me with great distain. "I guess I'm somewhat of a fatalist at heart," he remarked. "You have to have a sense of history and fatalism to survive some of these things. Life is, after all, one crisis after another."

"And death?" I questioned him.

"Not exactly the great equalizer," he said, adjusting the cuffs of his starch white shirt that was under a stiff black suit jacket. "Now, enough of this inane chatter. I'd like the two of you to stand at the back of the table."

No, we would not be invited to sit.

Not now. Not ever.

5.

It wasn't long before a massive, dark wood door opened and men and women began to flood the space. At first glance, I noted that they were some of the most interesting, if not the greatest, minds of our time. Most of them were also now housing their bones six feet under.

But they had joined forces here as the Higher Authority Board and this was perhaps their greatest accomplishment. I noted that it was an equal-opportunity calling and not all the same members were here that were present at our ITT sentencing. I could hear the women's heels clacking across the marble and the men plod along until they scraped their chairs away from the table to take their seats. Few smiled. Their dour faces were obviously letting us know that whatever was to be discussed was obviously of the utmost of importance.

The roll call was impressive. In cushioned leather seats sat the men and women of my textbooks. There was Roosevelt—all three of them, Curie, Hawking, Jobs (who had never mentioned his Higher Authority status), Emerson, Armstrong, and even Roddenberry. Was that . . . Sally? There were so many more, about twenty, and I recognized most of them. Anyone would.

"We want to help you, Mr. Reid, with this little housing problem you're having. We hear that you don't like the fine, although sparse, accommodations at ITT," Principal Dick began, taking his seat in the middle of the table. It was clear that he was our MC this afternoon. "That's why we convened the Higher Authority," he continued.

A chair was empty and it kept drawing my glance as I stood with Daniel at the far end of the table looking at the sullen faces. Principal Dick gestured grandly to that one chair.

"For your AWOL, or should I say, recently ascended Principal King," Dick announced. "May he continue on in peace."

Even some of the members of the Higher Authority didn't believe his act. "Let's get to it, Dick," said Hawking, and for a moment I wondered why he was here. When I last checked, he was still *alive*. "Special universal dispensation during the most dire circumstances," he said, looking at me, obviously reading my mind from the look on my face. Daniel was giving him the same strange stare.

My brow seemed to indicate that this wasn't enough on the explanation trail. So Hawking stood up from his chair, perfectly fit in body, and paced. "I love it here," he began. "I always feel like a million bucks." Then he launched into it. "My agreeing to be here is simple—a complete understanding of the universe. Why it is as it is and how it expands in the most glorious and unimaginable ways. Why it exists at all. Who wants it not to exist? That's why I'm here," he concluded, sitting back down in his large leather chair.

Under other circumstances, I would have loved to sit down for a Coke and a slice with this guy to mull it all over, but these weren't those circumstances.

"There is something we need; something of dire consequences to both the living and the dead. We need you to get it for us as there are few who could make this sort of journey and exist to talk about it," Hawking continued.

"Failure, as they say, isn't an option. Neither is nonperformance or incompetence," Dick interrupted. That was the windup. Here was the pitch: "The deal here is simple: You do what we want and Mr. Reid gets his ultimate freedom—an eternal get-out-of-jail pass from ITT, similar to what Miss Callaghan is now enjoying. We will ignore your previous indiscretions despite the fact they are most heinous. That should indicate how serious this situation we're embarking on is for all. You have my word when it comes to the promised outcome."

"Your word is worth shit," Daniel interjected in a hard tone. "You promised me that Callaghan wouldn't be involved in this . . . whatever it is."

"Yes, yes, yes, guilty as charged," Dick admitted. "That was an oversight. And you didn't get my word in writing—a mark of your stupidity." He pulled an envelope from his suit jacket and slid it across the slick table. "As you can see, Mr. Reid, it's all in writing now, signed by every member of the Higher Authority. There will be no going back on my word if you perform and get us what we want. What we all need. We even had our legal consultants cross the t's and dot the i's," he said.

"I advise you to give it a read when you have a chance," he continued. "I'm sure Mr. Jobs can walk you through the fine print. He has a copy in his Apple Bans." Steve had the new Ray-Bans with small computers in the lenses. It operated by eye blinks.

"Dan, I'm sorry," Steve said. "I had nothing to do with Walker being here today. I voted against it."

Daniel glared at him and nodded, while I continued to gather as much information as possible. My attention was momentarily diverted when I saw a small school bus pull up near the northwest side of the house.

"Choose not to embark on this mission in exactly the way it is presented to you and Mr. Reid's not just back at ITT for eternity. He will be sent away to a different realm—never to be heard from or seen again. No visitors. No parole," Dick threatened.

My hands began to shake and I couldn't stop them quickly enough. Dick smiled, satisfied that what he was saying was working.

"Why am I here?" I blurted out. It was the fifty zillion dollar question.

Dick just pursed his lips and said, "Miss Callaghan, I'm sure I speak for all when I say in the most polite way possible that Mr. Reid is no Rhodes Scholar. He was a B student at best. You got straight As from first grade until your death."

"You were a National Honor Society inductee," Dick continued. "You don't only have brains, but you proved yourself to be a true force amongst the worst demons in the living realm. Honestly, I don't think Mr. Reid would have survived a moment of it without your intelligence, savvy, and stupid blind luck at his side."

"Although, a smart young woman would never get involved with a man like Mr. Reid," Sally added.

I shot her a dirty look.

"We honestly believe that without your help again in the living realm, Mr. Reid doesn't stand a chance," Armstrong said.

"Now, let's give Daniel some props," Steve began. "Walker, I was against this, but there really is no choice—about any of it," he added in a soft, sure tone. "Think of it this way: We don't get a chance to do that many heroic things in life, but what about in death? You're about to get the chance to do something quite extraordinary. For the survival of humankind."

I didn't have the time to be bowled over by one of his graduation-like speeches.

"Just say it, Steve," I demanded. "What's about to take down humankind? Zombies? Vampires? Reality TV?"

"You went back. You homered. You got the kid. Major screw up when it comes to the rules, but you did that screw up well," Steve said. "Here we are now. And we have a problem. A big one. We could send a hundred kids back to get what we need, but quality is better than quantity. One homer is all we need—and we need it now. Humanity needs it." He paused, looking from Daniel to me and back again. "Do you have two homers in you?" he asked.

We were being asked to travel back—again—like some sort of DOA UPS service.

I took a long, slow look around the room at the tense faces.

"So what's the 'get'?" I asked. "Is this like when I was in eighth grade and we went to visit Lincoln's log cabin? Do you want something like the authentic Lincoln bottle opener? Or do you want your regular souvenirs like an 'I Went Back to Life and All I Got Was This Lousy T-shirt?'"

I blurted it out because what did I have to lose, except the man standing by my side looking at me in shocked disbelief.

Several chairs swiveled sharply in my direction. I had to be careful in front of this crowd. They could easily do any number of truly heinous things. Lasting, horrible things.

"You will be looking for something that could be used for one of two purposes—profound good or monstrous evil," Curie concluded. "There will come several moments where you will be forced to ask yourself, 'Which side am I on?'"

6.

The actual plan hit me like a million tiny slaps, one after the other, stinging with increased intensity as they were leveled upon us.

"Of course, this is a sensitive matter," Dick said, but it sounded to me like he was speaking underwater.

The rest of his speech was peppered with words like: "We have a serious situation" and "New evidence has come to light" and "Others will be searching, too." I was told that no further information would be given unless we agreed to the first step, which was going; and once we did give our word, and sign on the dotted line, we would be required to commit body, heart, and soul. In other words, there was absolutely no turning back.

As I watched those full green trees sway outside the window, I felt their nervous rhythm and began to shift my feet ever so slightly in a side-to-side sway.

Almost reflexively touching what looked like an old antique pocket watch, Dick kept hitting the lever to open the time piece's covering and then he looked down as if these moments were slipping by at an uncomfortable pace. "What you need to know," he continued, "is even a bit of a mystery to the board assembled here."

The mystery could wait for the paperwork. Dick produced a gold pen that seemed to shimmer in the late afternoon sun. Quickly, he shoved a piece of paper at us that had the official Higher Authority logo on top. I scanned the deal, focusing on the last sentence: IF MR. DANIEL REID RETURNS WITH THE HIDING IN HIS OWN PERSONAL POSSESSION—IN HIS HANDS—AND DELIVERS IT INTACT TO ANY MEMBER OF THE HIGHER AUTHORITY, THEN HE WILL BE GRANTED ETERNAL IMMUNITY FROM ITT. IF HE FAILS THIS MISSION THEN HE WILL RETURN TO ITT FOR TRANSPORT AND PERMANENT EXPULSION FROM THIS REALM.

I signed and shoved the pen into Daniel's hands.

His eyes never left mine. And he never even read the piece of paper. On blind trust, he signed his name as our eyes remained locked. Dick held out his wrinkled hand and I pressed the paper and then the pen into it.

Dick took this moment to launch into a fantastical story that made very little sense: The Hiding was no bigger than the size of a small box. In it contained papers that were a game changer when it came to what we knew of life and death.

"It will change everything we've ever known and had the courage to believe," said Hawking who added, "I heard whispers of this Hiding since I went to university, but I didn't want to believe it. Now, I must."

"There will be dark forces. The darkest ones. Darker than the ones you entertained on your first trip," Jobs told us. "The last thing they want is for a bunch of kids to find what they've been looking to retrieve for several centuries. We know they're looking for it now, looking hard, looking every minute, which is why we must act immediately and send what I like to call a task force. If they find it first, God only knows what will happen to all of us." He stopped and repeated it slowly. "God. Only. Knows."

The rest of it was like a steady buzz that kept reverberating in my head. I heard the most important particulars including when we would leave (the autumnal equinox), and why we would leave (to save us all—living and dead, whatever that meant), and where we would find this Hiding (they were absolutely, positively not sure of where for some reason, but had a longitude and latitude that was more than a guess.)

"Why autumn?" Daniel demanded, alternating between gripping the table hard, and then spinning away to pace like he was back in his cell.

"You need to train, son. With professionals. Not to be rude, but Miss Callaghan doesn't look like she could run a half mile let alone run from these forces," said a voice at the end of the table.

Insulting my prowess in gym class. I almost had to laugh given what I'd been through in the last six months.

"There will be no more swinging around, on a wish and a prayer, fighting demon armies with a bit of brawn and your scrappy little girlfriend by your side," this commanding voice added.

His voice sounded familiar and I looked hard into the steely eyes of the old war general, a man who guided his soldiers during some interesting times in the Middle East.

"No offense, Miss Callaghan," said General S, "But you got damn lucky last time thanks to Dr. King's knowledge of evasion and his great aim. You were almost toast at Lake Forest airport. We can't depend on luck this time around. We can give you weapons, and enough of them to sustain yourself. But first, you need training on how to fight and flee. For example, do either of you know how to use fire propulsion?"

"No, sir," I said, shaking my head. "They didn't get to fire propulsion lessons in gym class at Kennedy High—although it might have come in handy. Chicago is a rough town."

"I believe that's a joke, young lady, and it's funny," General S said. "If you'll let me talk me now, I'll remind you of how you escaped from your mother's apartment building. Piss-poor planning and near fatal execution proves you are damn lucky. And what doesn't help here is *where* we need to send you. New York is not a playground for candy-ass coddled teenage soldiers."

New York, New York. A helluva town. The song kicked into my brain.

"New York City. The Big Apple. The crime capital," General S barked and for once Daniel actually listened. "A direct trip to New York and back. It's a fast-moving place—a tough town—no matter what decade we send you into as your starting point. And I have to warn you that you will be visiting at least seven or eight decades in history and the time periods will rapidly shift at will."

"Shift?" I repeated, not liking the sound of that.

"You weren't in Chicago long enough last time to experience a time-period shift. You will have to stay in New York for perhaps an entire month What you probably don't know is that right now as junior-league spirits, you posses the most basic ability to make time shift. Why do you think you were able to bring back Riverview Amusement Park in Chicago when it closed in 1964? You shifted time," Dick said.

"Dr. King shifted time," I blurted out.

"Miss Callaghan, we have the records. You, specifically you, shifted the time. It's one of your gifts now," Dick said.

Before I could react or catch Daniel's glance, General S was speaking again.

"Let's say, for example, you need to dock at Ellis Island in nineteen-ten. Just by focusing on it, Miss Callaghan, you will make the period of time and the place return," he added. "As for you, Mr. Reid, you have other talents that will be discussed at a later period."

"Can we shift into the future?" I asked.

"Miss Callaghan, girl reporter," Dick mocked. "Not now. You can only go back. Of course, if you had bothered to stay in school here at the Academy, you could have learned that senior year during your Period Shifting courses. We save the field trips until later, but you took it upon yourself to do some independent study. So here we are, scholars."

"Dick," General S interrupted. "Why quibble now? Miss Callaghan, the time periods must shift because what we want won't come easily. The clues have been hidden across history—buried in time and entrusted with only those who could be trusted with such an epic secret."

"The great mind who discovered what we need to protect now

was actually quite crafty. He knew that someday there would be prying eyes," Rodenberry interjected. "That's why time must be pierced to find the clues. Time was necessary to protect the clues in the first place. It's not like he could hide *this* in his backyard in a box."

"Time will shift back and forth and as you prove worthy enough to receive what has been hidden—and fight off the forces who will try everything to steal each clue from you—you will get closer to your final goal," General S said. "Each clue is one step closer to a win for the good of mankind."

"Enough of the particulars for now," an impatient Dick interrupted, snapping his pocket watch shut again in a way that made the click sound like a cannon going off. "I gave Mr. Reid one of the clues."

Daniel took the piece of paper from the pocket of his leather jacket and placed it on the table. It was the same confusing few lines I read on the beach.

Mr. Sagan held out a thin hand and in a sure voice added, "I've repeated this many times in the past . . . but somewhere, something incredible is waiting to be found. And you might have heard these words before, but *this* is your true adventure of an after-lifetime."

"Carl, please," Dick said. "The less they know about it, the better. They just need to deliver it." To us he said, "This is not an epic adventure, although you might think so. It's a simple barter. You fetch. You get rewarded." He walked up to Daniel and poked him in his rock-hard chest. I saw Daniel's fist clench and his jaw set.

"It for *you*," Dick said. "A simple transaction."

"Now, let's meet the others because obviously we can't leave destiny up to just the . . . two of you," Dick added with great disdain, pressing a button on the table.

"We don't want any others," Daniel hissed. "No one mentioned others."

"You're foot soldiers, not generals," Dick said, jamming the button again.

"Seth, send them in."

7.

"The team will consist of eleven, including yourselves. We might add a twelfth at a later date, but for now it will remain eleven," Dick announced, allowing the bomb to drop slowly with each word.

Who were these others? Even the idea of working with a team seemed sobering and shocking.

"Your troops, as I like to call them, have been personally approved by this board based on their various strengths of mind and body. They were hand selected. Vetted," Dick continued. "Like the two of you, they were given the choice of accepting this amazing honor as we are calling it or face total banishment from this realm. The last thing I will ever do is argue with moody teenagers."

"What are their exact qualifications?" I demanded, reaching toward the table with some trepidation to take a notebook and pen. Yes, I would take notes.

"Miss Callaghan, good question," said General S. "Several will be the brawn. A few will be the brains. Several others possess unusual mind abilities that might keep you one step ahead of the demon forces. Some will be able to sense when clues or danger is near. One will serve as a blockade," he said.

"We'll bring in your team members—one at a time," Armstrong announced. "They're downstairs. Waiting."

I heard the first of many footsteps on the winding glass staircase that we had climbed hours ago it seemed. Quickly, I glanced ahead to see the first of our teammates. If my eyes weren't playing tricks on me, it was actually four girls, close in age, who stood in front of me. The tallest had crimson hair, bangs, and big doe-brown eyes. The next had white-blonde hair, blazing-blue upturned eyes, and the poutiest pink lips. Another had ink-black hair, dark, almond-shaped green eyes and ski-slope cheekbones, plus a smirk that seemed to be genetic. The shortest, and perhaps the baby, had a heart-shaped face, an impish smile, and a short, curly blonde bob. Her sweetness had an undercurrent. It felt like a poison.

They were each wearing tight miniskirts and mid-shirts. The baby, as I would now think of her, was in pink-and-black polka dots. Each was gorgeous, slim, and looked absolutely despondent. These girls were . . . warriors?

"From Frederick Reardon. Girls, please line up at the table in birth order," Dick said with great flourish. The girls looked at each other and then gave our principal an imperceptible amount of attitude that only someone the same age could recognize. It was in their catty eyes and the way they *slowwwwly* sauntered to the table. "These young ladies—sisters—have the precious mental capacity to see, feel, and plan ahead." Inside that riddle was the truth. The only thing that remained was the exact explanation of their freakishness.

Redheaded Claire V stood defiant and straight. The next in line, blonde Claire S was too close to her biggest sister, her long tapered fingers that were painted a gorgeous shade of magenta, almost clawing into her sib's arm. Dark-haired Claire A kept her hands over her ears and with her nose scrunched hard like she was seeing Motley Crue for the first time and it was just too loud for her. The baby, Claire C, looked at me like she could see right through me.

"Quads," Steve said. "But none of them identical in looks or size. And these girls were born with gifts." We learned that the initials after their names reflected "a little extra" given to them by their mother Lula Pitcher.

Steve broke it down by writing their names on a white board near the table. He scribbled:

Claire V: Clairvoyance
Claire S: Clairsentience
Claire A: Clairaudience
Claire C: Claircognizance

It seemed that Claire V was psychic, or a seer, who regularly witnessed the future for everyone except her and her sisters. In fact, events that were forthcoming for *anyone else* were played out in her mind on a constant loop. Claire S could easily sense other people's feelings because she actually "felt it for them." The scientific way to explain it is that she could pick up on someone's emotional state such as love, hate, low self-esteem, wigging out, etc. In turn, her emotions were scattered and constantly all over the place. She didn't own her own feelings, but borrowed them from others.

Claire A had the incredible gift of being able to hear voices inside the minds of others via telepathy. She could now hear the voices of both the living and the dead including the exact tone. She was an expert mimic, which meant she could also speak in those voices. But along with the good voices she would hear, Claire A could also hear the voices of evil, so all this made her feel like her head was stuck inside a stereo speaker. Even the sound of silence was deafening.

Finally, there was Claire C, who had the most difficult power to explain. She was the true mystery sister because she was born with claircognizance, which meant she just *knows*. No one had to tell her anything. She was the Yoda of the group. Rarely wrong, although it was possible, she could easily tell future prophecies. Her gift oddly didn't work for her sisters and their lives, but it worked for others. She was the breathing example of knowing too much for your own good.

A breathtaking beauty, the little imp ran a hand through her curly golden mane and did her best catwalk, hips swaying, as she beelined for Daniel and I. She had it down: The slight head tilt, million-watt smile, and swagger to spare. Despite the fact that she looked like a candidate for *America's Next Top Dead Model*, it wasn't the time to worry about her. So, I extended a hand in friendship or willed it to meet hers, and then stepped back a bit when she came closer to whisper something into my ear.

"Walker, right?" she began in a honey-coated tone.

I nodded. "How do you know my name?"

"Public service announcement, Walker: Whatever it takes, whatever is in you, whatever power you have, you must use it to not go back," Claire C warned, burying her face in my hair. "Don't show up on the day we leave. Disappear. Run. Hide."

But she wasn't finished. "And then I'll have your hot boyfriend all to myself," the baby blonde beauty concluded with a nasty smile.

My response was silence.

Oh, really. How do you know, bitch? I thought.

"I always know, bitch," she whispered back.

Quickly and with the sweetest smile, she returned to stand by her sisters and I could see her whispering into Claire S's ear. The one who could sense your feelings, S produced the saddest clown face and directed it my way. A tear slipped from her left eye and mascara ran. She didn't even attempt to blot it.

Dark-haired A, who could apparently hear voices, directed her attention toward Daniel. Reaching into her jeans, she produced two earplugs. Then she approached him. "You can think those terrible things about us," she said. "But you don't have to use that kind of language."

Daniel stood dumbfounded.

"These girls will count as four of your team of eleven. Up here, we affectionately call them the Claires," Dick said. "They're lovely girls who have had really hard lives."

Claire V spoke for the group. "We sense great danger ahead. But we're used to grave danger. I also sense . . . extinguishment. Vicious, heart-breaking extinguishment. But alas, it's the cost of the mission." She lasered her stare at me.

General S cleared his throat. "That's enough for now V," he said. "But thank you for your, uh, contribution."

"While we're at it, we'll introduce a classmate of the Claires who has been begging to go on this mission," Dick interrupted. "He's another esteemed student at Frederick Reardon."

Tearing my eyes away from these oddly aggressive girls, I focused on the stairs, which was fruitless. He was already here. In the room. I didn't see or hear him climb upward, but now I focused on what looked like an eighteen- or nineteen-year-old man frowning in his long, black winter wool jacket. He had an extremely narrow face—a painfully thin jaw and a long, stick-straight nose that he seemed to be directed at me, as if he were pointing.

"Tor," he said as an introduction, leaving his hands in his pockets.

"Nice to meet you," I said while Daniel and Tor traded hard looks. One thing was clear: they were sizing each other up for dominance. Tor didn't say another word, but I swore for a split-second the ground beneath us trembled and one of the candles on the table suddenly began to burn blindingly bright. Scolding myself for letting my mind run amuck (too many episodes of *The Twilight Zone*), I still jumped when a wick exploded with a tiny pop. Bright sparks of fire flew off the wax only to quickly meet their demise while suspended in the air. When my eyes left the candle, I looked at the others and no one seemed to be aware of what just happened. I wasn't sure, but I swore there was a candle on the table. And now there wasn't.

Tor's face in a word: bland. Maybe it was a momentary daydream—or not. There was no time to dwell on figuring it out.

"And the next member we've chosen represents another school or should I say institution," Dick continued. "In fact, you will be entirely familiar with the next several selections."

The way he said it, a chill ran through me because I didn't want to be familiar with any of the players. I didn't wish this on anyone, let alone a friend.

It couldn't be family. The idea made my blood simmer. There was no one in our little family who was even a hair qualified for realm jumping . . . except the youngest one.

"The next member was chosen by the GF," Dick announced. My eyes scanned the staircase and I could hear what was obviously a rather large young man lumbering upstairs as if his intent was to assault the planks with every step.

"No freakin' way. No way am I doing anything with these freaktards! Hey, is that food for everybody—or just the adults?" Eddie Wargo shouted, a human run-on sentence gazing at platters of sandwiches that had been set on the table.

When he was told that the food was for the board members only, Eddie became more agitated. He refocused and saw the two of us standing at the end of the table and threw his slab-like arms up in the air, as if a bad day was now the worst day possible.

"Kiss-ass Danny Boy. I don't even want to smell him," he announced, turning to the GF who had just laboriously finished the last stair behind him.

"Sorry, I'm late," the GF said. "Prison riot in the living realm in

Miami. Almost the entire juvie section—toast. Is that roast beef?"

"Hey, boss. Do somethin'," Eddie begged. "Tell these asswipes who is really in charge around here."

"Edward! You will represent me—and I don't want to hear another word. I don't even want to hear you breathe!" the GF barked, towering over his errand boy like a black bear.

That's all it took for Eddie to recoil as he wandered over to stand next to me. All the bravado was gone and in its place his head was down and his eyes registered defeat.

"It is my pleasure to offer Edward as frontline security for the mission. He certainly knows how to deal with adverse individuals. Growing up Wargo taught him how to fight first and ask questions later," said the GF.

Eddie's eyes registered petrified.

My own weren't exactly dancing with delight. Who were the last three team members?

"Well take a break for five minutes," Dick announced, sensing the tension was at a boiling point. Quickly, Daniel grabbed my arm and ushered me into a corner away from the rest of our new friends.

"Are you okay?" he whispered.

"I'll live," I said.

My poker face was firmly on, which wasn't easy because Claire C's words were like knife stabs.

"So what did the short one say to you?" Daniel whispered, hooking his fingers through mine. I loved that this was what he noticed about her.

"She thinks you have a cute ass," I said. "Now, let's go back and find out who else will be on the big, bullshit, save-the-world field trip."

There was no time to dwell on her words, or even try to figure out if she knew what the hell she was talking about. We had been reconvened.

Dick took time out from his team building to remind us of the rules once we crossed over. "All of you will work together until you must work alone," he said, brushing the sandwich crumbs off his suit jacket. "Only one of you will turn in The Hiding. The one who does will get the spoils. Each of you has made it clear what the spoils will be for you. Everyone plays for their own agenda."

Obviously, the Claire girls and their Freak friend could have cared less about Daniel's freedom. *It was absolutely essential that they didn't find The Hiding.*

"And now let's shift to the Academy side to see who has been recruited from the fine institution I've been forced to reshape," Dick said, smiling in his sickly way.

I should have known. The first to race up the stairs was Izayah in a white T-shirt and black shorts. The last time Iz was with Daniel they were punching each other on the rink. It just took one glance to right their world. Then he gave Daniel a quick fist pump. "Me for you. I'm realm jumping for the freedom of Daniel Reid," he said, staring at the GF. Iz couldn't help but add, "May the odds ever be in our favor, you son of a bitch."

The GF advanced, but Dick put out a warning arm as Iz stood by our side.

Shock followed. Light footsteps began to tap the stairs and suddenly Peter Reid was standing before us. Daniel bit out every foul word in the book and then stepped into Dick's face, but his younger brother got between the two of them.

"I demanded to do it," Peter said.

"Pete, get the hell out of here. That's an order," Daniel said in a deadly quiet voice.

"Bro, it's done. And it's not your call. I did the head of household thing when you were in prison. I don't take orders from anyone anymore—including you," Pete said in his usual quiet voice. Then he amped it up to repeat Izayah's words, "Me for you, bro. I jump for the freedom of Daniel Reid."

I moved quickly to throw my arms around both of them, despite Dick's warning glance.

Finally, the last person to arrive took her time up those stairs. Panting as she reached the top, she grabbed the banister hard and stood up straight. Her pride took her the rest of the way as her flattened flats carried her to us in a herky-jerky strut.

"Walk-*her*, I'm here, girl," said Bertha. "I don't know what I cans do, but I'm here doin' it. Me for you, Danny Boy! Me for you! Might as do what Van Halen said. Might as well jump, baby."

"You're out of your mind!" I pivoted and screamed at Dick. "She can't go! It's much too dangerous."

We were friends as close as sisters now and I knew Bertha couldn't run or hide, two of the main prerequisites of staying in one piece during a demon attack.

It was time to change tactics.

"Sir, I strongly object," I began to state to General S. "She's not fit for combat. Her heart can't take it." Once again, I got a quick lesson on the legality of this place.

"This isn't a court of law, Walker," Steve said in a somewhat sad voice. "You don't live in a democracy here. It has been decided. No appeals, kiddo."

"But Steve," I began to argue.

"But Walker, we know *you* well enough now to say without any condemnation that you lived a pretty sheltered life with your mother in Chicago. You didn't gut it out on the streets every single day for basic human survival. She did," Steve said, looking admiringly at Bertha. "She knows street life and New York is all street life."

Dick was smarting from all this back and forth and had to make his opinion known. "Of course, we have Mr. Reid, who was nothing more than a spoiled rich kid given every life's advantage by his hardworking, wealthy father who exemplified the power of the law. Despite his pampering, Mr. Reid woefully developed absolutely no respect for authority including the authority of the man who gave him life. That is perhaps the biggest sin of all."

Dick took a smug pause, obviously to relish the fact that he was making Daniel fume. "It's a good thing that I know the true story of the Reid dynasty," Dick concluded, pressing another button on the table. I wasn't sure why. The team was complete now. *Who else was hidden in the woods waiting to make an appearance?*

"I'm well informed when it comes to what really happened on the night of your demise—and all the nights before that one," Dick continued slowly as if this new topic was actually enjoyable for him. *Why would he choose now to stage an impromptu biography lesson on the Reid family?*

Dick pressed the buzzer again. "Please send our esteemed guest in," he said. A quick glance to the right and I could see the Claires high-fiving each other.

This latest guest took the stairs hard, two at time, as if he couldn't wait to get into the room. On a broad glance, I clocked him in at late fifties or early sixties. The polished patent leathers stopped at the top of the stairway as if he was sizing up the room before actually entering it.

There was something so familiar about him.

With jet-black hair and sunken gray eyes, this man was only about five feet five and had deep facial crevices that looked like old meat drooping from bone. Even more curious was that he had only one set of stubby fingers sneaking out the right arm of his expensive black Armani suit jacket. His other arm was mostly gone. What was left of it was in a sling made out of matching fabric.

He had no fingers and certainly no hand anymore on his left side. His left limb ceased to exist below the elbow.

"No!" Daniel said under his breath.

Glancing to the side, I saw that his face was drained of color.

"What?" I whispered.

He had a one-word answer that almost made my heart stop.

"Edward."

"Your . . ."

"My nothing," he bit out.

Edward Reid lowered his head as if he was in prayer and took his one good set of fingers to wipe something off his cheek. Then he walked a step or two closer to us and opened his one-and-a-half arms wide. His eyes darted from his oldest son to his second oldest, which marked his first acknowledgment of their presence. It was as if he was taking a pulse.

Nothing moved, including the air molecules in the room.

Finally, there were words.

"Daniel. Peter. My boys," Edward said in a low, elegant voice, befitting one of the country's most feared attorneys.

As a lawyer, he might have convinced a jury. As a father, an orphan child starving on the streets would have seen right through Edward.

And run.

8.

A clock ticked. I could hear myself breathing.

Daniel and his father stood, staring at each other for a long minute—something deep and dark passing between the two of them. I was sure I didn't know how deep it went, but it was laced with all things evil mixed with pure hatred. And then I saw Edward's thin lips break into the smallest, self-satisfied . . . smile. *He was happy to see his boys . . . dead. He was glad. Glad that he killed them.*

Detonation. It was inevitable.

Daniel's long soccer-player legs blasted forward on full force attack. "Don't hurt me!" Edward screamed as his eldest launched his entire body, hands lifted, aiming right for his father's thick throat. Edward ducked low. This gave the GF enough time to swing around, push Edward back, and the use his girth as a wall between father and son. Three guards struggled to hold Daniel in check. One went down. Then number two. Three was teetering. Daniel kicked again and it landed hard in the GF's ribs. Choking, he hit the floor because—as I had recently learned—he didn't have the reset.

I was the one who shocked them all. As I rushed forward after Daniel, a guard shoved me back so hard that I slid backward onto the conference table and directly into the hibachi, accidentally sending it flying off the table. The crash was epic as glass hit marble and soon bits of warrior bone and dust were forming little clouds as their particles danced in the afternoon sunlight.

Dick dove to save the urn, but it was too late. He only ended up slipping on Edward's sling, which was now also on the floor, and almost doing a header into a coffee table.

Even Daniel stopped struggling to see if I was hurt. On

purpose, I pretended to limp. Daniel lost no time and was at my side despite a stunned Claire V announcing, "She's faking it—and could use a good acting class."

Still, I whispered into Daniel's ear, "Deal with him later. On your terms. Without visitors." He pulled back and I grabbed him by the face and whispered again, "You can't go back to ITT now. I can't go on this mission without you. He doesn't matter. Look at him. Dammit. Look at him."

What remained on Edward was a bloody stump above the elbow that looked as if Lizzie had taken an ax and hacked away the flesh and bone.

The ashes of those warriors continued to rain on the floor while most of the Higher Authority got on their hands and knees to scoop up the precious bits.

In the end, it was two security agents who stood between Daniel and his father. This left Pete open to the kind of reunion he wasn't expecting.

"Peter, I'm your father," Edward shifted directions, limping up to the second in line with his stump still there for all to witness. "I only died three days ago in a terrible, terrible accident. You could say I was murdered. Show some remorse. I am your father."

Pete the pacifist and chess club member, who believed that most violence was unjustified, ignored a raging Daniel to gaze at the man who gave him life. I could see Pete's eyes were soft. His shy gaze looked down. *No Pete, don't. Don't choose him over your brother. Sometimes a line is drawn. Sometimes you choose.*

Pete seemed to be crossing to the other side of the line. Patiently and without fists drawn, he waited until his father came close enough to put his one good arm around his boy. Pete stepped even closer. Then he craned his neck back.

Pete spit hard in Edward Reid's face.

Hot saliva running down his left cheek, Edward took a small

step to advance, but the only muscle Pete moved was in his jaw.

It was fascinating in a way. I had never before witnessed the exact moment when a boy became a man. He couldn't age anymore. But Peter Reid grew up in front of my eyes.

Dick didn't seem particularly rattled by any of it and didn't really care if there were complicated family dynamics. He just motioned for a butler to bring Edward a towel. Then he stood at the head of the table again for a short explanation.

"It's unfortunate that Mr. Reid and his sons might not look at this as a bonding experience, but that's unimportant," Dick said. "What matters is that Edward Reid's recent death filled our need to have a team of top negotiators here. We're so sorry for your unfortunate 'accident' Edward, but your loss is our gain. The future of this realm and several others will require several excellent litigators including Edward, who is one of the best. He will be joined by two others.

"In fact, Kardashian just arrived. Perhaps we can all welcome him less . . . dramatically," Dick insisted. Under his breath, I heard him say to General S, "I certainly hope he doesn't have any brats in this realm. I detest family drama."

Edward was dead. He was here. My mind was swimming. *Murdered? Where? How?*

I felt Daniel almost vibrating with white-hot anger as Dick's butler was handing out thick packets to each of us. "Review the contents and we will be in touch soon with further information including your training sessions," General S said.

"Team dismissed," Dick shouted. "And could someone please get me another damn hibachi? Is that too much to ask?"

CHAPTER 12

1.

Dusk had fallen and we didn't race out of there. We raged out. Daniel didn't say a word our entire ride home. As we pulled the Harley up the driveway to our little house, I saw Bobby was on the front lawn playing with the dog. When he made the fast run to his biggest brother, Daniel hoisted him in the air, possessively cradling him in those wide arms. Pride and love mixed with old fears and frustrations.

"Has anyone come to visit you today?" Daniel demanded of the little boy.

"Superman. Batman," Bobby rattled off. "The usuals. I killed all the bad guys. Pow-pow!"

"Get in the house," Daniel shouted, carrying him to the front porch and setting him down.

"No way! I have to save Gotham City from the Joker," Bobby replied, pointing to a makeshift cape made out of a blue bath towel. When his biggest brother pointed hard to the front door, his bottom lip quivered. "But I have to fight the bad guys and I didn't finish my snack," he whimpered.

"Now!"

It was Jenna who poked her head out next. "Jesus, Jenna. Do you just let your little brother play unsupervised out here? You're supposed to be watching him! It's time for you to learn some responsibility!" Daniel snapped.

I could see Jenna's big gray eyes fill because she was a straight-A kid whose worst offense was leaving her cereal bowl on the table all day. She never got in any trouble. "I *was* watching him. I had to go to the bathroom. No one is going to kidnap him here," she blurted.

"Go to your room!" Daniel said, then stomped down the porch steps and began stalking around in the summer-scented grass.

"It's okay, Jenna," I interrupted, walking up the steps. "Just take Bobby inside and stuff him with more cookies. We'll be in . . . in a minute." Both were happy to comply while the dog nipped at their heels. Children and dogs always know to get going when the going is good.

"Callaghan, just get in the house!" Daniel said in a frozen voice. "Not a thousand questions. No, why is he here or how is he here. Just get inside, damn it. I need to think."

I could see Bobby peeking out a bottom window, so I paced around the porch, a move I was seasoned in doing since I arrived here.

"Why don't we just tie all the kids to a pole in the basement. Have the dog stand watch. You know, DEFCON Five," I finally said. "Roll down all the window shades. Keep the boogeyman away."

"Don't go there!" he roared.

"Oh, I'm going there!" I yelled back. "And I don't have a million questions. Just one. Am I part of this family—or not?" I boldly asked.

His head sprang up.

"Because if it's not, I can just pack up, grab the dog, and move next door. Technically, it's still my house," I said in my own low, steady voice.

An enraged Daniel took the three small porch stairs as one until we were inches apart. My head met the middle of his taut chest. But my eyes never left his hardened gaze.

"Callaghan, you need to learn when to leave me alone. And now is a good time to start," he said in a low, lethal voice.

When he grabbed me by both shoulders and lifted me off the ground to bring me bodily to the front door, I willed myself not to react. My legs were dangling in the air, my emotions running into the red. Then I remembered my Academy kickboxing class, wrapped my right leg behind his left, and found the weak spot easily. When I exerted force in the fold, the surprise of it made his knees buckle, which sent both of us tumbling down so hard that a board actually cracked. Our heads connected hard enough to cause a concussion in the living realm. Here, that old friend, the reset, kicked in.

"If I'm a full-fledged member of this family, I fight," I stated. "And he's never getting his hands on those kids. He will have to go through me. Not you. But me!"

Daniel rolled away, only to smash his hand into another plank, which cracked on impact.

"Shit!" Daniel said.

"Double shit," I repeated.

Undaunted, he rolled, flipping me under him until my hands were pinned somewhere near his thighs. "You keep struggling and I might like it," he growled. "A lot."

"Wait. I see the future," I said, mocking those horrible girls. "You're dreaming."

His warm hands now covered my entire neck, checking for

harm, as if the mere sight of his father would have somehow left me with scars.

Leaning up, I placed my lips on his and kept them there until I was sure he would remain quiet. Eventually, he twisted his face away. "You don't know who he is—what he is—how far he will go to get what he wants, which is everything," Daniel said and I could hear his anguish.

"I just want you to know who I am—and how far I will go—to make sure he doesn't get what he wants," I said.

I didn't have time to elaborate because the front door blasted opened.

"This is private," Daniel growled in a muffled voice as he allowed his body to go lax over mine. I could feel it. One molecule at a time, he was starting to accept that this wasn't just his fight.

Pete quietly shut the door.

"Why are you guys on the ground?" he asked. "Never mind. I don't want to know. I just came out to tell you that *we're* going to have to fight that bastard. I was too young the first time, but I'm never lying down again."

"There's no 'we' here, baby bro," Daniel said. "Obviously, I can't tell Callaghan what to do, but despite your little speech at mansion central, I *can* tell you. So get your sorry ass back into the kitchen. You don't know anything about our alleged father."

"Really? I don't know about the beatings?" Pete said, crouching over us. "I don't know about the cheating, the lying, the money laundering, the dismissed child abuse charges because he knew a Cook County judge? I don't know about the way he used to slap Mom around because he had a bad day? I guess I don't know because my room was next door to their room. Guess I don't know that he tried to make her abort Bobby. And Jenna. And Andy. I guess he just wanted to lavish his fatherly *love* on just the two of us."

"Lucky us," Daniel sneered.

Pete leaned down.

"What I do know, and I'm saying this respectfully and only once, is I get a piece of him, too," Pete said in defiant tone.

Then he offered me a hand because I was still lying on the front porch and Daniel had rolled away. Pressing my palm into his firm hand, Pete yanked and I practically flew upright.

Swearing, Daniel shoved Pete's hand away and stood up on his own volition. Having made my point, I decided to venture back into the house to check on the kids, but Daniel grabbed my right hand and pulled me to his side, while Pete took the left.

An alliance of three. That was the sight Edward Reid was greeted by when he pulled into our driveway.

2.

He drove a sleek, silver stretch Mercedes with overly tinted windows and chrome wheels. Edward missed half of the driveway and managed to park the car smack in the middle of our lawn. Now that it was dark outside, he half stumbled out of the vehicle and cursed when his designer uppers hit the marshy grass from the afternoon rain.

The short, broad-shouldered man with the oil-slicked black hair looked like a snarling pit bull who went through some sort of finishing school that didn't stick. He hid his venom under an expensive black trench coat. His only pinky finger was covered in a gold ring with a small yellow diamond catching the glint of a new moon.

He didn't allow his lame arm to slow him down. "I've learned to drive and fly with one arm," he said as a hello, although no one had asked.

How the hell could he even mention flying? It dawned on me in that moment as I took mental notes—and I was always taking notes—that he was a classic narcissist. It was *only* about him.

"Nothing stops a Reid from getting what he wants. Handicap, handicrap, I like to say."

I didn't want to be the one to speak first, but fate intervened.

"Miss Callaghan, we haven't been formerly introduced," Edward almost drawled, which didn't fit with his Midwest roots. Suddenly, he was advancing a few steps, but on second thought stopped as if there was an electric fence he chose not to cross.

"Call me Edward," he advised me.

"I call you a murderer," I replied.

He didn't even wince.

"Lovely that my eldest has found a girl in his own mother's image. Loud and uncivilized. In fact, you look like a breeder to me—in better times," he said, as I put my hand out hard to stop Daniel from flying off the porch. Edward took that as his sign to take a few steps closer, but not too close. Obviously, he thought he was winning. He reached into his jacket pocket, pulled out a Marlboro, and lit it, carelessly tossing the burnt match into the grass.

"Dick let me read your permanent record," Edward said, harshly blowing smoke out of both his nose and his mouth. "What a lovely history the Callaghan's have written during their time on earth. Madeleine and Sam Callaghan. Piss poor. Got hitched to live in poverty together. Excuse my ignorance here. Maddy and Sam first got engaged in New York City with a diamond chip that cost less than what I feed my dogs. But we digress. Your parents lived like animals in a one-bedroom hovel in the city. In Harlem."

It was true that my parents lived for two years in New York

before I was born, while my mother went to art school at NYU.

Edward kept loading bullets, pulling the trigger at will.

"So sad that your daddy thought he had a simple stomachache. Cancer. The great equalizer. Pity that he punched out so early. Age twenty-seven, wasn't it?"

This time I pressed my fingers into Daniel's thigh, willing him not to move. I wanted to see what else Edward had in his trick bag. I wanted him to use all the bullets in his arsenal.

"And then it was a fine, too-proud-for-welfare mess wasn't it . . . Walker, is it?" Edward said. "I'm sure you remember how the steel-mill lawyers worked their magic, so your dumbass mother didn't get a dollar of insurance money. Screwed her good. Medical bills poured in each month. Hungry bill collectors calling, calling, calling and demanding their money. Your father's car, repossessed. How many times were the lights turned off? Four times. And that was just in one year."

In the dark, my face flamed red. *Daniel didn't know any of the last round. He knew that my mom and I struggled—but not this. This was a world he didn't know. And didn't need to know. I felt the shame rise.*

And I could tell that he wasn't finished. Not by a long shot.

"Two years ago, you had walking pneumonia because your mother didn't have any medical insurance and you couldn't afford to go to the doctor. That should have killed you—not the car accident. Poor little wheezing Walker." With his one good hand, Edward grasped his throat and made wheezing noises.

Daniel lurched forward, but this time Pete stood in front of him.

"Then you came here after your little accident and latched onto my formerly rich son. Maybe you thought that he brought some of my money with him into the afterlife . . . or gold or privileges. If you couldn't live the high life in life you would live it in death," Edward concluded.

It was the biggest lie. But that didn't make me cry. A glance up at the look of pity in Daniel's eyes was almost my undoing.

I blinked hard. Breathing deeply and clearly, I remembered my own words. *Am I a part of this family or not? . . . You fight for what you love.*

"And you, Mr. Reid," I said, clearing my throat. "There was plenty of mob money to go around wasn't there? You used some of it to pay for your mistresses, your boats, and your plane. But we all know how that last one turned out. At least there was enough money to pay for five headstones lined up neat in a row. That's what happens when you kill your own children—all of your children."

In the blue moonlight, I could see Edward's face contort into rage.

"You killed your children," I repeated, slowly. "Their blood is on your hands. Remember their bodies in that field? Did you have to identify . . ."

I barely heard that creaky door open.

I heard the small voice coming from behind us on the porch. Bobby was in his Spider-Man pajamas.

"Daddy?"

Jake was next to him, growling like dogs do when they sense danger. He circled the little boy again and again to provide a protective shield.

Instead of running into his father's arms, Bobby looked at his father, couldn't tear his eyes away from him, and then began to sing in a hollow voice. "Hey you! Boo! Did you hear that sound? Is it a monster that I found?"

He sang it over and over again. In a flat voice. Without stepping forward.

Jenna and Andy now stood beside their little brother holding onto his puny shoulders.

If nothing else, Edward was a slick hustler. "Girls! Robert! Come down here. Give your old pops a hug," Edward said, changing his tactics. "I'm here. I'm finally here. I've missed your trademark Reid faces."

When they didn't move, he asked them, "Didn't you miss me?"

A long minute passed.

Increasingly infuriated, Edward spit out, "I demand that you come here right now and say hello to your father. A Reid is never this rude to their elders!"

The three children stood in place behind us. Edward took a few advancing steps and pulled out a white piece of paper.

"As you can see, I have an order from the Higher Authority," he said in his controlled courtroom voice. "I have the right to take my minor children with me anywhere I choose—including eventually to another realm. It's all up to me. They're mine! I am their father!" he bellowed.

"You are done!" Daniel said, finally taking a leap onto the lawn.

"Just do it," his father begged, moving even closer, but slowly. "One more outburst from you and I'll have you back at ITT tonight. Part of the reason I came here tonight was—"

"To make you lose your temper, Daniel. Don't do it," I begged. "We need you. I need you."

Before there were fists, there were white lights coming quickly down the street. I wish I could say that it was something otherworldly, but it wasn't. The glare was simply signaling the arrival of the Bentley driven by none other than our favorite Academy gate guard, Harold. He moved at a rapid pace to open the back door. At first, I only saw long, shapely legs followed by a short plum skirt and white silk blouse hugging curves.

Miss Elizabeth was economical about her movements,

slithering off the backseat and sashaying up to Edward despite the impediment of the highest suede purple heels I had ever seen in my life.

"Miss Callaghan, Daniel, children. I'm sorry I'm late. Academic planning committee meeting boring enough to suck the blood out of your veins," she began, waving one of her peach-sized diamonds in the air. "I can see that you're in the midst of an unfortunate family reunion," she added. "I'm here to help. As your counselor."

Edward was dumbstruck. "Are you really?" he began and my stomach churned. His gaze was lusty and raw.

"Yes, I really am," she said, holding an envelope, which she passed to Edward. "I'm also the head counselor of the Academy and my job is to tend to the children's emotional health, Mr. Reid. And I know their feelings are also of utmost importance to you. As you can see in this letter from our esteemed principal, Dr. Marvin King, the younger children have been entrusted into his care. He's away on business now, but wanted me to remind you that it's not in the children's best emotional health to be subjected to their father at this time. Perhaps, you can bond with them after lengthy family counseling sessions. That will be up to me to decide after a complete psychological profile. Of you."

Miss Elizabeth cast her violet gaze to the porch and commanded, "Bobby darling, Jenna, Andrea, please go into the house and close the door. Move like quick little bunnies."

They didn't need to be told twice. The kids were gone like three flashes.

"Mr. Reid," Miss Elizabeth said, moving closer to Edward. "I've been informed that you're here to participate in a special project. You're an advisor, which frankly doesn't make you a part of this realm or give you any parental rights. Death is the great custody rearranger."

"Dick personally told me that I could claim my younger

children. He IS the principal of the Academy," Edward retorted. "As a lawyer, I must object—"

"Perhaps you're not understanding me. My fault. I'm not explaining it clearly," Miss Elizabeth interrupted him, and then began to speak to Edward as if he were the child. "Dr. King wired us tonight." She looked down and produced a piece of paper from her small gold clutch. "As you can see, Dr. King sent word, which means he still IS the principal of the Academy. Dick is merely a glorified substitute. Just like in high schools everywhere, no one really gives a rat's ass about what the sub says," she said, handing him what looked like an old-fashioned telegram. Enraged, Edward balled it up and threw it down on the lawn.

"As I was saying, the children will remain in this house under the care of their two older brothers and Miss Callaghan," Miss Elizabeth purred in her usual self-satisfied way. "So all I can say to you now is . . . have a nice evening. Enjoy your time."

"This isn't close to being over," Edward shouted, twisting violently when the dog raced up and began to nip at his legs.

"It's over for tonight, son," Harold said, grabbing the smaller man by his hurt armpit and twisting like he knew what he was doing.

"I'll sue you for everything you're worth!" Edward screamed in pain.

To which Harold retorted, "What I'm worth is sue-proof."

When Harold slammed the Mercedes door, Edward fired it up and slammed it into reverse.

The last thing we saw were red brake lights swerving down our little street.

The first breath I took after he was gone was a shaky one. Finally, Daniel advanced onto the lawn and took a step toward Miss Elizabeth who was never one of his favorites. Yet, I had to smile when he offered his hand as thanks.

"Don't suck up to me, handsome," she begged off in her sweet, syrupy voice. "I still don't like you. But you can invite Harold and I in for a drink and I'll tell you what we know."

Everyone stood in silence as two shadows emerged from the distance. This time Jake's happily shaking dog body rotated in circles as Iz and Bertha came walking down the street holding hands. "Did we miss something?" Iz asked.

3.

A visit from Miss Elizabeth was like having the queen planted smack in the middle of your messy kitchen. "I'm so sorry ma'am," I said, scurrying to put the ketchup packets from Foxy's Hotdog Hut in the garbage. "I've never had to say this before, but I couldn't clean the house because I was in prison."

Miss Elizabeth just smiled. "Prison is what I call several of my marriages, dear," she replied, bouncing young Bobby on her lap. Jenna had managed to get him to change into Iron Man footie pj's and he had brought along his plastic superhero cuffs just in case he had to "get the bad guys." To him she cooed, "No way will that mean man get his hands on you. You're such a darling little boy. I'll hide you myself."

Bobby was obviously rattled by current events, but was enjoying his time snuggling with this sweet-smelling, soft mom type. "I'll get my superhero lasers out—pow, pow, pow!" Bobby answered, looking a little sleepy now. It was Pete who finally took him to his room after only a tiny protest and five kisses on the forehead from a legend.

Daniel left briefly—to tuck in and reassure the girls—but now he returned with Pete right behind him. He offered a bottle of vodka to Miss Elizabeth along with a red Solo cup, our finest glass in the house. Then he handed beers to Iz and Bertha, and popped one open for himself. He knew I was not a fan.

Harold walked in from the car with some pint-sized liquor bottles from the minibar and two crystal glasses. "You kids enjoy that beer—not that it will have any effect," he said. "Jack and his friend Jim Beam are mine. The taste brings back memories of a little bar in D.C. and some fine times with President . . . well, let's leave it there." He sat down at the kitchen table with Miss Elizabeth and me, offering her a finer glass for her vodka, while Izayah, Bertha, and Daniel remained standing sipping their beers.

I couldn't wait another minute. "Is Dr. King alive?" I blurted and Miss Elizabeth's smile was gone.

"We have absolutely no idea," she replied. "We can only hope."

I got it. They made it up to buy a little bit of time, which was genius of them.

"For the record, we haven't heard from Marvin since he went realm traveling," she said in a voice that was a hint accusatory. "We had to tell Edward that Dr. King sent word. It was the only way to keep him away from the minor children. I'm not sure how long that will hold."

"If it comes to it," Harold said. "I'll do what I can to protect them short of extinguishing that bastard, which, since he's Dick's favorite, might earn me a nice janitor's job at ITT." Always the gentleman, he added, "Sorry 'bout the language."

"What the hell is my father doing here?" Daniel demanded.

Harold's answer was equally unsettling. "From what we've been able to find out through our own intelligence, the Higher Authority has brought in some top negotiators for after—"

"After what?" I demanded.

"After you come back with this package they want from your

little 'vacation.' I don't know who they will be negotiating with or over what, but the call went out for three brilliant legal minds, which is why Kardashian is on board. You might have met him earlier today. The second is Edward, believe it or not. I'm not sure who will be number three."

"So, Edward Reid isn't going anywhere for the foreseeable future," Miss Elizabeth added. "We'll just have to do our best to keep him away from all of you."

"Impossible," Daniel said in a savage voice. "When he wants something, it becomes part vendetta and part quest."

"Son, tell us something we don't know," Harold said.

Quietly, Miss Elizabeth placed her drink on the table. Her jaw was clenched and I could see that she didn't want to be interrupted.

"The rest of what I'm about to tell you will go no further than this room," she demanded.

I looked at Daniel who glanced away into nothingness. Iz and Bertha shook their heads, as did Pete. I nodded.

"Of course, we sent a small, clandestine rescue squad for Dr. King immediately after your return," Miss Elizabeth explained. "If there was even a chance, we knew that we had to act upon it." Daniel's head dropped. "There is always a chance, Mr. Reid. Dr. Marvin King is capable of many amazing feats," she added, and their eyes locked.

"Let's move on to tonight," Harold interrupted in a gruff voice. He shifted on his small wood chair, and for a moment I thought he might break it. I noticed that he wasn't in his normal chauffeur uniform again, but instead black pants and a black sweater. Imposing was an understatement.

"Dark times are upon us," Harold said. "The Higher Authority has been corrupted. We're not sure how the current principal arranged to be here—but we're certain it was for only one purpose." He didn't pause. "They're sending you on this mission to find the final papers of one of the greatest minds of all time. All we know is that his final discovery was a complete mind blaster. It's nuclear. This man was studying the fine line between life and death, and what he apparently found will change everything."

"Dr. King knew a bit about it. In turn, he told a select, loyal number of faculty members, the ones he trusted the most," Miss Elizabeth said.

Harold took it again from there. "He couldn't share what these papers contained—I'm not even sure if he knew. He did know that they existed and were highly confidential. And our fine new Principal Dick was sitting in wait for the moment in some decade where Dr. King would be forced to leave the Academy. He needed the unique, one-of-a kind position as leader of the Academy to send an exploratory crew to find the papers. You see, Dr. King refused to unearth what was buried in the ages."

"How does a gate guard know all this?" I blurted, earning an admiring look from my crew, except for Daniel who—damn it—still looked at me sadly. I had to let it pass when Harold smiled broadly. "Maybe I'm not just a pie-loving gate guard—although the truth is I do loves my pie," he said with a chuckle.

"Harold Jackman, at your service," he said, standing up to shake my hand formally and nod to the others. It was the first time I heard his last name and for him to admit to the rumors. "Ex CIA. Ex Secret Service. Protected Roosevelt. The first and second one. Protected JFK. Took my day off when he went to Dallas. Fate's a bitch. Protected Reagan. Even protected Clinton. Let's just say that I'm a cat with nine lives."

"History has a way of making it right," Miss Elizabeth said. "Certain people are exactly where they're supposed to be to make sure."

"Then why are you *here*?" I asked.

"Very good, Miss Walker," Harold said, pouring himself

another glass of Jack and giving me the cheers toast. "I was sent here to protect the honorable Dr. Marvin King. My job was to keep him here for as long as possible, so what just happened couldn't happen. The idea was that no one else would slide into his role."

"It's our fault. We went back," I said in a sad voice. "And he followed us."

"And you set into motion the future," Harold said, shaking his head. "It doesn't take much more than one decision to change everything or to screw it up royally."

"Even *I* wanted to beat the crap out of you," Miss Elizabeth ranted. Then she stood to pace as her heels clacked across our kitchen floor. "There was nothing we could do about your incarceration. You brought that on yourself," she drawled. "There is nothing we can do about this impending mission. That's beyond our authority clearance."

Harold winked at me. "But," he added, "anything else is fair game."

"You've heard of running a little interference?" Elizabeth said. "Harold knows how to run a lot of interference."

And there was one more thing . . . because there always was.

"Dr. Marvin King went to college in the best city in the world. New York City, USA," Harold said. "He always said it was his second home and wished he could go back. If that man was going to run and hide anywhere, I couldn't think of a better place than where you're going. On your mission."

"The mission that might need to stray off course," said Miss Elizabeth, her violet eyes ablaze.

"Long enough to look for your real principal—and bring him home," Harold interrupted, finishing it.

4.

By the time they left, it was close to ten p.m. Izzy and Bertha hitched a ride to go back to the Academy with Miss Elizabeth. Daniel followed them out the door insisting that he needed some air to clear his head. No kiss. No other words. The last I saw of him, he was walking down the middle of our street into the murky fog.

From the kitchen window, I felt my heart shattering into tiny pieces. I saw the way he was looking at me while they were here. The information his father spewed changed his perception of me. He knew me as Callaghan, student journalist and demon buster. He didn't know Walker, the girl with the shabby clothes and worn shoes and garage-sale couch for a bed. The girl who ate dinner in the dark because the lights were turned off. I could see it on his face and it stung like a thousand slaps.

He felt something new for me: pity.

With nothing else to do except worry or cry, I checked on the kids and then plopped myself onto our bed to replay the last part of our conversation with Harold and Miss Elizabeth.

There was a plan. In a nutshell, we'd go back to school for a little while and pretend like we were just happy to be out of prison. Then on the autumnal equinox, we would go on our mission with our "team," but keep Harold informed of our progress along the way. "Steve will explain how," Harold had told us.

I wondered how truly far the World Wide Web extended, but my thoughts were put on permanent pause when I heard the front door slam. Hopping off the bed, I did the only girl thing I could think of and promptly locked myself in the bathroom.

I couldn't face him.

Why?

I looked in the mirror and everything looked shabby. My shorts were worn. My tank top had faded from a hundred washes. It looked poor. Suddenly, I was conscious of it. My eyes were dull hazel and my hair a regular reddish brown.

He was a rich boy. The truth started shouting.

He would have never been with you when you were alive.

Seconds turned into long minutes. Finally, there was no real choice, but to splash some cold water on my face and confront the new look in his eyes. I would have to absorb his pity.

When I opened the door, he wasn't looking at me at all. I found him sitting on the side of our bed his elbows on his knees. For a second, my heart melted because he looked so big, so lost, and so sad.

"Walker, I'm sorry," he said. *Was he talking about our earlier fight or the fact he had allowed our relationship to get to this point?*

"I'm sorry, too," I said, walking a few uncomfortable steps closer to him. "I should have given you some space to deal with your father returning. I can't even imagine . . ."

"Baby, I'm so sorry about what he said—not that I gave a shit about what he said," he continued.

"Are you sure about that?" I asked him, sadly. "We really do come from two different worlds."

Daniel nodded slowly. *Like he was agreeing with me.* And then he spun sideways as if he was going to turn his back on me—and he did. He moved away long enough to pull something from the side of the bed. It was a large box with a large red ribbon around it.

"It's not my birthday," I said, cheeks blazing for some reason.

"It's just something," he said, motioning for me to come over and open it. Then he sat back down on the side of the bed while I took the box from his hands. The ribbon slid off like it was made of air. And when I lifted the top off and pulled back the tissue paper, I saw a sea of blue.

I pulled out the most beautiful ice-blue dress with a flowing ballerina bottom of wispy tulle and a shimmering strapless bodice that looked like it was encrusted in hundreds of little diamonds. Gazing up at Daniel, my eyes filled. Next to the dress was a headpiece with tiny yellow-and-white jeweled flowers—just like the kind that were on the ground the first night we kissed in the woods.

"I walked into town and banged on a door," he said in a sheepish voice. "Myrtle opened up the dress store. I told her it was important. I picked it myself." Daniel walked slowly toward me and cupped my face. Leaning forward, he kissed me lightly on the lips. "Baby, I just wanted you to have something beautiful."

"I already do," I said.

When I walked out of the bathroom for the second time that night, I found his warm eyes on my long, flowing hair that was held only by the one braid I swept across the side to hold the flowered adornment. I did several twirls in front of him, never wanting the room to stop spinning.

"You're the most beautiful thing in the world," he said.

"But you haven't seen the whole world," I replied, still spinning.

"Yes, I have," he said.

And then he stood and held out his hand.

We didn't have a prom in our future or a graduation or wedding—things on our "never" list—but we did have a lot of dance space on our front porch with the broken board.

Daniel dimmed the lights in the living room and put some Sinatra music on low. He opened the big windows wide. We held hands as we walked out our front door.

He was in black jeans and a snug white T-shirt.

I was in a dream.

Love and lust mixed as he twirled me hard into his arms. When there was no breathing room left, he gave me a kiss that made me feel like the tulle had lifted me off the ground.

The moon was low and heavy that night and eventually we just stood there bathed in darkness, holding each other.

And swaying.

5.

I'm not sure how much time passed until I heard the voices.

"Don't kill us," the male whispered. My eyes popped open.

"Walk-*her*, girl, you look like a genuine fairy princess," Bertha said, standing in the grass. "Is this what you two do when we're not lookin'? You get all dressed up and go dancin'?"

In her bright-pink pajamas, Bertha busted a quick disco move, thrusting her hip one way and her arm the other. Even Daniel had to laugh.

Izzy was next to her and looked down at his feet. "Please don't kill us for interrupting," he repeated. "We couldn't sleep, so we walked back to the house."

Pete suddenly emerged from the front door. "I've actually been standing in the living room for the last half hour, but I didn't want to interrupt. You have to listen. There are things I have to tell you. I wasn't sure if I could say them in front of Elizabeth and Harold," Pete said in a rushed tone that meant business. "I hung back. Earlier today. I didn't walk home right away. I snuck back and I stood near the big house. You could hear everything because all the windows were open and Dick is a loud idiot. But I don't know who he was talking to."

"You heard what?" Daniel demanded.

"It's a suicide mission," Pete blurted out. "They're sending a big team because they don't really think most of us can make it. They think the Freak kids have the best chance of finding this thing because they have special gifts. Not a good chance, but still a chance."

"They're collecting human matter to protect the Freaks until they find this Hiding?" Daniel said.

"Eddie and the rest of us are nothing more than an army of bodies for the demons to destroy while the Freaks have a little time to stay out of harm's way and get The Hiding. We're basically bodyguards for them," Pete said. "Collateral damage. One-hundred percent expendable."

The air went silent.

Then Daniel put a hand on his brother's shoulder. "That was smart move on your part, Pete." Then he paused, looked at each of us, and ended the front-porch chitchat. "We've heard from the Higher Authority. We listened to what Elizabeth and Harold had to say. Now, let's do this our way."

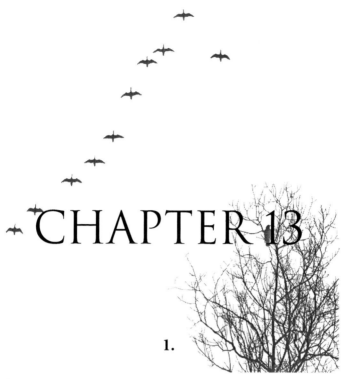

CHAPTER 13

1.

You're a ghost mapping out your trip back to life on a secret mission that will most likely lead to your ultimate extinction, so what do you have to be afraid of? Everything.

Daniel sat on the kitchen counter and I joined him after a quick run upstairs to change into jeans and a sweater. Izayah sat at the big wooden table shaking his head and muttering words under his breath. He went from rage to what sounded like a church prayer. Bertha struggled to her feet from sitting, sat down, and then lifted herself breathlessly out of that chair again. The warm kitchen still had the faint aroma of whiskey and hot dogs.

Then came the pronouncement.

"I ain't going," Bertha said, sitting again, her body spilling over the chair cushion like water cascading over the lip of the bathtub. "And don't correct my English, Walk-*her.* I ain't going. I'm not going. I'm never going. I'm politely declining their invitation into hell, thank you very much."

As much as I didn't want to admit it, the idea behind why we had to go intrigued me on some sort of core level. My father told me as a little girl that the only way not to be afraid is to take action. "Action trumps afraid," he would say when I didn't want to go to school or visit sour-smelling Aunt Ginny.

So, I would take action now and I grabbed the bulky pouch they gave us on our way out of the meeting and laid it on the table. Opening it, I dumped the contents, but it wasn't much.

There was some regular United States cash in there. A lot of it. I estimated about $5000 worth. And each bundle was obviously from a different era in history. Wedged between the bundles on the table were three typewritten pieces of paper.

Grabbing the first page, I began to scan it, which was my usual way of reading when I wanted to get to the punch line fast.

The sum total of all the words on the page indicated the following: There was something of great value hidden somewhere in New York City. It wasn't a thing. It was words on paper. No one was exactly sure of the contents of these papers, but it had something to do with the writings of Albert Einstein and something he discovered in 1935 at the height of the Great Depression. This discovery was made approximately two decades before his death, and he kept it secret for the last twenty years of his life. In fact, some thought it might have driven him mad.

The corresponding paperwork from Einstein's own private vault was so cataclysmic that even Einstein himself agreed that his discovery must be sealed and kept out of human hands. It was placed inside an insulated, airtight glass envelope that would be put into a special metal capsule that he personally designed. The metal was virtually indestructible and would withstand any natural element including water and fire.

The capsule was then burrowed deep into a place where no one could retrieve it without specific instructions. Just in case, there was a disclaimer from Einstein himself. Outside the envelope were these words: IF ANYONE SHOULD COME UPON THIS CAPSULE BEFORE THE YEAR A.D. 6939—THE YEAR OF THE RECKONING—LET HIM NOT WANTONLY DISTRIBUTE IT, FOR TO DO SO WOULD BE TO DEPRIVE HUMANITY THE LEGACY LEFT THEM. CHERISH IT THEREFORE IN A SAFE PLACE. THOSE WHO OPEN THIS EVELOPE WILL KNOW MORE THAN ANY MAN LIVING.

"Well, obviously, old Albert knew how to keep a secret," I said. And then I did the math in my head. This was the man who developed the general theory of relativity and was a pillar of modern physics. Einstein is the one who figured out that E=mc2, which was the world's most famous equation. I knew that he received a Nobel Prize in Physics. There were great minds, and then there was Einstein. In his death, his brain was even removed by scientists to discover why his gray matter was so extraordinary.

What in the world did he discover and why was it too much for mankind to comprehend until 5000 years in the future?

"It can't be opened until the seventh millennium, which incidentally will begin on January 1, 6001. Mark it on your calendars," I said, pacing around the room, while I continued to read.

"I'll probably still be at ITT," Daniel said, his boots clicking across the kitchen floor in long, catlike strides. "Or we'll be particle dust blowing around New York. Take your pick. It's a bright future—anyway you look at it."

"Keep reading," Izayah said, his frightened, caramel-brown eyes looking up at me from the spot where he laid his head in defeat on the kitchen table.

Page number two of our handout continued with a few

necessary particulars. Apparently, the "others" who helped Einstein hide his findings—and they were clandestine supporters—dubbed themselves the Shield. None were alive anymore. But in death, their spirits were suddenly missing or in hiding; and some had even sent out distress signals, although no one in our realm or any other could ultimately find any of them. Maybe they had chosen to go underground because evil forces could possibly torture The Hiding out of them.

They did what they were told to do. If it came to it. Contact the Academy for backup.

They had no idea that Dr. King was missing.

They had no idea that Dick would be waiting. For centuries. If that's what was required.

They had no idea that Dick was now here.

For Dick, getting his hands on The Hiding would make his first crime look like knocking over a kid's lemonade stand.

Dumb luck was on his side, and he didn't have to wait long. Around the time we were sent to ITT, the Shield had sent Steve a middle-of-the-night SOS—the first in at least six decades (since another scare in the 1940s involving Hitler trying to retrieve The Hiding)—indicating that they needed to move their secret, and fast. Steve wasn't sure if he should give the note to Dick, but in the end, it didn't matter. Dick, once again, was watching. Spying. Since his arrival, he made a habit out of hacking nightly into Steve's personal computer.

Dick promptly took action with the Higher Authority, which offered to send a team to help The Shield relocated The Hiding. Informed that Dr. Marvin King was no longer "available" or even at the Academy, the Shield went dark for a few weeks, but then surfaced again with another SOS to Steve. Evil forces were circling, they wrote. Reluctantly, they would accept Dick's help. They had no choice, but they still had their concerns about working with anyone who was not Dr. King.

They sent this message:

"In the absence of Dr. Marvin King, we will only be able to offer clues as to the whereabouts of The Hiding. If and only if we deem the couriers you send of the highest moral caliber, and if their bravery matches the mission, then we will lead them on a journey that will ultimately reveal The Hiding. If we deem them unworthy, then we will extinguish them ourselves as they will then know too much to continue on in any realm."

The Shield noted that they "would always watch, always wait, for the right moment of revelation indicating The Hiding was in safe hands." They wrote, "This is our sacred mission. We will also know when the time is running out and evil might find Einstein's discovery. If and when that happens, it will be of utmost importance that The Hiding is placed into the utmost of good hands, for evil begets evil. And this type of evil will destroy all of mankind—living and dead."

There was silence, so I took it upon myself to pull out page three, which gave some specifics of the mission. It seemed that the subsequent clues would remain in the living realm in what these Shield members called "what remains of the Biggest City as we cannot judge what will or will not be standing when the looking begins. If the city no longer stands, the looking might seem easier, but not necessarily so. Those who look will find a New York of the past, as time is always the best way to hide true secrets."

"One clue will lead to the next," I continued to read aloud. "And a deeper explanation of the first clue will be provided to the first person deemed morally worthy after passing through the portal. There will be an initial test of bravery involving an element of destruction."

"I don't do vacation. I ain't going," Bertha piped up again.

Then Pete spoke up, and made my already pale face go white.

"There is one more thing I didn't tell you earlier," he said, looking at the kitchen floor. "It's the worst thing." He took a breath. "Our father personally picked Daniel and I to go. To extinguish us once and for all."

The room felt suffocating.

To try and clear the air, Izayah finally said, "Maybe we can run." But his slightly hysterical tone betrayed his large form.

"There is nowhere to go—and they would find us," I replied, putting my hand over his arm. "If we say we won't go now, it's ITT for eternity for all of us. We have no choice, plus we have to secure Daniel's freedom. That's more important than their Hiding."

Daniel pushed one of the empty chairs into the table. The fury in his eyes made my heart stop.

"Yes, we have to go," he said. "But what happens there, in the living realm, is up to us. Walker and I have been there. They haven't. The Freaks don't have a clue of what lies ahead. Dick said it himself. 'You will work as a team . . . until you don't.' Everyone in this room is *our* team. The only team."

"And I promise you one thing," he added, savagely. "Once we get there, we won't be anyone's front line."

2.

It was almost midnight when the rest of them went to sleep and I snuck out of the bed I shared with Daniel to log on to the computer. No one but Steve had a multirealm email pass, but we still had educational Internet privileges. Jumping onto Wiki, I typed, "What was Albert Einstein studying before his death?"

Images popped up of the mad professor with his rebellious white mane of hair while countless biography entries materialized at my fingertips. During the Great Depression, Einstein was actually studying mathematical models that could explain all the laws of physics and various realms. It was noted that he would wander around with his notebook, often meandering into traffic, where he would stop, look down, and write some mathematical symbols down. One scholar wrote, "Out of those symbols came the most explosive ideas in the strivings of man to fathom the mysteries of the universe."

Before dying of an aortic aneurysm at age seventy-six, it seemed that old Albert was considering a four-dimensional universe in which the conventional universe of the past, present, and future, vanished into a mere subjective shadow.

He was also looking into the physics of what actually existed beyond our universe. Other than that, his neighbors outside of Princeton, New Jersey, reported that he was simply an eccentric old man with long hair, a pullover sweater, and wrinkled slacks, who wandered around in a knitted stocking cap, and with no socks on, because his toes were abnormally large and poked through them.

"Look deep, deep into nature, and then you will understand everything better," he said in one of his more cryptic statements. "The most beautiful and profound emotion we can experience is love," he wrote. "It needs to be protected—over the ages."

It was Daniel's protective nature to wait in the shadows, watching over me, and I could feel him there. Then I felt him closer, his chin on my head, his own eyes peering over at the screen.

"Maybe we should figure this out in the morning," he said with a yawn.

I wasn't really exhausted, but remembered how it felt to be tired, so I put my arms around his shoulders and he carried me and my confusions and fears to bed.

3.

In the midst of our drama came the one constant: Monday morning and school. It felt like a day where anything could happen and it probably would. The Academy worked like that. Existence worked like that.

My mind drifted. Most of all, I wasn't sure if we'd have a warm welcome back. We had been gone for seven months, thanks to our little vacation at ITT. It wasn't everyday that two students returned from maximum-security lockdown, and I knew there would be questions, innuendos, whispers, and fingers pointing. What else was high school for?

"Think they'll have another assembly for us?" Daniel said as we trudged through town on our way to the hill that would take us to The Academy. Main Street looked glorious, painted pure white from last night's expected August snowstorm. "I've lost track. What day is it?" Daniel asked, reaching out to pack a snowball before it all melted in the seventy-degree heat.

When I told him it was August first, he stopped walking, which meant I put on the brakes. The snow dripped to the ground.

"Problem?"

"It's not a normal day," he said.

"Is there such a thing? Or is it just another special day of livin' the vida morte," I said sarcastically, adjusting my backpack and only imagining all the makeup work that would soon be crammed into it. It felt strange to walk next to the tall pines, to wear a backpack, to plan a day, or to feel the fresh air again.

"It's parents visiting day," he announced fast like he was ripping off a bandage.

My heart began to quicken as I saw proof in the form of a poster on display at BB's True Value Hardware (The Place Where Your Household Blues Go Away). It simply said: THE PARENTS ARE COMING! THE PARENTS ARE COMING!

Was it possible for my mother to come back here—even for just a day? *My mother!* Since I had last dismissed spirit-hunter Cass, I hadn't heard a word about my mother and I missed her desperately.

"You're thinking about your mom," Daniel said in wistful tone. "I'm sorry, baby. Your living parents aren't invited because, well, they're just not capable of showing up. There's no e-ticket express train here. They're alive. You're not. But your dead parents, grandparents, aunts, uncles, you know, well, that's something else. Some of them even receive a written invitation."

"Do they all show up?" A shield seemed to come down over Daniel's eyes.

"It's just like life," he grumbled. "Some parents are there and some are eternal no-shows."

I knew that Daniel was hurting. The parent he didn't want to see was already here.

"Your mom?" I asked, gazing up into his eyes as we started up the hill. He was good at lowering the shades when necessary.

"Guess she's out in the field somewhere. Racing one of her horses. You know, busy," he said with a hint of sadness. "Dad always banned her from the parent-teacher conferences because he wanted to see what kind of screw-ups we were becoming. He attended to make his demands and harass the faculty."

I nodded, but didn't let him see my sadness.

"Maybe she just can't," I suggested. "Not enough frequent flyer miles."

"Maybe," he repeated, putting a finger to his lips when Bobby snuck up on us to shoot his sponge arrow into his big brother's back. Daniel raced backward to tackle him and then hold him upside down in a snowbank, his spiked black hair becoming soaking wet. Amid the shrieks of young laughter, I got lost in the "what ifs" of it all.

Then reality set in. My father never left my mother's side.

It was better that way. At least that's what I tried to convince myself.

4.

It was my "best friend" Demanda who was the first to celebrate our homecoming at the Academy. She cornered me in the expansive entryway that smelled like gardenia candles and musty first-edition books that had been there for centuries . . . and counting.

"Well, well, well," she said, a vision of tallness in a short, blinding-blue mini with a hot-pink midi top. Her white boots screamed go-go dancer. Or hooker. "Look who we have here. It's the ex-con and her felon boyfriend." Naturally, Daniel was out of earshot, making amends with Walter, when she bounced up to me, ponytail dancing in some sort of persistent draft. Apparently, neon was still "in" even here. Or maybe she forgot that the 1980s were over, although I heard some of the brothers Gibb had started an a capella harmonizing club.

"De . . . I mean, Amanda," I said in a flat voice. "You're still here."

"Where else would I be, Walker," she huffed. "Cabo?"

"Better touch up your roots before you say adios," I said.

I just managed to poke the bear. She looked me up and down—and then again in her typical insolent way. I was sure my new jeans and loose blue shirt didn't measure up. Nothing I ever wore was good enough for her clique.

"Lockdown chic? You might want to change out of your jail clothes before you come to class," she said.

I never won one with her. Never, ever, ever.

When Daniel returned from saying hello to a wandering Steve, Demanda turned on the full-wattage megacharm to rush up to him and throw her especially toned arms around his shoulders. The amber light from a gargoyle-shaped sconce threw her face into sexy shadows.

"Danny, I was really worried about you," she said to Daniel who had the standard warp-shields up. Gently, he took her arms and removed them like someone unsticking octopus tentacles. When she ran a concerned hand over his arm, he just shrugged her off again, winked at me, and disappeared around a corner.

"Okay, later, at lunch. Want to hear all about it," Demanded yelled.

We were interrupted by Tosh, who slid down the big banister and did a ballet leap to split the difference between us. I wasn't much of a dancer, but I caught her when she pivoted into my arms to hug me hard. "Walker! I really missed you!" Tosh cried. "You okay? You want to talk about it?"

I nodded "no," so Tosh moved on.

"Where's Pete? Is he with you?" she not-so-casually asked, gazing over my shoulder. "I spent some time at your house when you were gone, helping with the kids, you know."

"Really?" I said, a slow smile forming. I had never known her to be a 'kids' person.

Before I could get into that one, I was interrupted again.

"Hey, hey, Walker Callaghan, where for art thou been, girl? You in one piece?" yelled my favorite music teacher, Kurt. I smiled and then got closer to give him a hug. He was his usual mess of unwashed jeans and rumpled flannel. "You got class in about three minutes. Move it. Today, we have a real treat. Skynyrd. Live. In the music room. Ronnie Van Zant is a real pain in the ass, but I love the guy. Just don't tell him. And don't be late."

With my fingers, I played a few licks of air guitar, which delighted Kurt. What other class (and in what other place) could you get the undisputable true behind-the-scenes story of "Stairway to Heaven"?

My world was clicking back into place. I could see Miss Elizabeth standing as regal and royal as ever in a violet form-fitting suit that matched those killer eyes. She had highly arched black brows and lipstick the color of summer cherries. Say what you want about her, but she walked as if the world was her stage. Always the consummate actress, she didn't betray the fact that we already had our reunion.

"Guts and guile," she purred. "You're just like me. We can survive anything, although I'm not a fan of one-star accommodations. Was it really tacky at ITT?"

Miss Elizabeth was the only one who could call a maximum-security prison tacky.

"Worse than Motel Six," I said, leaving out the part of how my mom and I lived in one for a few weeks while we were trying to figure things out.

Miss Elizabeth physically shuddered.

"If you want to talk about it, I'm here," she added. "And you could always move into a dorm room here at the Academy and stop living with that nasty boyfriend—or not."

"Or not," I said with a smile. "And he's not that nasty."

"Shame," she said.

5.

The morning was so busy that it flew by in a blur. There were a few mentions of ITT, but mostly good-natured ones. Gracie and I almost blew up the home-ec room when Julia tried to teach us to flambé. Arnie did blow up half the room in science and dedicated his sonic boom to me. "This is how I planned to spring you, my lovely," he said with a shy smile. It was sweet how the little fire starter wanted to pitch in to help. By noon, my stomach was rumbling and I couldn't wait to grab an extra slice of blueberry pie for myself and deliver one to Harold at the front gate. There was something to be said for going back to your old routine. It was as comforting as the big glass of milk that went with that pie.

My plans hit the skids when Daniel circled back to our lockers with a look on his face that said he was resigned to the reality of the situation.

"Callaghan, you need to come to the gym with me. Let's just get this over with," he said. "Parents visiting day begins in five minutes. Don't make too much out of it." Actually, the morning had been so busy, I hadn't had time to really think about it.

"Many of them are no-shows. You can't let it get to you," Daniel added, grabbing my hand in his as if he could take a little edge off what was about to happen. He squeezed it hard.

"Shall we raise our shields?" I attempted a *Star Trek* joke that Daniel immediately got since, before ITT, we would stream vintage episodes as a post make-out middle-of-the-night treat. There was something to be said for a place where you didn't require any sleep.

"Shields up, Captain," he replied in a low voice.

I stared straight ahead when Daniel swung open the heavy

wooden doors of the gym. What I saw next was one for the record books.

There were thousands of students and several thousand more parents in the expansive room. Some were milling around and others greeting their long-lost kids with hugs, kisses, and a never-ending supply of fresh tears.

Miss Travis was beyond busy making connections. With a megaphone in one hand, she announced, "Students, if you don't see your parents, do not despair. We're at capacity in the gym and the overflow parents are in the foyer, the music room, and on the front lawn."

"Walker, dear, you're home. What a relief! I wore three new holes in my favorite red sweater worrying about you," a harried Miss Travis said to me with a hug. She gave me a quick once-over. "No worse for wear either." Her gaze diverted to my right. "Mr. Reid, I never worried about you. I knew you could take care of yourself despite the horrid conditions. It was criminal that they sent you there in the first place."

"I've been personally keeping watch over young Bobby," she affirmed. "What a charming, highly energetic child. I believe I've lost my heart to him. We even made mud pies last week."

Daniel shocked me when he leaned in to hug her. Her next action mortified Daniel. She leaned up slightly and placed a kiss on his cheek.

"I heard about your time. Hard time. The GF . . . such a repul . . . individualist," she said, catching herself. "But that is over now and it will never be discussed again."

Daniel looked down.

Miss Travis smiled at me warmly before giving me a crystal circle no bigger than a silver dollar. She handed another to Daniel. "Dears, if you have any parental visitors then the sensor will light up red. If not, do not despair. Just resume your normal school day.

As they're fond of saying, whomever they are, there is always next year."

I could tell by his frown that Daniel had been through this routine before.

"Never. She has never visited," he said, reading my mind. I could see the hurt, but I didn't have time to linger. Instead, I jumped when my disc flashed bright red. Daniel nodded, followed by a wry smile. Then he said, "I'm going to find Pete and the other kids. This usually hits them hard."

"Say hi to your uberprotective father," he said, but without any real gusto because Daniel wasn't exactly my father's favorite person in any realm.

Feeling crazy nervous, I managed to move around the room as I felt my sensor get warm and then warmer. Then I saw him leaning against the back wall by the basketball net.

My father was nervously shifting his 250-pound frame. It did warm my heart to see that he was in his Sunday best. Just like in the living realm, he looked the age of his death . . . twenty-seven. The truth was, he didn't look much older than Daniel. Or me.

I wasn't sure if the idea of seeing me caused that reaction or maybe it was his itchy-looking dress shirt, pressed pants, *and* a tie. I had to smile because he did shun proper dress shoes for thick-soled, well-worn work boots in mustard yellow. Just in case he needed to build something. Or protect someone.

I would like to say that my growing maturity was the first thing my father noted during our visit, but that would be a complete and utter lie.

"Dad!" I yelled and flung myself into his welcoming arms.

"Babe," he screamed, scooping me up like I was four again. He twirled me so many times that I should have been dizzy.

All I wanted was for it to never end.

6.

As we walked outside the gymnasium, Dad, the least fancy person on the planet, shunned the endless stream of private cars that would take us anywhere we wanted in the realm. Instead, he asked if we could just take a walk together, something so easy, simple and taken for granted. Soon, we were strolling on the school grounds without a care in the world.

A guy on a Schwinn bike slowed when he spotted us. "What can I do you for, son?" Dad asked, although he was the same age, give or take a year, as the biker.

"I'm Paul," said the handsome, sun-kissed blond with a Zen smile. "I'm the new coach of the cycling team. Just out for a ride and thought I'd say hi," he said. This Paul looked so familiar to me, although Dad was clueless.

"What happened to your hot rod?" I said, immediately reconsidering my choice of words. "Sorry, I shouldn't bring that up. What a shame, all things considered."

Paul just smiled and shrugged.

"You know something? I hate cars now," he said. "Two wheels will do."

The last I saw of Paul he was waving after cranking that bike into max gear.

We strolled leisurely and I took Dad past Harold, who bowed his head and took off his black cap in respect. Then we made our way onto Main Street where we saw that the coffee shop had a sign in the window that declared: WELCOME PARENTS. CAFFEINE WON'T GIVE YOU A BUZZ ANYMORE, BUT THE COFFEE STILL TASTES GOOD. THE FIRST TO THE LAST CUP IS FREE.

Dad always had broad shoulders, even when he was sick, but now they were all filled out again and shockingly muscular. He looked like a football player with arms that seemed a mile wide and a smile that drew you in and made you want to stop and live in it for the next year or two. He also oddly remained the world's biggest optimist despite the fact that at a young age (just like his daughter), he was given a personal punch out.

"So how are your grades, babe? Straight As?" he asked, walking down the street with one of those mitt-sized hands around my shoulders. I saw a few of the teachers giving him double takes, since he was technically a hunk, and it made me smile.

"We don't get grades," I said, "We're here to learn, but I think I'm doing pretty well. My unformed brain is soaking it all in. Like a sponge."

"Take what they're doing here seriously, babe," he said. "You'll need all of it. For later. I'm not just a steelworker now. I know everything about quantum physics."

I knew not to ask. He wasn't about to tell.

So, we reverted to a topic that was both safe and sound. "I'm absolutely starving," I said, motioning to the local diner, Joe's, which was advertising its two-for-one meatloaf special in honor of parent's day. Of course, it was ridiculous because it was also free, but Joe couldn't resist offering a daily lure.

"I could eat," he said, patting what was a washboard flat stomach.

"I could always eat," I said, and Dad gave my hundred-pound frame a doubtful smile. "Burned off a lot of calories doing all that realm traveling," I joked, and he did something he had never done in our lives.

He put me in a mock headlock, promising, "We'll talk about that in a minute. But first, I need mashed potatoes with a tub full of gravy."

Roxy Paine, the six-foot hostess with the mostess, gave my dad the hot-and-hungry once-over while escorting us to a booth covered in Vegas-style red vinyl. I knew Roxy (heart-attack victim) since we were constantly getting take-out from Joe's, but didn't expect the extremely curvy redhead in her 50s to bend down and heavily flirt with Dad. But Dad and I still managed to order between the batting of Roxy's eyelashes.

Minutes later, our plates loaded with sizzling meat swimming in gravy, we squirmed in our booth as we circled each other in conversation that was more like an interrogation.

"How's Mom?" I asked.

"How's that boyfriend?" he volleyed. I could feel his exasperation at the mention of the B-word.

"Fine, Dad," I said, shoveling in my overcooked carrots and potatoes. I figured if I was chewing, there might be less talking.

I could see his expression soften.

"Your mother," he began, sipping his coffee, "well, she's doing much better. She hired some kid. Good kid. Why can't you get a boyfriend like that? You know . . . helpful?"

I let that one fly for far too many reasons. "Are you still there with her?"

"I'm there every day. I'll be there tonight. Hanging out with my girl," Dad said, his eyes low and misty. "She's still watching *Jeopardy* every day at six. Sometimes when she's not looking, I change the channel to the Cubs game. I think she believes her TV is on the fritz—but not really!" Dad chuckled at that one. "Babe, she took three steps on her own last week. No cane," he said, his voice thick. "I was standing next to her screaming, 'Come on, Maddy, you can do it!'"

I nodded. Smiled.

"Her helper, Cass. He's like a trainer. Been working her hard all summer," Dad said. "He's helped get my Maddy back on her feet. I love that guy."

I didn't have time to react to the actual saying of his name because the front door slammed. A few female heads in the diner popped up in that appreciating kind of way. Daniel was imposing in black jeans and white tee with his black leather jacket on and his hair slicked back. He considered windblown to be actual grooming.

I knew he wasn't here for the free fries.

Zeroing in, he walked our way almost too quickly.

"Mr. Callaghan, sir," Daniel said, stopping at our booth. He looked at me and then extended a hand to him. At first, Dad didn't move and I held my breath. Would he really snub him again—like he did in the living realm? The clock ticked.

Finally, Dad reluctantly lifted a hand. The workingman and the athlete shook hard almost as if it were a contest. Dad still glared at Daniel, establishing the pack order.

"Are you just going to stand there all day or pull up a chair?" Dad barked. No, Daniel would not be invited to join us on our turf inside the booth. He would remain outside the circle, but at least it was some sort of progress.

For the first time ever, I said a silent prayer that Daniel didn't kiss me.

Survival prevailed and he didn't. Instead, he smiled warily and said, "Callaghan." Both my dad and I popped our heads up. "I knew you would take your dad here."

Then he sat and returned his focus to Dad who said, "So, what do you have to say for yourself?"

"Nothing much, sir. Just existing," Daniel said.

"No troubles since you got back?" Dad asked. "No repercussions?"

"Nothing worth discussing," I quickly lied.

"You're living in the dorms?" Dad continued, asking me, but looking hard at Daniel.

"Yes," I lied again.

"No crazy crap on the horizon?" Dad wanted to know. He slammed his coffee cup down just a little too loudly on the saucer.

"Just developing our minds," I said.

"Well, that's a relief," Dad said, turning to Daniel in a way that said he wasn't entirely convinced, which is why he continued to say what he came to say. But this time he wasn't talking to me.

"My Maddy told me all about your fancy background, soccer star. For some reason I can't quite understand, she speaks fondly of you when she talks to me at night," he said to Daniel. I remembered being a little girl and through the paper-thin apartment walls hearing my mom at night have whispered conversations where she told my dad all about her day.

"Mrs. Callaghan is an amazing woman," Daniel stated while my hopeful eyes darted over to Dad.

"I hate a suck up," Dad replied, tossing a menu at Daniel just a little too hard. It hit him midchest and bounced back onto the table. "This ain't a five-star joint, rich boy," Dad challenged.

"Roxy," Daniel said as she walked up, his eyes still locked on Dad. "I'll have a double cheeseburger, fries—extra crispy—and onion rings. In other words: the regular. Oh, and a chocolate shake. Be kind with the whipped cream."

"This one," said the gum-smacking hostess gazing adoringly at Daniel, "is a bottomless pit, but it all goes to the right places."

Dad looked repulsed.

"You have good taste, Walker," said the middle-aged hash slinger, her eyes ping-ponging between my men. "Ever think of sharing the wealth?"

"Rox, that one is my dad," I said, pointing to my booth mate.

"They make 'em handsome in the Midwest," she said with another gum crack.

"Roxy, hun, I'll have a second lunch," Dad said. I couldn't believe that they were even going to turn eating into a competition.

“Triple cheeseburger, cheese fries, and rings,” Dad said, patting his flat stomach.

“Bring me a chili dog with my burger,” Daniel challenged.

“And a cup of the clam chowder,” Dad added. “No, make that a bowl.”

Their eyes remained locked like two wolves circling each other, although neither was moving.

They ate for an hour and when it was over, Dad asked for the bill, and of course, there was none. Out of reflex, Daniel rubbed the bottom of my arm, which caught you-know-who’s attention. I wondered if there would be a rumble in the back parking lot.

Again, there was an air of “anything could happen.”

Our anything happened at the front door when we were leaving. As my dad stepped through it, he collided with a man looking down at his phone and texting. A cigarette was planted between his lips and he puffed hard.

Edward Reid used his one good arm, with phone in hand, to brush off any imagined dirt on his sling while his superiority weighed heavily in the air.

“There should be a worker’s exit,” Edward huffed, locking eyes with my father, but looking at his boots. “I should report you to management. Deliveries are in the back!”

“Here’s an idea,” Dad retorted. “Take your eyes out of your ass, pal, and shut your mouth.”

Daniel did the only thing he could do under the circumstances, which was take my arm and help me through the door before his father zeroed in on us.

Before I could do the complete half circle back to the sidewalk outside, I saw Edward’s lips moving and my Dad taking a step that closed the gap between them to inches. Roxy raced over and soon Dad made his way outside.

“Who the hell is that rude jerkoff? Don’t tell me he’s a teacher,” Dad said.

"You could take him," Daniel bit out. His smile was wicked.

"Damn right, I could take him," Dad said. "That's the first intelligent thing you've ever said to me, young man."

"I'd like to beat the shit out of him myself—not that there would be anything left after you were done, sir," Daniel said. This time Dad actually nodded. And slapped Daniel way too hard on the back. Daniel returned the backslap and I waited for the world to explode. But it didn't.

They were both young men. And now they finally had something *else* in common, besides me: Hating Edward.

7.

A few minutes later, Daniel headed toward home as I was still keeping up the "I live in the dorms" ruse. It was Tosh who appeared out of nowhere as I showed my Dad around the Academy's lower floor.

"Hi, Mr. C," Tosh rambled, earning a warm grin from Dad who liked her on first sight. "Is this your roommate?" Dad asked me with a happy smile. "And best friend," I added. One thing about Tosh—she was quick. "Uh, Walker, I think I left my English book in *our* room. I was just about to go get it. Why don't you guys join me and we can show your dad the dorms."

We ushered Dad to the dorm area and he missed her wink. I kept Dad busy showing him the common areas while Tosh popped into "our" room for her supposedly wayward English book. Fibbing to my father would never have been my first choice, but I was getting used to giving up first choices. By all accounts, we had settled into a very normal father-daughter flow now—if you didn't count the various interruptions and half-truths.

When we took up where we left off downstairs, Dad sputtered as we passed my favorite guidance counselor in the hallway. "Is that Elizabeth Ta . . . holy hell . . . who's that with her? That guy from *Dirty Dancing*? Your mother loves that movie!"

"Our new dance teacher, Patrick. I'll introduce you," I told my dumbstruck father.

The Academy tour took an hour—time that moved far too quickly. As the sun began to dip low in the sky, I walked him outside where a bright night moon was beginning to glow summer pink. The air was warm and fragrant with the smell of orchids and summer jasmine. I knew that as soon as Dad started walking away he would slowly disappear . . . *I just knew it.*

I wanted to ask a million questions, but I didn't.

I wanted to watch, but I couldn't.

All I could do is hug him hard. And try not to cry.

"Babe, please," he said in a serious voice as that summer sunset backlit his face. "Let me tell you something. And I know you don't want to listen to me, your father, because I never listened to my father, who probably didn't listen to his father . . . but you need to listen to me now."

He had my attention.

"You were lucky to come here in the first place and crazy lucky to get back here. Damn lucky," he said, closing the space between the two of us until it was only inches again.

"Don't you ever try that again," he implored, gazing down at me, his eyes as intense as mine. "Don't you ever do it. Someday you'll be able to do it—go back—but not now. You stay here. Don't let that boy screw everything up for you because he likes to live on the edge. You still have a future. A bigger one than you ever imagined. You promise me, babe," he implored. "You look me in the eye and promise me."

I guess I had one more lie in me.

CHAPTER 14

1.

The following Monday was a clear day and the damp of the night had been replaced by what felt like a soft, southern breeze—although I wasn't quite sure what we were south of anymore. We had been officially excused from school that day, but it was far from a day off. No sleeping late. No sitting around in our jammies. As instructed, I Googled (it works everywhere) the directions to a place that was past the rock quarry and far from the woods that marked my personal perimeter here.

We were going on a field trip.

The mandate read: MONDAY. 6 A.M. TRAINING SESSION. NORTHGATE MOUNTAIN. TRANSPORTATION WILL BE PROVIDED.

We shunned their little school bus action and took the black Harley out for another spin. The comfortable rumble of the motor was relaxing, and so was the feeling of wrapping my arms around Daniel's back and just holding on.

I felt like a feather attached to granite. He felt so big and firm across the shoulders and his usually hard gaze softened when he slowed the bike and then turned around for no real reason except to look. For such a rough-looking type, he was so tender underneath. It reminded me of something my mother used to say. "Walker, always be nice to tender people," she advised. "Tender people are rare and must be cherished."

He was someone to cherish.

His hard side kept me off-kilter. Without warning, he sped through town and then a few hairpin twists later, the Harley was chewing a path into the deep and shadowy woods. The way I was pressing into Daniel's flesh, molding myself against him, produced a wolf whistle from the front.

The air, the wind, and my man—why did it have to feel so good when it might soon be gone again?

I gave Daniel's chest an unexpected squeeze and let my mind wander. *What if we didn't find The Hiding? Where could we go? Where could we hide?*

In the distance, I could hear the rushing waterfall and it sang a pleasant morning song as the water crashed into the rock. Day seemed to morph into night thanks to the dark shadows of the protective granite rock walls that framed us. The rock looked like it was millions of years in the making and I wondered who had passed this way. Our sanctuary here was fleeting as the bike zoomed ahead and settled on a small forest road that led even further up to where the land flattened out.

In the distance, I could see it.

The small white building in the middle of woods looked like a glorified garage. It appeared to be the kind of place where you took your parent's car if you dented it and needed a quick fix without them ever knowing. When we got closer, I could see a hand-painted sign on peeling wood that read: JOHNNY TAMALE'S GYM.

After swerving into the small gravel parking lot, Daniel swung a leg off the bike and then gave me a hand to help me slide off. I could see he skipped grooming. In his black leather jacket, dark jeans, and aviator glasses on a face covered in three days of shadow, he looked almost primal.

"Just another day at the gym," I said, looking around without moving.

In black leggings and a matching black T-shirt, I let my long dark hair fly wild on the bike. Now, it was a tangled mess that kept falling into my eyes. Tenderly, Daniel took a finger and brushed a few strays out of my eyes. "Remember Callaghan," he said, reverently, "We're not here to make friends."

"Got enough friends," I confirmed.

Speaking of which . . .

Narrowing my eyes in the morning sun, I could see an old-fashioned yellow school bus, like the kind they had in the 1950s with the round fronts, chugging up the twisting road. The driver obviously needed glasses since he stopped inches in front of us creating a cloud of choking dust. With an exasperated belch of air, the bus doors burst opened, releasing some sort of built-up pressure inside.

Manners-challenged Eddie Wargo, in a hideous blue velour 1980s jogging outfit, pushed his way to be first off the bus. There wasn't enough velour in the world for his large, jiggling stomach, which hung over the pants like a pouch.

Stumbling down the three muddy bus stairs, he landed in the gravel with a loud thud, which created another plum of gravel smoke.

"Howdy-hi kids," Eddie called out to us. "You think they're serving breakfast in . . . what the hell is this? A garage? I'm training at a chop shop?" Somehow I knew that Eddie had never seen a gym in his life.

I watched as he readjusted a large backpack on his shoulder and then, on habit from my months at ITT, tensed when he reached into it. I wondered if he had a weapon, or worse yet, another velour outfit. He actually came brandishing . . . snacks.

"Twizzlers, losers?" he offered, ripping open the plastic and shoving five strands into his big mouth. He loved the fact that they were dangling from his teeth, making him look like some sort of giant prehistoric beast. Daniel put up his hand to pass, but I actually accepted a Twizzler. I didn't trust Eddie, but I knew that this was no time to alienate him either.

"Thanks, Ed," I said, forcing myself to nibble on the end.

"It's us against those Freaks," Eddie said in too loud of a voice. "At least I know you two creampuffs." Dare I say that he was actually coveting an alliance with us? "You know I've always liked you, Walker," he said. "I don't mean in that way. I mean as a professional."

"A professional what?" Daniel bit out.

"A professional dead person. No hard feelings about the past," Eddie begged, offering a beefy hand. Daniel knew that it was wise not to put him in the Freaks' corner, too. He shook. "No hard feelings," I said, shaking his pillowy hand, knowing that in the living realm it was a numbers game. The more people on our side, the more chances to defeat a bloodthirsty demon.

Iz and Bertha quickly stepped off the bus and I smiled at her hot-pink workout ensemble. Iz had on more Michael Jordan sportswear than I ever knew existed. I wondered if there was an outlet mall in this realm. Pete arrived next, swinging around the side of the bus. He left our house when it was still dark outside, opting to walk. It was the new grown-up Pete in dark Ray-Bans, long black basketball shorts, and a white T-shirt. He smiled at me as he approached and said under his breath, "Check out who's coming off the bus. Walker, we're not in Kansas anymore."

"Damn," I replied. "I thought we were in Michigan."

Descending was one of the Freak U students and he didn't tumble off the bus, but elegantly strolled as if he was sightseeing along the Champs Élysées in Paris. He was wearing what looked like OCD-pressed white workout pants, a starched white T-shirt, and a long dark trench coat. *In the middle of summer?*

"Just what I'd wear for a day training in the woods," I whispered to Pete who tried not to laugh. This newcomer's eyes were covered in steel gray, wraparound sunglasses. A black skullcap made his angular, bony face seem even more forbidding.

I didn't have time to study him. He was instantly in my face, standing far too near, invading my space and now speaking in low, insistent tones.

"I beg your pardon. Our introduction was quite informal the other day, please forgive me," he said with grave concern.

He had a pronounced English accent and I noted that his teeth were slightly crooked, veering right. The rest of him looked like a GQ ad, from his short, spiked, almost white hair to the designer high-tops on his feet. The shoes were so white that I was sure they had never left the box before today.

"I'm sorry. I don't recall your name," I said, wary of the finishing-school manners. Yet, there was something about him that demanded your full attention, especially when he was this close. When he took off the glasses, I connected with eyes that were so dark they were almost black.

"Tor. Licensed, bonded, and dangerous to know," he said, like it was a fact. And he didn't smile.

I took him at face value and knew this wasn't an introduction. It was a warning.

2.

The structure in front of us was in a word: bleak. It was a single story, ramshackle building, featuring a façade of old aluminum siding covered in thick coats of peeling white-gray paint. Where the gravel from the parking lot ended, there was about ten feet of acid-washed asphalt that fronted the shack.

"It's a relic," I said, wondering if we were also being condemned as we walked through a warped metal garage door that was ajar in a crooked way like someone either ran into it or kicked it. A small sign next to it it read: ALWAYS OPEN TO SELECT HUMANS. OTHERS ENTER AT YOUR OWN RISK.

A few steps inside and the verdict was in. The place smelled like old cigarettes and foul body odor. There were half-full spit buckets and old sweaty towels everywhere, but not the plush cotton variety. These were threadbare and when I ran my finger over a supposedly clean one in a pile, it felt like brand-new sandpaper.

It was Africa hot in there—with no hope of air conditioning or even a fan. I pinched my nose to deflect the rancid smell of sweat and said to no one in particular, "The fate of the world starts here? In this pit?"

Everything inside seemed to be expired. There were the deflated, cracked vinyl red mats and the sagging boxing bags that hung haphazardly and half lopsided from the ceiling. Forget state-of-the-art treadmills and spin bikes. I saw two broken-down bikes that were partially covered in rust so old that it had eaten holes in the metal.

A few ragged posters were tacked to the wall boasting long-ago heavyweight fights in Atlantic City, Madison Square Garden, and of course, Sin City aka Las Vegas. Life-size cutout replicas of the greats including Rocky Marciano, Ali, and even my hero, Rocky Balboa, were obviously there for inspiration. "Eye of the tiger, baby," Daniel remarked, which earned him my best eye roll.

"French toast! I knew I smelled something good in here!" I heard Eddie shout as he raced to a folding table in the back. *Who could eat in here?* Bulking up seemed to be part of the plan because the table was covered with fortifying foods including steak, eggs, bacon, hash browns, and extra-thick slices of a banned substance in the living realm known as white bread. Eddie even body checked poor pink-lady Bertha in order to be first to fill his paper plate as high as possible. One thing about him: He made the most of the moment.

I waved away his offer to scoop greasy hash browns onto a plate for me. "Thanks anyway. I'm Irish, and I'm still on my own personal potato blight," I said, glancing around as I made a few additional mental notes.

The light interrupted me. A streak of sunlight made something on the opposite end of the garage glitter and I did a quick double take.

The entire back wall looked like a showroom of medieval weapons with every conceivable primitive manmade torture device hanging on display. During a quick, silent inventory done only with my eyes, I could see various versions of Dr. King's infamous throwing stars, several actual flamethrowers, spears, swords, and several shining, gold-bladed axes that looked like they could take down the biggest monsters.

"Nothing like doing a little cardio while holding your flamethrower," I whispered, and Pete laughed as we stared at a treadmill that didn't even have an "on" and "off" switch, but large metal rollers covered by a torn black track. The ripped part was put back together with silver, multilayered duct tape.

Pete laughed and ran a hand over his military style buzz cut. Daniel's only concession to the day's events was slicking his hair back. Badass all the way.

"I'm not runnin' no stairs or chasing some dumb chicken around a yard. Chickens are for soup and not for exercise," Bertha declared, flailing an arm toward those life-sized cardboard cutouts. I thought I knew what she was talking about, but as usual Bertha filled in the blanks. "I've seen *Rocky* about two hundred times. I know how this physical fitness goes," she said, alluding to the scene where Mickey makes Rocky chase a chicken to develop his speed.

Looking at my amused face, she closed her eyes and said, "Walk-*her*, this ain't funny, girl. Alls I can do is glare at those demons. Or cuss at 'em. If cursin' counts, we got this thing."

I was the one who thought about cussing. It dawned on me that my powers of observation were actually lacking. I didn't wait to see everyone and everything that slithered off that bus. And, yes, there were more. The Claires, the four sister bitches, had finally sauntered off the bus like they were waiting to make an entrance.

Instead of coming directly into the gym, they had lined up, standing side-by-side, and sashayed behind the closest tree for a few minutes, puffing Marlboros and creating clouds of smoke. From my vantage point near the garage door, I could hear the conspiratorial giggling as they got their game on.

With their cigarettes in hand, they finally joined us inside, puffing and applying bubble-gum-pink lip gloss that was passed to each sister like it was part of a primping routine.

When Izayah gave dark-haired Claire A a look, she gave him a slow, appreciative once-over before confirming in *a voice that sounded exactly like Izayah*, "Smoking can't kill me now. But the way you're looking at me? Well, I think my heart just stopped." Then she put her hands over her ears. "I hear you," she said under her breath. "But you can't possibly be infatuated with *that fat girl.*"

How dare she insult Bertha? Luckily, Bertha was out of earshot trying to find a bathroom to hide in.

Impish Claire C, with her short curly locks, pranced past the breakfast spread as if she was walking a catwalk. "You don't have to be psychic to know this means heartburn," she said frowning at the fried Jimmy Dean meat products. The sisters coordinated their workout gear and were dressed in various versions of skanky-sexy including tight tanks, scandalously low crop tops, and barely there booty shorts.

Focus. What was their dog and pony show details? Then I remembered the briefing on them in the packet.

Claire V, short for Claire Violet (full names were printed on the gym's chalkboard) was the one who could see the future. She came clad in a breast hugging, neon tank top and the shortest shorts known to mankind, her long auburn hair in a high pony and half of her rear end hanging out. Claire S, short for Claire Sophia, was the one who could sense people's feelings. She hadn't zeroed in on mine because I thought her bright-pink leotard and matching pale-pink tights were hideous.

"Excuse me," she said in my direction. "Bright pink is very in this year. Don't try to dilute your fears by focusing on me." She was dead on. But how could I control what I was feeling—or her radar when it came to picking up on my thoughts?

For a moment, I thought I could actually count the Cheerios she ate for breakfast because the straightening-iron blonde was that emaciated. "Don't feel sorry for me either. The only disorder I have is piss-poor fate," S said.

I still hadn't said a freaking word.

Claire C wore a tight black jumpsuit zipped down to way-way-way past there—there, being her bellybutton. She had nothing on underneath. The shaggy blonde ringlet curls presented an innocent picture and the sky-blue eyes pushed it over the edge. My arm hairs stood up when she pranced toward me.

She planted the fakest smile en route. And with a look that clearly said, "You're pathetic," she transferred her sexiest gaze to Daniel. Her big, ultrabright smile made my stomach churn. Gracefully, she took one long, slender finger and flicked a small bead of sweat off her pale brow. It made her frown as in—how *dare* sweat enter her world. She put that same bony hand on Daniel's arm, a friendly, not-so-friendly gesture that confirmed she had set her sights on him.

"Bored, aren't you?" she said to Daniel.

But she was looking directly at me.

3.

Daniel ignored her to grab us two bottles of water from a metal tub. I smiled. Walker, one, Claires—as I would now call them—zero. However, like in most out-bitch-each-other triathlons, my moment of victory was short-lived.

We were interrupted by a salty, gnomelike, portly creature, who stood no bigger than five foot two. This man had a thick flash of pure white hair that would rival Santa. His belly was hanging over extremely high-waisted pants that seemed to hug his heart and stopped below his shoes.

"Just open my grave and stuff me back inside," he snorted, wiping his pock-marked nose with the back of his wrinkled, almost mangled-looking hand. The pants served as the rest of his tissue.

Quickly, he began to sneer at Bertha, the Claires, and then me.

"Broads—and lots of 'em. I can't take broads in the morning—or noon or night for that matter," he growled in a way that made it sound like he had gargled half the parking lot.

"Sorriest bunch I've ever seen in my life or death," he said, taking a quick look around the room. "The muckety-mucks keep askin' me what I think. Well here's the rat's ass truth. Somebody better call off this fools' journey. That's what I think, yessir, Bob. And somebody better get rid of the broads," he hissed. "No good can come of a journey with broads."

"How do you really feel about it," I whispered under my breath, figuring the last thing the old coot had was decent hearing.

His senses, it turns out, were in fine working order.

Shockingly agile for his age, he turned on what looked like some sort of specially built medical shoes and stared at me while wiping that pitted nose again with his hand. Then he shook his head like a dog that had just escaped his yearly bath.

"I tells ya how I feel about it," he said. "Broads mess with your mind, wreck your legs, and invade your head. And they run like . . . broads."

Great. We were going to be trained by some sort of sexist, sweaty Yoda. His only redeeming quality revealed itself when an actual gym dog rambled to his side and I watched him reach down to ruff up its fur. I knew she was his when he called her Peg. She was an old terrier with a white beard who moved extra slowly, but kept up with her master.

"She's a broad," I whispered to Daniel. "The dog, I mean."

"Broads. Always gotta get the last word," he mocked in a low voice.

"Who is that crazy lunatic?" Izayah whispered to me. "He looks familiar in a weird way, but I can't place him."

"I'm Johnny Tamale and this is my house," he hissed at us, his rheumy eyes sending trickles down his cheeks.

He had a small, melon-like head, which neatly balanced on his neckless body. His eyes slits were again locked on me. "Girlie, do you have any muscle on those bones? I mean, look at you. Bean pole!" he sneered at me.

He put up that gnarled hand like a stop sign. As in—I don't care enough for you to answer.

"Like I said. I'm Johnny, a no-good boxing bum," he introduced himself again, focusing back on his original agenda.

"Who are you? Mickey from *Rocky*?" I asked.

"Bean pole, they based him on me," he said with a mixture of pride and disgust. "You think I'd get a shout out, a damn percentage of the profits, an autographed poster of my boy, Sly Stallone. A ticket to them Oscar Meyer Weiner awards!"

His rant was short-lived, and quickly he went back to business. "Rule numbers one," Johnny rasped, addressing the entire group. "There are no shortcuts when it comes to training for your immortality. Rule numbers two, keep your mind clear and just listen to ya trainers. Unlike every other flippin' teenager in the universe, pretend that ya don't know it all because yas don't. Yas don't know shit."

He looked at Daniel and gave rule number three, which sounded pretty damn familiar.

"Keep your hands and the rest of ya to yaself," Johnny said, then glanced at me. Walking slowly up to the group, he poked a gnarled finger into Daniel's chest. For a minute, I thought the old guy might get decked, but I could see a certain level of respect in Daniel's eyes.

"Women weaken legs. Just remember that. *Women. Weaken. Legs*," Johnny ranted like a madman. "I gave Sly that damn line and now I'm taking it back. So take ya romance and put it where the sun don't shine."

"Mr. Taco, I'll lay off the broads, too," Eddie promised, dropping his fork for a second as cold eggs fell to the ground. Peg chose to trot over and have a morning snack.

"You don't have to worry about weak legs, Eddie," Izayah taunted him.

"Hey," Eddie replied, looking genuinely hurt as he grabbed a muffin. "I came here to be friendly. If I wanted abuse, I could've stayed at ITT."

"Shut up, all of yous!" Johnny said. But he was interrupted before he could lay into Eddie.

"Johnny, nice to see you again. We'll let the team settle in for a few more minutes," General S said, walking into the gym in his freshly pressed whites while the old man just grunted. Not exactly a master of manners, Johnny grabbed one of the breakfast steaks with his bare hands and walked away nibbling on it like a cookie.

"We're wasting time. Let's line up by schools," General S said, doing a quick roll call. "Daniel, Walker, Pete, Izayah, Bertha from the Academy. Check," he said, actually checking our names off on his clipboard. "Eddie, ITT. Check. Tor and the Claire sisters from Frederick Reardon. Check. The others are on their way including the Fusions and the kid."

I looked at Daniel. Once again, I found myself wondering, "Others?" There were more surprises in the form of invited guests.

"Yes, others," Claire V murmured to me. "Try to keep up—if you can, Walker."

Her gaze was directed at General S, as it was his mind that she was reading. "Oh, this should be good," she said to no one in particular. "You know one of them. Well, well, well."

4.

A thin shadow passed under the crooked garage door and my jaw dropped when my eyes connected with the owner.

"Just what we need!" Johnny shouted. "Another bean pole."

To General S, he added, "Don't you feed these kids?"

He was beyond the definition of skinny, but I would have recognized those baby blues anywhere. He looked confused and discombobulated, which was typical for fourteen-year-old A.E.

"Um, well, okay," blurted the painfully thin boy with a slightly acne-covered face and blond bangs. He was talking to no one in particular.

"Why am I here? I guess I know why. I went back. Like Daniel and Walker, I know how to do it, technically speaking," he rambled. "Gonna zip it now. But one thing: it's sure nice to see blue sky again. Can I just sit outside in the sunshine until someone needs me?"

His eyes were so round and . . . hopeful. His needs were so simple. The kid would risk being extinguished for a little fresh air and to feel the warmth of his old friend, the sun. That was everything for a young boy who was being caged in a glass box for eternity. "Is that a dog?" A.E. squealed with delight.

Like an eager pup, A.E.'s eyes also brightened when he actually saw Daniel and me, and he tossed up his bony hand to wave furiously. I returned the favor and added a warm smile.

He was just a kid—and he wouldn't last two seconds after we went through the portal. He was lucky the first time around during the pork-chop fest at his house. But luck runs out. I wondered how long ours would last.

It was slowly becoming clear why each of us was here: Daniel, A.E., and I had the knowledge; Eddie, Pete and Izayah were the brawn; the Freaks were there to do whatever freaky thing necessary to get what was needed. We were just the front lines, a means to an end that would certainly create our ending.

"I've heard that you're the smart one," said General S with some admiration as he towered over A.E.

The kid just shrugged as he approached the food table with some hesitation. Since his gaze was directed at his shoes, he fumbled a half-open box of cereal, pouring most of it on the floor. He cowered a bit, obviously hoping that no one would beat him for that slight infraction.

"I'm so sorry," A.E. cried and I kneeled next to him to help him clean up the mess while Peg offered her help, too. He quickly poured the rest of the box down his throat and looked like he was swallowing without even chewing. It was almost as if he thought someone would take this good food away. The truth was, he was barely fed anything where he lived now. I don't know what possessed me, but I cut up half a steak for him as if he was Bobby's age, and he didn't protest.

"Is that real milk?" he said in an amazed voice. "Can I have just a little? Please? I haven't had milk in years."

"We're the odd couple from ITT," Eddie said, laughing at his own joke. "Me and the kid. The brain and the bruiser."

From his position on the floor where he was eating muffin after muffin, A.E. responded, "It's not that I'm so smart. I just stay with the questions much longer. I'm just passionately inquisitive."

It was such an A.E. thing to say.

I gazed at our friend in a vintage royal-blue Nike shirt with the white swish logo. He wore a sickly pair of light-green sweatpants and red Keds. I'm sure his training outfit was born out of mismatched prison leftovers.

"Son, why don't you just stay passionately quiet," said General S, who informed the rest of us, "This is your newest team member—a last-minute addition. He was working out the particulars with the

Higher Authority last night. Say hello to everyone, son."

"Greetings from Neptune," A.E. said, biting his sugary bottom lip.

"Bitch boy," Eddie blurted.

"Do we have a problem, Edward?" General S said into a megaphone that had his initials on the side.

"A mega one, sir," Eddie whined. "I don't want to go on a kill mission with the biggest ass-kissing eighth grader in the universe."

"Arse kisser? OK, interesting, Eddie," A.E. began. "Did you know that more than forty thousand parasites and two hundred and fifty types of bacteria can be exchanged in one kiss. According to your definition, I'm a bacteria-ridden parasite made even worse by my lip placement—on an arse—and hopefully not your arse because that might have more parasites than most."

"This kid makes my brain hurt," Eddie said in a confused voice. And to A.E., he yelled, "Stop being . . . smart!"

The banter was short-lived. An old clock ticked and it was now time to commence training. It turns out that *hurting* was actually the name of the game. Johnny paddled across the concrete floor while carrying a wooden crate that advertised some kind of spicy Louisiana hot sauce "guaranteed to blow your mind and taste buds." I wished it was filled with something to put on our steaks, but that was far from the truth.

The old man began to hand out something I knew only too well from my time on D Block.

"Put 'em on or I'll put 'em on ya," he said. "Just make sure they're nice and tight. Give 'em an extra squeeze for good luck."

"I know someone I'd like to squeeze extra tight," murmured Claire V, looking at Daniel and then glaring at me. I didn't have time to focus on her taunts and dares.

The crate was filled with those same infamous anklets that were slapped on our legs before we entered ITT. They were taking away our reset because it didn't exist in the living realm. We were told that the anklets would be removed each day for the Academy students, so we would have the reset at home. Suddenly, I was thankful for small favors.

"Gentlemen and ladies, those of us at the Frederick Reardon School have historically chosen to shun the reset, which is why we don't even need those anklets today. The device is permanently implanted in us," Tor informed the group.

This was news to me, so I asked, "Why do you, historically speaking, want to feel pain?"

"Pain is our constant friend—our *compadre*," he said with a slicing glance. "When you've spent a lifetime being bullied, you're used to feeling pain. Not feeling it would be strange."

Claire A filled in the blank. "As nonconventional members of society, first in the living realm and now here, our special traits have always gone misunderstood by most. This means tremendous pain is always in our vortex. You live with that type of pain and in time, it feels comfortable. Normal."

As I digested those particulars, my new pal Johnny jammed a metal anklet at me and slowly I leaned forward to place it below my calf. Like it was made of molten lava, it burned through my flesh and sunk deep. *Agony!* When it burrowed into my actual anklebone, my body broke into a cold fever sweat. I would sweat again at the end of the day when Johnny would use a remote device to remove it.

Moments later, I accidentally walked into that wooden hot-sauce case and saw stars from a very human phenomenon known as a bitch of a stubbed toe.

Clutching his sides, Eddie wouldn't stop cackling.

"Should we get Walker a weedle Band-Aid for her sweet girlie-girl skin?" he mocked.

I winced, gazing at him with disgust when he blew me an

impromptu kiss. When I glanced again, just a split-second later, it wasn't a kiss. He was simply standing there with his blubbery bottom lip gasping for air because he shoved almost an entire onion bagel into his big trap. As I turned back, Tor was smiling at me.

"Enough mollycoddling," Johnny yelled. "I ain't here to babysit ya losers . . . and all these broads."

5.

General S loved to address the troops. "This mission, in a word, stinks like . . . well never mind," he said. "But we're here for the next few weeks to give you every physical advantage because everything is on the line."

"We've had what you might call bad luck in the past with these missions," he divulged.

Bells were going off inside me. *There were other missions?*

"We sent an earlier crew of mostly professors and elite, adult combat veterans. Your Dr. King went on an early mission," he said, laying another brick. "We found that sending elders wasn't exactly the type of troops we needed. The clues failed to present themselves from the start. The Shield, the group protecting what we need, didn't trust adults. They could smell the lack of patience. They could sense the desperation."

"Remember," he continued to instruct, "what we're looking for is hidden in history. There are those who will vigilantly protect it and deny clues to those with the wrong agendas."

So they decided to go younger.

"There are times when youth is the secret weapon," said General S.

"Why?" Daniel said, his face illuminated by a shaft of morning sunlight. "We're expendable? There are thousands more waiting at these schools to do your bidding?"

"No, son. In this case, it's about purer motives," General S retorted. There was total silence. General S focused in again on Daniel. "Still, I wonder if you know true selflessness. I've heard that you have a PhD in selfishness."

Daniel just glared at him.

"The only thing worse than ignorance or arrogance is ignorance *and* arrogance," General S snapped. "I would advise you, Dan, to put both of your specialties on hold while I introduce your trainers. Most were imported. You will give them your utmost respect."

With his words, I heard the most hideous sound of metal grinding on metal. It was the crooked garage door opening full and diamond-like sparks rained into the air as the track almost flew off its hinges.

With the sun hitting their backs, a team of twelve men and three women blasted into the gym like they were going to tear it down and eat the steely remains. They had one thing in common. The kill in their eyes.

Once inside, they stood in the far corner of the room in a perfect line, and when my eyes adjusted to the natural light still seeping in, I could see that many were also in uniforms that defined them.

There were US Navy Seals, Israeli Commandos, British MI5 agents, and Russian Spetsnaz fighters—among many other nationalities and fighting icons.

"Hope you kids ate your veggies last night," said a man whose name tag read Tig. He sized up the Claires like *they* were being served for lunch. He was a US Green Beret in khaki's and a muscle shirt threatening to explode. Tough didn't even begin to cover it.

"The most badass soldiers to ever live," Daniel whispered,

noticing my fascination and utter enjoyment of anyone who would dare make a Claire feel uncomfortable.

"These are the greatest handpicked warriors in any realm. They also gave their lives for their respective causes," boasted General S, slapping a few of the Seals on the back. "They were invincible—until they weren't. You're here to learn that kind of killer instinct."

Glancing around, I saw those Spetsnaz fighters fingering their sniper rifles and AK74 Carbines. A few had those trademark Makarov pistols. The Green Berets held good old-fashioned shotguns.

In another corner, I saw what appeared to be three overweight guys in black pants and long, black leather jackets. "Mafia killers," General S. remarked. "Homegrown from the great state of New Jersey."

One named Mario looked at the Russians, rolled his eyes, and said, "What are yous guys lookin' at? Ya got a problem, I got a solution."

I jumped when the one actually named Tony cocked a long silver weapon that he caressed like a lover. "Fuggedaboutit, Mario," he said. "These morons couldn't find their way out of Trenton."

"The sawed-off shotgun—bang, bang, bye-bye," Mario said in a pleased voice. "Made in the good old US of A. Of course, it can't compete with a Thompson submachine gun, but those are just too noisy. Why wake up the dead? Get it?"

Tony almost split his polyester pants when he doubled over laughing.

"You can't fit a tommy gun into your purse either," said Claire A.

"With our brains, we can create weapons out of just about anything," said his leather trench-coat-wearing friend, Tiny, who was actually quite large at about six foot five. "Kiddies, lesson number one: The baseball bat," continued Tiny, holding a well-worn Louisville Slugger by his right side. "Works like a muther every single time." He jabbed a fat finger into the air and A.E. looked like he wanted to crawl out of his own skin. Tiny laughed and yelled, "The bat weighs more than yous, kid. Maybe we use you as a ball." A.E.'s eyes got wider. Tiny slapped his own leg and shouted, "Just messin' with yous!"

Next to approach us were two buff younger men with short, spiked haircuts and the brightest of blue and green eyes. Their faces were long and angular and their bodies were lean like Olympians. They spoke with delightful Irish accents that came directly from what I imagined to be lovely towns in the Emerald Isle, birthplace of the Callaghans.

"I thought we'd get a little training help from these blokes, too," said General S. "Meet Liam and Aidan. Irish Republican Army. The greatest guerilla fighters to ever live and die. Hello lads."

"Ye party—let's get it started!" Liam shouted, his brawn defined in a body-hugging black spandex workout suit.

"Where are your green outfits? You know? The luck of the Irish?" piped up Claire V who punctuated her interruption with well-calculated hair flip and some not-so-subtle lip licking.

Liam looked game and gave her a quick up and down followed by a not-so-brotherly wink. Then he turned his attention toward me. "Ha-ware-ya, young lady?" he responded. I thought that translated into "how are you" but I wasn't really sure. "By the way, we don't wear green, Miss," Liam said in his thick Irish accent. "Our green is in here." He pointed to the vein in his right arm. "Our blood runs green."

"Attention!" commanded General S. "I still have to introduce the Yakuza, our friends from Japan. Extremely organized and with a strict code of conduct and honor. They use street fighting, pro wrestling techniques, and judo, which they will demonstrate now. I just need a volunteer."

It was as if everyone stopped breathing.

Undaunted, General S pointed to Izayah like he meant business. "You . . . yes, you. Son, you will do ten laps around the woods for not immediately standing up to volunteer. And when I ask again, you're going to raise your hand first to learn from the Yakuza—while you still can raise your hand."

"In fact, five miles for each of you to start," General S commanded "And you better be done in the next fifty minutes." My heart broke for Bertha. She wouldn't be done in the next fifty years.

Forty minutes later I was still outside, running and panting when I saw another bus—a dark, slick BMW slicing through the woods at top speed. Slowing my pace, I watched curiously as the driver stopped in the gravel lot and then worked his way around to the back of the bus. Carefully, he removed five silver wheelchairs from the back and placed them in two neat rows.

What emerged from the bus was beyond curious. I saw five lean, wide-shouldered, ripped young men slowly and carefully make their way on their own volition. But thanks to nature, or what was fated for them, it wasn't easy. Each young man had a condition where their lower extremities were completely fused from thigh to shin, but apart from the shin down to their bare feet. I couldn't even call them feet. There were oversized toes, but they were webbed. This configuration caused them to walk . . . .no, waddle . . . like human ducks.

They were, in a word, *fascinating.* Each sported some sort of wild, longish hair pushed off wide foreheads and handsome faces. All of their locks were in vivid blues, greens, purples, and pinks—

the colors of the sea. Some of the men had the same pops of color on their carefully trimmed facial hair, which made them look like half men, half ocean creatures in a way.

In my life, I had never seen a man with an aqua beard in deepening shades of blue and bright-green eyebrows. Another had a large green-and-blue braid on top of his head and facial stubble of hot purple.

"Some call them Fusions. I call them Mermen," said a dreamy Claire A, catching up to me at my slow pace. "They're from our school, of course. Which is one of the perks of our school, naturally. Men of land and the sea, dreamy. Just imagine a Friday-night skinny-dipping session with them, although strangely you're not. I can sum it up in one word: Shivers."

Without the reset, I was finding it hard to breathe after doing five miles, so I just nodded.

"Sorry about my sisters. They can be bitches, but they're really not. We just shun new people. It's easier that way. You know, shun first or be shunned," she explained, huffing and sweating. Jutting her hand out, I returned the favor and we shook warily.

"Walker."

"A," she said. "We go by our middle initials. I know you're wondering, but don't ask. Not yet."

For once, my name wasn't the one in question. "Yeah, I know, you get a lot of shit about your name," A said. "We're the opposite. We don't put up with shit—ever. And yes, you will remember that forever."

I couldn't win.

"No, you won't win," A confirmed.

Distraction was my only chance.

Purposely my attention diverted to watch as the Mermen shunned the chairs and continued their waddle-walk steps toward the interior of the gym building. They looked like normal young men from the waist up. What was in the middle was anyone's guess. They were also mostly naked, except for what looked like a small cloth in front and back to hide their particulars. The rest of them was sculpted, sinewy perfection, much like the rippled muscles and lines that defined Daniel.

"They can live in the water or on land," A said in a dreamy tone. "Their dorm room is a beach house."

"Men with oceanfront property," I attempted a joke.

"Don't think you're funny," she replied.

General S filled in the rest after we reassembled in the gym. "Meet the Fusion men," he formally introduced them. "New York is surrounded by water and swimming demons are the worst. These men aren't going with you on your mission, but will train you in the aquatic arts."

Water sports, however, would have to wait.

Our master teacher had arrived.

6.

He stood shirtless in front of us, small in stature with sinewy muscles that looked like an elaborate road map of glorious victories. There were the trademark thick black bangs and pursed lips. His dark eyes narrowed as he nodded, which would serve as his introduction.

He was *that* Bruce.

The legend.

The man.

Even Eddie bowed, not even knowing why he was doing it.

"Good morning," Bruce said. "Let me begin by stating our collective mission. Our mission is to embrace the vole."

My head swiveled to the side to look at Daniel. It was exactly what he said to me in the woods on a cold night not so long ago. Looking down at his feet, I could see Daniel grinning in a way that set his entire face on fire. This wasn't supposed to be cool at all, but suddenly it was actually getting pretty damn close.

"Embrace the vole?" Pete repeated, obviously not even sure why he was speaking out loud, but it was enough to catch Bruce's attention. With liquid moves of someone propelled by air, Bruce whipped around and stood inches in front of him.

"Embrace the vole," Bruce repeated. "To risk everything in the hope of great rewards. You will also 'go the vole.' That means to try every possibility under heaven and earth to do what's needed to be done."

"Embrace the vole," Daniel repeated, slowly, casting his eyes to the side. I could see the look of seething jealousy on Claire C's face, but she didn't have time to dwell. All of us said it together like children in a primary school, although we weren't told to do so. Blank-faced Bruce nodded and I could tell our quick response pleased him.

"You are wondering how this is possible, how can you embrace the vole and I ask you to begin by looking at me. *Really* looking," he said. Bruce pivoted hard and now addressed A.E. "I am not the biggest. Not the brawniest. I didn't take on fifteen opponents at a time with my fists," he continued. "I did it with my mind. And it was not the mindset of 'I'm going to smash your face in.' Instead, I would say, 'If you can smash my face in, I will openly shake your hand.' But when I smash your face in, I hope you *aren't* capable of shaking mine.'"

His voice, calm and low, caused shivers to race up my spine. I got it. Eddie didn't. He looked so hopeless and lost that I leaned over to whisper to him, "Eddie, they can't shake. They're done."

"Oh," he said, slowly. His meaty face looked happily confused.

"They're already dead," I said.

Bruce zeroed in on me. "You might think you're too small. Or you dwell on the fact that you're not extremely muscular. Or female."

"White. Black. Child. Man. Woman. It doesn't matter," he said. "You win by walking into a room and visualizing your opponent defeated. You do this before the fight even begins."

Tor was asked to stand.

"You can also send the mightiest force reeling backward by getting into his or her face and hitting with a one-inch punch," Bruce said, standing inches away from the towering Freak force. For his part, Tor looked bored.

"Not a full swing," Bruce said, "But a one-inch punch to the right spot is the kill shot."

If nothing else, I was a great memorizer.

"If you do it fast enough, they will be lucky to know it's coming," he told us. "The brain doesn't have enough time then to tell the body to block or evade."

With those words, he popped Tor one in the kisser that sent him reeling back until he fell over a folding chair with a thud. Peg the dog raced up and Tor violently pushed her away, causing the canine to whimper. Tor didn't give her a second thought. He removed what looked like a white handkerchief from his pocket and calmly attended to his bleeding nose. The look he gave Bruce said that he wanted to rip out his organs.

When I gasped from the sheer violence on Tor's face, he set his focus on me. When I looked away and set my eyes elsewhere, I swore that I saw Bertha licking her lips. Certainly, she couldn't crush on someone who looked like a British serial killer.

One of the Navy Seals broke the tension. "You will learn to fight your fear with knowledge. Let your opponent underestimate you. That is your most powerful weapon."

The Japanese Yakuza spoke next. "A warrior understands his surroundings," he told Daniel, and then pivoted toward the Claires. "She knows that there are no failings."

"Your death is not your worst nightmare," said the Israeli Commando, addressing Pete.

"It's your unleashing," the MI5 agent informed me.

We half-assed sparred for the rest of the day, but I mostly evaded, which wasn't hard because quaking A.E. was my partner. No one was spared. A sweaty few hours later, my eyes glanced to the side of the room. A tall man with all-American good looks was suddenly sitting in one of the Mermen's wheelchairs. I didn't see him come in, but he had the loose, relaxed face of someone who was in no rush. Smiling at me, he stood easily, casually sauntering over to us, which made Eddie audibly gasp.

"I'm here to talk to you about fear," he said in a smooth, soft voice. "Fear can be paralyzing. But the truth is, some people walking around with full use of their bodies are more paralyzed than I used to be. What we'll do here over the next several weeks is help you beat your deepest fears."

"Thanks, Super—" Eddie began with an ear-to-ear grin.

"Kid," he said. "Just call me Chris."

CHAPTER 15

1.

Being dead, I wasn't sure if I couldn't grow physically stronger, but I did. Over the next two weeks, we spent every extra minute at Johnny's gym where we sprinted, sparred, and sweated until I felt dizzy and my muscles were on the verge of collapse. On the weekends, we practically lived in that garage stink. And it wasn't just to build our bodies. One such rainy Sunday it was Bruce who explained how we would defeat the demons in the living realm.

"Miss Callaghan, let's try the one-inch punch," he said, grasping my hand and moving my thumb to the outside of my fist. He placed my new fist precariously close to his face and wanted me to deck him. I couldn't even give him a dirty look, let alone punch him.

"Do it," he commanded as we stood in the ramshackle boxing ring. The others waited outside the ropes, watching. I knew how ridiculous it looked. The legend and the girl in her favorite Mickey

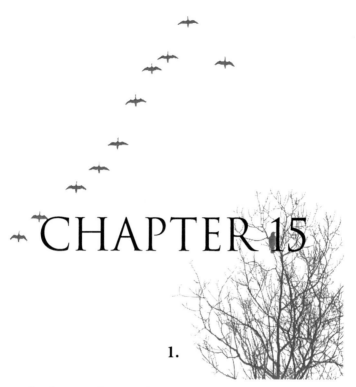

Mouse T-shirt and black shorts defying him.

My fears held me back as my fist remained an inch from his face, but not moving.

"I read your permanent record," Bruce began, an object of stillness in the ring.

My hand began to shake.

"You've been conditioned to take it. Take whatever life had in store for you," he said. "You were taught to allow the carnage and then acted as a one-girl clean-up squad for your mother. You had to take losing your father. Take losing your home. Take losing your pride when you couldn't afford a backpack or hot lunch at school. Taking it no longer applies, Walker. You have the power now."

Just thinking about it made me want to cry. Bruce stepped closer to me. I moved back. He invaded again, pressing me back toward the ropes. "How long are you going to just take it, Walker?" he taunted. "Are you an eternal victim?" He walked closer again, and I evaded until my back was again on the ropes. "You didn't live life on your terms? Why not start now?" Bruce whispered.

I closed my eyes and popped Bruce hard in the nose. Our master trainer reeled back. "Harder," he commanded, lifting my fist and placing it almost between his eyes. I hit him. And then I jabbed again. Bruce didn't wince or bleed. Like an arrow, he just stood there. "Again," he commanded. My fist sprang off his flesh.

"Bertha, get in the ring," Bruce said, switching things up.

"No!" my mind screamed.

Bruce set it up the same way with Bertha pushing and me stepping back. "Strike first!" he yelled, but I wouldn't. I couldn't. And when we got close enough to the ropes, Bertha had no choice but to pull her club-like arm back and clock me so hard in the face that my cheek started bleeding and I saw stars.

"Very good, Bertha," Bruce said. "Walker, give me twenty laps outside. I'm very disappointed."

My head low, I complied. "Walk-*her*, Walk-*her*. Girl, I didn't want to," Bertha cried after me and I looked back at her, blood running down my face.

When I came back, I ran into the Claires who were doing sit-ups by the hundreds in the corner. Two of them worked out at a time while the other pair took photos. They were wearing what basically looked like bathing suits. None of the trainers seemed to care. In fact, the two IRA guys were giving them lusty looks.

"We should send your boyfriend a shot," V said, glancing in my direction. "We also love to do hot yoga. We made a video."

The IRA guy named Liam zeroed in on me. "Are ye makin' friends or training, Walker?' he demanded.

Why was it always me?

He was tall, sinewy, and lean with a buzzed haircut and a jaw like a razor's edge. When he took off his black sunglasses, his searing green eyes had a merry twinkle to them and dimples that looked like they were carved.

"Let's get on with it my *rùn stor*, you're up next," he said, reaching down with a treelike arm and hoisting me to my feet.

What followed was about three seconds in the ring with Eddie who put my mood into the red TNT zone. He was unfriendly Eddie today and asked me about "that little bastard kid" I had with me the day I came back. This time, I didn't back up an inch. I punched him in the melon with all the stored-up fury of the day. His meaty head snapped back so hard, I thought it would detach and roll out of the ring.

"Buy this girl a pint!" Liam cried, raising a fist in the air.

Maybe he didn't like Eddie or maybe those freedom fighters were on my side. Later, when I checked a Gaelic dictionary, I found that *stor* meant treasure and *rùn* was Irish for secret.

2.

During breaks, I kept my sanity by wandering outside to smell the fresh, clean pine scent of the trees. There was something affirming in taking off my shoes, closing my eyes, and just existing.

One such afternoon, it was Tor who snapped me out of a lovely daydream of spending a rainy day with Daniel curled up on the couch. "If you weren't so sensitive and needy, you might actually excel at the physicality," he opined, leaning against one of the large pines in the woods. I didn't plan to see him. He was just there—sent outside to do thirty laps for insubordination. What else was new? And naturally, he just took the Tor show outdoors, where he was doing absolutely nothing.

As for his words, I looked at him as if he just slapped me. My rational self screamed that he was provoking me—and that I just needed to walk away. But I couldn't. Didn't.

"Excuse me?" I said under my breath. For a horrid long moment, he gave me a slow up-and-down glance that was more cutting than any words.

Tor's angular cheekbones and semipointed chin were frozen. I noticed that a pronounced blue vein ran down the center of his forehead stopping at that extremely defined, narrow nose.

"Did you know that you have coward written all over your aura?" he taunted with impeccable control.

"You have psychopath written on yours," I said, not sure where that came from except that it was true and somehow sprang from my lips.

He was one of those Teflon people. Impossible to insult. Tor just advanced a few steps closer while I held my ground. When he was close enough, he purposely blew out his next breath hard. Like I disgusted him.

A turn of his pristine, white athletic shoes later and he was gone.

I stood there barefoot, feeling like a fool.

There was nothing else to do, but wander back into the gym where Daniel was busy in a weapons class with the MI-5 guys. My eyes wandered over to Izayah who was nearby doing weighted squats. *Yep, that was it. I'd ignore him and go talk to Iz.* The young Denzel look-alike stood squarely in the middle of his mat, a large pole and weights on his back, and with the little finger dexterity he had left, promptly gave me . . . the middle finger.

I blinked twice. *No way did he just flip me off. He would never.* On second glance, I could see that he was smiling and giving me the same kind of encouraging thumbs-up he used to send me when we played hockey together for the Academy.

When I looked away, I saw Tor. Again. Just staring.

"Young lady, you're in the ring next," one of the Seals interrupted me.

Claire V was waiting for me. I forced my mind to do a quick round of "what if." *What if* I beat the living shit out of her? *What if* the rest of her snotty sisters were reading my mind right now? *What if* they ganged up on me and sliced me to bits with those stilettos?

Claire C stood by the side of the ring to offer her sister moral support. "You know he loves when you go badass," she muttered under her breath. Who was the "he" in question? "Your boyfriend," C clarified. "We already did a training session with him this morning when you were off communing with trees. It was blocking and evading, although I prefer to think of it as melting and moaning."

She accomplished what she intended. I was jealous. And

distracted.

In the end, V didn't really need to play any mental games with me. In the ring, my mind was elsewhere, as in checked out, and she demolished me with a roundhouse kick to the ribs (to show who was stronger) followed by a hard slap across my face (just because). Anything was game here.

The Claires stood on the sidelines air kissing each other.

"Break," said a dejected Bruce.

Of course, Daniel was allowed to rush in and check for wounds. "At least she didn't bite you. Then you'd need a rabies shot," he said.

I loved that he never made me feel weak or less than. Still, there is no shot for the loss of pride.

The decision that Daniel would be next seemed predestined. "There are no limits," Bruce told him. "There are only plateaus, and you must not stay there. You must go beyond them." Swallowing hard, I waited for Bruce to pair him against Tor or Eddie. That wasn't in the training manual. Yet. What followed was Bruce showing Daniel *how to fight himself.* "Mr. Reid," Bruce said. "You are your worst enemy. But you already knew that."

Daniel was instructed to do the same high kick about a million times until his leg should have fallen off. "I fear not the man who has practiced ten thousand kicks once, but I fear the man who has practiced one kick ten thousand times. Give me another two hundred," Bruce said and I honestly wondered if Daniel would be forced to accept defeat. Not in this afterlife-time. He was like a machine. That gave Bruce time to lower his leg and move way.

"And since you like to look, it's time that you do," he said to me. "Give me one hundred of those kicks. Maybe next time, you won't underestimate those initialed young ladies."

"But I can't possibly—" I began.

"Miss Callaghan," he retorted. "Sometimes you have to stop thinking so much and just do."

I had no choice.

I did.

3.

Lunch on our third Sunday of megatraining was a simple affair at our picnic tables in a wooded area near the gym. Claire V, who changed each time sweat hit her ensemble, emerged from the ramshackle two-stall bathroom in electric-blue booty shorts to show off her fabulous six-mile-long legs. Sashaying close to our Academy table, she didn't mind making her crush on Daniel obvious. Her game plan was nothing new. She walked extra slow by him in the name of looking for a cold water. She was the pranciest of the sisters, and played that "poor pathetic me" game to the hilt.

"Why don't we just give her an IV of ice water?" I grumbled under my breath to Bertha who shot off a few death rays to Claire A in pink leggings who did her own personalized runway walk in front of a clueless Pete. He would not be broken. Tosh had actually started eating lunch with him at school before training began, and I thought our Pete might be seriously infatuated with my school friend. Another clue was the ten million odd questions he was always asking me about Tosh.

"Do you think Tosh likes comic books?" Pete inquired today, wolfing down his second sandwich.

I noted that Daniel took little notice of the Claires, who were now busy preening over their specially ordered meal. Their names were clearly on each box in black marker. No one else dared to touch the freshly caught sushi platters sent expressly from their favorite chef at Freak U.

"Sweetheart, more wasabi," purred Claire C to one of her sisters who did her fetching. Pleased with the results, she stared at Daniel and then licked her full lips slowly before inserting the fish roll like she was trying to bring that tuna back to life.

After the fish fest, she stuck out her bubble-gum-pink tongue and said to Claire A "We finally got Chef Harland away from that deep fryer, right, honey?"

The way they addressed each other made me sick—*honey, darling, sweetie, baby, angel.* And the waves in my stomach weren't just my reaction to raw fish.

Daniel must have sensed my displeasure. That's why I felt him look at me for a few seconds too long.

One second. Two. Three.

He was still looking.

It was a lover's gaze and it felt like a warm summer breeze. In that second, I imagined his hands caressing my shoulders and sliding down my arms.

In reality, Daniel stood up and then leaned down to whisper into my ear, "Callaghan, what am I going to do with you?" Then he showed me by burying his face in my hair and gently biting my ear lobe.

I couldn't help but feel very, very lucky. But that was short-lived in the outdoor lunchroom from hell. Tor was giving us one of his lethal stares. The slim, tall one, who was wearing a long beige cashmere sweater today over white shorts and a polo, wasn't unnerved when I stared back. He carefully took off the sweater, folded it over a metal folding chair, and spread out his own personal yoga mat in the grass. After a few cleansing breaths, he twisted his legs behind his head.

Limber and loose, Tor was like one long muscle. His skin was the color of fresh milk. Of all of us, he appeared to be the most ghostly.

After he finally unwound himself, he walked over our way, which was a given. He was repulsed by the Claires, and Eddie and A.E. were just prison riffraff to him. But he knew we could be provoked. His words, however, were quite unexpected. "Did you know that the average person walks past a murderer thirty-six times in their life?" The transition created the desired results. I willed it not to happen, but my eyes widened.

"We're still not sure who or *what* killed me. But I was murdered. That much I know," Tor said.

This time I could read Daniel's mind. He was obviously thinking, *Too bad someone else got to you first.*

Without an invitation, Tor sat down in enemy territory: Our picnic table. Bertha was the first to speak up. "I was murdered, baby," she said. "Your story can't top my story. Stabbed to death in juvie. Asshat, we have a winner . . . and a loser."

Tor would not be one-upped. Could not. Let the street girl win? It went against his code of what I suspected was dishonor. For some reason he insisted on telling us his story, and I hated the part of myself that was morbidly curious enough to want to listen.

DEATH STORY: Tor

AGE OF DEMISE: 17

I shall begin by stating the obvious for anyone not oblivious. No one here in this realm, no matter male or female, boring or freak, has a story quite as epic as mine. It spans oceans and countries. And it ends in a box. In time, you'll understand. If anyone could ever truly understand why a life ends abruptly at . . . well, suffice to say, it ended as quickly as it began.

"We have to leave this place," my mother said. Her face looked feverish and her voice a mere whisper, although there was no one around to hear us. It was 1915 on our farm in Russia, in a time before

the Revolution and minutes away from the end of the tsars. We were in the middle of the Great War with Germany and Tsar Nicholas II faced a fatal weakening of his regime. Like any king losing power, he grasped at anything that could keep him in on the throne. Anything real. Anything possible.

We lived in a time of rumor and innuendo. As a young boy who was considered "different," I was often the topic of talk. This was no information age, but the talk spread as quickly as the economic crash. Yet, it wasn't economic reasons why my mother decided I would stop going to school in our small war-torn town. It was too dangerous. "We just can't risk it," she said. "He'd be such a powerful . . ." My father finished her sentence in Russian.

The word was weapon.

That November, I remember there was no wheat, no potatoes, and virtually no animals to hunt. We had such little fuel for heat in the small farmhouse that my mother had inherited. I was outside collecting the last of the apples when they came. I was only nine at the time.

"We're academics," my father cried to the soldiers who all but burst down the front door. On second glance, they weren't soldiers, but the Tzar's secret squad, a group so arcane in their thinking that occasionally they arrested or killed each other by accident.

"We have nothing. We know nothing of the Germans," my mother begged. "All we can give you is apples."

"We came for the boy," said one of the men, shoving her hard into the coal-burning stove that had little coal. "We know about the boy. He cannot fall into German hands."

"What boy?" my father repeated. "We have no children."

"We know that boy," my mother said in a low enough voice that they believed her. "That family keeps him hidden. Continue down the road for ten miles and you will find him."

They had no reason not to believe her. I took care of the rest. That secret squad was secret no more. Their ruler found them all hanging side by side from the tallest oak trees. When they came to our farm to ask, my father said, "We have never been visited by soldiers."

A few weeks later, my mother sent me out for rabbits one morning. I saw the soldiers approach and like my mother always told me, I hid deep in a hollowed-out tree until there was a chance of safety. Two cold nights later as my fingers turned blackish, I returned home. My father had been beaten and my mother's cheeks were still stained with tears. She was pacing at the door. "We've been waiting. I've packed the essentials," she said. "We'll leave in the storm. They won't come out in the storm."

We walked that night under the shroud of darkness. In the cold and the snow. We walked until field became town and we reached the unlocked basement cellar of my mother's dear friend whose husband had died in the war. The deal was struck years ago. She needed money and we needed papers. It was the perfect marriage of motives.

Tall, lanky, and blond, all three of us were transformed from Russian Nationals to natives of the Bonny Prince's England. At least on paper. My mother kept those papers safe in her clothing as we ran together. On foot. On horseback. On a train. Hungry. Cold. Tired. We stopped near the administrative center of a town called Kursk where the nice man gave us food and shelter for an afternoon and checked out our papers. He nodded. The journey would continue.

In our tattered dark wool coats, we walked the final miles until we reached the small train station. If all went well—and I planned that it would—we would travel by rail first to France and then England where we would find a new home. The dream meant going through a metal gate with a guard in the form of a burly policeman who had to check our papers before we boarded the train.

She pushed me in front of her, so I was the first sight the guard would see when it came to our little family.

"Torsk," my mother called to me. "You do what you do."

Barely looking at me, he stared down at his clipboard. "Family name and town of origin," he barked.

When there was no answer, which fit my plan just fine, he was forced to really look at me.

"Little boy," he said in perfect Russian as he blocked the entrance to the train. "Where do you live? What is the purpose of your travel?"

"I live in Plymouth. On the southern coast of England," I said in the most perfect English accent that I had never practiced a day before in my life. He stared at me and I stared at him. His doubts mixed with mine. Why was I in Mother Russia? I didn't need to answer. Without knowing why, the guard stepped back several inches until those inches became feet. He was out of the guard booth and walking backward toward the train. I continued to stare up at him as my parents and I climbed under the metal arm.

"I must stop walking backward. I must," he whispered under his breath, stepping even further back. Just one more step. One more step until you arrive, *I thought.*

He took that step off the platform and was impaled by the front of the 7:00 p.m. train arriving from Paris.

"Come! Toropit'sya!" I called to my parents in Russian, tagging at my mother's skirt. "Their confusion is our victory."

With all the guards preoccupied, we walked onto the train like we were aristocrats going on our winter vacation to more temperate climates. Without asking where to go, we found three warm beds in a half-empty train car. And my mother took the first breath she allowed herself in days.

"Tor, you must be like the rest of the boys now, moya lyubov," my mother said. "Assimilate, not annihilate."

I did not assure her because I didn't want to lie. She was my mother.

Until she wasn't.

The train was my sweet freedom from Russia and from prying eyes. Quickly, we made it through the checkpoints in the Ukraine, Hungary, Austria, and Switzerland until we arrived at the Paris train station. In the Ukraine, a nosy Russian soldier stopped and asked to see our papers. I handed him what he wanted, but he didn't have time to read them. Suddenly, his mind was consumed with his dying wife and his bleak financial life.

He fell to the ground after suffering a fatal heart attack.

Luckily, I grabbed the papers away from him before the other guards arrived. By the time we arrived in desolate Hungary, we were allowed off the train where weary local police guarding the dilapidated train station interrogated you as you arrived. I didn't have time to get a good look at the officer assigned to our car. Instead, my gaze focused on three local teenagers. One shot that nice officer in the neck.

In Austria and Switzerland, no one bothered to ask us anything. By the time we reached Paris, my mother was beside herself. "It was war," I reminded her. "Kill or be killed." Luckily for us, the French gave us free wine and cheese as we boarded a boat to England. We lived in Plymouth for eight years until I was asked by the headmaster of the school to leave immediately.

He didn't just mean school.

He demanded that we move out of the country.

I was seventeen, and would never see England again.

The New World was calling.

America.

The year was 1923 and my parents had enough money from our fruit orchard to book travel for three on the SS Monroe *to the New World. It was a hellish three-week journey in icy waters in cold, damp quarters where you could never get warm. The nights were the worst because the little cot beds were crammed so tightly and the darkness was filled with the sounds of hacking coughs and lurching contents from stomachs too upset to hold down a meal. Even the healthiest among us didn't stand a chance.*

And then as the murky morning fog parted like curtains being drawn, I saw it.

Liberty.

We arrived at Ellis Island, and quickly we were told to leave the ship, line up, and retrieve our things. Luckily, my parents were strong and my father pulled two steamer trunks, containing everything we owned in the world, along the sturdy wooden planks of the dock as it rained ice. We were led into what they called the Great Hall, a carnivorous, frightening place of endless chatter and moving bodies. It was where every immigrant had to pass through as their last walls between them and the New World.

The Great Hall was like a theater of life and death or should I say sickness and health. My mother kept a tight hold on my hand as we were tagged with the ship's number and told to climb endless stairs on our way to medical inspection. Once upstairs, the hallways were narrow and clinical with white tiles on the floors and walls. It was hot and stuffy up there, not to mention claustrophobic and mind numbing with people speaking in all languages as they pushed the line along.

"There are ten thousand people who pass through these stations every single day. Over eighty percent are successful," we were told by a kindly American nurse named Dorothy. "Don't worry, hun. Your chances are very good."

We were led up into a small box of a room where a doctor and a nurse would see us and deem us healthy for the New World.

"America can't take on the world's diseases," the nice nurse told me. "We have to screen you for tuberculosis, trachoma, and cholera. So strip off your clothes." She gasped when she saw the scars from

my beatings in the various schoolyards. In another part of the room, my mother and father were getting the same inspection as I held my breath. A chalk mark on the back of your wool coat meant you were sent to the Ellis Island Hospital and would not be admitted to the New World now or perhaps ever. Many who were branded as infirmed threw themselves into the icy water, choosing to commit suicide rather than go back.

I couldn't even look at my nurse, but occupied myself with the doctor who would decide if my mother's cough was a result of weeks spent on a freezing cold ship or a far more insidious disease. I tried to make eye contact with him, but it wasn't necessary. Miraculously, mother was told to gather her things. She passed the health inspection.

Another type of doctor was now standing over me explaining that he examined what was inside the mind. He shocked me with the coldness of what looked like gigantic metal tongs that he attached to my head. "This is to measure the circumference of your brain," he said as I squirmed. No one else's head was being put through this test. Was it a bad luck of the draw—or something else? I tried to gaze up at the doc, but he was stern. "Look straight ahead, young man," he said, adding, "People of different races have different types of heads. Some of the people have heads filled with the disease of mental illness. The minute you walked in here I could see a certain arrogance."

"Ignorance is a mental disease," I said in Russian, adding. "I am far from ignorant."

The doctor nodded and whispered into my ear, "I also come from the Motherland. And I am not ignorant either."

He put a large chalked X on the back of my small wool coat.

"Mentally unstable," he wrote on my chart. "Needs further examination."

I was admitted into the Ellis Island Hospital. My mother was hysterically screaming and crying because she was only given mere seconds to say good-bye for now. "Do not worry. We will come back for you. We will get you out of here," she said as my father dragged her away. He never looked back at me.

After all, it was their new life, too.

"What is my disease?" I shouted at the nurse as the hospital orderlies dragged me out of the room and outside, across a grassy section covered with snow. I could see the lights of New York City, illuminated like candles on a cake. It was so close, but it might as well have been across another ocean.

My America was the secret hospital at Ellis Island, a three-story, red-bricked building with locks on almost every door. I wasn't placed in the contagious disease ward where the tuberculosis patients hacked their way into each day and gasped into the night. They had their horrible two sinks, one for cleaning and one for expelling sputum.

Instead, I had a bed in what they called the psychology ward with its long, drafty corridors. My sunlight now was slivers of later afternoon that were allowed to beam through the vent shafts. There were rows of beds where men and women lay moaning and screaming, white medicinal scarves wrapped around their heads to remove the demons, and often their hands tied behind their backs with rope. There were such sad eyes. And crazy ones, too. Sometimes there is not enough rope in the world.

There were other boys my age there—nasty, psychotic boys—prone to fighting and fits of rage. Some weren't sick, but merely surly and had attacked the nurses and doctors. Branded socially ill, they were sent to the psych ward for further evaluation. As time passed, our nurses were the only ones who felt pity as the boys' families had certainly abandoned them. There would be new boys in the New World.

We were like discard animals.

On certain days, they allowed us to roam free as long as we didn't leave the hospital building. One day, six months later, during a spirited attempt to see a naked girl, we wandered far to the back of the last of the beds in the TB ward and found a room we knew was off limits, which is what made it so inviting. It was labeled the Autopsy Theater.

"Come on, Tor," said my friend Ethan. "I dare you!"

The theater was unlocked, but it wasn't really a theater at all.

It was just a large, dank room with what looked like a large concrete block, the size of a king's dining table, in the middle. Upon closer inspection, it was stained with large pools of blood. There were expansive fixtures overhead to hold candles and what looked like a massive wooden filing cabinet that was built into one of the walls. I counted ten darkly painted drawers and could smell something extremely foul coming from that section of the room. Rotting chicken came to mind.

"That's where they put 'ya," said one of my new Polish friends, Mikel, who had snuck in, too. "They put you on ice once you close your eyes for good on the way to heaven. An' I hear they keep you on that ice block to cool you down for the last time before you're sent down to hell."

"A motherless bastard like you, Tor, is probably going to hell," he said with a wicked laugh.

"Motherless?" I repeated.

"They have a new life," Mikel taunted. "They're something you will never be: An American."

I stared at him hard, but couldn't contain my rage. In that moment, I knew with certainty that he was right. There was never a letter. Never a visit. I knew that my mother and father would never be back. They had moved on. They were young enough to have more children.

Normal children.

Suddenly, my anger could not be contained. Mikel was older, stronger and I shouldn't have hit him. But I put my fist into his right eye. Fists were not enough. On the wall were various knives and other things needed to conduct 1920's autopsies. Reaching back, I found an ax on the table and swung hard at him. His fist connected with my neck and gasping hard, I heard the ax fall to the ground. When I finally had the breath to cry, he had already gripped my collar and was now shaking me violently. My head flopped back. When it lolled forward again, I could feel the blood rush hot.

Mikel flashed yellowish teeth, growling, "I'll put you out of your misery now." There was a large butcher's knife behind us, and he used it to slice my arm, the muscles of my bicep now dangling outside the skin. "You'll kill him," Ethan cried. But when he came closer and saw all the blood, I heard him whisper to Mikel, "Now you have no choice. You must kill him."

Assaulting a fellow patient was grounds to be sent back to Europe on the next ship.

But he didn't slash me again. Already I felt dizzy from the loss of blood, which was why Ethan and Mikel were strong enough to lift me and stuff me into one of those wooden drawers in the wall. "Put him in the highest one in the corner, where they won't look," Ethan whispered. "Maybe they'll think he killed himself. Put the knife in with him."

At first, I fought by flailing my legs. But the blood continued to rush. My head was swimming in a dizzy haze. The boys stood on a chair and hoisted me, shoving me into a drawer. Then they slammed it shut. The last I heard, they were running, their hard shoes clomping across the tile floor.

It felt so good to close my eyes. I vowed to only rest a few minutes.

The orderlies found my body ten days later on the next scheduled autopsy day.

They smelled something odd in the wall. The boys forgot the ice.

There was never a record of my stay at Ellis Island.

History likes to omit what needs omitting.

"Bullshit," Daniel said, grabbing my hand as we stood up from the picnic table and began to walk away. I didn't have time to react.

Tor just stood in place.

I wondered how quickly he came here. And when. If he died in 1923, that meant his stay at Frederick Reardon was nearing a hundred years.

4.

Another week passed, and I decided to let the Tor story go. It was none of my business and there was enough to keep my mind occupied and my body hurting during the daylight hours in the woods.

One of my most unusual sessions began in the woods one day after school. Suddenly flanking me on the right before one of my runs was a middle-aged African-American man in navy Lycra pants and a matching tank top. His face was round and those deeply sunken eyes were a friendly molten brown. I had never seen him before, but now we were both standing together on a pile of discarded pine needles.

"I meet a lot of ghosts, but not too many angels," he flirted with me, but it was harmless and charming.

One of those eternally positive types, his face didn't just smile. It burst into rays of man-made sunshine. "I'm your track coach, Willie James," he uttered as if it wasn't so much a fact, but a promise. "I saw tapes of your last performance in the living realm."

"Tapes," I choked.

"You have no idea," he said with the deep laugh of a Broadway tenor. "Big Brother is watching, angel, in ways you can't even fathom. Always has been. Always will be. I got some tapes of you running for the school bus in the living realm, and it wasn't pretty either."

"So, why do I need a track coach now?" I inquired, flashing back to my disastrous days at Kennedy High School where our gym teacher in a big army-green parka would demand that we dress in skimpy shorts and tees. In the freeze of zero-degree December, we were forced to trek outside and run laps around the football field.

"Angel, back there or anywhere, a good life motto is when you can't fight, you run like hell. Run like the wind," he said, reaching inside his shirt to produce what looked a lot like an antique silver medal.

"Never got a gold that year in Berlin—my one life regret. Here, I have no regrets. So let's start," Willie said.

"But Mr.—"

"Willie or you'll break my heart, angel,'" he insisted. "All the cute girls call me Willie. You're so cute, you might have to call me Will or Wonderful."

"Berlin. That was the Olympics of . . . nineteen thirty?"

"Nineteen thirty-six. Stop procrastinating. I know a playa when I see one," he said with a grin.

"You run and I'll tell you the story. I'll start with how Adolph Hitler himself was there in the stands. Those were not good times for a black man. I'll tell you all about it. But first you need to keep running. Can't walk forever, Walker. Bad joke. Let's do this."

"Willie," I said, now chugging along in the woods, swatting a bug away, and feeling like the afterlife's biggest dork, "I don't know if they told you, but I don't really do sports. I'm not the physical type. I like to read. Sitting down." Then I began to stammer. "Sometimes laying down . . . and reading. Not running."

"I want you to run like your grandmother," he instructed and when I began to protest again, he put up a hand in a good-natured, but firm way. "Everybody has a grandmother. Even Charlie Manson had a grandmother and she's waiting for him in . . . well, that's gossip. We won't go there. The point is, I want you to run as slowly right now as humanly possible where your feet are barely even moving." He sounded as earnest as a kindergarten teacher. "I told Dr. King the same exact thing many moons ago when I taught him how to run again."

I knew he was talking about Dr. King's bad leg that was partially amputated in the living realm from diabetes. "Had to get the feeling of that gimpy foot outta his mind," Willie said. "Most of running is in your mind. Got to clear your mind, too. You're too young for that much fog in there."

"One question first," I insisted, looking him square in the eye. "How fast can Dr. King run under the best of circumstances?"

"Fast as an Olympian. Like me. But to do that you have to start here," he said, running so slowly in front of me that it looked like he wasn't even moving. I tried it and found that my feet were itching to move faster. "Don't give in. You keep it grandma slow," Willie insisted.

We ran in slow motion through the pine-scented trees that reached deep into clouds. At times, I forgot we were even running because Willie had me enthralled with the story of how he met Dr. King.

"Had a little too much weight on him and rocks in his head, all right," Willie said. "It was the night that school shooter took poor Dr. King out—but let's not go there. Dr. King arrived at the Academy and the first thing he wanted to do was test his gimpy leg. But not in front of anybody. So, he decided to go running at night, so none of the kids could see him gimping along. He was ashamed of his legs even though they worked now. He just wasn't so sure he could trust it. He was chugging along, dragging a perfectly good foot. I was training in the woods, stopped and said, 'What are you doing, boss? Why are you pretending you have a draggy leg? You don't have one no more.' Well, Marvin . . . I mean . . . Dr. King stopped in his tracks, looked me dead in the eye, and said, 'I don't know.'"

"It was the beginning of a beautiful friendship," Willie continued. "I ran next to Dr. King on that cold, dark night and in time he began to pick up that bad foot. In no time, he was running, but slow like I made him. Finally, one cold night, not that it mattered to us, he stopped on our thirty-third lap around the property and asked, 'So how far did we go Willie?' I told him, 'Boss, about ten miles! Keep goin.'" Willie laughed as I chugged along slowly.

"I was doing some custodials at the time at the Academy. Dr. King brought me up to his office and sat me down," he said. "He asked if I'd like to go running again. Every single day."

"I told him as long as it didn't interrupt my work," Willie explained while running backward to check my progress. He moved in microspeed.

"And then Dr. King said, 'Well it won't, because you are going to work as the new track and field coach here at the Academy.' Every single night when he wasn't busy or occupied with student arrivals, Dr. King and I had our nightly run and philosophizing session," Willie said. "He had a soft spot for you, Miss Walker. Said you reminded him of his daughter. That man might have seemed hard, but I always knew when he played favorites—at least in his own mind. I do hope I have the chance, and honor, to run with him again soon."

I couldn't *not* ask him.

"Willie, if Dr. King had to run on the bad leg without the reset—and please don't ask me why—could he do it? Would he have it in him?" I asked in a rushed voice.

"Miss Walker," Willie said matter-of-factly. "I know what I'm training you for. And as for Dr. King, well let's just say I taught him everything he knows, which is a lot of knowing."

Willie motioned for me to stop and gladly I put on the brakes.

"You're going back to New York. Some of the very best years of Dr. Marvin King's life were in New York. I don't expect he'd stay in Chicago with all that riffraff on the demonic front. My money is he'd sneak out of town. New York has a lot of nooks and crannies. It's good for hiding. An old ghost could get lost there and stay lost. Until the time was right and he could run for the right portal."

"You really think it's possible Willie?" I asked, chugging along. I had a lot of training to do, and I would take it seriously.

"Walker, it's the possibility that makes me wake up every morning. Not the guarantee."

5.

That night when the kids were asleep, Daniel and I went for a midnight swim in our lake. My mind was clouded with thoughts of our New York mission and Daniel was on the razor's edge of tossing his body off a cliff to de-stress.

Swimming sounded like a better option.

I was wearing a saucy little black bikini that just showed up on my dresser, as did several little goodies these days. One day there was another pretty dress; the next I found sexy new jeans. Of course, I could have gone to town and "bought" all of them for free since that was the going price here. But it meant more to receive them. Daniel didn't say much about it. But he smiled each time I did a quick twirl to show him how much I appreciated his thoughtfulness. "The bikini wasn't thoughtful," he growled. "I'm a selfish bastard."

It's true that the bathing suit was one of his most outrageous gifts. There wasn't much of it except some well-placed triangles. All things considered, I was overdressed for the occasion. Daniel got to the lake, casually stripped down, and dove in wearing a smile and his tats.

A lemon moon was drifting softly in the background as I wrapped my legs around his middle. It dawned on me that this was the same lake I had fallen into so long ago. Back then, I couldn't wait to get out, as I was sure I was drowning. Tonight, I had run through the woods hand-in-his-hand dying to jump in.

Everything was different now. With my legs still secured on Daniel, I did a graceful backbend until the upper part of my torso was floating with nothing but love and passion shining on my face.

"We should probably go back. Get some sleep," I murmured, the water gently lapping my sides.

"I'm not that dead," Daniel growled again, his hands wrapped around my waist. He lifted me forward until we met in the middle. All I could do was feel.

It was summer.

Summer always means love.

CHAPTER 16

1.

The next day was Friday and we had to keep up appearances, which meant another day at school. As usual, the morning was chaotic enough with Bobby going on and on about his new teacher 'prentice who was now his "bestest friend in the entire world."

"He looks like a big panda-bear man without the furries," Bobby insisted, dropping down on all fours to show us how real bears navigated terrain as we all walked to the Academy. Jenna, Andy, and Pete broke away early when they saw their friends.

I stuck with Bobby on our way to a small elementary school on the property for smaller kids who arrived with their older siblings. Bobby was quickly accepted in every single way. He had his teachers, friends, and real knowledge. The kid was reading like a ten-year-old. "I'm crazy 'vanced," he told me. "Almost a genie."

"Genius," I repeated.

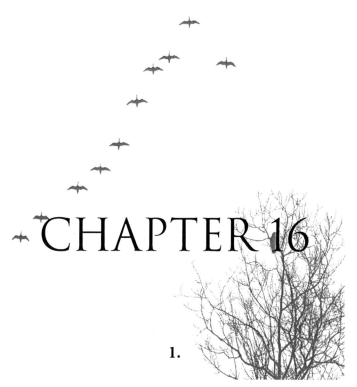

"Yeah, a genie," he said, racing around me like he did earlier this morning when I tried to get him to take his pants off his head. I was a lenient "parent" and allowed him to jump on his bed, which was his favorite spot thanks to a new Star Wars comforter. I had to smile. The genie owned my heart.

A few times, he actually called me "Mom" by mistake, but always covered it up in his maniac little way by making fake fart noises with his mouth or doing a quick cartwheel. When he said it again today, he said, "Sorry, Walkie, I know I didn't come from your tummy, but I don't really 'member lots about my mommy. But I know she was pretty—from the pictures Danny shows me. So . . ." His face was flushed with embarrassment like we were entering unknown waters. "So, you're it," he said, tagging me like we were playing a game. But we weren't.

"It's okay toad-face," I told him. "You better learn some good stuff today because I want a smart kid in my house."

"Auggie said I'm 'tremely 'telligent," he repeated after we said good-bye to Daniel and the rest of the brood. Bobby was actually dragging me by the hand to meet the one who he had dubbed his new *bestest* buddy.

He wasn't the main teacher, but like Bobby gushed, the new teacher's apprentice, which basically meant he was a glorified student intern.

What else can I say about the first time I met Auggie O'Connor? Let's start with the physical. He was a big teddy bear of a guy at about six foot four with an equally wide frame that was solid, but not chunky. He looked to be about seventeen with a sweet, handsome face, sprinkled with freckles, that was meaty and full—thanks to the fact that he pulled his long mid-back strawberry-blond hair straight off his forehead, capturing it in a leather ponytail holder. My first thought on meeting him was that he was a little *nuts.* Hanging upside down with three kids on the monkey bars, his large melon head touched the stones underneath. The ponytail sunk into the sea of pebbles.

"You look like bats," I said, grinning.

"I don't want to be Batman," he retorted, still hanging. "Maybe Batshit, but that's not a good superhero name."

Even upside down, Auggie's smile made me grin.

"He's an amazing creature. The little upright wombat next to you," Auggie said, still upside down, which delighted Bobby to the point he ran around like a lunatic screaming, "I'm a bat from the black lagoon! I live in a cave. I breathe in rain and spit fire!"

"And such a calm child," I joked as Auggie righted himself by falling hard on his back into the pit of rocks. The kids loved it and began to dance around him like this was some ritual.

"Gotta love the reset," he said, shaking himself off and offering a big, meaty hand that looked like a catcher's mitt.

"Auggie," he said.

"Walker Callaghan," I replied.

"Really?" he replied, looking at me quizzically. "Bet there aren't many Walkers around here."

"So far, I'm a limited edition," I replied, but Auggie didn't laugh. After all, he was a bit preoccupied. Giving me the "just a sec" finger, I watched Auggie race over to catch three kids who decided it would be fun to face-plant off the top of the slide into the rocks. "No Supermanning kids," he instructed, and I gave him an admiring nod. "Or Superwomanning," he added. Turning to me, he said, "The last thing I am is dead and sexist."

Later, after a short talk about Bobby's academic progress, I hugged my little wombat and went to class knowing that the big bear 'prentice had our little guy's back. That was the way it was up here. People pitched in. They cared.

In an unexpected good mood from hanging with the kids, I hiked to class the long way, purposely stopping by the Academy

Stables, a serene place where powerful creatures were allowed to roam free in the meadows. Breathing in deeply, I smelled musky horse and sharp pine combined with freshly cut summer grass—but that wasn't all. It was layered today with the pollution of car exhaust. Before I could figure it out, the spooked horses in the pen bolted as a silver Mercedes screeched to a halt inches away from me.

The driver barely cracked the window as if the pungent, animal-scented air might sicken him. He was curt and made his agenda known without any polite padding.

"Get in," said Edward Reid.

2.

Sometimes the only thing you can do is open the door and slide. Edward certainly wasn't going to do the polite thing and push it open for me. Once the heavy Mercedes metal clicked shut, he took off slowly, not saying a word, but just driving. He had a way of directing the car forward while looking at me, which made me feel queasy.

"Miss Callaghan, I've been biding my time and waiting for a little face-to-face with you. Just you. I'll take your eagerness to jump into my car as a sign that you also have *things* on your mind," Edward said.

It was his opening statement. The car was obviously his court of law.

I was actually speechless as he continued to drive under a summer sky filled with pregnant rain clouds dusted dark. It made me uneasy that we were advancing in the exact opposite direction of the main Academy buildings. "Where are we going?" I finally asked in the calmest way possible. Edward refused to answer. Despite his short stature, he filled the space in a way that made me feel like I wanted to roll down a window and jump out, mid-ride.

Edward's one good arm, his right, loped over the steering wheel. Today, the coat was off because of the humid air. His wound, and it was odd to see one here, was covered by an expensive long-sleeved shirt with the lower unoccupied fabric blowing back and forth horrifically thanks to the heavy wind of the car's cranked-up air conditioner. It was that cold in the car, but that's not why I shivered.

"You remind me of my wife," he finally said to break the silence again. The quiet that followed was hysterically loud. No radio. No outside noise. Just the steady wind from the car's ever-pumping vents.

"In what way?" I posed, forcing myself to say *something*. "How do I remind you of Mrs. Reid?" I said her name slowly. Deliberately. I knew he didn't want to be reminded.

"In a way where men like myself, and now my son, are tricked into believing in some level of compatibility."

He was going right in again and I knew I couldn't match the master lawyer. But I could give him the type of answer he wanted. "Now, I'm totally confused," I said in a voice that best mimicked Demanda. It wouldn't hurt to let him think that he was in charge.

"Let me spell it out for you, Miss Callaghan," he said, slamming on the brakes, which caused me to jettison forward and almost smash my chest into the dash. He didn't apologize or ask if I was harmed. My safety was the least of his concerns. "As I was saying," Edward began again. "All that apple-pie, Chevrolet, blue-collar, beer-guzzling, red-white-and-blue, can-do spirit you wear on your sleeve. It won't help you or my eldest on your fool's mission."

"And what will help me, Mr. Reid," I said in the same confused voice.

"What will help you, Miss Callaghan, is cutting the proverbial crap. Why don't you drop the act? Besides, like I said, I've read your permanent record. You're a straight-A student, and far from stupid," he said in a blunt voice. "So let's start again. I wanted to have this little meeting with you, so I could actually help you."

"And what will help me, Edward?" I bit out.

"A representative," he announced.

"A what?"

"What you need is someone in an advisory position, like myself, to plead your case to the Higher Authority."

"Plead a case for what?"

"Mercy," he said.

3.

He had driven as far as the outer reaches of the meadows where the Academy kept prize racehorses that few were allowed to ride. I could see New Zealand's Phar Lap and even Secretariat—plus Seabiscuit himself doing gentle lopes across grass so green you wanted to roll in it. A light rain was dripping now and the drops rolled casually off the horses' manes as they stood watching. I've always felt that horses were mystical creatures. And now I knew I was right. The wisdom was in their eyes. My hand was suddenly rubbing the horse pendant that I almost never took off now, the one that belonged to Mrs. Reid. Maybe it would give me the kind of strength that it gave her back in the days when she had to face off with her husband.

Oblivious was one word for it. Cold was another. Edward didn't notice my choice in jewelry.

"Walker, if I may call you that," Edward continued from the confines of our private chamber inside the Mercedes. "I've been dead for what seems like a nanosecond. But I still like to move fast. So, I'll cut to the proverbial chase because who knows how much time we have anywhere."

I didn't care about his real reason for sequestering me today. This time I interrupted him because before we went any further. I needed to know—and someday Daniel and Pete did, too.

"You survived a plane crash. Don't tell me that something far less dramatic brought down the great Edward Reid. In other words, why are you here?"

"I wondered when one of you would get around asking," he taunted.

Since I asked, I'd be the one to get answers.

Death Story: Edward Reid

Age of Demise: 52

Son of a . . . It was a scandal wrapped up in innuendo and gossip. And the best part was no one gave a damn about me. I was the famous one, written about constantly in the Trib. Why didn't they rush to find out how I was recovering? What about my time in that hospital bed with the leg fractured in three places? Of course, I demanded to go home after only a week in ICU. A Reid never lies down. Never.

As for the children, it was, in a word, unfortunate. I might miss some of them, but a Reid also faces the sharp point of reality: they were gone. Although I preferred to remind the nosy reporter from the Chicago Tribune *and the suck-up, social-climbing writer from* Vanity Fair *that the children were now with their mother. Isn't that where children are supposed to be? There was a certain poetic justice to it, if you thought about it . . . over a nice glass of Merlot.*

Of course, there were the strategic photo ops. I was wheeled to the grave sites—six in a row at Lake Forest Cemetery—in my chair where in the brutal January weather, windchill of eleven below, I managed to stand, drop my head into my chest, and shiver. Some said that I cried. And perhaps I did. I was that cold and the windchill was a bitch.

By spring, it was time for my cast to come off—and retire the grieving father act. Get on with it, I like to say. The divorce that followed was necessary because when one life ends, it opens what remains to new possibilities. And Mrs. Brittany Reid was starting to bore me, as they all eventually did. She was happy to settle for a condo in Boca, her jewelry, plus a small settlement. For better, for worse, for richer, for . . . now. She ended up telling the National Enquirer *that I was so distraught over the loss of the children that I retreated into my own private hell. It was the nicest thing she had ever done for me. She earned an extra $50,000 for that one.*

I was back on the market, childless, burden free, and ready to embrace life as a single mogul. There was only one thing that ate away at me at three in the morning in that big drafty house. I could fly. I was an excellent pilot. Damn those who said that I wasn't. Didn't they know it was all the kids fault? They were the ones who couldn't move their lazy asses fast enough to beat that winter storm. They sealed their own fate.

My fate was to buy a brand-new plane, but this time I went for a prop plane that my new instructor, Jeffrey, told me was a lot easier to control. For f— sake, every movie star on the planet was flying around Los Angeles in them. If it was good enough for Harrison Ford, it better be good enough for Edward Reid.

This time, I took all the flight lessons. I paid Jeffrey an exorbitant amount to take me up in the air to practice. He commended me when it came to my excellent attention to detail, especially because I kept him on payroll. One might say I became OCD about it. Before each flight, I would even walk around the plane, making sure my equipment was top-notch. I would prove them all wrong. I would solo.

It was one of those warm summer nights in Lake Forest where the air was thick, as was the boredom. I had sprung another client from Joliet Prison, and I wanted to celebrate. Antsy for a challenge, I drove the new Lamborghini to the executive airport to check on my plane. "I might not take her out tonight, Mr. Reid," Jeffrey said. "Tom Skilling on WGN said thunderstorms are rolling over Lake Michigan. They're even shutting down a few runways at O'Hare."

"Nonsense!" I said. "Tom Skilling couldn't predict rain if it was falling on his bald head!"

"Mr. Reid, there is no one else at the airport because of the storm. I'd strongly advise you to—" Jeffrey warned.

"I'd strongly advise you to keep your mouth shut," I retorted. In that moment, it all came flashing back. I would not be rattled by these naysayers.

He needed that monthly stipend after Afghanistan and walked away when I went through my preflight check. It was my favorite part. An air of excitement came over me. It wouldn't be long before I'd climb in the cockpit.

The Piper Twin Commander. She was silver and sleek. She was mine. My baby was always waiting for me. Silent. Ready for my hand. I loved to stand in front of her, admiring her gleaming beauty.

Thunderstorms, my ass! The sky was black and clear.

I heard it before my eyes allowed it to register. It began with a slow twirl, which became faster and faster. I was standing on the ground. How could it be possible? The plane was whirling to life. Dumbfounded, I watched as the blade speed became supersonic, not even stopping when it sliced into the skin of my left shoulder. My baby cut deeply into my flesh, above my elbow, and lopped my arm clean off.

My eyes glazed while a hot fire ignited my left side.

When I crumbled to the ground, in front of my plane, I forced myself to look into the near distance. My arm was only several inches away. Out of reach.

My mind knew what to do: Jeffrey would put it on ice. The surgeon would sew it back on. I would be back flying in no time.

But it wasn't Jeffrey who calmly walked to my side.

A young black man, about fifteen, and wearing a White Sox shirt, slowly removed himself from the cockpit and casually approached as if he was shy. "I've been critically injured," I cried, blood pouring out of my arm and shock setting in. "You must call for help. Do you know who I am? Take my phone from my pocket. Call an ambulance, you stupid—"

"I know who you are, Edward. Now it's time you know me. I'm Antoine from the South Side," he said, reaching out, but not to shake my other hand. He was invading my suit pocket.

He was going to rob me?

But he didn't take my wallet. Instead, he reached for my phone and once he found it, raised it up in the air, then threw it hard to the ground where it cracked open. That wasn't enough. I watched him place it under his Jordans. He smashed his foot down hard.

"You got Abe 'Killer' Burke from the Outfit off those murder charges yesterday," he said. "Congratulations are NOT in order."

By now, I had lost feeling in the top part of my body and my legs began to shake violently. I could smell the steely scent of fresh blood that was inching toward a nearby drain. "Please. Call 911. I'm a very rich man. I will give you whatever you want," I panted.

The blood started to pool and flow back toward my face now.

"But we're not done with our story," said the young man. "When you got Killer off he came back to the projects and shot the only person who could testify against him the next time. That man was my daddy."

"Please! You will be set for life. Call 911," I begged, my breathing feathery light now.

"Why would I want to talk on the phone when I can talk to you," he said, sitting down in a metal folding chair where the mechanics ate lunch. He reached into his pocket and produced what looked like a baseball magazine. "In fact, I'm going to sit here, read about the Sox's chances this year, and watch a different kind of justice—street justice," he said.

I moaned.

"The truth is I was going to shoot you, but you made it much easier. You were standing there livin' large. Like you owned the world. Standing there. In front of the propeller. I lucked out with the buttons," he said. "Tech school. Paid with your tax dollars."

He had a question for me. I didn't have the energy to object.

"How could you even fly again? You're the guy who killed all his kids, now aren't you?"

"I'm an excellent pilot," I gasped.

When I woke up, I was somewhere else. Not here. But then I was summoned.

You know the rest.

But I didn't know. I didn't know where he went or why he wasn't made whole again.

I didn't know how I could even continue to look at him, and it had nothing to do with his amputation.

Most of all, I didn't know how much longer I could pretend to be stronger than I was feeling. I was usually a master at this art, but he made me feel small and diminished.

I also knew one more thing and it gave me that ounce of bravery: I had one last question.

"I still don't know the real reason why you summoned me here today," I stated, purposely not giving him any reaction.

"I'm here to save you, Miss Callaghan," he responded. "I can fix it so you don't have to go on the mission."

I couldn't hide the shock that registered on my face. *He was giving me an "out" while sending off his two oldest sons to their final extinction.*

"You do remember the demons, Miss Callaghan, don't you?" he began. "Surrounding you. Engulfing you. Devouring you. Extinguishing you."

Yes, I remembered.

"Plus," Edward almost whispered, going in for the bloodless kill. "Wouldn't my son be more focused to survive those attacks without you? You're the ultimate anchor around his neck."

Drawing a deep breath, the master manipulator felt he was winning. And there was a big part of me that knew Daniel would protect me . . . against all odds. He'd sacrifice himself first. It weighed heavily on me, infiltrating my dreams at night. I remembered the portal in the living realm and how he fought the demons, so Bobby and I could return here. Daniel was a breath away from never returning.

"And may I ask, how will you 'live' with yourself for the rest of eternity knowing that your actions led to my eldest son's eternal demise?" Edward stated, then paused for a moment. "Could you," he began again, going in for the win, "really live—or whatever you do here—with that? Could you go on?"

He took my silence as his answer.

"I could work a deal," Edward continued. "I can always work a deal."

Right then, it sunk in. *He thinks that "saving" me increases the odds that his sons won't come back.* It was official. Edward Reid was the devil.

Five words silenced him for a moment.

"Why are you really here?" I asked again.

He was slow with his response, the lawyer in him knowing that he had the jury in his back pocket and now it was just about making everyone squirm when it came to the terms of the settlement.

"This isn't *just* about me," he began, our eyes finally connecting. "It has occurred to me that my other children have become quite fond of you. From my one detestable counseling session—and I hate shrinks—I was told that they would be devastated if they lost both of their worthless oldest brothers and their new surrogate mother."

"Yeah," I stated, "I'm freaking Maria from *Sound of Music*."

Edward smiled as I dug my fingernails into his Corinthian leather.

"I have a settlement offer for you—of sorts," he proposed. "What if I told you that I'd give you *some* of them?"

Some of his children?

"I have no use for girls," he said in a matter-of-fact tone. "I told my wife Maureen time and time again that I didn't want to raise a barn full of children, least of all girls who are always whining, shrieking, crying messes. If I could dump the girls at some eternity orphanage I would. Giving them to you is the next best thing. "

"You can have them," he offered like he was giving away free puppies. "I'll tell Miss Elizabeth it's in Kelly and Andrea's best interest to stay with you. Forever."

"Your daughter's names are Andy and Jenna," I corrected him. Edward just shrugged. "And since you're hoping that Daniel and Pete don't survive the mission . . . there is just one question left? What about Bobby?" I asked.

"My youngest son is nonnegotiable. He's mine," he said, tossing his lit cigarette out the window he momentarily cracked. "He's the true unformed. Impressionable. Moldable. Malleable enough to be salvaged."

"Salvaged?" I repeated.

"Young Robert Edward Reid, named partly after me, is small enough to convince that his eldest brothers left *again* and betrayed him *again* just like they did when they left him at the crash site for all those years. I plan to take him," Edward said, filling in the blanks. "He's my son. The true Reid heir. I can mold him in my image."

The fury racing through my blood was so intense that it seemed to boil in my veins, causing my hands to shake. Wiling them to stop trembling, I allowed my head to lower, hair falling forward and shielding my face like a veil. Slowly I looked up.

Our eyes locked.

"Give me your word and I'll go to the Higher Authority. I'm the master at working a deal," he said with a self-satisfied smile.

His expression said, *It's in the bag.*

Edward held out his good hand. To shake on it.

I held up my hand.

"I give you my word," I said, keeping my fingers just out of reach. "You will never see your children again."

I dropped my hand and continued. "I will go back to the living realm to complete this mission with your two other heirs, Daniel and Peter. And when we come back here with whatever the Higher Authority wants, one of the conditions of giving it to them will be that none of us, including Bobby, will ever see you again."

He sat deathly still. His eyes seared into mine.

"Hell isn't a good place to raise children," I taunted him.

My moment of victory was short-lived.

With his good hand, he grabbed me by the back of my neck and drew me even closer as he yanked my hair back. "Who will fold first?" he hissed. "Who is stronger?"

"Me. You can only play one hand, Eddie," I said, purposely shoving him until his stump hit the car window.

"You little bitch," he screamed. It was enough time for me to grab my door handle and slide right off that fancy leather into the warm embrace of the rainy outdoors. The smell of wet grass and free, pungent champion horses was never sweeter.

"I'll make sure to give your children, *all* of your children—the heirs and the spares—your best regards," I said slamming the heavy door.

As he pulled away, I shouted, "Enjoy your time here—however limited it might be."

4.

I didn't follow big Willie's advice.

I sprinted down a dreary dead-end road, accidentally stumbling upon a path that took me all the way to the back door of the Academy's gymnasium. Hands trembling, I ripped off my clothes and slid into my regulation uniform of white cotton shorts and a matching tee with a big A on it. My first class was PE and Walter was the one who noticed the mood.

"Walker, you wanna just kick my ass? You look like you woke up on the wrong side of the bed. Maybe you woke up on the floor," he joked, tossing me a regulation hardball from a bin of baseballs. One word came to mind.

"Dodgeball," I said, a wicked gleam in my eyes.

"Badminton seems like a piss-poor idea," Walter retorted, chuckling as he grabbed a large bin filled with regulation major-league baseballs.

"Break up into two teams," he shouted. "Tosh, you're one team leader. Amanda, you're the other." Over my shoulder, I gave Walter a nod. It was almost as if he was setting it up in my favor. Then the "almost" was scratched. "You owe me for this Callaghan," he said.

With her posse of long-haired princess types surrounding

her, including that new poser, Legs, from the bus accident, Demanda had that usual condescending look in her baby blues—half dismissive, half pure hatred. With one pristinely manicured fingernail painted navy blue, she flipped me a quick bird from the other side of the line where her team of future Miss Dead Teen USAs were setting up.

"*Orange is the New Black* looks weak today," she whispered to Ashley, one of her favorite blonde minions who gave me patented ECA: eye contact abuse.

"I heard that over at ITT, Walker had a big prison social life. Lot of maximum-security boyfriends," Demanda cooed as she practiced aiming in my direction. Then she blew me a kiss.

Walter blew the whistle.

It took only a minute. With all the rage still inside me from my morning with Edward Reid, I wailed on her. She aimed for my face and I flinched fast, zeroing in on her midsection. There's no six-pack in the world that could defeat a regulation major-league baseball.

Turns out my new professional training for the mission, and hours spent trying to find a specialty, had made me surprisingly limber and shockingly fast. My aim was dead on.

The IRA guys were actually working on my arm, handing me throwing star after throwing star to practice. I remembered their words. *Focus! Put the enemy into your scope! Stack the odds.* The latter is why I spit into my hands, rubbing the oozy fluid on the ball for a better grip. Then my right hand flew backward for the windup and I put her in my scope until . . . bam! Not only did the ball smack Demanda hard in the forehead this time, but it also bounced and—thanks to all that spit—burrowed deeply into the crown of her hair. She had enough spray in that 'do to make the ball really stick.

Demanda screamed at the top of her lungs, which sounded

like a fire drill—but we didn't have those here. She wasn't hurt. The reset took care of that issue. Humiliation, however, had no reset. Arms, legs, chest, and face burning crimson red, she recklessly dug into her hair to find the ball, burrowing it deeper into her bun. When she pulled much too hard, a thick patch of stick-straight golden-blonde hair was victimized and stuck to her hand. In her fury, Demanda yanked it completely by the roots. Her freak-out reached epic decibels.

"Oh my God!" Demanda shrieked. "Someone call 911. Wait, we don't have 911! Help! My hair! You bitch!"

When I passed her later on the bench, I did the one thing that I knew would make it worse. I looked into Demanda's eyes and laughed. Loud enough for her to hear, I kept walking and laughing. Finally, I said, "Ah, the bad hair era continues. Such a pity, baldie."

"What did you call me?" Demanda demanded.

"Baldie. You know. That would be your prison name," I replied, continuing to walk as I said, "Remember, I was in there a long time. Learned a lot of things that you might find really upsetting at best, or hazardous to your already fragile mental health, Demanda." It was the first time I actually called her that to her face.

I wish I could say that it didn't feel good—it didn't. It felt great.

5.

In music class, Kurt was attempting to teach us how to play the bass guitar. "Walker, you're not supposed to rip the strings off the thing," he said, demonstrating again as I sat alone at a back table. Daniel was off somewhere. Cutting class again. What else was new? I was used to it and gave him his space.

Where he went and why he was seldom in class was his business, and today I was glad. The last thing I wanted to do was tell him about my encounter with his dear old dad. Go hunting—that's what Daniel would do. He'd hunt Edward down, maybe punch him a few times, and then land himself back in ITT.

I skipped lunch because small talk and tacos with Tosh and Gracie or a celebratory high five over the Demanda situation didn't seem to be in my wheelhouse today. Instead, I wandered back to the elementary school, my stomach in a ball of knots, despite the lovely warm day. I was worried about Bobby. What would I do if Edward showed up there to keep his eye on the little "heir"?

It turns out the only vehicle outside the picture-perfect red schoolhouse was a sunshine-yellow school bus. Needing a little extra confirmation, I snuck around to the back where Bobby was shrieking that he was Spider-Man and racing through the fenced yard with five other little hellions at his heels. The little guy didn't see me and it was better that way. It was his time to just be.

Because the hand was so suddenly and firmly planted on my shoulders, I couldn't run.

Jump reflex: 12.

Concern clouded his handsome face and he quickly dropped his hand to his side.

"Harold!" I sighed with relief at the sight of my favorite gate guard.

"Got a minute for a little one-on-one?" he said, motioning me to follow him down a white stoned path that led away from the elementary school. It seemed like all I had been doing all day was walking these grounds and having conversations that I didn't necessarily want to have.

In boots, a short skirt, and a T-shirt with a flannel over it, despite the heat, I was setting the pace for Harold who was in pearly white athletic shoes, basketball shorts, and a black tee. It was a far cry from his gate guard's uniform and I admired the way his sinewy forearms burst out of those shirtsleeves.

"I'm on break," he said, easily keeping up. "Maude Travis monitors the gate from twelve to one, so I can do my run. No one dares cross her. The only bad thing is she sprays that Jean Naté perfume all over the place. Drives me nuts."

Despite my day, I had to laugh.

"One must keep the body in maximum working order for all future journeys," Harold said, shadowboxing the air. "You never know when you're going to have to deal with some scumbag, piece of you-know-what ex-lawyer from Chicago in a silver Mercedes."

He knew. He always knew.

"Don't worry," he said. "I have my eye on that little boy. That bastard won't touch him—or take him. Or convince him to go with him. The kid is much too smart. That boy knows with every molecule of his pint-sized being that you can't trust a poison mind."

"He had a private talk with me today."

"I know," Harold replied. "Near the stables."

"Jeez, Harold. Do you know what I had for lunch? Do you know my old blood type?" I had to admire the guy. He had a lot on his so-called plate.

"You didn't eat lunch, but Tosh is still waiting for you. You were O negative. So let's get right to it. What did Edward Reid want from you? What crooked line did he want you to cross?" Harold demanded, walking backward now, as he looked hard into my face. "Brief me."

It was an order from an ex-CIA agent. The only thing was, I wasn't so sure how "ex" Harold was when it came to being official.

I felt hollow as I told him Edward's terms.

"I am going with Daniel," I concluded. "That's nonnegotiable."

"But now you're wondering about what happens when you leave? Who will protect the boy? You'd make a good agent, Walker,"

Harold said. "But since you're a student and I am . . . what I am, I'll tell you exactly how it will go."

Harold stopped on a dime, which meant I put on the brakes.

"The boy is not going anywhere—with anyone," Harold said.

"How do you know that?"

"You don't have QX clearance, so I can't tell you," Harold retorted.

I stopped for a moment to consider it.

"In other words, chill," I said with a slight smile.

"Officially . . . chill," Harold said. He was not smiling.

I wasn't sure if the QX clearance could answer my real question.

"Do you believe in evil, Harold?"

Harold took a few steps, then stopped again to lean on an ancient oak tree. "Yes, I do," he said, staring off into the distance. "I'm not so sure that evil isn't here now. Maybe it's not just inside of one person, but it's a feeling buried deep inside each of us. The question remains: Do I let my evil come out and play today?" He paused then added, "Evil is also infectious."

"And the weapon against evil is . . . ?" I asked him.

Harold's already low voice became even lower.

"When we die, Walker, what remains of us? Answer: our bones. Inside them is the essence. The marrow. Why do people say that they feel it in their bones? *Because they do.* That feeling helps us separate good and evil."

I stared up at him.

"Remember, they buried your bones, but not what really lurked inside of you, which is the essence of you. That's what ascended. What was inside. That's what's here and what will move on—along with that pretty smile. That essence is what fights evil," Walter said.

Then his eyes sparkled, although clouds were covering the sky.

"Edward knows that you have the marrow to mess up his game. It scares the crap out him—and it should," Harold said. "His wife had the same thing. He knows who you are because he met someone like you many years ago. *He married her. Created children with her he couldn't control.* Now, he wants to get rid of who you are. *What* you are. *What you will be.*"

His words didn't empower me, but stuck in my throat. I didn't want to be anything now but a student at the Academy living with Daniel and the Reid family. Edward's mere presence threatened to take it all. One tear slipped. Mortified, I didn't brush it away. I allowed it to fall to the ground.

"I never cried over anything that didn't love me," Harold said. "Think about it." And with that, he righted himself and jogged away.

6.

By the time I finished my last class, the sun was low in the afternoon sky and the towered peaks of the main building burned amber bright like they were washed in gold.

Safe in the warmth of the Academy library where I would do a little research on Edward Reid (information is power), I was only half listening to librarian Maya who nervously handed me a small electronic device. "Remember Walker, no drag racing. No bumper cars. And for God's sake, buckle up tight and keep your hands inside your pod. They can lift up to a hundred and fifty stories in under three seconds."

The stacks—packed with books and research on all subject matters under the sun and beyond—were located in the towers of the library and were only reachable by machine. I knew from past adventures that the towers reached over two hundred stories up in the air, making this the tallest library ever created. The grandness was breathtaking.

"I know you took a lesson last year, but you've never driven before, so here are the particulars: The top of the pod is made of glass. Make sure you look at all your sensors. They will tell you if someone is above or below you," Maya added, nervously. "In other words, don't crash. Crashing goes on your permanent record. You crash and you lose your pod privileges for six months."

Maya waited until the end to ask the ten-million-dollar question. "You did drive in the living realm, didn't you dear?" the kindly librarian asked, running a hand through her short black hair. Her tone remained several notches beyond simply concerned.

The truth was I was a city girl who was afraid of that kind of harried driving and cabbies who looked like they were in the middle of a video game and set on demolition. We didn't have the extra money for a second car and it was just easier to take busses and trains everywhere. Mom doubled as a pretty good limo service—on call 24-7.

"I'm an excellent driver," I stated, looking everywhere but into her eyes. It was true that the few times I drove around a suburban parking lot, I didn't crash into anything or anyone.

Pressing an electronic starting device into my hand, she just shook her head and pointed to the extreme back of the library. It took a few minutes to wander over there, but once I arrived, I knew I was in the right place. The pods, all 200 to 300 of them, were lined up against a wall that went straight up as far as the eye could see. It looked like a used car lot for UFOs.

I'm not usually aspiring to get to higher surfaces (okay, I have a small fear of heights), so I took a deep breath and approached a blank-faced, middle-aged newcomer to the Academy named Garry (from his nameplate). He looked up from his book on Eastern philosophy and mindlessly pushed a button on his desk.

Too soon, a driverless pod filled the open space. Garry moved his two hands in a quick, sweeping motion, indicating that he was busy and I needed to get going now. He sounded bored when he read me the list of rules from an index card. "No joy flying. No drag flying. Don't go too fast. No playing bumper pods with friends or enemies."

"I'm here alone today," I said. "No friends."

"My friends tell me I have an intimacy problem. But they don't really know me," Garry said. He didn't give me time to laugh. He just shook his head and added, "Oh, and no food or beverages in the pod. Do I have to search you?"

"I'm not even packing a water," I said.

"I don't really care," he said as in good-bye.

I was *ready to go, oh no.*

Breathe. My ride looked like a souped-up silver oyster with a half circle of glass window on top. "Buckle up," Garry said as an afterthought. "Don't purposely crash into people. Don't blast the radio."

"There's a radio?" I shot back.

"Hit the button that says radio. Hit the arrow pointing up to go up. Hit the arrow going forward to go forward," Garry said. "It's just like driving a . . . pod."

As the pod hovered next to me waist high, I bit my bottom lip and tried to be dainty when it came to climbing in. But the little silver oval was too high and hovered near my waist. Lifting one foot in a skirt wouldn't work. There was no choice, but to stand on one of those little plastic library chairs and hurl myself in. When both feet were inside, I plopped down with a thud.

The pods were built for one, and the seat was so low that I felt like I'd fall through the shimmering, iridescent floor.

The next sound I heard was the glass top sliding down over my head like a retractable convertible roof. Garry made a circle with his hand. Then he did it again. On the third circle, I got it. And I searched for (and like the tech dork I am eventually found) the button to roll down the driver's side window.

"I only have twenty other pods checked out, so there won't be much traffic," he said. "But keep your eye out for other students. Even with the reset, running over a pedestrian isn't the way to deal with your hormonal issues."

Nodding, I checked out my instrumentation panel. There were only four arrows, up, down, forward, and back. *Piece of cake.* On the floor at my feet, there was the "go" pedal and the brake pedal, which was labeled "stop." How hard could it be?

I said a silent prayer as I tapped the go, putting my pod into drive. Obviously, you didn't leave your finger on the up button for too long. Jettisoning at least twenty stories up in a nanosecond, my head flew back, but the reset kicked in before the whiplash could. Somehow I maneuvered enough to not crash into a lower ceiling painted by Monet.

Harnessing my inner Han Solo, I alternated between the go and the brakes as I sputtered midair, turning myself around in several quick circles. I could imagine all the freshmen down below laughing at me. It was official: I was the afterlife's worst driver.

"Damn!" I cried, my hands flying up to my face when I crashed into the lower ceiling for real, half expecting the glass to shatter, but, naturally, it was indestructible. Slowly, I lowered with the down arrow until I was back on the floor by Garry. He looked annoyed.

"Danica Patrick," he joked into my still-open window. "Put it into up mode. Then you lift with the go. You're a worse driver than Letterman."

With shaking hands, I complied as the pod shuddered forward. That's when I realized my feet were on both the go and the brake at the same time and I removed the scary foot: the one on the brake.

Pressing down much too hard on the go pedal, I jettisoned forward like a bullet. Maya's face came onto a small screen on the blinking dashboard. "Dear," she said in a terrified voice. "The speed limit is thirty-five."

That's when I glanced down and found there was an actual speedometer.

Easing my foot off the go, somehow I got the hang of driving straight and eventually arrived at the actual stack I was looking for. "Don't be a moron," I reminded myself, slowly working the go in preparation to move up. Lights began to flash both red and green on my instrument panel and I had no idea what they meant. Hitting the up arrow, I flew up forty stories, but my stomach didn't lurch this time.

"You're driving," I told myself with glee. Then it dawned on me. "You're not driving. You're flying!"

Breathe.

The crash came quickly when the other driver roared up from behind and rear-ended me. I wasn't hurt, in fact, the seat belt made sure I didn't even move an inch. As a native Chicagoan, it was still my duty to whip around and scream at the idiot driver who had eyes in his rear end. It took a full minute of thought to figure out how to spin this thing around—and I sent myself into two double spins before I braked.

The driver's eyes were vibrant and alive. A faint smile played on his full lips. With a daring nod, Daniel backed up and hurled into me again. Then he punched it until I couldn't even see him anymore, which left me with only one choice. I punched it until both of us were hovering at the hundred-story mark.

He rammed me again, playing bumper cars with a state-of-the-art personal spaceship. To my left, I saw we were only in the K stacks. In front of me, Daniel's gray eyes danced merrily as he laughed. That teasing spark meant he wasn't done. His face blipped onto my computer screen. "Stardate, twenty-first century, in the midst of the great unknown," he said in his best Trek voice. "Just wondering, fleet commander, if you're wearing the red bra or the black one. I could easily volunteer to become your humble alien slave."

"Daniel!" I shouted, shocking him when I dropped ten stories and found myself in the F section next to books on frogs and Maynard Ferguson.

Yes, I had this!

With a conspiratorial grin, I even figured out how to send my face to his computer. A push of the right button and he ran those gray eyes over my face. I stayed suspended in the air hovering breathlessly. His jet-black hair was slicked back and he put his silver aviator shades on. I removed my own ponytail and shook my hair out.

"Ever made out in a pod?" he asked and as I blushed, he shot straight upward again. This time I chased him all the way to the top where the Z stack had research on zoology and zircons. Daniel wasn't smiling now.

"Look up, baby," he said, pointing straight up into a rainbow-colored stained-glass ceiling at the top of the tower that contained the most vibrant reds, greens, blues, and yellows. I could see that the top looked like some sort of map with the blue being a river or maybe an ocean, the greens the treetops, and the sky bright yellow. The dipping sun above leaked through the glass making everything up here glow.

Where was this place on the glass? Did it even exist? Or was it just a beautiful surprise for those who dared to fly high enough to find something glorious that came from curiosity? The colors shimmered on Daniel's face and I couldn't resist coming back onto his screen, closer, and closer, to blow him a kiss.

"Baby, go down to the W's. You can't miss it," Daniel said in a deferential voice before saying, "Over and out, beautiful."

I dropped. Then hovered. The plaque next to the W featured a very familiar face and a quote that read: "You're only given one little spark of madness. You mustn't lose it."—Robin Williams.

I shot back down to ground zero. Grinning.

It was our shop teacher, Chuck, who met me down below. "Remind me to tell you, fly girl, about the time I broke the sound barrier," he said, helping me out of the pod's cockpit despite the fact that I never did any research on Edward.

Daniel parked next to me, jumped out, and Chuck slapped him on the back. Daniel was holding a book called *Thermodynamics*. "You read? Wonders never cease. I'll see you back in the shop, son," Chuck said.

Daniel wrapped his arms around me, our shadows merging. Then he kissed me on the top of my head. "Got a little thing to do,' he said.

I nodded and he kissed me again on the lips, pulling back to mouth the words, "I love you."

The law of thermodynamics indeed.

7.

It was past dusk when all the frolicking was done, which meant I had a long walk through the woods before I could set foot in our warm, cozy Craftsman on Burning Tree Court. Outside the library, a curtain of black had fallen over the dense growth of evergreens in the near distance, painting them in silent shadows. I knew these woods well now, from the sky-blocking trees to the strong scent of wood, greens, and pungent lake water that filled my nostrils when I walked here. Yet, I rarely ever navigated these parts alone. Today there was no choice.

When I stepped off the last blade of Academy grass and entered the thickness of all that green, I imagined I was falling off the face of the world. As usual, the woods were possessive, swallowing you whole the moment your feet were firmly planted on the mulchy dirt path.

The night sucked me into its breath as I tried to find a familiar trail. For just a moment, I allowed my shoulders to go lax and my breath to even as I became one with this private haven. A night bird cried out a hello. Water from the lake slapped the shore. Branches rustled and roared as the green, lively summer leaves danced in the light wind. I closed my eyes for a moment and thought I heard them whisper, "*Walker . . . Walker . . . Is it you?*"

Despite the last hour of frivolity, this day had weighed heavily on me. Edward's words about not going on the mission still rang in my ears. I tried to shake him out of my head and find a distraction, but there wasn't a moon yet and there was never any starlight here. At night, the blackness was so dark that you couldn't imagine it ever being light again. It was like walking into a dark tunnel with no end and no beginning. There was just the middle.

"Remember those demons!" Edward had said, and I saw them like they were here with me now, their teeth dripping and eyes burning bright red. My feet began to move faster and I crunched over the rocks and fallen twigs. The leaves sang out to me again, "*Walker . . . Walker . . . come back. Or stop. We'll come to get you.*"

"No!" I screamed into the woods, and my voice reverberated, making it sound shallow and distorted. "No, no, no! I can't do it again! I can't! I can't!" I sobbed as tears raced down my cheeks. Somehow I had made it to the lake and fell to my knees by the murky shoreline, my lower legs sinking into the thick mud.

In that moment, I just wished I could make it all go way.

I never wanted go on this mission. Yet now I had to go. I couldn't let Daniel go alone.

Burying my face in my hands, I continued to weep as the warm lake water splashed up and caressed my face and the tips of my hair. I heard the branches breaking behind me. And then another rustling. A sigh raced through the trees.

A guttural moan brought me straight to my feet while the seaweed in the lake laced around my ankles like a tether.

"Who's there?" I tried to shout. My voice was thin and tinny. Then my lungs clogged and I couldn't take another breath. I whipped around a hundred and eighty degrees to stare into the blankness, my eyes still clouded with tears.

Holding my breath, I listened as the woods continued to breathe. Nothing was out of the ordinary. No one was here. The woods beat to a real rhythm. Maybe it was a raccoon or skunk doing their dinner trek. I saw a fish come to the surface of the lake, flip, and then dive under the water. I was the one who didn't belong.

Pine needles began rustling furiously now. A bigger tree branch on my right snapped hard, but it might as well have been a shotgun going off. In that moment, something wide burst from the trees and the mud around me became quicksand.

I couldn't move and now it was . . . yelling my name.

"Walker, Walker," he grunted.

Then he was upon me.

8.

He advanced from the new night, reached out, and dug into my shoulders like he would forever anchor his fingers in my flesh. I kicked out, connecting with muscle and bone to no avail. He came back fast and hard, spinning me in a way that made me feel like down was up. He used that time to reach out as if he was going to gouge me. "You were going to take this little guy home with you," he said, lifting a small creature off my shirt pocket. "But he already has his own little waterfront condo. Frogs are people, too."

I knew this man. Then it dawned on me that I *barely knew him.*

"Auggie?" I croaked. Something had to be wrong. "Oh my God, is it Bobby? Is he okay? Did someone take him? Is he hurt?"

"Little man is fine," Auggie insisted, looking nervous and scared at the same time. "I walked him home hours ago. Nice dog, too. I love Labs."

"Thanks—and sorry for kicking you," I muttered.

"Didn't think you'd remember me," he stammered.

Well over six feet with a wide frame, how could I forget him? His sweet-handsome face was meaty and hopeful as his long strawberry-blond ponytail danced in the light evening breeze.

"Were you following me?" I demanded.

"Guilty as charged," he admitted. "I've been looking for you since the day I got here, if your name really is Walker Callaghan. I knew I'd run into you sometime, but I didn't know when or where. Then you came by this morning and . . .well, you're the one."

I didn't have time for this.

"I have to get home," I stated, neatly dodging around him as I started to walk again. The last thing I could stand today was someone else's drama. "It's nothing personal, Auggie, but I can't today. I just can't," I said. "Maybe another day. We can talk when I get back from—" I stopped myself.

"Going somewhere?" Auggie asked.

"Home," I replied. It was the truth.

It turns out Auggie wasn't just big, but he was fast. He blocked me again and insisted, "No, you have to listen to me. Believing me might be another thing. But you have to listen."

He motioned for me to sit down on a hollowed-out tree log. When I didn't, he bowed in front of me like a servant dealing with a princess.

"Please," he begged. "The last thing I am is dangerous. I mean, look at me. Not a dangerous bone in my body. Just a lot of dependable ones."

I *was* looking at him now seated on the forest floor and the truth was he looked more lost than me. I don't know why, but reluctantly I sat on a log. Then I listened to him, which would mark the first of many times I would listen to someone destined to become one of my closest friends here, there, or everywhere.

Auggie wasn't just special.

He was beyond.

Death Story: Auggie O'Connor

Age of Demise: 18

So, okay, here we go. I don't know why I feel nervous. But I do. Okay, here it is: My name is Auggie O'Connor and I'm from Austin. Deep in the heart of Texas. I was a high school senior, am, a senior, I think, and really into superhero comics and playing tuba in the marching band. I think that makes me a renaissance man.

Anyway, someone has to play the tuba and I was just a tuba playing kind of guy.

I'll fill in a few more blanks. I have, I mean had, three little sisters and two brothers, so that explains why I love kids. I was just never good with kids my own age. Even when I was a kid, the rest of them called me fat, lardo, fat-ass, dumb fat-ass—well you get the picture. I was never really that fat. Just big. I was the biggest toddler. I was a giant at preschool. By second grade, I was the biggest kid in the class. I always prefer to say XXL. More Auggie to love. Not that I'm suggesting you love me. I'll go for like or interested in.

On most afternoons when I was a-alive, still weird to say it that way—working on it—but when I was alive, I used to take my XXL self down to the local Starbucks with three or four of the kids who were probably driving my mom nuts. Mom was bipolar, so it didn't take much, and Dad was bye-bye. Anyway, we'd go to Starbucks and I even played the tuba for all the people until someone complained to management, which was usually in the first five minutes. I also had a wicked way with the electric guitar. Most of all, I loved to write songs, and not boy-band stuff. I didn't go in just one direction.

My music asked real-life questions like: How? Why? Someone wrote on their blog that I combined philosophy with heart and a lot of soul. There was also a really good beat thanks to my younger brother Jerry who played drums. The kid always knew a sick beat.

My mom used to say that I was someone who loved strangers. She was right because I was always collecting strays. Stay dogs. Stray cats. Stray people. I always asked anyone new to come to my side of the table at lunch. I had this stupid slogan: Your drama is my drama. I know. Dumb, but I meant it.

The hair was my thing. So what if some of them bullied me for it. It was just an extra layer. My Teflon.

A few months ago, my mom got a call from her sister in California. Did I want to come out on spring break to visit my cousin Jeremy? I didn't really want to go hang with Jeremy, the egomaniac college football star. And he obviously didn't want to spend break with his geek cousin, the one he barely saw. But Mom made me. His mom made him. The rest will go down in sad family history.

Jeremy was all about the socializing. One night, he took me to this party on Venice Beach. It was mostly college kids from UCLA. They had a bonfire and a keg. For a minute, I actually felt accepted. This really pretty girl with dark hair danced with me on the sand to the Ramones "Teenage Lobotomy." It was suddenly the best night of my life. No one knew me here. I could be anyone I wanted to be. I could be that guy. I could be Jeremy.

The rest of the guest list was a mix of stoners, jocks, and babes—I guess the usual beach-party combo platter. But for once, Auggie O'Connor was also on the menu.

The party was Bring Your Own Poison. Jeremy and I had brought Miller Light, nacho-cheese Doritos, and cheap Dominos pizzas. Some of the other guys brought crystal meth and ecstasy. One brought a bottle of Xanax, and of course, there was pot, wine, and beer.

I didn't want to do it, but Jeremy kept saying to me, "Auggie, come on. Don't be a douche that crosses state lines. We always knew you were a pussy." I really didn't want to do it, but then Mark, Jeremy's friend, got me in a headlock in front of that dark-haired girl, poured half a beer over my head and started shouting, "Girly man with the strawberry hair. Prove it to us that you don't get your period."

I didn't want to be that guy anymore. I wanted to be the cool, out-of-town Auggie. So, I did something I had never done. Ever. I gave in. I stuck out my arm and Mark wound an old shoelace around it. Then he jammed a needle in.

I hated shots. Cried when I was a kid. What was I doing?

It was too late.

I heard that dark-haired girl yell something about it being a really bad trip. The only other bad trip I had ever been on was to Tucson to visit my aunt. And I felt this current trip go from bad to worse. My heart was racing, my knees buckled, and I fell to the sand. "I don't know this kid. I had nothing to do with it," Mark said before walking away. All I can remember is Jeremy disappearing and this new guy running over and wiping out the foamy stuff in my mouth with his bare hand, so I could breathe.

"Stay with me kid," he said. "I called 911. Just hang on. We're here together. Hold my hand and breathe."

I could barely speak, but I answered his questions. "Have you ever done heroin before?" he asked. "No sir," I whispered. "I'm Auggie O'Conner and I play tuba. I don't do heroin."

"I got you son. I got you. Just keep talking to me," he said. "What else do you like to do besides play tuba, kid?"

Where was the air?

There was no air.

Was he sitting on my chest. It felt so heavy.

"I want you to know something," I barely whispered to that nice man. "I'm not going to make it." And then I started to cry a little bit and he squeezed my hand harder and said, "Yes, you are, Auggie. You're going to be fine. You're a tough kid. A big guy. I'm sure you have a real big heart. Just breathe with me here until the good guys arrive."

It felt like I was winding down. I didn't want to breathe anymore. I could feel my heart beating at half time now. My head felt like someone was holding me underground.

"Sir," I said to him after he did mouth-to-mouth and took away a little of the pain. "Sir, tell my mom I'm really, really sorry. I did a dumb thing. And I love her. Tell her I love her."

"Auggie, you stay with me, dammit," he demanded in a savage voice.

"But I don't know you," I whispered. "Why would I stay?"

"Then let's get to know each other. I'm Cass. I go to school in Chicago, but I'm home this weekend for break. I grew up on this beach. I lived on it. Surfed on it. Slept on it. This is my turf. We're going to call on everything that is good here to get you through the next few minutes. And then one day, you'll pass this on when you see another kid in trouble."

"But I won't be here," I said. And I knew that much was true.

He wasn't smiling and neither was I. It was too much and I couldn't think about this anymore. "I only have a few minutes," I said, remembering the real me. I was a renaissance man who collected strays. This strange guy holding me was a stray. I knew how to do this.

"Tell me something more about you," I whispered as my legs began to shake violently. He held my legs down as he cradled me like a baby in his chest.

"Auggie, you listen to me, dammit" Cass said. "You have your whole life ahead of you. You must stay."

"Can't," I whispered.

"Okay, okay, okay," Cass began to ramble, still holding me.

"What do we do now?" I could barely say.

"I don't know," he said.

Then he checked my pulse.

"This is so wrong. So freaking wrong," he kept repeating. "But if you slip over, and I don't want you to do it, but if you do, I need a favor kid."

I could only stare at him as he spoke. "I've been carrying something around for a long time waiting for the right moment, which this isn't going to be. It can't be this moment."

"But if it is," I said.

"Her name is Walker Callaghan. You can't miss her. She's real pretty. Real smart. Give something back to her. For courage," he said. "She's going to need it."

Cass slipped something in my pocket and the next thing I knew I was flying high over the Pacific Ocean and into the setting sun. I swore I heard myself playing one of my original compositions in the background. It was the most beautiful thing.

When he was finished, Auggie O'Conner turned and my tearful hazel eyes fell into his shimmering smile.

"Here, Walker," he said, pressing something into my palm with trembling big bear hands. "I don't know what it means. Maybe I'm not supposed to ever know. You never have to tell me. Just take it." He hugged me tightly. "But someday if you want to talk about it, I'm . . ."

As he pulled away, I felt my lucky green rabbit's foot in my hand again.

Auggie O'Connor.

Ass-kicking, realm-crossing delivery boy.

CHAPTER 17

1.

I cried most of the way home. That's why Auggie walked with me—no, make that behind me. He walked the entire way two steps behind until the woods spit us out at the far end of a mostly pitch-black Burning Tree Court. I thought I'd shake Auggie now, but he continued to move in step with me. We went past all the little houses with the warm yellow lights glowing from their kitchen and living room windows.

Our house was all lit up, which was why it was easy to see Daniel in the front yard pacing like he was bulldozing the driveway with his booted feet. "What is it baby?" he said, his face flooded with relief when he saw me. He did a quick once-over, inspecting for damage and then drew me in hard until my face melted into his chest. When he ran his hand over the back of my hair, it was just about my undoing.

Knowing he would need someone or something to blame, I

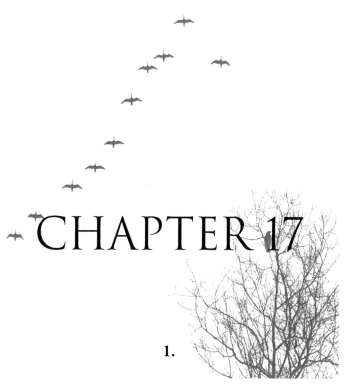

watched him look hard at Auggie who was still just standing there, a hulking bundle of nerves.

"What the hell? Did he do this to you?" Daniel asked in that possessive voice, still rubbing the back of my hair. I shook my head as in no, but Daniel wasn't satisfied. "Aren't you that guy from the pee-wee school?" he demanded. "You better have a good, and fast, reason why my girlfriend is crying."

"I swear, dude, all I did was walk her home. I didn't want her walking through the woods all upset. She was upset enough already and I didn't want anything bad to happen," Auggie rambled. "Don't hurt me."

"Upset about what?" Daniel shouted now.

"We're all good now. Aren't we Walker? We're good, right?" Auggie pleaded.

"He's good," I sniffled, my tears making little wet spots on Daniel's T-shirt. "This is Auggie. He's a nice guy. He brought me something."

There was only one thing I could do before Daniel flattened this gentle giant. I pressed the rabbit's foot into his large hand.

"Greetings from the other side. Special delivery. From Cass," I sniffled.

"You've got to be shitting me?" Daniel said under his breath. Viciously, he threw the rabbit's foot into the grass and missed it when Auggie gingerly moved forward to pick it up.

"Not that anyone wants my opinion, but I sense bad blood here," Auggie said to no one in particular. An epic glare from Daniel didn't stop his nervous chatter. "Not that you have anything to worry about Mr. Reid," Auggie said in a too-chipper tone. "This might sound like the makings of a love triangle, but everything points to you." He put his hands on his mouth to mock the sound of a cheering crowd. "We have a winner! The crowd goes wild," Auggie said, trying hard to somehow lighten the mood.

It was enough to make me stop crying. He was trying that hard. "I don't know what happened. I died and this dude on the beach I never met before helped me. Then he slipped the thing in my pocket," Auggie explained.

"Did he kill you?" Daniel demanded.

"Kill me? No. I took care of that job myself," said a sad Auggie, which earned him a curious look from Daniel. "I'm sorry Mr. Reid to be the bearer of the rabbit's foot. I don't even know what it all means. Don't shoot the messenger. I mean, really. Don't shoot me or hit me. Please. I take care of your little brother during the day. He can vouch for me."

"Don't call me Mr. Reid. That's my father," Daniel spat out.

It was actually Auggie who stopped Daniel cold.

"Yeah, I met your dad," Auggie said.

It was like a bomb going off. Daniel's head swiveled hard in my direction and then back to Auggie.

"You said that you never had anyone ask about Bobby," I demanded.

"I didn't want to upset you. That's another reason I walked you home, Walker. I wasn't sure where you lived and I wanted to talk to Mr. Reid. I mean . . . Daniel. You're listed as the official guardian of Bobby," Auggie continued. "I needed to tell you that earlier today someone named Mr. Edward Reid in this big silver car came to the school saying he had permission to sign the boy out for the day."

"Son of a bitch," Daniel cursed.

"You didn't . . ." I began.

"Of course, I didn't allow it," Auggie assured us. "I said and I quote, 'Mister, you're not on the approved list.'"

"I bet he loved being told that news," Daniel said.

"No, no, he definitely did not love it—or me," Auggie said. "Edward said and I quote, 'Move your fat ass out of my way Lardo or I'll beat the crap out of you.'"

"And you said?" Daniel demanded.

"I said, and I quote, 'Mister, now you've gone and done it. You pushed my buttons. You're going to need a written letter now from Miss Travis to approve you even coming into this school or on school grounds,'" Auggie said in a tone that sounded a bit . . . defiant. For him.

Then his face fell.

"Look at me. I'm genetically a large person. I didn't ask to be six foot four, but I am. And I'm proportional here, give or take a few bags of Cheetos," Auggie explained, spinning around like he was a model. "I look good, if I do have to say so myself."

"You told Edward you ate Cheetos?" Daniel said.

"No, no I said and I quote—and I'm sorry if this was inappropriate—but I told Edward, 'Get the hell out of here or I'll call a Code Nine, which means suspicious person entering and loitering around the children.'" He looked down at his toes. In the glow of the moon, he continued to glance away when he said, "Sorry about the language. I don't usually say loitering to anyone. It's such a hall-monitor word."

Someone needed a long moment to digest.

"Well then, Auggie, right? I will say and I quote, Auggie, 'I'm grateful to you for taking care of both my little brother and my girl,'" Daniel said, holding out his hand. But it wasn't enough for the proportional one who yanked Daniel in for a back slapping bear hug of a good time. Daniel looked like he was being mauled by Gentle Ben.

That's when the door burst open and Bobby was suddenly in his glory. "You came to see me! You came! Can Auggie stay for dinner? Can he?" he cried.

2.

It turns out that he wasn't our only dinner guest that night. Iz was already inside, sprawled out on the floor watching *Breaking Bad*. A few minutes later, the doorbell rang and I was shocked to see my school friend Tosh standing on the other side of it. She was in a short blush skirt paired with a cap-sleeved shirt in hot pink. She even wore a tulle tutu. "Hey, Walker," she said, looking past a protective Daniel who filled the frame. "Hey, Daniel. Sorry for the drop in, but I'm here on a mission." She pressed a large yellow envelope into my hand.

"From Miss Travis. Said you must follow the instructions and not bring it up at school. Whatever that means. She said to take what's inside with you always and have it handy. Whatever *that* means. And she said to open the envelope in private—and tell me nothing, which is just plain rude, if you ask me, which you didn't. Hey, is that pizza?" Tosh rambled. "I'm starving."

It was pizza and Izayah came out of the kitchen with a giant pie in each hand. It wasn't long before the table in the living room was covered with pies, glasses, and large bottles of Coke. Iz didn't skip a beat. He handed Tosh a plate and grabbed another to fill for himself.

"Why don't you stay for dinner?" I said, laughing because she was already eyeing her second slice. The truth was I was glad to be doing something normal for a change. Tosh made herself right at home and Andy and Jenna were thrilled to have another girl in the house to fill with soda and school gossip. And when I glanced at the dining room table, I could see Auggie cutting Bobby's pizza into small pieces. Was he really hand-feeding the kid? "Another piece of coal for the train! Open wide, conductor!" he cried and Bobby laughed between bites.

"Tosh, do you know Auggie?" I asked. "He's new around these parts."

"Hey, Augmented, didn't see you over there," Tosh said with a full mouth. I found out they had a lit class together taught by that nice lady writer, Nora, whose lucky students got to write screenplays instead of term papers.

"We're in glee together, too," Tosh said between bites. "We have that hot teacher, Cory." I knew from our lunches that Tosh's fondest conversation was the varying degrees of the opposite sex.

The real surprise was Pete who disappeared for a moment and returned in new jeans and a black sweater. Pete had his hair styled longer on the top and shorter on the sides just like Daniel. Did he really gel it up? The answer was yes. The same could be said for his new love of musky cologne.

"Hello, Peter," Tosh said, smiling up at him. "Someone took a shower."

"Natasha," he said, smiling nervously. "Can I get you something new to drink? We have soft drinks, beer, and wine." He brought her a Coke in a wine glass with a lemon wedge on the side. The sheer artistry created in the glass made it look as if we were at a five-star restaurant. When I asked him for another drink, too, he tossed me a can.

"Welcome to the Reid zoo," he said which made Tosh laugh. "All we do here is feed the animals."

A man of few to no words, Pete was suddenly talking in short paragraphs about school, hockey, and the upcoming end of summer dance. And when Tosh beamed a smile back up at him from her spot on the couch, I swore I saw our boy blush.

A few minutes later, back in the kitchen, it was Iz who wouldn't let him live it down. With Tosh in the living room out of earshot, I heard Iz torment poor Pete. "That's a lot of woman for you, *Peter*," Iz said. "But, obviously you like her, so why don't you wander back into the living room and actually ask her to that dance."

"Shut up. She can hear you," Pete whispered, refilling Tosh's drink and this time cutting lime wedges.

Why is it the worst days make you really appreciate the best nights?

3.

Auggie had quietly eaten a whole pie all by himself, which wasn't an issue here. You just called Mr. Rosati's pizza delivery service in town and five more were delivered free of charge. It was Bobby who flung open the door to get them. "Want a tip?" he told the delivery boy. "Don't smoke."

"Bobby!" I said, but the delivery boy just laughed.

I figured that Auggie wasn't just hungry in the conventional sense. He was actually friend-starved. By the end of the evening, his grin had absolutely nothing to do with the half gallon of Chunky Monkey that he polished off either. He easily assimilated into the family, especially when he put Bobby on his back and gave him horse rides across the living room while Daniel got on all fours and pretended to be the swamp monster attacking them.

"He seems like a good guy," Daniel said, taking a break for a quick kiss and the rest of the pepperoni pie. The look of concern still hadn't faded from the shadows that covered his face. "You okay, baby? Has this thing today freaked you out?" he asked, scanning my eyes for signs.

"Who cares about Cass's latest circus act? Now that I have

the rabbit's foot, I'm guessing that will be it. Having it helped him connect with me. Now, he has nothing."

"He has your mother," Daniel said, glancing out the window and holding me tighter.

"Someday we'll go visit your mom again—when the time is right," he said and I nodded into his shirt. He didn't have time to say more because someone was tugging at him. "The evil monsters have drinked up the entire river. They're barfing up green stuff at Auggie. Come on, Danny! We need you," Bobby yelled.

That left me alone in the kitchen to clean up, but I wasn't alone for long. Iz was suddenly there, stacking up the dirty glasses and hauling paper plates into the trash. "You don't have to do that. I love mundane tasks. I might even mop the floor," I said. I waved him away, but Iz wasn't budging.

When he pulled up a kitchen chair, I knew he wanted to talk.

"I couldn't help but overhear," he said. "Not some of it, but most of it. This house has thin walls. Plus, Dan told me about this jack-off Cass. How you met him. How he's *alive.* How he's obsessed with you, hot stuff."

"Please," I interrupted, waving a soapy sponge in the air.

"I know Daniel hates it, but this Cass is like a one-way connection to your mom, right?" Iz continued to poke around.

I stopped, turned off the water, and fessed up.

"He shows me what's going on with her," I said. So far, he had mostly shown my mother walking again, which thrilled me. What didn't thrill me, well, never mind . . ." I knew I had to leave that one alone.

"Come on, Walker," Iz said. "You can tell me."

Wandering over, I began to rip little pieces of cardboard off the pizza boxes. "She's visiting psychics in Chicago. She was trying to find a way—any kind of way—to communicate with me," I said. "It makes me sad because she never gets anywhere. She just pays more money and goes home even more depressed."

"Listen, Walker," Iz said, sliding his chair closer to give my shoulders a squeeze. "Sit down for a sec. No really, sit. I have to tell you something."

Scraping a kitchen chair, he motioned for me to join him at the table. At first, I resisted, but Iz had a fine way of wearing you down.

"It's no secret I've been here a little while," he began, looking into my eyes. "I don't even keep track anymore, but there's no change of address for me. At least, not yet. I guess I'm still working things out."

I wasn't sure of where he or this was going.

"The longer you stay here, the more you learn—and I don't mean learning about math or science," he said. "You learn how to do things. Ghostly things. I know we don't like to talk about that here, but let's be honest. If you hang out in this realm long enough, they even put you in classes to learn those ghostly arts. There's a senior wing to the Academy that would blow your mind. They don't even allow the rest of us in there."

"How do you become a senior?" I asked.

"In the past, it was when Dr. King said you were one," Iz relayed.

"I'm not a senior," he added. "But I am an observant pain in the you know what. Which brings me to the time a year or so ago, but who's counting, when I was doing a little manual labor for Dr. King in his office."

It turned out that Iz decided to cut shop class because he didn't like building things. The big man decided that his punishment would be building perfect shelves in the outer part of Dr. King's office. "I was there for a month pounding and hammering nails. The reset was my best friend," Iz said in a disgusted voice. "It was long, boring work, but occasionally there was a perk."

My curiosity piqued.

"Dr. King always left the door to his inner office open, and I learned all kinds of things. Heard all sorts of sob stories. One day, there was this girl who was bawling her eyes out. She begged Dr. King to allow her to speak with her father one more time. He said no and she went bananas having a breakdown."

Iz paused and lowered his voice.

"Finally, Dr. King said he would make her a senior, which meant that she would learn how to Dream Trip."

I pulled my chair closer.

"Dream Tripping is a way of actually going back to the living realm without physically going through a portal and having to fight the demons," he said. "Anyone can do it. From here. And it's allowed. But only when we're emotionally ready."

I leaned forward so hard that my chest almost slammed into the table.

"Think of it like breaking and entering," Iz said. "All you need to do is stage a little dream road trip. In your sleep, you leave your body and join them. But you're not entering their dreams. You're entering their realm temporarily as an observer. They're wide awake, living their lives, and you're watching. You can only stay for the shortest amount of time, but it's something."

This time, Iz leaned in. "Come on, Walker. Weren't there times when you were alive that you looked into a crowd or across a room and swore you saw your father? Then you looked again and he was gone?"

I nodded. "Once at school. I looked at someone else's father on one of those field trip days and saw my father's face. But on second glance, I was wrong," I said.

"No," Iz said, emphatically, "you weren't wrong."

He didn't stop there.

"You can do it from here . . . anytime," Iz said. "Remember when Dr. King told you not to even think about returning to the living realm? Well, he didn't want you to accidentally Dream Trip too soon because it's quite a trip."

"Tell me what I need to do," I begged.

"I imagine you think about everything before you go to sleep—like we all do. In your case, it's school. Daniel. School. Daniel. Daniel. Daniel," he said, as a hint of a smile playing on his mouth. "That schizoid thinking is common, especially for people our age. We literally have a million things racing around our brains."

"To Dream Trip, you have to focus. Listen to your breathing. Go inside. Think of just that one person . . . and keep thinking of them. Singular thinking. Think of only them as you drift off to sleep. It's almost like you're setting a dream GPS and pointing right at them," he said. "You're on a Dream Trip and they are the destination."

"Does it work every single time?"

Iz shook his head no. "It's tough to remain that focused," he said. "Our age and hormones and a million other things stop us."

"Do they see you? Can you talk to them?"

Iz shook his head yes and then no.

"Let me put this in theater terms. At first, you're simply a cameo. A bit player. You'll see your mom and she might see you lurking in the background. She won't even be sure it's you at first, but that's okay. Just the idea that it might be you will make her real happy. The first time she sees you in a crowded airport or at the supermarket or in your own backyard at dusk, she will wonder. Was it really you? Was it her imagination? Is she really that tired? Did she have that third glass of wine? But she knows deep down, instinctually, it was you and she will be overjoyed. Even a split second of you or a vision is better than nothing. And then she won't be able to stop thinking about it, which is key. It helps link her to you the next time."

"Why?"

"Because the next time, she will believe it a little more," he said.

"And belief is your rocket ship when it comes to bridging the gap."

"And to answer your question," Iz continued, "no, she can't hear you—at least not now—but you can hear her thoughts or words. You can feel her emotions. Her life in that very moment will be crystal clear and you'll hear and see it all. Even if it's just a glimpse. As time progresses, you might have the gift to say a few words that she hears. Not everyone can do that. Not every living mortal hears it. Can you conduct conversations eventually? Beats me," he said with a shrug. "I'm not that far along. I really don't know."

"This is a lot from just building a shelf," I said with a smile.

"I'm a real good builder," Iz said. "And I'm a dreamer."

"The best—on both counts, I'm figuring," I said. Then I asked him, "So, you do this on a regular basis?"

"Nah, not every single night. I don't want to burden my dad with nightly sightings. He needs to move on with his life. But I do it from time to time when I get a feeling that he needs me," Iz said. "Literally, I've been here long enough that I'll be going about my business, letting my mind wander, and—bam—I'll feel that my dad needs me. That's when I try to do it."

"When I first started doing it," he continued, "I'd sit far away in the hockey stands back home. After I died, dad insisted on going to watch my old high school team the Hawks every single Saturday. I'd watch him look at the ice at Hawks Stadium with tears in his eyes. He was looking for me. He felt the void. Then one day, he looked and for a few seconds, I was back. Just for a few seconds. I saw Dad do a double take. He was the only one who saw me."

"And then?" I asked breathlessly.

"The farthest I've gotten is one evening a few months ago when I felt Dad struggling. I just felt it in my bones. So, I visited and found him sitting at the kitchen table with a pile of bills in front of him—the mortgage, electric bill, and taxes. Then he wandered upstairs and sat on my old twin bed in my musty old room. The room looked exactly the same down to the pair of socks I left at the bottom of the bed. The garbage by the desk was still full with balled-up papers.

Dad was sitting on that bed, crying. Then Mom came in and said to him, 'We have to move, John. There is no choice. They're going to foreclose.' But Dad cut her off. 'This room is all we have left of the boy,' he said. 'The bank will have to pry me out of this house.' After my mom left, Dad started looking through my old sports photo album. I didn't go in the room, but stood in the hallway. Dad popped his head up, saw me silently standing there, and it was like a jolt going through him. He stood up to follow with a strange look of wonder on his face. The next thing I did was wander outside to the front lawn and Dad followed, looking at me quizzically as I darted away, motioning for him to 'come on.' I moved all the way down the street to the local park where Dad took a seat on a bench. When he looked across the baseball field, he saw me standing tall by all these kids who couldn't see me. I took a ball from the ground. I wasn't sure if I could do it, but I tossed it hard and it landed by Dad's feet."

"A sign?"

"I thought I didn't know how to do anything, but move and stand. I guess as time passes, you can do more, which I have to say is pretty damn cool," Iz said.

"So then what happened?"

"Then Dad picked up the ball and looked at me. I looked at him and smiled. Dad blinked and I was gone. My alarm rang here and I had to get to class."

"Did your dad sell the house?"

"Miss Travis told me he put it on the market later that month. When I checked back in on him, he looked better. He even told my mom that I didn't live in that bedroom anymore. 'Our boy lives everywhere,' he said."

I put my hand over Iz's as I filled in my own blanks. I told him how Cass simply showed up, offering me little slices from Mom's life like the coming attractions from a movie. I told him how he often stood and smiled like he controlled the world's most potent remote control.

"Screw this manipulative SOB. If you learn to Dream Trip, you can learn a lot more," Iz said. "You can learn what's she's thinking. And feel what she's feeling."

"What do I do?" I rushed him.

"Remember to focus just on her when you're ready for sleep. As for the rest of it . . . relax. Rest. Remember," Iz said. "Just let go, Walker. Surrender. Let it come to you. It's actually easier the first few times—before you really start to think about it."

I felt the whoosh of air as Daniel sailed through the kitchen with an armload of dirty plates. "Baby, we have training tomorrow morning," he said, as Pete and Tosh followed in behind him. "So, let's kick out Bobby's human horse and turn in."

Iz gave me a wink and stood up. "Good talk, goalie. I'll walk them back to school. Although if anything goes bump in the woods, smart money is on Tosh kicking the crap out of it. Be careful with that one, Peter."

"Please!" Pete said, moving past Daniel to toss the rest of the plates.

Just as if he had been part of this crew for a long, long time, a winded Auggie, hair half-pulled out of his ponytail, popped his head in.

"Auggie, we gotta be up early tomorrow for . . . a thing," I said.

"So get out," Daniel said in a good-natured voice. "And thank you, man."

"You need a babysitter tomorrow?" Auggie replied.

I looked at Daniel who said, "You're hired."

4.

An hour later, the house was pitch-black and Daniel was out cold. Maybe it was too many hours slaying a swamp monster or some gentle making out, but all was well in my love's bed. With one leg over mine, he was spooning me with his face buried in my hair.

It was no time to think of another man, but I heard Iz's words clear as day. *Relax. Rest. Remember. Surrender. Let it come to you.*

The deafening sounds of the night made it impossible to relax. *Tick, tick, tick* went a garishly loud clock. There was moaning from the hallway where the dog was in the middle of a really good or bad dream, his nails scraping the wall as he ran wildly in his slumber. Bobby liked to talk in his sleep and I heard him say aloud, "Santa, are you there, Santa?" The green rabbit's foot, now on my nightstand, seemed to tremble.

Breathe. Listen only to your own breath. Think of only her. Mom. I love you, Mom. You're the best mom in the entire world. Mom, we don't need him. Mom, I can try to check on you. What were dreams made for in the first place? Mom.

My eyes rolled back and I crossed the threshold.

The house was garish red including a stained sofa and crimson scarves that covered the small lamp near the table with rose-colored candles. "I hear a voice calling out to you from the Other Side," said Madame Sofia, her long black hair a wig left over from last Halloween.

The small flame flickered and the Madame said in the worst fake Russian accent in history, "Did you feel that cold breeze enter? It's a sign. She's here."

"She is?" Mom said in the most hopeful voice. "I knew she would come."

"I'm getting a commun-ica-shun," the Madame enunciated. "Did you lose a sister?" Mom shook her head no. "Was it a friend?" Mom shook again.

"My daughter," Mom offered. "She died." Even the great Madame was brought up short but recovered quickly. She was, after all, a professional.

"Yes, yes, your daughter died young."

"Yes!" my mother cried.

"I see water. It was accidental drowning," the Madame tried.

"No," Mom said.

"Bad boyfriend," the Madame tried.

"No," Mom said. "Car . . ."

"Accident," filled in Madame Sofia. "I see it. I see it all now. The car burst into flames. I feel the heat."

"Yes and no. There was no fire," Mom said.

"Your daughter tells me she was joy riding with friends and she's sorry."

"No, no, no," my mother cried. "I was with her. Are you sure you have my daughter?"

"And you feel such guilt," Madame Sofia added. "Your daughter says that she loves you and forgives you. That will be seventy-nine ninety-five. Tips are encouraged."

Mom was trying so hard to find that elusive, thin thread between us.

"Here I am, Mom!" I shouted, but she couldn't see me in the dark room even though I did exactly what Iz said to do. I stood in the background, but Mom looked right through me.

Dammit, it didn't work.

At least not for me.

All I could do was watch. And churn.

The dream began again with a time check.

Three in the morning. Greektown in Chicago. Mom rises out of bed, quickly maneuvering into her tiny bathroom to put on a white skirt and light-blue T-shirt. I stand by the bed. Just standing. She looks right through me and walks next to me without a second glance as she reaches for her glasses.

"Mom!" I call out to deaf ears. "Where are you going? It's the middle of the night.

Quickly, she unlatches the deadbolt and slips outside of her apartment into the blackness. She walks past her little blue Honda and down the street, which is a dangerous thing to do in a big city when everything good is sleeping.

I can see it on her face. She doesn't care.

A man darts between two buildings, stopping, lurking. He sees her and moves closer. I race across the street and try to physically push him back, but he walks right through me. Doesn't see me. Doesn't feel me. He comes closer to Mom who looks right at him. She stops, but doesn't scream. "You need something lady to help you get through the night?" he asks, adding, "We all need something. Maybe someone."

She brushes past him and I say a silent prayer of thanks that he doesn't follow.

Mom walks down the empty street as the panic rises within me. The black Escalade slows down to follow her, garish oversized red brake lights blinding me. Then it stops.

A man rolls down a window and says in a deep voice, "Do you need a ride, pretty lady?" My mother, the most cautious woman on earth, flicks her auburn hair back, which falls in long waves now. She hasn't bothered to bind it and it makes her look a decade younger.

"Take me anywhere . . . everywhere," she says, walking around to the passenger side.

She slides into the car like she does this all the time.

The man has his hand on her leg. Her eyes are glazed like she doesn't even feel it. He inches the hand up and she doesn't even try to stop him. They're on Lake Shore Drive, which winds around Lake Michigan, but you can't see the water because a summer fog has rolled in.

"Where should I pull over?" the man asks, but he's not really asking. In my mind, I begin to scream, "No, Mom, no!"

She can't hear my words, but says to him, "Pull over here. Now. Let me out."

"Pretty lady, that's not the plan for tonight. Plus, we're in the middle of Lake Shore Drive," he says. "I want something dark and private." I check the speedometer and it's well past sixty. They're flying down the highway.

"I can't pull over just yet, pretty baby," he says. "Give me a minute and then I'll give you my full attention."

Mom does the impossible and grabs the door handle, pulls it forward and the car door springs open. The man swears as Mom dangles one leg out, the car still speeding along the dark highway. She swivels, attempting to dangle the other leg out of the racing car.

"What the hell!" the man screams as she tries to jump. Jamming the breaks, he pulls over into the emergency lane.

"Get the hell out, lady! You're too crazy! Plus, I'm married," he says and Mom tosses him a vacant stare before she steps out into the misty fog.

"Move, Mom!" I shout, as she stands too close to the right lane, a Mustang narrowly missing her.

Mom doesn't stand there for long. She hears the crash of the waves on the sand. And she heads for the water.

Mom takes off her cheap drug-store sandals and tosses them as far as she can throw them. The early morning seagulls descend thinking this is food, but fly away after nibbling at the faded pink plastic.

She's walking on the beach now, past where two bums are sleeping on fishy-smelling sand. They don't even stir when Mom walks closer and closer to the waves.

The fog is so thick now that even I can't see where the sand ends and the water begins. Mom still doesn't care. First, she gets her toes wet and then her ankles. Soon, she's waist deep in the water, her white skirt soaked, and still walking impossibly forward. The water eats her alive, consuming her waist, her breasts, and then her neck.

I know what she's doing.

My mother is going to kill herself.

The water caresses her chin and laps at her bottom lip.

I'm floating next to her. In my Mickey Mouse shirt and nothing else. Screaming on the top of my lungs. "Go back, Mom! Go back! You were sent back for a reason! Oh, Mom!"

The night is crystal clear and soft. And that's when Mom turns one wet cheek to the right, lake water raining from her eyes like tears.

"Walker?" she says in the most hopeful voice.

"Cass!" I scream.

He's in a cab, tossing a wad of cash at the driver who has recklessly pulled over on Lake Shore Drive.

He has thick thighs and strong, runner's legs from his years as a Marine and he knows the water. He sees the sandals and keeps moving, feet churning up the sand as they pound to close the distance.

Cass doesn't walk into the water, but races through it, diving hard when it gets deep. The fog swallows him, but he doesn't need sight.

He twists his body hard in the direction of the wavy brown hair.

"Mrs. Callaghan! Maddy. Just stay there," he shouts as he becomes one with the murky lake. His trajectory is like a bullet. He has her on lock now.

My mother is in shock. "Cass . . . how in the world? Cass, oh Cass," she cries opening her eyes wide.

He has her. In his arms. Carries her like a baby to the sand. Gently, he places her down on an old orange towel that someone left behind. Her feet crumble.

Mom falls to her knees. "I saw her. I saw her!" she cries. "I saw Walker."

"I know," Cass says on his knees next to her. "I see her, too. She's right over there."

All I can do is stand inches away.

Shaking.

5.

"Baby! Baby! Wake up."

What happened next was only right. I told Daniel all of it because he deserved to know. I told him that it was easy or—like Iz said—the idea that I didn't know enough to overthink it sent me right in. As I divulged, he held me hard.

And he broke my heart.

"I want to be the one to save her—not him," he said under his breath.

"Like you saved me?" I whispered, burying my head in the crook of his arm, which was my personal dream catcher for tears.

6.

Much later, I fell asleep again although I was almost afraid to do so. I couldn't stop thinking about my mother. My thoughts were pure and organic—the kind that later on would probably be harder to conjure.

The sky in Chicago is milky blue, but the fog has lifted. I drift back and my mother is still sitting on that beach, her face washed clean of the pain.

It was possible to reach her.

She knew it. I knew it.

I was still possible.

Mom gazes into the distance, her beautiful face calm and serene. I stand close, then sit next to her. Willing her to notice. Wanting her to know.

As the sun slowly comes up over the lake, it creates thousands of tiny sparkles. In that light, I see him. He stands nearby, ankle deep in the foamy surf, long blond hair still wet and wavy down his back, wet shorts and no shirt. He saved her. I would never forget it.

I need to thank him.

Cass opens his arms and I go to him. I hug him. It's not a lover's hug, but one created from gratitude. Despite my intentions, I feel it bonding us. So desperately, I want to resist.

He isn't as sure that this is about gratitude. He pulls me in tight as a lover would.

I allow it for only a second and then yank myself away.

"No promises. Just now," he says. "Close your eyes. Be with me."

I open them.

Daniel is sleeping next to me.

It was almost morning.

CHAPTER 18

1.

By morning's light, all thoughts of Cass and my mother had been tucked away. My new schedule demanded it, although I found a way to carve out a little thinking time.

It just didn't last long.

I smiled at the sight of Auggie and Bobby fighting over a box of Lucky Charms at the kitchen table. They were taking turns digging into the box for the fake tattoo prize.

Once Bobby won, he was off like a rocket. His plan was to tattoo his entire arm before his brothers and sisters woke up.

Making myself a cup of coffee, I leaned against the sink in my trademark black leggings and matching training tee and asked, "So, Auggie, what did you miss? *Who* do you miss?"

"Well, Miss Walker, if I may call you that," he said with that XL smile. "I was accepted at Arizona State on a band scholarship. I was going to rule the universe, one tuba tune at a time. My goal was to get a million hits on YouTube and ask this girl Ella to the prom. So, Ella is probably going to the prom with some chapped-lip trumpet player. Ain't fair, if you ask me."

"I also had four hundred and ninety-seven dollars saved up for a car," he continued. "I guess that went to my brother, Jerry. I miss him and I bet he blew all that dough on Candy Crush. I worry about my brother and my dog, Max, who has probably died of a broken heart by now. I long for Max."

Auggie was nothing if not an open book, which was fine. It was nice to take a waking trip into someone else's head.

"My mom—and I miss her the most—keeps sending out Facebook messages warning parents to talk to their kids about drugs now. I'm not the only one. Another kid at my school died right after me because he took a pill he thought was a Xanax. It wasn't."

Then he added, in a whispery voice, "Anyway, that's cool of my mom to keep my name alive. She tags the posts with 'Auggie O'Connor' so my friends will read them. That's the killer thing."

"What?" I asked.

"I'm reduced to a cautionary tale," he said, shaking his head and collecting the cereal bowls. By now, Pete had come downstairs in his workout gear for training, which consisted of an old Rolling Stones concert shirt and biker shorts. He picked up the box on the table. "Really, Bobby, you ate all the marshmallows? What's lucky about this cereal now?" Pete demanded. Bobby just licked his lips.

Auggie not only cleared the bowls, but also insisted on washing them as the first of his babysitting duties. It dawned on me that we never really told him when to show up. He just did.

Pete took his cereal into the living room and Bobby was out walking the dog. This gave Auggie time to finish his story. "So anyways, my mom keeps posting a lot of things. She posts pictures of me as a little boy in my baseball uniform with really bad bangs she cut at home. Really? What girls will look at that picture and feel badly that I'm outta there? I want sympathy. I want reevaluation."

"I bet they're thinking, 'We had our chance with Auggie O'Connor and blew it,'" I said with a laugh.

"You think?" he asked with gusto. "Do you think they're thinking: prom remorse?"

I had to laugh. Auggie really wanted that afterlife fan club.

His smile quickly faded. "The day after I, you know, died, my mom received a package from school in the mail. It was my eight-by-ten mug smiling up brilliant at her. School pictures. Senior year," he said with a wince. "You know the photos where everyone has that promise of a bright future in their eyes. I was king of the world—at least my world."

"Aug, you still are," I told him.

"It's funny what I used to worry about," he said. "I never had a dad, so I'd always worry that something would happen to my mom. I'll never forget that when I was five, I asked her to promise that she would never die."

"And what did she say?" I asked.

"She was the one who told me that I'd never really be without her," he said. "She said that we should agree on a symbol of this promise. My mom had long hair that was always flying, so I said she should be a kite. Mom said if she was ever gone, I should just go outside and fly my kite as high as possible and she would grab it from the other side. And it would be like we were holding hands. Still."

Without skipping a beat, I grabbed one of his strong, yet boyish, hands and led him out to the garage.

Half an hour later, Daniel found the three of us running down the middle of the street, our kites flying high. With Bobby at his heels, Auggie was surprisingly light on his feet, almost like a dancer, and joyous when his kite caught the warm summer wind, making the white string jump. It pulled hard. "Yep," he said, grinning.

"What's going on?" Daniel asked.

"Nothing. Everything," I said.

2.

Somehow it was already nearing the end of September, only two weeks away from the autumnal equinox. The joy of the early morning was met with the foul, dirty underwear stench of Johnny's gym, which at 9 a.m. was full of those in maximum sweat mode. Eddie already had an eight-inch saber slash in his arm from a session that included weapons. For once, I had been rooting for Eddie. His opponent, Tor, had an uncanny way of making eye contact for several long moments to the point where I felt my skin begin to crawl.

As he bandaged his wounds, Eddie just looked on the bright side. "I've been at ITT longer than I was alive—and I have worse scars from the GF," he said. "This is a vacation."

"Ever think of getting out?" I asked.

"A Wargo on the outside or above ground? Nah," Eddie said. "I don't even think about it."

Bertha had walked up silently because she wasn't the biggest Eddie fan and now she had been ordered to get in the ring with him. She was dripping from thirty minutes on a bike, but determined.

"Knockout technique number one," said Cleve, one of the MI-5 agents. "Strike a sensitive part of the body and use maximum force. Animal force."

I heard Bertha growl.

"Aim for the head," Clive instructed. "Brains are rarely firmly placed in there. Find a way to shake the brain so it swims in its own juices."

Eddie just stood there. "That cow will never take me," he said with an arrogant sneer.

Bertha wound up, filled with the rage of Eddie's beatings while she was at ITT. I was shocked when she sunk a fist deep into his very, very low midsection.

"Or you could go for the element of surprise," she said with a satisfied smile. Once he could catch his breath, Eddie wheezed, "Truce."

"Don't ever piss off a short girl. We're tiny little ninjas of death. The perfect height to punch you . . . you know where," Bertha said, advancing. It took everything in Eddie to cover the jewels and back way the hell up.

Exactly how Bertha was such a good punch didn't shock me. "Street girl stuff, Walk-*her*," she said. "A case of eat or be eaten. You have to keep your wits frosty and your hands in fists."

I didn't doubt she could take care of business. As for me, I wasn't doing any business as I slogged through my morning. Somehow I clamped down my taste buds and finished my eggs, so I flung the paper-plate Frisbee style into a faraway trash can.

"Girlie," a voice boomed. "Yes, you, girlie. Look alive!"

It was unmistakably Johnny, addressing me the only way he knew how. "Howja learn to do that?" he asked.

"Do what? Eat cold eggs? What am I doing?"

"C'mere girlie. Yes, you. Do you broads need a written invitation?" he shouted, pointing at me with his twisted, wrinkled finger. Given no choice, I followed.

His sweat jacket was slightly askew and his pants were about a size too big, but he belted them midchest like old men do. I wondered how they even stayed on as he clomped out the garage door of the gym and down a muddy trail into the woods with me at his heels.

He was shockingly swift for a man his age, which I guessed to be somewhere in his seventies. Like a nimble, fast-moving elf, Johnny led me down a rambling forest path until we reached a small wooden cabin-shack that looked like a place where you'd keep lawn mowers. The outside seemed to be home to every rusted-out tool in the universe.

"My house. Don't even think of coming in. I haven't had broads in it since nineteen sixty-two!" he barked, motioning me to stop in my tracks while he went inside.

It was hard to picture any "broads" frequenting this shack, let alone its owner.

Johnny quickly reemerged and what he returned with wiped the smile off my face.

He was pointing a gigantic knife at me.

"Go ahead, girlie. Take it," he said impatiently.

Either I was stabbing something or he was about to grill steaks. My guess was the first choice.

"Hold it by the handle. It won't bite."

Cautiously, I reached out and took the knife from him.

"What should I do with it?"

"Butter some bread," Johnny sneered.

"Really?"

"If you could take a moment from your busy schedule and focus, you'll listen to me and throw it," he barked.

"Throw it where?" I asked.

"Anywheres—but at me or at you or at Peg," he balked, noting the dog was curled up in a ball in the sun by his feet now. "There's ten thousand trees around us. Just throw the damn thing at one of them—and stop yapping!"

So, I did and I killed a tree. Well, maybe I just wounded it. This made Johnny smile and duck back into the house for what seemed like the longest time. This time he returned with an ax. "Are you housing a serial killer in there?" I demanded and his look told me to shut my big trap.

"Same thing, kid. Do it again!" he said. So I shrugged, grabbed the ax handle, and whipped it hard at an unsuspecting maple tree.

"Think we'll get syrup? To go with our bread?" I posed and Johnny actually . . . smiled.

"Stop running your gums," he said. Then he was gone (again) into the little cabin, which meant I could gaze up and get a few rays of sun before he returned with who knows what . . . a chainsaw maybe?

He emerged when I was still sunning myself. "What are we doin' out here, having a little beauty session!" he yelled. "Open your lamps and look what I gots here!"

What I saw surprised me.

It looked an awful lot like Dr. Marvin King's wool trench coat, although his was black and this one was smaller and charcoal gray. When my mouth fell open, Johnny took it upon himself to shoot me the kind of look that said I was jumping the gun. "Only got a few of these left and I think this one just might fit you," he said, motioning me with his wrinkled hand to come forward. Even though it must have been eighty degrees outside and I was wearing leggings and a T-shirt, I put on that winter coat.

"I'm not cold," I announced.

"Pocket," Johnny commanded. "Reach in carefully. Don't want you to bleed all over my nice coat or start with the eye drips because you cut your delicate hand."

"It's like a Hallmark card around here. Thanks for the concern," I said, gingerly reaching inside until I felt them. The throwing stars, exactly the same as the ones used by Dr. King were cold, hard, and extremely sharp.

"I've been watching you, girlie," Johnny said. "Watching you for quite some time. I think you got the aim, maybe even the skill.

You definitely have the balls—and I love a broad with balls."

"I have no balls," I retorted.

"I know balls—mostly because so few of you kids have them anymore. Most of you are soft with all your video games and computers and chitchats on your machines. You sit on couches. You binge on nonsense. Get awards for breathing. And yous grow up with one thing: No balls," Johnny said. "But you have balls . . . more balls than most of the guys and definitely more than the broads. Besides, someone's gotta work these," he said. "Can't trust those Freak girls with them. Personally, I'd never trust any of those Freaks. They're mongrels, if you ask me."

"They're different," I said to the most unPC person ever born.

"They're uncivilized and ruthless 'cause they had to be to make it. It doesn't make 'em someone I'd close my lamps around. There might come a moment when you'll be glad old Johnny showed you how to take care of business," he said.

"What business is that?" I asked, quietly.

"Survival!" he shouted.

In the end, he took me to a tree just a little beyond his living quarters. On that tree was a picture of our new principal with several slice marks through his rather large, rather pale forehead. It was the first time I laughed joyously since last night's situation with my mother and Cass. "Not a fan of Principal Dick?" I asked with a laugh.

"He's the head mongrel. Maybe even the devil. Time will tell—as it always does. Now pay attention and stop this chitchat!" he yelled. I shut my mouth and Johnny spent the next hour explaining aim, lifting my arm back, and helping me narrow my vision to throw the stars and hit my mark.

"It's like playing Frisbee—with a victim, explosions, and sometimes buckets of blood. Now that's my kind of fight," he said with a malicious laugh. "Aim for the heart. Busts those demons up permanent-like. Works on Freaks, too, in case you're wonderin'."

When my training session ended, I paused before placing the weapons safely back in their pocket. "They're almost mythological," I said, glancing down at the 14-karat gold stars that sparkled in my hands.

"Become your own myth, girlie," Johnny said. Then he walked away and with his back still turned, put up one hand in parting.

"But what about the coat?" I yelled.

"It's been waiting for yous since you arrived here," he said. "I'll have the rest of the stars sent to your house for you to pack. Have the balls to use them, girlie. Listen to your gut. You'll know when to throw and when to run."

3.

I had nothing else to do, but sling the coat over my arm and walk back to the gym to face the rest of what had already been a brutal morning of sparring. Ass was kicked and imaginary trophies were won.

As I approached the gym, I heard loud cheering from inside and wondered who was in the ring now. It was the same sound children emit when someone is having a schoolyard brawl before the teacher rushes in to break it up.

When my eyes adjusted to the soft lights inside and the stench of fresh sweat hit my nostrils, I glanced into the ring . . . and my heart hit ground zero.

Daniel was raging a war. I could see his sharply defined jawline and his grim, hard mouth. He swore under his breath when Tor gave him a curt nod that was almost a dare. Daniel answered by wrapping his wide hands on Tor's throat as together they fell with a seismic thud to the mat. Both were dripping ample blood and sweat.

Raw and dirty, the fight blazed on as Tor dug an elbow into Daniel's midsection and then found himself the winner of a vicious head butt from the man who slept next to me.

"I've thought a lot about you, which is unfortunate," Tor grunted. I could see Daniel clawing at the air, and I imagined that's what he did in the Hole. Each moment just dug him deeper into the dark as Tor stared him down almost hypnotically.

When he was sure his prey was off-kilter, the bastard wound up quickly to punch Daniel hard in the right temple. A gasp flew out of my throat as Daniel's neck snapped back. After shaking his head like he was trying to reset his scrambled brains, Daniel shouted, "You've been on my mind, too."

"You're sleeping next to her and dreaming of me?" Tor taunted, glancing momentarily my way. "If that's the case, Walker darling, you should visit me on the island and really get your freak on."

"Here's a preview of my dreams," Daniel hissed, lifting one of his strong soccer-player legs and kicking Tor so hard on the back of his head that his bodily fluids showered the repulsed Claires.

The Freak's knees buckled, but he willed himself to stand upright just as quickly, although I noticed that his left front tooth was now embedded into the mat.

"Pity you're already deceased," Tor taunted, his eyes inches from Daniel's as they took turns spewing obscenities to each other. Tor continued to stare and I saw Daniel blink once and then twice as if his vision had suddenly gone blurry. Tor used those seconds to deliver a lethal front kick to Daniel's ribs. At the last minute, Daniel arched his back almost perpendicular with the floor, forcing Tor to fall forward, jamming his knee into his own face.

"Yes!" I cried under my breath, spontaneously clapping.

Claire C wandered up with her sister Claire V. "Might be fun to get between them. Something to do on the trip. I love a vacation romance," Claire V said to which her sister simply tossed me a saucy smile.

I felt the sweat fly off Tor who rebounded nicely by smashing a fist into Daniel's face. But that didn't stop the darker of the two. Daniel swung around hard, ramming an elbow into Tor's solar plexus, which caused him to hit the ground. He rebounded fast, smashing his foot into Tor's pointed chin. "Mess him up! Mess him up bad! Rip his lungs out! Pull his hair!" A.E. shouted from the safety of a folding chair halfway across the room.

Undaunted, Tor returned a kick to Daniel's shinbone and then almost landed one on his crotch, but Daniel dodged while Tor ricocheted into the ropes.

I found myself pacing hard on the sidelines, bashing into one of the Mermen who sat in a wheelchair. "Just chill, baby," Chayne said. "No one hates that SOB Tor more than us. Remember, we live with him. You can't even drown him. Believe me, we took him out in the ocean and tried."

I wondered why Bruce wouldn't just stop the fight, but our master teacher allowed it until the bell rang. At that moment, Tor's head was tilted and Daniel had his hands wrapped neatly around his throat. I could see he was about to press his Adam's apple.

The *ding-ding-ding* of the bell sounded and Daniel removed his hands, cupped his palms, and smacked them hard against Tor's ears. Finally, he was the one who was temporarily disoriented, and Daniel plunged a fist into his face. Tor hit the deck hard. It took the three XXL Mafia guys to peel Daniel off him including the one named Mario who yelled, "I thought Tiny here had the bad temper! I don't know if we should adopt you or shoot you."

"No one is shooting anyone," Bruce insisted, pointing to me. "Walker in the ring."

"And you," he said to Daniel. "Stay in the ring. You're far from done, son."

4.

I stared at Daniel, praying that time would suck us into some sort of void. Looking across the ring that I was forced to enter, I felt myself begin to visibly shake. *Why were they doing this?*

It was almost as if Bruce read my mind. "Your worst fear is seeing her hurt. And vice versa. But you must. You must see it. Feel it. Get over it," Bruce instructed, handing Daniel what looked like a jagged-toothed hunting knife.

"I want you to imagine she is one of the demon forces," Bruce said. "Do not worry about consequences. Later, we'll put on the reset and she will be fine."

"This is bullshit!" Daniel said. His eyes went dark very fast and a hand curled into a tight fist. For a quick moment, I imagined him striking Bruce and then being escorted away.

"It's an order," Bruce said. "And I want you to make swift, lethal moves. Take her out. Go for the wounding shot."

"Of course, she is welcome to do the same," said a Russian trainer, handing me the same hunting knife. "My money is on the devushka." Translation, I found out: girl.

Trembling, I stood inches away from the man I loved wondering, "What now?"

Of all the people in this room, I knew who was the most powerful, although I was sure that he would never use that strength on me. I could see Daniel's grim, hard mouth. His gray eyes narrowed.

The IRA guys approached me with three gold throwing stars. "Let's up the ante. Shake that shit out of ye head, lassie," said Liam. "I got a pint on you winning. You have the stars and the knife. He just has the knife. Now, let your body go loose and do what you were taught today. We'll slap the reset back on your boy if you hit the wrong spot. You won't cut anything off you need."

That earned him a hearty laugh from most of the men in the room.

"I won't do it," I said, defiantly, allowing the stars to drop to the mat by my feet.

"Oh yes, you will, Miss Callaghan." I wasn't sure when he had arrived, but I knew that voice. In a dark gray suit, Principal Dick looked out of place, especially with that pointed chin and low-hung head. He should have been a comic-book character instead of one of the most influential men in the realm.

Dick patted his sweaty brow with a white handkerchief looking like he loathed being here, but at the same time needed to check on our progress. He stood as far away from the action as possible, against one of the ugly gray back walls with a poster of Rocky on it.

"This is quite a lovely showing of commitment from the two of you, but now it's time to fight. I want to see what you've learned during this crucial training time," said Principal Dick. "If either of you proves unready then I'll remove you from this mission."

"Really?" I posed.

"You'll be so far up shit's creek that a speed boat set on a hundred won't help you find shore, Miss Callaghan," he said.

"I'm a great swimmer," I said, locking eyes with the man I hated the most next to Edward Reid. Then I added for good measure, "I hope you're recording this."

Dick ignored me.

It was Daniel who quietly picked up the throwing stars and put them into my still-trembling hands as Bruce rang the bell indicating that it was time to stop talking and start fighting. By now, the entire team had gathered ringside as Daniel and I stood in place. Frozen.

The clock ticked. A minute passed. A fly buzzed.

"Do you want me to take one of you away—with me?" Dick threatened.

We moved toward each other because there was no other choice.

Daniel stared into my eyes, holding the knife and then raising it in striking position as we did a gentle exploratory dance around the ring. I held one of the stars in my throwing hand and two of the stars in my left hand, where I also grasped the knife. Daniel nodded and I lifted my arm the way Johnny showed me.

My head cocked to the side, I allowed myself to get lost in the dance as we circled each other. For a minute, I pretended that we were back on the front porch keeping time to some imaginary music.

We went in another circle with a despondent Eddie shouting, "Somebody kill somebody. Let's get this over with and have lunch."

Daniel struck first, grabbing me hard by the fat in my upper arm and ramming me against his chest. I heard the slice of the knife ripping through tender, young skin and tears formed in my eyes from the pain. Daniel continued to hold me then stepped back. Dropping the knife and the stars, I grabbed my stomach with my left hand and held my midsection as blood dripped to the mat below us.

I wasn't the one bleeding. Daniel had sliced his own arm, although no one could see it under his long-sleeved black training shirt.

"Very good," Bruce said. "But not a lethal blow. Walker, you must return the strike. You're fighting for your existence. He's a demon. Destroy him."

My eyes locked on Daniel who danced me around another thirty degrees with his right arm firmly placed over his bleeding one. Slowly, he lifted that same arm with the knife in it, aiming the point at my heart. Narrowing my eyes, I refused to look at the weapon, but remained locked on his face.

Then I threw my remaining star as hard as I possibly could.

Which was harder than I thought.

It landed inches above Principal Dick, embedding in Rocky's mop of dark hair.

"I'm done," I announced.

"We're out," said Daniel, who started to leave the ring but on second thought flung the knife viciously, sticking in the wall inches away from Tor's face.

When we walked out of the garage, our not-so-beloved Principal was still checking himself for puncture wounds.

5.

Burning Tree Court. Late afternoon. When we got back to the little white Craftsman, Auggie, Bobby and the dog were in some sort of front-lawn competition for the world's loudest being. I had to laugh because the kid always had his priorities straight. "Can you teach me some moves? And I'm real hungry. What's for dinner?"

Auggie grinned and plopped down on the grass in the front yard. "Yeah, what's for dinner?" he said with the same hopeful face.

Daniel, his arm perfectly fine after the reset, pretended to tackle Bobby and I promised a cheeseburger was in everyone's future. In the youngest Reid's little universe, everything was pretty much perfect: a little wrestling, a cool canine, and two all-meat patties on a bun.

Our house was expanding, but not in square footage or bathrooms. Out of nerves over the mission, Iz and Bertha were practically living with us, too. At night, they set up camp on the two living room couches. I hung back to wait for Bertha who was clomping up the street. "Stupid school bus," she hissed. "You think they would drop us off at the driveway and not down the road." The reset was back, and I noted that she was moving quite swiftly.

"For what we're doing, they should send a limo," Iz said.

"With Beyonce inside," Bertha said. I knew she was testing him.

"I don't need Beyonce," Iz said, running off to tackle Daniel and Bobby.

Bertha wasn't someone who ever hid a feeling. Her smile could have been used in a power outage. "Uh-huh," I said with a smile "He don't need no Beyonce."

Inside the house, alone for a moment, I hung up my new coat in the closet and then braced against a kitchen sink piled high with dishes. I started shaking as my mind drifted to being in that ring with Daniel.

I didn't have time to dwell on the day. Daniel was suddenly there, in the kitchen, filling up the space. He grabbed me by the hand and without a word locked the two of us in the dark kitchen pantry. I was very much aware of his presence and he covered the distance quickly.

"Do you need Beyonce?" I asked.

"I need you. Alone. Right now."

A beat passed. And the pantry seemed to be overheating.

"Hey!" I heard Bobby yell. "What are you doing in there?"

"Long day at the office," he said, touching his lips to mine.

"Brutal," I whispered between kisses. "But things are getting better."

"They usually do." He fit his mouth to mine and made it better.

That is, until Bobby slid his fingers under the door, which was just plain Bobby. Then he slid a picture he drew of me at school, which made me smile. He sailed two Matchbox cars toward our feet. We refused to come out, which made him go to Plan C. When he shoved the day's mail underneath the door I couldn't look away.

The envelope was midnight black with small, white handwriting. It was addressed to Daniel, Pete, and me. The return address: Frederick Reardon Establishment of Academics and Kinetics. Daniel saw it, too, reluctantly bent down, and ripped it open. Shrugging, he used the thin shaft of light coming in from a crack in the door to read what had been sent.

"Baby, we've been summoned," he said in a gravelly voice. It was his shock tone.

"Where?" I said, blandly.

"Freak freaking island."

Grabbing the white card in his hand, I read it aloud: YOU HAVE BEEN INVITED TO SPEND THE NIGHT TONIGHT AT FREDERICK REARDON. NONCOMPLIANCE WILL BE DEEMED RUDE AND RECKLESS. CONSEQUENCES OF THE HIGHEST DREADFULNESS WILL ENSUE. MEET AT THE BEACH PROMPTLY AT 7:30 P.M. FOR YOUR TRANSPORT. REGARDS, H.H.

"Harry Houdini?" I posed. "Is he their principal?"

Daniel grabbed the card from my hands and before I could say another word, put the invite in his mouth. He held it with his teeth and ripped it in two with his hand.

"Callaghan, it's not 7:30 yet," he said, letting the paper fall to the kitchen floor.

He crushed his lips to mine again. Burger night and future Freaks would have to wait.

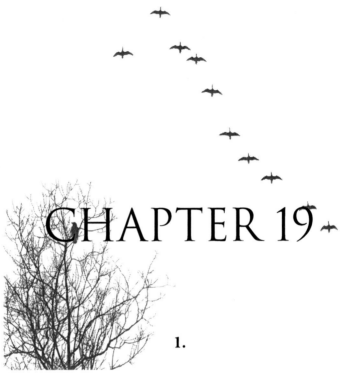

CHAPTER 19

1.

The beach was murky that night making it look like we were walking through a blue-white gauze. I waded through what I imagined to be tiny fingers of dense fog as I followed the sound of the water harshly slapping the shore.

It didn't take long before I was standing in a place where that turbulent sea crashed down on my toes. For a split-second, it reminded me of my mom in Lake Michigan when the water called to her, too. I wouldn't let my mind go there. There was too much here. *Thank God for Cass.* No—I wouldn't think that either. *I would never go there again.*

We were sleeping at Freak Island tonight. As usual, there were no choices and only threats and demands.

Packing for a sleepover didn't feel familiar. I was never that girly and Friday nights were never spent in front of the TV in sleeping bags in someone else's den. I was den-less. You don't exactly invite friends from school to sleepover when your bed is Aunt Ginny's pull-out couch. It dawned on me that Bertha and Tosh had replaced the few girlfriends I had back in the living realm.

Time moves us and acts as an eraser.

In many ways, there was too much to think about now. Where would we sleep tonight? What would we do on the island? I wasn't even sure what I had shoved into my backpack, now resting on the frosted grains of sun-bleached sand. All I knew was that my shoes were off, my yellow sundress was damp from the dryer (why I wore a dress for a boat ride to an island was beyond me), and my nerves were on high alert.

The treacherous tidewaters sloshed hard through my toes and I wished that the liquid was colder. How convenient to just put it all on numb. If only I could freeze every fear and then chip them off like icicles waiting to fall and then shatter. But tonight was about confronting fears. And I couldn't numb myself to the Freaks. Johnny warned me.

Looking into the whiteout, I couldn't see Daniel, but I heard boots pacing hard up and down the shoreline. He was in black jeans and a black T-shirt with his favorite aviator glasses on like a mask. Maybe that was his plan. Hear no evil. See no evil. Internalize no evil.

I gasped when without warning Bertha was suddenly in my face. "I told them . . . I told them . . . Yessir, I did, damn it, damn it all to hell," she kept ranting under her breath while she faded in and out of my vision stomping around on the sand.

"You told them what, B?" Pete asked. As I came closer, I saw the man-child was sitting in the wet sand, playing tic-tac-toe with himself.

"I told them I wouldn't go there. Ever. Never ag . . ." she began and her words evaporated into the air. "What did you tell who, Bertha?" I asked her, but she never answered me directly. "Never again. Never again," she began to rant again as she wore out the sand.

When she looped by this time, I reached out and grabbed her arm gently.

"So, you've been there before?" I asked. "You said never again. You've been to Freak Island?"

"Don't pay me no mind, Walk-*her.* Don't pay me no mind. I'm just rambling," Bertha said. "My mother used to say, 'Bertha, you're such a rambler.'"

"But you didn't know your mom," I said, quietly. She had told us she was a toddler dumped off at the hospital where she'd been born. I couldn't help it. Once I started with the questions, the red lights started going off in my brain.

"My foster mom. Gots lots of those."

"I'm sorry, Bertha," I said, looking down at the water. "I'll shut up. I'm nervous, too."

"No worries, Walk-*her*, baby," she said. "Just your way of dealing with your jingle jangles."

Iz collected some ammunition and began to show us how to skip rocks. He was good, which wasn't surprising. "I think I hit something out there," he joked. "Maybe it was Jaws."

"I ain't getting on no boat," Bertha announced. "I've seen all those horror movies. I believe in Sharknado. They eat everything. Even the steering wheel of the boat."

I had to laugh again. This was the Bertha I knew.

In the distance, I could barely see what looked like amber headlights slicing through the mist, but it wasn't a boat. This came from the road. When the vehicle reached the beach's parking lot, I heard angry voices followed by shadows walking closer. Every molecule of me tensed.

"Did I miss anything, kids?" he yelled into the night.

"Oh, kids? Where are you? Come on! You guys. Don't be

asswipes," Eddie Wargo shouted. No one spoke. "Hello! Are you out there? I can't even see your footprints. Don't do this to me, man. Someone say something. Fog gives me the creeps."

It was Iz who in a low voice faked a moan followed by Daniel who went animalistic with a wolf howl.

"That's not funny! Come on, you guys. I got you stuff. Sour Patch Kids, anybody?" he offered in a petrified, but still hopeful way. "I got Twix, too. From the GF's private stash. The big bars. And Snickers."

He broke me down. I put up a hand, which cut through the mist.

"What the eff is that?" Eddie cried. "Don't hurt me! Are you one of the fog people?"

I heard Pete, Daniel, and Iz laughing hard now, although they tried to muffle it.

"Eddie," I said. "It's Walker. Move toward the sound of the water. I'll take the Twix."

I could hear Eddie's feet moving like a herd of buffalo stampeding. When he actually ran into the water and screamed on the top of his lungs, I thought I'd never stop laughing.

"I don't swim, Walker," Eddie whispered, handing me the goods. "I don't even float. You have to save me if I go in by accident."

"That'll cost you the Twix and the Snickers," I said.

A.E. was somewhere and when I called out for him, I heard a wee voice in the distance followed by a . . . poem. "Fog. Oh the fog. The fog that wouldn't rise. So thick, swallowing me whole. Leading to my ultimate demise," he chanted.

"Just what we need," Daniel said. "Edgar Allen Poe Jr."

A.E. just giggled and tripped over his own feet in the sand. "I made that up. I love the beach. My mom used to take me when I was a little boy. But never at night. Say something someone. I'm all turned around. Wait. I hear the water. Never mind."

Finally, I saw the stick-figure legs in shorts no less, wobbling toward me. "I wish we had time to build a castle," the kid said. "But that's okay. I just want to stand here. I love the fog. I'm also an excellent swimmer."

"We don't have to swim there," Eddie balked, nervously. "I don't even do baths."

"Yeah. We know," Bertha said, pinching her nose. "Why don't you stand downwind?"

Everyone from the Academy and ITT had arrived, which begged the question: Who was the other person?

A large figure appeared in shadow as he lumbered with purpose and hard strides down onto the beach. He wasn't walking on the sand, but crushing and grinding it underneath him.

When the fog momentarily parted, I saw the bright red nose and the white painted face.

My breath caught.

"I need to tell you something," Eddie whispered. "We have a new driver and babysitter."

2.

John, moved closer, which caused Iz and Pete to meet him halfway, almost blocking the rest of us. A rancid smell caught my attention and I knew it was from the fact that he was in his janitor's uniform. But he had his full clown face on.

Without asking, he began to collect all the backpacks. "The GF sent him," Eddie said.

John disappeared again into the fog.

"I thought he'd eat us on the way over," A.E. whispered.

Eddie told the rest. "After he delivers the backpacks, he's been told by the GF to wait here. Until morning. Partly, it's to take us back, but mostly it's to make sure that no one from our side gets any funny ideas and decides to escape the island in the middle of the night.

There were now two unwelcome choices.

Freak Island or a freak named John on a deserted beach.

There was no choice after he spoke. It was the first time I heard him speak. But it wouldn't be the last.

"Get. Into. The. Water," he wheezed as if he used every last ounce of lung space on those words.

I chose *the* Freaks—not this freak.

He cleared that beach in under a minute until he was the only one standing on the sand. Even with the fog, my eyes remained on lock with his feral ones.

In the mist that was lifting, he licked those ruby-red lips.

3.

A choking Eddie pushed past A.E. to wave something in the air.

"It was on a pole. At the top of the beach. I saw it when we pulled in," Eddie interrupted, holding a piece of paper in his hand as he continued to cough. By now, all of us were at least waist-high in the water.

"What does it say?" I called out, silent swearing because the water was actually that cold.

This time Eddie was silent.

"Eddie, speak!" I called to him as long, slick seaweed began to wrap around my feet. At least I hoped that it was seaweed and not something underneath moving around my toes.

"I'm not reading this stupid thing. Who cares what the Board says now. We're all done for it in the water," he cried, holding the note high as he waded deeper.

He wouldn't read it. Then it dawned on me. He *couldn't* read it. *He couldn't read.* Why did that instantly break my heart?

"Eddie," I called out in a harsh tone. "I want to read it. You hear me? I want to be the first one to read it. Just stand there and don't you dare read it. Just, uh . . . sing something until I find you."

His voice was filled with guarded gratitude.

"What do you want me to sing?"

"Whatever you fancy . . . Michael Bublé!" I yelled, still not seeing him. Daniel had my left hand tucked firmly in his right, as we went deeper into nothing, water stroking my neck and this time something was actually nibbling on my knees.

"It's a nice day to start again," Eddie Wargo croaked. "It's a nice day for a white wedding."

Just what I needed.

A moonlit swim with creatures and Billy Idol.

"Is that a stingray?" A.E. shouted.

"No, keep swimming," Daniel replied.

When Eddie came close enough to hand me the note, I grabbed his other hand, so we wouldn't lose him again. I could see the grateful look on his face—and this wasn't about the swimming.

Our eyes locked and I gave Eddie a quick nod. I read, "Your travels have begun to an island with no boats. Swim toward the ascending moon until you reach another shore. The Higher Authority."

"No freaking way!" Eddie screamed. "If I take another step, my head will be underwater. I can't hold my breath. And I don't have no reset."

I couldn't focus on Eddie. Something else dawned on me.

Those who made it would be soaking wet and vulnerable when we arrived at Freak Island.

The Freaks were evening the odds.

"Callaghan, stay close," Daniel said, reluctantly dropping my hand and slicing through the water toward Eddie. "Pete, you got A.E.?" he called out.

"Yeah!"

"Iz, you got Bertha?"

"No, she's got me."

But Daniel never had to save that Wargo. A head popped up from the water followed by four others.

"At your service," announced Colin, one of my favorite Mermen whose big, square-jawed mouth smiled large.

His bright purple hair in a man-bun was dripping, but he was obviously enjoying a regular evening swim. His buddy Connor, a fellow Merman with aqua hair and a rainbow beard, was easily treading water next to him. He zipped a quick circle around us.

"I'll take Walker," Connor said with a lusty laugh. "Think of us as your underwater Uber, princess."

"I got Callaghan," Daniel announced. "You got Eddie."

"Thanks. For nothing," said a dejected Connor.

Moments later, I saw Connor's arm around the big guy's neck. "I'm freezing," Eddie cried. "I have that hype thing."

"Shut up. You don't have hypothermia," Connor sighed.

Almost like he was motorized, Colin was off with poor A.E. in a headlock. That left Daniel and I free to follow their bubbles, which was all we had as a map. We couldn't see a damn thing as we swam hard through what looked like a black inkblot.

Underwater, I opened my eyes, but only once did my vision clear.

Luckily, I didn't see any sea creatures.

I did see Bertha who was under the water, swimming deep and

alone. What I saw of her shocked me. She was moving hard and fast, her belly looked absolutely flat and her legs supermodel long. She was . . . thin. I knew then that these waters probably contained mind-altering properties. Why wouldn't they? Maybe they were turning us . . . into them.

My mind was moving at warp speed when my knees scraped rough sand.

We were there, but not the there I expected. In my mind, I saw us being greeted by throngs of Freaks in every shape and size and condition. I pictured moaning Freaks mindlessly wandering in all directions like the walking dead.

The solo little girl on the shore was our first sight.

Or should I say sights?

4.

There wasn't even a hint of fog on this side where a mellow type of summer night had bloomed complete with a yellow slice of moon hanging low.

It cast a soft spotlight on a tall girl sitting on the beach shoveling sand. She was alone as far as my eyes could see and talking to herself in a voice that wasn't so low either. "Shut up!" she said to no one in particular. "Duh. Don't you think I'll tell you if I see anything."

It was an odd time to play on the beach, but I was a city girl, so what did I know? Although I knew looks could be deceiving, this girl appeared to be perfectly normal. I calculated her age to be maybe thirteen or fourteen. She had lovely, blemish-free alabaster skin and thick dark bangs that fell into her face while the rest of her pixie cut curled at the neck. She was wearing a sweet, white nightgown that billowed in the kind of soft island breeze that felt like a caress.

I noted that the sand here wasn't beige, but onyx black and the girl sat in it without a blanket just looking out at the water.

It might have been cinematic if I gracefully emerged from the surf with a hair flip and shimmering skin. "Greetings from the other side," I would say.

Instead, grace was the last thing I accomplished as I clomped out of the water, removing bits of seaweed from my hair. I could see Daniel clawing his way out of the foamy surf. His clothes were so formfitting now that he might as well have just walked out naked.

A sputtering Eddie was next, and Connor dumped him like a sack of potatoes in the dark sand. He curled into a ball, chocking like he was about to cough up a lung.

"Keep this up and I really will drown you," said a disgusted Connor, who took some time to stand up and right himself before he waddled away. "Hey D," he said to the girl.

"Fish boy," she replied. "Looks like you caught a few."

Where was Connor going? There was only beach. I didn't even see a building or any lights. I saw him lurch into the darkness and then disappear from sight.

Looking back toward the water, I saw that it had taken on a strange amber color like liquid rust.

"Duh. It's from the trees," said the little girl, putting her shovel down as she stared out into the orange. "The trees leak an acid that goes into the water. We think you best not stand in that water too long or your feet will turn the color of orange juice." She giggled at her own joke. "Your whole body will turn orange like a giant . . ."

I was at a loss. *What else was orange?* "Like a giant cheerleader with a really bad spray tan?" I proposed.

"No," she said. "I was thinking that you'd look like the fires from hell."

"Oh," I said. "I wasn't going that big."

When she stood, that billowy white cotton nightgown danced joyously and I noted that she also wore white knee-high socks and once-upon-a-time-ago spit-shined Mary Janes, now caked in the black sand. She had a bright-yellow bow on top of her head making her face look elementary-school young. Her tall, gangly body didn't fit.

"Greetings from this side. We want to welcome you," she said in a wee voice, her milky-white legs carrying her closer to the water. "We hope that you like it here at Frederick Reardon," she said.

We? There was only her there.

"We weren't really supposed to come down here to be the first to see you, but we don't listen too good. We're always in trouble." She waved her hand in a swoosh-like motion, as if it was the kind of trouble easy to make go away.

"We're so happy to meet *you*," I said, holding out a hand, but she kept a bit of a distance, eventually sidestepping me to step into the water. I saw her feet turn the color of a carrot and quickly glanced down at my arms and legs, which thankfully were still flesh colored.

In the moonlight, I saw her big eyes well up, tears threatening to run.

"Aren't you happy to meet *her*, too? She never did anything to you—at least not yet," she said. "And it's rude to play favorites. We hope you're not one of *those* rude girls. We hate rude girls."

The place was already living up to its name—and no one even had tentacles. Yet.

The girl only went ankle deep into the drink. Then she held out her right hand, but not to hold mine. Instead, her arm jettisoned sharply to the side and her fingers curled. Then she began to swing her arm gently like someone *else* was holding it.

"Look into the water," she said with an amused lilt to her voice. "Then look at me. And then look into the water again."

That's when I saw her.

There was one girl standing in the surf. She was visible to the naked eye. But when I looked into the water's reflection in that sliver of moonlight, there was two of her. Standing next to each other. Holding hands—right and left hands clasped.

I saw it clearly. One girl. Two reflections.

5.

"Duh. We're twins," she blurted, smiling widely and then giving me a little eye roll as in *isn't it obvious?* The one in the water didn't talk or smile. She just nodded. Repeatedly.

"Molly and Matilda Malone, but you can call us Deuce," said Molly, the one on dry land. "We're from Boise. No other sibs. And we get doubles on everything like desserts and Christmas presents . . . and punishments. We don't mean to be bad. We just have, according to Ma, 'rambunctious spirits.'"

I could feel Daniel's laser stare on the back of my neck. "Nice to meet you . . . both," I said because I saw them. Both of them. "You're Molly, right?" The girl who was apparent nodded happily. "And you're Matilda," I said into the water's reflection. My reward was a large smile and the kind of wave you do when you only scrunch the first few digits of your fingers.

For a long minute, I didn't know what else to say and neither did anyone else.

"Awkward silence!" Molly finally exclaimed.

"Your sister is shy?" I inquired.

"Why don't you be more obvious about it," she scolded. "You know, she can hear you."

"Please," I said, clearing my throat. "Forgive me. I can be shy, too."

Bertha was less cool about it. "So, run this by me one more time. You're like soul sistas? I'm down with that. I have soul sistas, like imaginary fly girls who I talk to when I have a problem," she blurted out. Bertha was so nervous here that she couldn't stop talking now. "But what's with the water trick. That's freaky," she blurted. "One time I thought I saw one of my soul sistas, but then I realized that the mirror at the bus station was cracked and it was just more of me."

Oh, Bertha.

Deuce looked seriously hurt. "We're not soul sisters. We're not tricksters. We're not fakes or creeps. We're sisters. I was born. She was absorbed. We had one mother named Miranda. We're identical twins. I saw her being born—even if others didn't," she said.

The word that stuck in my head was *absorbed.* "Back it up a little Deuce," I said in a sweet voice. "What do you mean by absorbed?"

"You ate her?" Eddie said in horror. Then he turned to us. "She ate her! When she was inside!" he insisted.

"Haven't you heard of it? It happens all the time," Deuce said matter-of-factly. "A mom is pregnant with twins. After just a few weeks of carrying her babies, the doctor says, 'I'm sorry. It's sad. One doesn't have a heartbeat, but don't worry. It will just go away. It will be absorbed.' Matilda went away, as far as the doctors and my mother were concerned, but not really. Inside, we held hands. And I watched her fade, small parts of her becoming one with me. Technically, I didn't eat her. Later, I saw her being born. I've seen her our entire lives. She's part of me, but not really. She's also her own person. And sometimes she lets others see her, too." Her rosy bottom lip settled into a pout. "You got a problem with it? Because whoever created us doesn't."

"No, no, problem, Molly—I mean Deuce," I said.

"Do you have a name?" she said, walking a bit closer, touching my hand. Her hand was warm. Something invisible touched my other hand. There was no mistaking the fact that I felt it.

I managed to say my name. "Walker."

"Weird," Deuce replied.

This time I pouted back while gently returning my hands to my side.

"Sorry," she said. "We don't mean to judge. The others do enough of that. And anyway, we already like you, Miss Walker."

I wasn't that much older than her, but I could sense a respect level from them both. Molly cocked her head to the left and put up a finger. "Matilda is telling me something. Hang on. She has been annoying like this all day. Just blah-blah-blah-blah-blah. Diarrhea of the mouth, Ma used to say."

"Okay, okay, I'll tell her," Molly said after a brief moment. "Really? You want me to tell her all that . . . right now? Okay, okay. Don't bug me. Ma always said you were the bossy one."

"Matilda wanted me to give you some good advice for your night here," Molly began.

"Run," Daniel bit out.

Ignoring him, I leaned down.

"So my sister said, 'Tell the pretty girl be real careful because now you're the different ones. Normal is the disease here.'"

6.

Before I could let that last one sink in, I heard the revved-up roar of heavy vehicle approaching. The black all-terrain SUV seemed suspended momentarily in the air as it crashed its way from a ridge above down to the sand. It was the kind of drop that off-roaders only wished they could do because it was like flying a car off a cliff.

A heavy door opened and then it was slammed.

A tall man in an expensive beige suit was the first out of the vehicle and with each step, I saw him pump a small plastic bottle he held in a death-grip.

The fine smell of two-dollar disinfectant caught in the air.

"Thank you, Deuce, for being here to greet our new friends—although you and little Matilda were told to go to bed," he said in a deep voice. Deuce didn't seem to be afraid and tossed him an adoring smile.

"What is my punishment, H.H.?" Deuce asked.

"Go clean your room with bleach," he replied and punctuated his words with a wide, affectionate grin that made it seem as if he was ready for his close-up.

No doubt about it. He was movie-star handsome and tall, at a few inches over six feet. I saw him gaze down at me—still dripping water and shaking off seaweed—with unconscious disgust. His hand shook convulsively when he forced himself to shake mine. It wasn't pleasant for me either as something was sprayed into my hand. He shot me with that spray disinfectant. Going down the line of us, he did the same act with each. A shake and then a cleansing spray.

He made me feel like a walking germ.

H.H. was neatly pressed and had the most perfectly coiffed dark hair. His brows were thick and he possessed a royal, Roman nose. A glance back to his hands revealed something a bit off: His fingernails were overly long and curled into loopy Os.

"I'm Howard," he announced with great gusto. "You know, the aviator! Precious time is wasting!" he boomed, checking and then rechecking the massive gold watch on his wrist. "There are stairs over yonder—about a hundred of them. I'd invite you in my car, but you're just too dirty. Happy climbing, kiddos." With those last words, Howard took large steps and soon was sliding back into his vehicle. The last I saw him, he sitting at the wheel, disinfecting.

As for us, we took our germ-ridden selves to one corner of the beach where a staircase sported *at least* a hundred rotting wooden, wobbly, beachy stairs.

"The adventure continues," Daniel whispered into my ear and added, "You go first. At least I'll have a good view."

"I think that's a compliment," I muttered.

"It was," he said, hoisting me by the buns up the first three stairs.

The view at the very top did not disappoint any of us.

"Welcome to Freak Fantasy Island," Daniel said.

CHAPTER 20

1.

It was a tropical paradise complete with so many varieties of fist-sized flowers that I couldn't even begin to try to name them all. Breathing deeply, I allowed the fragrances to fill my senses: jasmine, orange blossom, and the heady smell of what looked like a field of lilacs.

I wish I could say that the grounds were manicured and lavish, but they were wild and overgrown like the perfect deserted island. They were also filled with dense, low scrub growth like you would find on any island, and trees with branches and leaves dipping so low that it looked as if the twigs would dig into your flesh and rip you away.

The showstopper was illuminated by what appeared to be twirling searchlights. Even from a distance, it looked like the world's grandest and tallest luxury hotel plopped right into the middle of this lush habitat.

Squinting, I could see that the building was made of pristine white brick that wasn't that weathered from the salty spray of the ocean. This impressive structure emitted a sparkle that made it look glamorous and special. I felt myself moving faster, but then reminded myself of who lived in that place.

I wasn't the only one rethinking this thing. We were still about half a mile away and Eddie was huffing, puffing, and complaining when faced with yet another physical challenge. "Don't they have a shuttle? Even the Holiday Inn has a shuttle. Motel 6 probably has a shuttle," Eddie whined. "I wonder if there will be free soap and those little shampoos. I'm stealing as much as my pockets hold."

"World traveler," I retorted. "Why don't you write a nasty e-mail to Travelocity saying, 'Hi, I'm dead and I resent the fact that there was no ground transportation to my accommodations.'"

"Once, we stayed at a HoJo's. Now, that's class," Eddie muttered as we trudged in the dark through bramble and bush until we reached the longest cobblestone driveway. As we got closer, I could smell blooming magnolia trees just ahead of us on each side of the drive, their sugary scent making me want to inhale deeply.

There were silent doormen in black uniforms who stood in service. We were still soggy wet and molting as we approached the front of the magnificent building. Up close, it looked like a place I once saw in a picture of New York City. It was a dupe of the historic hotel where presidents, world leaders, and movie stars hung their hats for the night called the Waldorf Astoria.

The front entrance was grand like the one in the Big Apple and featured large gold angels with oversized and outstretched wings attached to intricately etched 14-karat-gold doors. Large sparkling-gold light fixtures hanging beside the doors appeared to hail from another century as they contained real fire within. I could see the mini blazes lighting the way inside . . . but into what or to whom?

I could see a few students about a hundred feet away on the pristinely manicured grounds sitting with their backs toward us in large white wicker outdoor chairs. Some were on their tablets or reading books with what appeared to be levitating candles that provided a glowing amber light. I expected tails and wings on the student body, but even on second and third glance (or tenth) they appeared to be resoundingly normal. At least they looked human from a distance.

Much like our Miss Travis, there was a greeting committee of one, but he wasn't like our beloved welcome wagon.

For one thing, he was much younger. And he had ink-black hair and a matching dark 'stache. His dress code was bold to say the least. His shirt, what there was of it, looked like it was made of about a hundred red shoelaces tied together. His skin-tight pants were made of bright cherry-red leather. "Bet you didn't know cows came in this color," he said as Pete's eyes popped and the poor kid began to choke on his own saliva from nerves.

"Another one bites the dust," he said. "Sorry, I use that one all the time."

"Really . . . ?" Daniel began.

"Yeah man, I'm Freddy," he tossed out and I quickly looked at Daniel's face for a reaction, but there was only blind fan adoration.

Our host didn't mince words as he continued to play getting to know you. "People are apprehensive when they meet me," Freddy said. "They think I'm going to eat them."

"Are you?" Pete tossed out.

"Excess is part of my nature. Dullness is a disease," Freddy retorted.

I had met my fair share of former celebrities here, but this man was a rock legend. My body even seemed to know that fact. I couldn't bring myself to offer him my jittery hand.

We will rock you, indeed.

"Why are you *here*?" I blurted out, immediately chastising myself for asking him anything. Why would he be at Freak U?

"If you must know, when the offer came in it was for a teaching position at the Academy, but I turned it down. Conformity doesn't turn me on," Freddy said. "I like to hang out with those on the fringe."

"I see it in your eyes," he said to me. "You're a fringe girl."

I shook my head and smiled.

"Liar," he said, winking at me like this was now our secret.

"You're still the biggest star," I blurted.

"I know," Freddy said, shrugging. "One thing I've learned is that you don't want to be a star. You want to be a legend. Am I right?"

"One hundred percent right," I said.

Clearly, Freddy was all about future forward. "We're having a late supper at ten and Howie will toss his cookies if you attend with all that water and dirt on you. He's eternity's biggest germaphobe, but I love that rich whack job. So, let's get to it. I've assigned each one of you to a student mentor to help you clean up tonight. Your bags are already in their rooms."

"Rebel with a cause," he said to Daniel. "You're with Tor. Don't piss him off. He's already in a foul mood, but what else is new?"

"Hot mama, Deuce will help you," he said to Bertha who kept looking around like she wished the soft ground would swallow her whole.

"Felony, you're going with Toxic. Just don't touch each other. His skin is actually toxic to the touch. Touch it and you will feel sick, plus you don't have the reset, big boy," he said to Eddie. "Here, you puke, you clean it before Howard sees it—or you'll be spending a night in what I like to call the zombie pit."

"Little bro, you'll go with one of the three-sixties. They can see you coming and going. Ever hear of eyes in the back of your head? They got 'em." Pete looked intrigued as two hippie-like dudes walked backward out of the hotel, parted their hair in back, and then said with their mouth, located in front, "Follow us. Just don't get turned around."

"Denzel, you're with the Mermen," he rattled off. "Genius Boy will go with you."

"That leaves Walker," he said in that strong voice. At first, I was hurt. No nickname from my celeb crush?

"Bitchin' name, Walker, if you ask me," Freddy said.

A line kept running through my mind, *"I see a little silhouetto of a man, Scaramouche, Scarmouche, will you do the Fandango? Thunderbolt and lightning. Very, very frightening."*

There are no accidents. In the next minute, I knew why I thought of that song with those last lyrics.

"Walker, you'll go with the Claires," Freddy said. "God speed."

2.

The ultra-glamorous lobby of Frederick Reardon could only be described in one word: extravagant. The snow-white walls showcased priceless works of art and there were countless sweeping staircases covered in red carpeting leading way, way up. Even the floors dazzled. What else can be said of walking over what looked like millions of one-inch glass tiles carefully handcrafted into multitudes of sparkling, iridescent mosaic patterns? It was like gliding over diamonds and precious gemstones.

The sight of pint-sized Claire C marred the beauty. She was perhaps the worst of the Claires because, thanks to her clarcognizance, she just *knew*. Everything.

Without a word of greeting or hello, the little pixie with short blonde hair dug her bony fingers into the flesh of my upper arm and dragged my dripping body through a sitting room with oversized, purple velvet high-backed chairs and dark wood tables. She kept yanking me along until we passed several couch areas and a cappuccino bar and arrived at an elevator bank in the back. The solid gold doors slid open. I made a mental note once she started pushing buttons. The living and learning floors were numbered into the thousands.

Claire C had pushed me inside the elevator and then jammed a button that read: THE TOWERS.

"Your stuff has already been delivered to our room. And my sisters have already gone through it."

She speaks!

Warning bells were going off in my mind. With a sarcastic smile, Claire C informed me, "You'll clean up in one of the bowls. Or go down the hallway and take a shower. Your blue dress is your best and only choice. Who packs only a blue dress and running shorts with a sports bra? Did you come here to go jogging in a dress?

"I didn't give you permission to go through my things," I said in a quiet voice as the empty elevator car began to rise.

"We didn't touch a zipper," she said. "V went through it. *With her mind.*"

This was worse than TSA.

"What's with the rabbit's foot? Into dead rodents or something?" she asked, but didn't give me time to answer. "Oh yes, your father gave it to you originally and then it was recently returned to you. S knows you have mixed feelings about that and my sister V can't figure out why. She can't clearly see who gave it back to you—and from where. Strange. It will come to her eventually."

"Fascinating," I said, blandly.

My mother's never-ending positivity tried in vain to break through my current attitude. I could hear her say to me, "Keep an open mind, Walker." But I couldn't—and I wouldn't. I knew I was stepping into a snake pit.

When the elevator stopped, C pushed past me to rush out and I had to run to keep up with her. At this clipped pace, she made her way down a long, narrow hallway where her kitten heels clacked over the sparkling black stone floors. The lights were so dim that I could barely see in front of my rapidly moving feet. Twice, I sneezed. It smelled that strongly of lemon and bleach. Howard's touch.

We stopped in front of Suite 17,721 with gold-colored double doors that had a tiny peephole in the middle. Claire C didn't bother knocking. "We never lock it. Why would we? Awake or sleeping, V always sees who's coming. So, sweetheart, you can never surprise us," she boasted and then narrowed her eyes.

Swinging the door open wide, she stepped back, put her fist in the small of my back, and shoved me inside. Two faltering steps in and I knew I was in trouble.

3.

It was like stepping back in time.

The air hung heavy in the warm, dark room with the only light trickling in from oil lamps on small, sculpted walnut nightstands that were placed next to four pristinely made single beds.

Each bed was framed by a turn-of-the-century white wrought-iron headboard and covered with an elaborately embroidered quilt in pinks, greens, and purples. When my eyes adjusted, I saw a large ivory-colored porcelain bowl next to each bed with a matching water pitcher inside of it.

The beds were lined up on the dark hardwood floors in a neat row with a scratchy looking wool rug in muted colors next to each. Standing in her section, which was no bigger than a sliver to turn around in, Clair A was washing the day off her face. She lifted a simple cloth towel and dipped it gingerly into her bowl, pioneer style. She had a mirror hanging over her nightstand and it was so old that parts of it were blackened from age, yet it still served as her only reflective surface. Gazing into it, she made a duck face, grabbed a cherry from a small silver tray, and bit into it in a way she thought was sexy. Then she painted her face with fresh cherry juice, concentrating first on her cheeks and then her lips.

Claire V was carrying something that smelled foul. Upon closer inspection, it was a small off-white bowl with a handle and yellow liquid sloshing inside. I remembered it from my history books and this was nothing more than a chamber pot, invented in the days before toilets. V carried it to the biggest window, leaned outside, dumped the pee, and then wordlessly slid the pot back under her bed. *Why were they living this way?*

There was no closet in the room, but a large walnut wardrobe and a low cupboard with a sideboard top, plus a matching antique dresser with a scratched mirror above it. There was no TV, computer, phone, or any electronics. On one wall was a painting of a woman in a dark cloak framed in a heavy, somber frame. Her eyes seemed to trap me in some kind of net that made it nearly impossible to look away.

"Welcome—not that we had any choice," said my nemesis V, the one who spent all of her training time staring at Daniel and salivating. "I knew you were grimy and waterlogged, but I didn't expect you to look this sloppy," V continued. I was so stunned by the surroundings that I was a blank slate.

In the corner on the scratched wood floor, I saw my steel-gray backpack, which looked like an alien amongst all of the relics. So did the Claires who were mostly flopped on their beds in modern clothing of leggings, short skirts, and cropped tops. All four were lined up on one side and I stood in front of them.

I refused to ask any questions. Of course, more than a little part of me did want to know, but I fought it hard. The less I knew about them, the better for my mental health. To avoid interaction, I stared at the portrait and the woman with the piercing almost-amber eyes.

"Our mother," said Claire A with pride. Obviously, she heard what was going on in my head. "You're thinking you don't want to know," she said. "But you desperately do. You always do. Want to know, that is. It's your freakdom."

I forced my lips to shut.

"I guess in the interest of bonding, C can allow you to use her washbowl to clean up and we'll explain a few particulars to you while you attempt to look human," she said.

C motioned for me to join her by her bed and standing almost on top of me poured some lukewarm water from her pitcher. Handing me a clean towel, she bumped into me hard, almost daring me to complain about their old-fashioned system of hygiene or the cramped quarters. *Were all the rooms this small or did they prefer it this way?*

As the gaslight near me flickered, I picked up the washcloth knowing that this way, it would take hours to get rid of the seawater and stink.

Claire A fanned herself with a piece of paper as she sat with her back to her headboard. "I know what you're thinking. And you couldn't possibly understand. But we feel better this way. It reminds us of our life. Our *first* life."

"You can't die twice," I said, repeating the fateful words Daniel said to me when I fell into the frozen lake not so long ago. I didn't say anything more because the small cloth I was holding was green now. I felt dirty and trapped—and they wouldn't stop talking.

"Every rule has an exception, Walker. I guess your boyfriend didn't fill in every blank," A said.

Claire S, smiled and said, "You're extremely nervous now. You want to run out of here and grab a hot shower. But you don't want to appear chicken shit, I know. But you're also intensely curious. You know your heart is racing and your mind whirling. You want to hear the story—and you hate yourself because you want it too badly."

"Shut up S," said V. "I'll tell it. Let's just get this over with so we can go eat."

4.

Death Story: The Claires

Born: 1911

Died Together: 1928, 1945, 1962, 1979, 1996, 2013

Claire V, the first born by one and a half minutes, sat on the edge of her old, thin feather mattress and took it upon herself to school me.

Not that it's any of your business, Nellie Bly, girl reporter, but we were born in 1911 to Lula Pitcher and . . . no one else. We like to believe that we don't have a father, and maybe we don't. Stranger things have happened. The point is we don't see a father for us, although we don't see, hear, and feel everything. Just most things. But I digress.

Let's start again.

Lula entered this world under a cloak of normalcy. She was the daughter of a shoemaker and a dishwasher in the late 1800s. Her address: Old New York. Unfortunately for Lula, she had received the type of gifts that couldn't be returned.

Not that it's your concern, but as a baby, Lula didn't have a mobile above her crib. So instead, she summoned baby birds who arrived nightly through open windows and flew circles over her laughing face. Even at that age, she had the gift.

By age three, she was hearing voices late at night. By six, ghosts were visiting her in the wee hours with messages and memories of lives past.

By age eight, she was looking into the future of others and seeing their lives play out like a picture show in her mind. By ten, Lula learned how to cross back and forth from the shimmering light to the extreme darkness, telling no one of her travels.

However, and you don't get to pass judgment, but when her father took ill with consumption and the family became poverty stricken, it was her own mother, Penny Louise, who told Lula, "You must use what you were given. Our survival depends upon it."

To that end, Penny set up a room off the kitchen and painted those windows black. She moved a small wooden table into the center of the room with a chair on one side and another one opposite it. The same lone candle sat in the middle, burning brightly for years.

Word spread about the odd little girl dressed in the black cloak. Some called her a witch; some said she was divined. Despite their superstitions about what was called black magic, the neighborhood fishermen and washerwomen almost nightly tapped on that dirty window, but only well after dark. They would bring small bowls of sugar, eggs, a baby pig, or a loaf of freshly baked bread.

Penny reminded each: "You will go blind and hungry if you speak of my daughter in any way or discuss what happens here. If you try to harm her, the consumption will come to your door, slither under it, and down your throat."

In turn-of-the-century New York, magic was considered a sin. In nearby Salem, Mass, women were being hung as witches and the penalty for practicing any kind of magic in New York was either throat slitting or the hangman's noose.

For her commission and survival, Lula would sense their pain, hear their unspoken words, and see their futures. She knew the moment their children would be born and the day when they themselves would draw their last breaths. She told them when to sail, when to plant, when to marry, and when to run.

She predicted war and peace; droughts and floods. She calmed their fears, tickled their fancies, and warned against submitting to the darkness in their souls.

As time passed, Penny finally told Lula that she also possessed some of these gifts, but had kept them carefully hidden for her own safety.

"But you, my child, possess so much more," she marveled, explaining, "We come from a long line of witches and wizards who were banished in England and sailed for America. Our birthright dictates that spiritually we fall under the governing of the Patriarch of Paranormal in London for they are the one responsible for sending us here.

Penny then gave her daughter a letter from that board that began with these words: "This must be burned three separate times upon reading. Even when you believe the ashes of this letter have been burned, you must burn them again and again."

Then the Patriarch wrote: "It is clear to this board that Lula Fair Covington is a rare combination of clairvoyant, clairsentient, clairaudient, and claircognizant, meaning that she possesses the most powerful four quadrants of magic. She can see the future, read minds, sense other's feelings, and know in a way that is boundless. It is crucial that her body, mind, and gifts do not fall into the wrong hands—and equally important that she never be allowed to reproduce. It is divined that her own children would possess even stronger gifts and thus live the most heinous existence both in life and after. This potent magic must end with this bloodline. It cannot be allowed to splinter recklessly into the future."

What followed was a potion that would ensure Lula could never conceive a baby.

Penny complied with the burning although she never made the potion. Instead, she enrolled Lula in a religious school, but the nuns returned Lula to her home at the end of the first day insisting, "She doesn't belong. We must insist she never come again."

A month later, the town found Penny upside down. She was dead, her body pickled in the barrel of brine outside of the vegetable stand. How it happened was never known.

Orphan Lula, now seventeen, was left the black hovel of their house. Neighborhood children refused to play on that street. Maybe it was the gargoyle that Lula placed on the front step that terrified them. Or perhaps it was the sight of the strange young woman who occasionally went outside in her long, swirling black wool skirts, dark shawl, and heavy hood. Her eyes burned as bright as the gaslights that lit the streets.

Underneath that hood, Lula was actually beautiful—with piercing amber eyes, black hair, and a slightly longer-than-usual nose, which most said predicted shrewdness. Lula was quite the shark, a young woman who secretly managed her rapidly growing powers to the benefit of her growing list of "clients."

Politicians from near and far now came calling to find out who would be elected the next president. And the president himself visited in the wee hours to ask what would happen if he went to war. Mothers of sons lost at sea begged Lula to call out to their boys. Spinsters wanted her potion of attraction. Crews about to go on voyages would arrive in the dark of night to ask if they were safe or would find any treasure.

"Fools, if I knew where money was buried, I would be a rich woman," she'd cackle, insisting, "No mere mortal knows all or there would only be one mortal."

She was rich in other ways. At the old age of twenty-one, under those dark skirts, she was hiding an amazing secret. She was pregnant.

Four babies were born.

It was unheard of in those days.

Quadruplets. All girls.

She named each of us Claire with a different middle name: Claire V, Claire S, Claire A, and Claire C. Ever the proud mama, Lula knew that her girls were special.

Extraordinary.

As we grew and developed, Lula put us to work in the family business as "welcomers."

We would receive clients and then serve them the all-important tea as Lula was now reading tea leaves. Most importantly, we would collect the money. If payments were resisted or threats of violence mentioned—many came not knowing why and then resisted—one of us would race up the back stairs and start pulling a heavy chain across the floor that corresponded with the ceiling in the drawing room.

I recall one man running from the house, his face drained of color, screaming into the night, insisting our home was haunted. Of course, he threw his money down on the front step. Why tempt fate or irritate the one the town called "the witch"?

As for the tea, I was the first to observe how Lula would whirl it around and then invert the glass in the saucer. The tea grounds naturally fell into the bottom of the cup and these formations then told her the future. It was simple: If the grounds went their separate ways, one was to be unfortunate in love. If the leaves stuck together, one would be happy and wealthy.

A long line of straight leaves meant imminent death.

We were late into our sixteenth year of life when Lula was finally arrested for witchery and the practice of illegal magical acts. It was a cold winter's day with the sky spitting snow and the corrupt judge sipped his tea at the courthouse where her fate would be decided by a mere man. After the last drop, he summoned Lula to his chambers, asked for a quick reading, and then sentenced her to life in prison.

It was days away from our seventeenth birthday.

We were allowed to visit Lula the next day, which was brutally cold as a nor'easter brewed. We feared she'd freeze, as the jail had no heat. That's why we smuggled in hot tea along with her favorite china cup and a saucer. Through the jail bars, Lula asked us for only one thing.

"Hold hands, my darlings," she said. "I want to read your futures."

Gazing down, Lula screamed loudly.

The tea leaves formed into four straight lines.

By morning, Lula was found hanging from the rope in her jail cell. A journal found on the floor offered a last entry that read: "Death is never the end, even if it comes again and again and again."

Two days later, upon our first seventeenth birthday, all of us woke up in these beds, but they were unfortunately located in the middle of burning hot ashes. The town set fire to our black hovel and it quickly burned with the witch daughters inside.

We emerged dead, but unscarred. Four sisters in white gowns that weren't even charred.

Pristine.

Eleven months later, a farmer's wife in Des Moines had the longest and most celebrated birth in the small town's history. She had quadruplets.

"I'm sorry. All girls," the midwife apologized to the farmer.

The girls were named Claire with different middle names.

By age two, we would wake in the middle of the night, hold hands, and sing an old folk song. The only problem was that neither the farmer nor his wife had ever taught us the song.

By age three, we knew how to read and speak perfect French. By age five, we did numerical equations at a high school level. By the time we went to school, the other children dubbed us witches. The farmer and his wife decided it was better for us to school at home.

A few days before our seventeenth birthday, we were found together in the cornfield. In the dirt. Dead.

Some said the cows went mad and attacked. Some said that horses trampled us. They was no blood; no marks.

We were all face up.

Pristine.

"It was almost as if they expired," said our newest grief-stricken mother.

Ten months later in Berlin, a spinster schoolteacher trying to hide her affair with a married soldier found out she was pregnant.

She gave birth to quads.

5.

"We're the anomaly here," V said, quietly. "Every seventeen years something or someone kills us. All of us. Together."

A added, "And then nine to twelve months later, a couple somewhere in the world has nonidentical quads and it all begins again."

S chimed in. "We've lived through the Roaring Twenties, the Great Depression, World War II Victory of Europe Day, Vietnam, Justin Bieber, Harry Potter and Teen Mom. Each time we're born to a new family."

"We have pictures of most of them. Some of the families were lovely. Some not so much," A said, shuddering. "We try as hard as possible to be normal. There's nothing worse than when your own family tells you that you're a Freak—or worse yet, thinks it and treats you accordingly."

It was Claire C who brought me to the walnut étagère by the window to take a short trip down their memory lane. There wasn't a speck of dust on the frames and it became obvious that one or several of them took loving care of their lengthy history. On that polished, antique table, there must have been forty framed photos crammed onto the wooden surface.

"That was Lula," C said, pointing to a faded black-and-white photo of their once-vibrant mother and then she quickly moved on. "That was our Roaring Twenties family, the Mercers, the farmers in Iowa."

"Oh, and here's us at the end of World War II. In Times Square no less," said A who had wandered over.

V boasted, "That was me with the solider. Getting the kiss. He was so dreamy. I was just sixteen and on my last few days. Shortly after, we died."

"I loved the seventies," said Claire S. "The bell-bottom pants! Disco! I could do the hustle better than John Travolta."

"And then there was our last family," said Claire C. My eyes drifted over a photo of a beautiful blonde mother with stick straight hair on a beach, and a beefy, square-jawed father in an American Air Force fly suit.

Between them were the four Claires in cute one-piece flowered suits. They must have been six or seven. Standing next to them with a surfboard in his hand was a slightly older, taller brother. Their mother held another little baby in her arms.

My eyes moved to the next framed photo, which was the last on the table. It was the Claires maybe a year ago on that same beach with the parents. Everyone was about a decade older.

The Claires were in skimpy bikinis now and the brother had also filled out. His long, unbound, wavy hair fell over his broad, shirtless chest and flowered Hang Ten Hawaiian shorts hung just below his six-pack. He was in the middle of the photo with his muscular arms affectionately draped over V and C.

"Stop staring, greedy girl," C said. "That's our brother. Cass."

My world slipped away.

6.

I closed my eyes and he immediately came to me with the type of speed that made me feel dizzy. I wasn't sleeping or dreaming. This was real.

"Walker, listen hard! Listen fast!" Cass implored. "I'm begging you. Don't give the picture another look. Don't tell them that you know me. You can't *even think* about knowing me. They will destroy you!"

What the . . . ?

Then my mind cleared. *Son of a . . . He knew this all along.*

"Just think of Daniel," Cass begged. "Damn it, I can't believe I just said that."

This time I obeyed, as my mind flooded with images.

"Please, sugar, I'm begging . . ." Cass implored, but I cut him off. My eyes flew open.

"Like my sister said, aren't you a greedy little porker?" V taunted. "You have that delicious Daniel and now you're looking that way at our brother. Control your hormones, little girl."

"I didn't mean—" I began.

"Dinner is in thirty minutes. I'll walk you to the shower down the hall. You still look like you rolled around in sludge," C said, pinching her nose hard so she didn't have to smell me.

7.

A quick trip back to my own century with water slicing across my face in the ultraclean and modern shower wasn't enough to calm me. *Cass was . . . IS . . . their brother. They were . . . ARE . . . related.* I felt like a mindless zombie when I stepped out, grabbed a heated towel, ransacked my backpack, and somehow dressed for the next shock.

After, I ran out of there and took a sharp left in search of an elevator. It made me want to scream when I found myself in what looked like a labyrinth of small hallways that twisted and turned to the point where I felt like a rat in a maze. *He was their freaking brother. He knew them well. He knew I knew them. He played me.*

Again, my rational self tried to give him the benefit of the doubt.

He saved your mother.

He played you.

There wasn't time for further internal discussion. I didn't mean to run into one of their classmates, but it was unavoidable since this was their territory. I *really* ran into him, but I was the one who bounced back, nearly falling into one of the walls. This Freak was fresh from an evening workout, sweating and slightly annoyed. I was forced to look up at someone who was over six feet tall, beefy like a bodybuilder, and had large, almost intoxicating caramel-colored eyes and curly reddish hair that flowed to his shoulders. He was frowning in his Harvard shorts and red Frederick Reardon sports hoodie.

Those soulful, oversized eyes scanned mine.

There was something about him staring at me that made me physically tremble.

"Excuse you," he said in a deep voice that made him sound almost aristocratic.

Screw with me pal and I'll flatten you.

But I didn't say that.

"Excuse me," I said, trying to nav around him, but he moved in the same direction, blocking all escape. I was forced to stop in my tracks. At least I could look past him. He couldn't block that . . . could he?

I stared past him at the wall, and suddenly it was as if the creamy expanse turned into a movie screen. A bright light flashed in my eyes that made my legs rock back.

When I could focus again on the wall, the movie was playing, at least in my mind.

I didn't see an actress, but myself . . . my older self. I knew it was me a few years from now, looking more mature and . . . kissing Daniel . . . kissing Cass . . ." *Not Cass!* I shook my head to rid this from my mind. When I glanced at the wall again, I saw myself with my much older mother, who was maybe seventy now, sitting by the edge of the bluest water I had ever seen in my life.

The bright light flashed again. The show was over.

"I'm Chronos," he said.

"What the hell was that?" I bit out.

"You tell me," he said, glancing down at his watch. Without another word, he brushed past me and was gone.

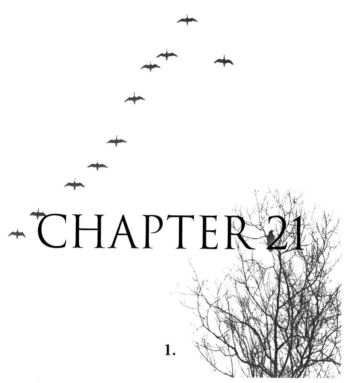

CHAPTER 21

1.

"Baby, what is it?" Daniel whispered, as he met me outside the elevator on the ground floor before dinner. "You look like you've seen a ghost."

His words were lost on me because I was mesmerized by the entrance of their dining hall, which was appropriately called the Odditorium. Daniel proved a potent distraction for tonight's menu. He was stunning in dark slacks, a white dress shirt, and a matching black dinner jacket. It was the first time I had actually seen Daniel in a suit and it took my breath away.

"You look amazing," I stammered.

"What's wrong, Callaghan?" He trapped me in his laser stare. He knew—he always knew. I could see his eyes searching for clues.

Forcing myself to mute the Cass news, I forced a smile, shook my head, and whispered, "Just on Freak overload."

"Liar," he said, putting the word into my ear. But he didn't push. He would later. That much I knew.

"Silence is better than bullshit," I said. "I'll tell you tonight."

He soothed my long hair back to murmur, "In case you were wondering, I took out Tor. Drown him in the ocean." When I rolled my eyes knowing he didn't mean it, he reluctantly grabbed my hand in both of his and guided me inside the grand dining room.

The Odditorium was glorious with rows of crystal chandeliers and hundreds of dark wood tables covered in ages old Irish lace and featuring fine ivory and rose-colored china and ruby-red goblets.

It appeared as if the entire far wall was on fire. "Our version of a fireplace," said a helpful student. Also illuminating the darkness were thousands of small votive candles that seemed suspended in air and floated a few feet above our heads all the way up to the top of a peaked, dark-beamed ceiling.

The table setting was lavish and expansive. Tropical flowers including red hibiscus spilled out of low crystal vases and the smell of late summer jasmine made me long for a hammock, a good book, and a breezy day where your worries were carried away by the wind.

This wasn't a carefree day, but a formal late supper and there were name cards at our seats. An extremely tall girl who must have been over nine feet ushered us to one of the head tables near the front. After taking my seat next to Daniel, I could see that we would be eating dinner with some our training "friends" and a few newcomers that already made me cringe.

A large purple banner overhead was filled with loopy gold letters that read: HERE WE ALL ARE: UNIQUE. INFINITE. RARE. NECESSARY.

2.

Bertha arrived in a gorgeous blue velvet dress she picked up from Myrtle's Dress Shop in town. I had never seen her look lovelier with little diamond pins in a high-pitched updo. Her lips were glossed, but her look of quiet desperation remained. "How many more hours until we blow this Freak stand?" she muttered, taking her seat at the dining table. "My skin is crawling."

"Eight more hours until sunrise. Hang in there, B," I whispered.

Even more eye-popping was the site of Eddie Wargo squirming in what looked like an overly large black rental tux, which he wore with his regulation black prison shoes. A girl with more arms than necessary was helping him to the table, and even the big lug from Booneville, Alabama, was perturbed.

"Keep those flippers away from me," he said in his most polite tone, which was loud and offensive. Pete and Izayah were quite the picture in matching gray suits, and I noted that Claire V and C, in figure-hugging black evening dresses, were personally attached to the testosterone.

My eyes diverted to Freddy in a navy tracksuit with ample cutouts across his chest and along his legs. He was playing DJ tonight and it surprised me that he was playing Beethoven's Violin Romance no. 2. When we got closer, I said, "You're cheating on rock and roll."

He shrugged and said, "I'm just a musical prostitute, my dear."

Then he threw his hands in the air, forcing me to take it all in. Each time my eyes settled, it begged a second look.

"It's not dinner," Freddy said, proudly. "It's a theatrical event."

3.

Deuce was seated next to us at the table even though she wasn't on the team. So was Chronos, in a white sweater and black pants, watching and observing a few seats down. The Claires and the still-sneering Tor flanked him. "Do you think a butter knife would qualify as a bad-ass ancient weapon?" Daniel asked, trying to make me smile. I faked it for him.

It turned out that late supper wasn't a democratic type of affair. Wait staff didn't ask what you wanted, but delivered what they felt you should have based on a quick assessment of your body type.

Daniel was served a large T-bone steak, as were Pete and Iz, while Bertha, A.E., and I received white fish and rice, which suited me just fine.

It was Eddie was who given the wild-card meal.

"I ain't eating this . . . what is it? It's black and it's . . . moving," he said in horror.

"It's squid in their own ink," a lanky waiter in a formal English accent informed him.

"Why don't I just eat a pen," Eddie said. "Got a Bic . . . and some ketchup?"

"That could be arranged. We have a student here who only eats plastics," the waiter retorted. "But what is catch up?"

Deuce was served a vegan dinner of quinoa and assorted veggies. The seat next to her was empty to the naked eye, but a meal of fried chicken and waffles was delivered to it. I saw Molly lean over to cut the food for the empty chair, never touching a bite. Then I understood why when my eyes caught the shine of a wide butter knife.

In the reflection of that knife, I could see Matilda as clear as day, sitting stick-straight in a sweet yellow sundress with big black daisies on it. She had a sparkling blue headband in her hair.

Despite the fact that I tried not to stare, I saw a waffle piece lift *apparently* all by itself from the plate, followed by several crispy pieces of heavily battered chicken. The red crystal water goblet was next to lift and then tilt, although not a drop of liquid spilled. Not a morsel of food fell. Practical matter would suspend in the air and then disappear. Even odder were the chicken bones, daintily returned to the plate.

Meanwhile, Molly was now happily preoccupied, chewing her zucchini and chatting with Bertha. Later, when the wait staff passed with a silver water pitcher, I saw Matilda leaning forward as she took in every word while blowing little kisses in Pete's direction.

Freddy wasn't kidding. It was a visual feast.

Howard ate alone at a private table at the front of the room about four feet in front of everyone else and encased in a glass booth.

The sum total of what I knew about the leader of this place came from Chronos who, without being asked, gave us a history lesson. "His father was the inventor of the Hughes Rock Eater, a drill bit used for drilling oil wells. Inheriting millions as a young man, Howard started Hughes Aircraft and Hughes Helicopters, which were sold for $5.5 billion," he said.

Claire V interrupted him—much to his displeasure. The viciousness in his eyes made me do a quick double take. "He was also a moviemaker and ladies man who had relationships with several teachers and one-namers including Katherine, Bette, Ginger, and Ava," she told us.

Chronos cut off her frivolous take of his personal life. "Later in life, Howard became a little crazier and even lived for five months in a screening room in Hollywood. When he was really old, he kept his urine stored in jars in his room and wore Kleenex boxes as slippers due to his paralyzing fear of germs," he said. "He came to Frederick Reardon as a young man again."

Obviously, he still had oddities including an obsession with peas. Even from where I was sitting down, I could see him arranging his peas on his plate according to size. The rest of his eclectic dinner tonight consisted of several Hershey Bars, a mountain of shelled pecans, and a pitcher of frothy milk.

A man ran behind the glass booth with a jar and a large swatter. "His only job is to catch flies. Howard is petrified that they'll spread germs," said Claire A. "Even right now, I hear him wondering if a black dot on the wall is just a dot or something heinous."

Chronos sat opposite Pete, which meant he was far enough away for me to avoid entirely. But his voice was loud enough for whole table to hear. Clearly, he was finished with the Howard talk and decided to move on.

"Did you know when a person dies, they have seven minutes of brain activity left. It's the mind playing back the person's memories in a dream sequence. Interesting, isn't it?" he said. Then Chronos not-so-innocently inquired of Peter Reid, "What do you remember from the night you perished?"

"A field. Snow. Our father crashing a plane," Pete said before putting on the verbal brakes. "Why am I telling you any of this?"

"Yeah, why are you, Pete?" Daniel said.

"People always tell me," Chronos said. "It's a curse."

"Then you know I want chocolate cake for dessert," Bertha said.

"I know quite a lot about you," he answered.

Chronos kept his gaze on her and I could see that Bertha's eyes were riveted as she looked at one of the white walls. He was doing it to her. Showing her a movie where she had the starring role.

When she looked at me again, there were tears in her eyes.

4.

Well after midnight, after more strained bonding with our team that resulted in absolutely no bonding at all, we were safe in our own private quarters. Howard wasn't one to judge. The Academy and ITT students were shown a wing and instructed to sleep in whatever room "made immediate sense."

Daniel and I didn't have to pretend and took the corner room way at the end of the dark hallway. It was elegant, like what you'd find in a five-star hotel room with a soft bed covered in a cloud-like white comforter. The bathroom was marble and glass with a tub for two. I tried to keep the mood light, so he didn't pry into what upset me before dinner.

"Girls like a guy who takes charge," I told him, shimmying out of my dress until I was wearing just a thin white slip. "Ask her out. Plan the date. Take her to a freaky island. The only thing missing is flowers."

"Callaghan," he said, glancing down at an imaginary watch, before he sat down and sunk into that bed. Yanking his shirt over his head, he tossed it on the floor, followed by his pants. "I gave you a full two minutes. Tell me what you should have told me two hours ago." He was imposing with that bare chest and I felt myself gazing, which made him smile.

"Let's put the Freaks to bed and then you to bed," he said with a wink. "Tell me."

And I did, knowing it would ruin the mood. I told him about the Claires, which made him scrunch his eyes in disgust as I described their room and their strange bathroom habits. That was only my opening act. The big show was telling him about their mother Lula, which, if nothing else, was a good story. Of course, I saved the best for last.

"Then they took me to a table to see their family history," I said in a quiet voice. "There were pictures of people from various decades."

"I can imagine who you could shake out of their family tree."

"The funny thing is they looked quite normal . . . and then . . . there was one person I knew," I said. "That you know."

He looked mildly curious. "I don't care," he said.

"But you do," I countered. "Cass is their brother."

Silence.

"Cass. He's their brother."

Silence.

"You've got to be . . . no, it can't be possible . . ." he said under his breath. "He's the brother of those Claire girls." I could see him try to process the layers of insanity.

I tried to explain how, when, and why, but Daniel was already up and stalking around the room like a caged lion. "I should have ended this in that college dorm room a long time ago," he said in a lethal tone.

"In front of Dr. King? And by doing what? Hello, we need to use your room to hide out from demons and you looked at my girlfriend so now I'm going to kill you?"

"You have a problem with that?" Daniel demanded. Then he punched the wall hard enough to make a large hole in what was once pinstripe wallpaper. His eyes were dark, dangerous and his anger was palpable. I knew I should just leave him alone, but it was impossible in these cramped quarters.

Looking for any escape, he nearly unhinged the white, slatted French doors that led to a terrace overlooking the beach. I followed him out there and the warm, summer breeze felt feathery light and sweet despite the mood being so bleak.

"F— me!" Daniel shouted to no one and nothing. He was basically in his birthday suit, which never caused him any concern. I watched as he glared at the water lapping at the shore.

"There's one more thing—because there always is," I said and his head whipped around. "He came to me for just a minute and insisted that the girls, the Claires, can't know." Silently now, I waited for the next explosion.

When he didn't say a word, I added, "He said they're dangerous."

The look he gave me was ice.

We were quiet for several long minutes as I watched the night birds scream victory after sourcing their midnight fish from the choppy waters.

"Know what else is dangerous?" I finally said, wrapping my arms around his naked back. I pressed my lips to his shoulder, but he didn't turn around. Then I ran a hand down his back. And when that didn't work either, I was mad enough to rip what was left of my slip down and let it fall to the floor. We had established a new dress code.

"Walker," he said.

"Daniel," I said.

"You should just leave me alone," he said.

"And what if I don't want to leave you alone?"

He didn't say a word. All I heard was the sound of the water and rushing air. Then he whipped around and I felt furious hands digging into my waist. He lifted me and soon I was balancing on the balcony railing and it felt like free floating with his arms banded tight around me. The waves crashed below us and I gasped when he buried both hands around my bum and descended on my mouth, fury and passion fusing.

We didn't think about anything but flesh, the water, and the rush.

It was well after two a.m. when we decided to slumber in the big bed, but I couldn't sleep. By three, I was still wide-eyed, which was bad. Even worse was when the fever dreams began the way they did on those nights when the mind becomes a theater of the perverse.

5.

The moon was liquid and it cast a spotlight on the thick flakes of snow that were taking a one-way header to earth. The little blue Honda was a twisted heap on the road, wispy trails of smoke waving some sort of white flag of surrender.

An ambulance with a blue strip down the side now housed my mother and two medics. Punching it, it began to speed away, tires spinning on the ice-covered roads of the Chicago suburbs.

Running faster than I ever had in my life, I made my way to what I thought was the center of the road. "Mom!" I screamed, my legs agile, flying. "Mom!"

Then I slipped. Fell hard.

I was in the middle of Milwaukee Road, on my back and under a blanket of stars. Why wasn't I cold? Why didn't I hurt? I poked my arms, my legs, my face and they felt fine. So were my eyes, and they focused on the jack-knifed truck in the shallow ditch. Something inside of it moved and I tuned in to the sickening sound of bone scraping against metal.

The dead deer stood her ground in the middle of the road. Eventually, she cocked her head toward me and took several cautious steps closer as I remained in my supine position. I wasn't sure why, but when she was near enough, I rose to my feet and smiled. Her feet smacked the ground and she was off, running hard with me racing behind her.

It became a game. I ran faster to keep up, dashing at a breakneck pace as we entered the dense woods, dodging around the tall elm and maple trees that had been there for seventy or eighty years. Before long, we were keeping pace with each other, girl and doe. The woods were deep and when I stopped to look around, I was stunned. There were hundreds of sparkling orbs in front of me, tiny clear balloon-like circles illuminated from within. I stared at them as they hovered and lingered. These weren't lights, but felt like guides of lives past.

A full moon caught lower sparkling images that looked like glittering marbles from a child's game. It was the illuminated eyes of a multitude of deer. There must have been hundreds of them.

A branch broke and I heard the whisper. It was human. Eddie Wargo's strangely tall, painfully thin father sat in the snow several feet away with his back supported by tree bark. He was moaning, but he wasn't bleeding or broken. For a man who just lost everything in a fatal truck crash, he didn't look much worse than I imagined he did in everyday life.

"A fine thing. A fine thing," he kept repeating. "Look at us. Dead. Dead as doornails. A fine thing isn't it? And it's snowing. I hate the winter."

I could see the deer were migrating closer to me; farther from him.

The dream faded for a moment until I heard human footprints crush over the last of the white-colored autumn leaves. "I knew I'd find you here tonight, Walker," Cass said. He stood tall and wide in faded blue jeans and a sky-blue winter parka, long blond hair wild in the whipping winds. "It's common to go back in your dreams to the night of your death. Most people do this during times of extreme emotional trauma."

"I hate you," I growled. "I want you to go away for—"

He interrupted me before I could forever dismiss him.

"Why?" Cass demanded. "Why do you hate me? Because I did the one thing that I knew could protect you from my sisters? I didn't tell you, Walker, so you wouldn't think about it. So you wouldn't think about me. So you wouldn't think about the possibilities—and I know you do. If you think about any of it then they will know. And they will destroy you because they'll assume you know about them—really know about them. There is so much I can never tell you. Things they've done. Horrible, horrible things."

"They hate me," I blurted.

"Not as much, sugar, as they hate me," he said. "The last time they died, it was my fault."

Branches cracked. The deer retreated.

Daniel stepped out of the shadows. He was in black, his shit-kicker boots on, and holding an enormous limb of a fallen tree. "You son of a bitch," he said, hoisting the branch and roaring toward Cass. The former marine didn't hesitate. Jumping hard, he grabbed the lowest, equally large branch of the nearest tree, and ripped it from the trunk.

"Bring it," Cass said.

Using the branches like a sword, Daniel swung hard at his opponent's head, but missed when Cass dropped and rolled in the fresh snow. He righted himself in time to use his branch to hack at Daniel's legs, narrowly missing his knees and smacking into a nearby tree. Daniel hoisted his weapon to his shoulder like he would slice forward, but then flipped it, using the blunt end to drive it into Cass's midsection. It hit skin and Cass folded, but only long enough for him to reposition his hands and swing for the fences. The collision of Daniel's rib with tree branch made me scream at the top of my lungs. Seeking revenge, Daniel swung with all his might. With each hit, pieces of their tree branches broke off, splinters raining.

"That was just round one," Daniel said, viciously throwing his sword down, as did Cass. Daniel rammed a fist into Cass's face; the night caller returned the favor with a brain-shaking blow to the side of Daniel's head.

"You're alive. Why her?" Daniel shouted.

"Life is finite," Cass growled. "Eternity is forever."

The doe bolted into the air and I sat straight up. Cass was gone. I was in bed next to Daniel who was already upright and staring at me hard.

"Callaghan, why couldn't you have stayed asleep for another five minutes? I wanted to give him his eternity," he said.

"What did you . . . just . . . do?"

"Beats the shit out of me," he said and I believed him. "I think I just fell into your dream."

He ran a hand down my back and we were silent. Was it Freak Island? Or was this something else we could do with time and practice? There were more questions than answers. "I wish you could fall asleep again—and I could finish the job," Daniel said.

Suddenly, the darkness of the room was paralyzing and the air was suffocating. I heard the clock ticking garishly loud. I knew I'd never close my eyes again on this island.

"Let's get out of here," Daniel said with a wicked gleam in his eyes.

"We can't leave the island," I reminded him. "We have the child eater waiting on the other side and we're his version of a Grand Slam breakfast."

"We're not leaving the island," he said in a way that sounded like a dare. "Earlier tonight, I noticed that this place has a basement. Callaghan, let's go on a little reconnaissance."

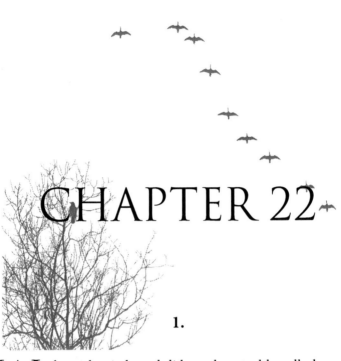

CHAPTER 22

1.

We dressed quietly and did an uber-stealth walk down the long hallway, pausing each time we heard any sound. Finally, we reached the student elevator, stepped inside, and then I cursed when the lowest floor read: LOBBY.

"Damn it. I saw a basement level, baby. I really did," Daniel whispered.

I punched the open button, stepped out, then crooked a finger, bringing him back into the hallway. "The service elevator," I mouthed, and raced across the hallway. I punched its button and luckily it was only a few floors away and came swiftly. Quickly, we walked into the no-frills cube that was used for official Frederick Reardon business. Scanning the endless row of floors, I saw them: There were actually two lower floors.

LL

RR

"What's RR?" Daniel asked, and since I didn't know, I pushed LL figuring we could always go lower.

With a wobbling jolt, the elevator took the express route down tens of hundreds of floors as my stomach tried to keep up. Slipping a hand into Daniel's large one, he squeezed hard. "We've really lost it now. What in the world are we doing?" I asked him. Adrenalin was pumping hard.

"Sightseeing," he said with a wide grin. "Besides, I was never one for the official tour. They never show you the good stuff."

With his hands now on my waist, he was holding me steady when the elevator car careened to the end of the line. The jolt at the bottom made me wonder if we had crashed somewhere in the middle of the universe, but that wasn't the case. The elevator read LL in bright red letters.

There could have been some serious turning back.

But then those heavy elevator doors opened. All I could do was wonder who or what would greet us as we hit rock bottom.

2.

We weren't stopped. That was the first shock.

I imagined guards guarding other guards, but there were none. My eyes darted everywhere. I saw no one. There was just what looked like a sterile white waiting room with a large wraparound desk and a white chair that was empty.

There was a white coffee cup with no fresh brew. Next to it was a white phone with what looked like hundreds of lines, but none blinking red as if the act would disturb the color coordination of the room.

Breathing in, I could smell it. It was the unmistakable scent of hospital.

Years ago when Aunt Ginny had her gallbladder out, I was forced to visit her repeatedly at Chicago General. That horrid smell of sickness and strong disinfectant still haunted me. This place had that same foreboding feeling enhanced by the foul odor of rubbing alcohol.

Daniel and I made our way past that waiting room, ducked through heavy double doors, and found ourselves in some sort of brightly lit patient unit. But this wasn't for the rest of the student body. The infirmary for Freak Island students was on the fifth floor. There was a special button in the elevator since these students didn't have the reset and chose to feel pain.

The LL was something else.

This unit was white and sterile from the nondescript linoleum floors to the pristine white walls void of any pictures or even posted notices. Just like in any other hospital setting, there was an uneasy silence that made you want to shout at the top of your lungs. This corridor was marked by what looked like endless white doors, each containing a small glass window about the size of an index card. Close-set wires in the windows prevented break-ins or breakouts.

I could tell that Daniel was looking for a nurse on rounds or a doctor tending to an emergency. But it was as if the place had been put to sleep for the night.

What remained was what was in those rooms. We passed the first one and I had to look inside. My mind screamed "no," but my hand was on that knob, twisting gingerly. It hitched. It caught. What was hidden was locked in there.

I raised an eyebrow when I heard a grinding noise, but it was just the service elevator whirling into action, ascending to higher floors. Then my heart sunk. We were trapped down here now. I didn't even see a sign for a staircase. There were no signs because there was no exit.

Daniel walked slowly in front of me, with one hand out as if he could somehow shove me away from any surprises.

"This is where they must keep the people they study," Daniel whispered. "I don't want to even tell you how close I was to coming down here. After my second month in the Hole."

Shivering, I refused to think about it.

"That's just part of it," I whispered back. "I bet they keep the real oddities down here. The ones they can't let mix with the rest of the student population. There's odd . . . and there's odd/dangerous."

"That sounds promising," he said.

Inching up to the first little window, I tried to glance inside, but it was futile. The window was too high, so no one could sneak an easy peek. Daniel moved behind me, lifted me, and then carefully moved closer to the window. It was pitch black in the room, which was why I pressed my face closer and closer until my skin was touching the glass.

Someone else had the same idea.

An oversized black eye filled the window. It was on the inside, which made me physically rip my face away. "Callaghan, are you okay?" Daniel whispered, pulling me back and putting me down. I shook my head yes.

"Do it again," I insisted.

Slowly, he lifted me again, leaning me closer to the window. The eye was still there, the size of a whale's eye, with wiry black lashes. It blinked; I stared. Then it was gone, replaced by what looked like a half human, half snout of a nose. It blew to fog up the window and I willed myself not to react. When the window cleared, I could see a thin stream of fire coming from that nose. Then I heard a click and white extinguishing foam was released from the ceiling.

"Just some kid . . . smoking," I said, knowing if I told him the exact truth, we would turn around and leave this floor.

"Keep going?" he whispered.

"Yeah," I said.

A few doors down, he repeated the routine, grabbing me by my middle and lifting me until my face was in one of the little windows. This one was dark with only a hint of white light coming from the far right corner. But I could hear someone or something lumbering inside and he or she sounded like they took up the space. Then a match was struck and I saw a young woman bathed in candlelight. She had light blonde hair, wide shoulders, and an ethereal look on her face. Putting down the book she had been reading in the dark, I watched her deliberately turn around. In the next moment, she disappeared.

It's just a girl reading. No biggie. Don't let your imagination run wild.

Thwack! I almost hit the roof when something inside slammed into the door so hard that I saw an indention begin to form on our side. The handle slammed down, and I prayed the lock would hold. Three more *thwacks* hit the walls. It sounded like a bulldozer ramming into steel.

"What the f— was that?" Daniel said, ripping me back.

"Get me back up there. It's getting good now," I whispered hard.

Worse than my response, he complied.

I cursed my always-morbid sense of curiosity.

It turns out the truth doesn't always set you free.

Thwack! The entire door rattled.

The girl inside the room was whipping it with her Jurassic-style tail.

Before Daniel could notice my rapid breathing, I jumped out of his arms to the floor. "I guess these rooms contain the kids with more severe curiosities," I said, as I dragged him down the hallway. "More rooms to visit. As Howard would say, 'Precious time is wasting.'"

"Callaghan, you're a lunatic."

"At least I'm with the right person," I said.

He was about to lift me again when we heard something so foreign now that I stopped cold.

A baby was crying.

3.

We had no choice, but to walk in the direction of the cry. As our feet moved forward, the fluorescent overhead lights became dimmer and dimmer as if where we were going needed shadow and not light.

"Stick close," Daniel said.

I was so close that I stepped on his boots once, then twice. He stopped once and I crashed into his back. Then we heard it again. It was the high-pitched wail of a newborn human being. "It's not a baby," I whispered. "It's babies." The cry was not singular.

We passed rows of those little white rooms and resisted jumping when we heard odd scratching, thumping, and moaning sounds coming from within.

When we got to the almost proverbial end of the road, I saw two double doors that were propped open by white folding chairs. They were the second-to-last doors of a dead-end hallway. The crying had stopped and now I heard the gentle creaking of well-worn wood moving slowly forward and backward. Almost hypnotically, I walked through the doors.

It was a nursery not unlike the kind you'd find at any hospital in the living realm. There were three rows of clear plastic bassinets, each occupied by a squirming or sleeping infant. Each appeared to be one or two months old. Some were cooing, a few gently crying. On the white walls were gorgeous needlepoint art pieces created with love. There were pictures of ducks, trees, and even, alas, clowns. A complex feeding schedule had several red checkmarks indicating that little Joyce, Margaret, Joseph, Thomas, Charles, Frances, Willie, Eugene, and others had their meals every few hours.

She sat in the corner—a tiny figure at about four foot five, plump, and maybe seventy years old. I assumed she was their caretaker or nurse and I knew she saw us from her original glance our way. She didn't stand or scream. Instead, she remained sitting in a white rocker holding one of her babies.

"Dears, you can come closer," she said in a high-pitched voice. "Didn't much feel like getting up to greet you, which is so rude. Please forgive me, but the children have been so restless tonight. Maybe they know there are strange beings on the island—and by strange I mean the two of you and your friends. With all that is holy, I'm bone-weary tired," she said, smiling down at the infant. "But this one just won't stop crying unless I hold her."

The baby in her arms was beautiful, with big blue eyes, fuzzy blonde hair, and perfectly rosy skin. Her feet kicked inside the blanket the woman had swaddled her in. I could smell the baby powder and pink lotion.

The woman continued to rock as the baby in her lap nuzzled close. "Babies can sense disturbances," she said, gazing up at Daniel and giving him a hard once-over. "I get a good vibe from you, handsome. You can stay," she said, then turned her gaze to me.

Her brown eyes narrowed, but I didn't turn away. Instead, I did a quick scan of her weathered, lined face and choppy gray hair cut in a close crop. She wore what looked like a blue flannel nightgown and a big wooly gray robe.

"I've heard about you," she said, giving me the once-over three different times. "Mr. Howard told me about how he has high hopes for you. By the way, I'm Midge."

"Walker."

"I know."

"Go look around, Walker," she said. "It's best you know now. These are very special children."

Daniel shrugged his shoulders and stayed back by Midge. "So here at Frea—" he began. "I mean, here at Frederick Reardon, the students can have babies?" he asked her. I walked toward the rows of infants slowly enough, so I could make sure to hear the answer.

Midge just laughed for several long seconds and said, "And I thought I was punchy. The dead having babies! That's a good one. I can't wait to tell that one to Freddy later at the five a.m. staff meeting."

"I'm sorry," Daniel said.

"About saying such a stupid thing," Midge said, eyes twinkling.

"No, I'm sorry that you have staff meetings at five a.m.," he said, returning the smile.

I was never much of a baby person because my mother and I moved around so much and I didn't do that much babysitting. But I always loved kids, and used to think that someday I'd have two or three.

For a moment, I allowed myself to dream as I looked at the next sweet face of a baby girl named Margaret who had a thin dribble of saliva coming out of her mouth. Without asking, I grabbed a nearby towel and gave her a wipe. I didn't linger and moved on to a boy named Charles who was peacefully sleeping in only thin cotton diapers with a little blue blanket he had kicked off scrunched at the bottom of his bassinet.

I stopped at a baby named Eugene because his little arms waved in the air. I gave him my large smile and put out a finger. Quickly, he wrapped his tiny fingers around it and began to squeeze. Then his face turned red and his mouth twisted as he began to cry. It broke my heart and I wanted to pick him up, nuzzle him, and comfort him.

I wasn't sure if that was allowed. Still, I couldn't help myself and lowered my face to his. "Oh, Eugene, it will be okay. Maybe you don't like your name. Someday they'll call you Gene. Like Gene Hackman, the famous actor. Now that would be very cool," I said.

It was working. He stopped crying and I moved even closer, hoping to hear him coo or maybe even laugh.

But he twisted his face into a vicious sneer.

"What are you looking at, bitch?" he said.

4.

Reflex made me want to jump back, but I couldn't because he still had my finger in his now steely grip. The harder I tried to pull away, the deeper his little fingers dug in. They were like little blades and I could see my index finger turning white.

"What did you say?" I whispered.

"You heard me, bitch," he said. "I don't like Gene Hackman. I'm more of a Brando man."

Then he opened his mouth and I saw an entire row of discolored, but pronounced jagged teeth. Eugene popped his head straight up and lunged fast toward my finger. Baby or no baby, I pulled hard to the right, which tossed him on his side. In a rage, he used his tiny hand to push himself to his feet. Now standing, he lunged toward my face, and I used my free hand to shove him back. He toppled, but Midge was here now, gently lulling him back to a prone position. She swiftly stuffed the nipple of his bottle into his mouth. He still had my finger in a vice grip and it took all her might to pry off his fingers.

"This one," she said, chuckling, "is a bit out of sorts."

"What is it?" I cried, recoiling even further back and watching the blood flow back into my finger.

At last glance, I saw Eugene bite the nipple off his bottle and spit it out of his bassinet onto the floor. Then he chugged his milk, holding the bottle in both tiny hands. When he was done, he stood again and shot me double middle fingers.

"He's one of the Agers," Midge said, as if naturally *this was the obvious and only explanation.* "It's not his fault. Not his fault at all. He didn't ask for this. None of them did."

Daniel didn't ask for this either. In the commotion, Midge had handed off the baby in her lap and young Victoria wasn't a happy camper. Daniel looked helpless as the little girl twisted hard and then scrambled out of his arms, jumping onto his chest and digging her hands into his skin like one of the chest huggers in that movie about aliens. The baby then grabbed onto his T-shirt and used it like a rock-climbing wall, swiftly moving upward toward his face. I screamed and Midge raced on her short legs to them, tossing a cotton diaper over Victoria's face. She twirled the baby off him as if she was twisting the cap of a bottle.

"Victoria, you stop playing, you little monkey," she said.

In Midge's arms again, the little girl demurred until she was put back into her plastic box. "Now go to bed all of you," Midge announced. "If you want to go swimming tomorrow, you'll mind your afterlife mama."

To the two of us, she pointed to a little office on the side.

"It's where I keep the hard stuff like formula . . . and bourbon," she said.

5.

I took a seat next to Daniel on a small couch in the office, ignoring all of the pint-sized bite marks in the leather. Midge poured herself a tumbler of bourbon then two more. "Why not?" Daniel said, knowing it would have no ill effect.

"Make mine a double," I said, joining in.

"They're Agers," Midge repeated without much fanfare as she sat down in a reclining chair and propped up her pint-sized feet. "What I'm about to tell you will sound incredible or deplorable. That's for you to decide," she said.

We nodded and Midge seemed sufficiently convinced.

"It began during desperate times," she began. "World War II. The Nazis were winning. World domination was in their grasp. At the same time, they were doing unfortunate experiments in the camps. Hitler wanted to create the ultimate army of young men. He was secretly working on a scientific program to halt the aging process at age twenty-one when a young man was at his maximum strength. The tides turned. The Nazis began to lose. It wasn't long before the United States captured the scientists involved and brought them to America where their presence was kept highly secretive. It turns out they couldn't find a way to stop aging altogether and lock it in place. But they did discover a way for children to age in a very nonconventional way."

"I'm not following you, Midge," I said.

"Most parents want their children to grow up, mature, and

move away from home to start adult lives of their own. It's a normal rite of passage," she said. "But there are other parents who mourn the fact that their children will someday grow up and leave them. These scientists found a way to stop it."

Daniel shook his head.

"First, it was through injections and then medication. A child in the program would only advance to age to fifteen or sixteen. At that point, the medicine they had been taking since birth reversed the process and the child would slowly age backward. Bones and bodies would slowly shrink, but the child's mind, cognitive thinking and verbal skills, remained intact as a teenager. At every age level, they would think and feel as if they were still sixteen," she said. "Eventually, their bodies would return to an infant stage. The process would then begin again and they would grow up."

"What happened to these kids?" Daniel asked.

"They always lived with their parents, although eventually the parents had to move to remote locations and homeschool them because of the attention and questions," she said.

"It went on and on until the inevitable happened," she said. "The Agers began to take care of their aged parents. As time moved along, they had to live through the eventual death of their parents. When all of the parents were gone, the children in the program found each other and lived on a commune together in Oregon. En masse, they made a pact. They would stop taking the pills and injections—when this began they were given several lifetime supplies."

"And they died?" Daniel asked in a horrified voice.

"Not in the usual way. Some had heart attacks at age five. Strokes at age seven. Death from old age at age ten," she said. "But each was singled out from the start. We knew that they would come here to Frederick Reardon."

"Now what?" I asked.

"Even without the medicine, they're healthy again. Curiously, the aging and de-aging is just naturally happening to them still. We don't know why," she said, glancing at a large calendar on the wall.

"These are in the infancy period now, which enrages many of them. Imagine having the mindset of a sixteen-year-old, but you're stuck in the body of a baby? Imagine having the emotions of puberty, but being trapped in this small shell?"

We sat in silence for a few minutes. I had an eye on the nursery. Just in case. From the corner of my eye, I saw that mean little Eugene standing in his crib now, but his wobbly legs didn't support him. Just like a bowling pin, he eventually toppled.

"Man interferes with nature. Man makes the world implode. I'm just here helping to clean up the mess," Midge finally said.

"Speaking of messes," she added. "You've come this far tonight. Care to go a little further?"

I looked at Daniel.

Midge looked at me. "I know you brought it with you," she said. "We gave it to the Academy and Miss Travis gave it to Tosh."

My mind flashed to the night that Tosh stopped by our house with a manila envelope. Inside there was a small brass key with a note on plain paper that read, "The key is to keep the key with you at all times."

I reached into the pocket of my jeans, which contained my rabbit's foot and that key.

"There's a little more hallway left," Midge said. "And one more door. It's your choice, but really . . . why stop now?"

6.

It took us about three seconds to get out of there and suddenly we were back out in the white corridor with only one door left. I didn't sweat anymore, but I imagined my forehead covered in beads of it as we walked about fifteen steps and now stood in front of the last small window.

"Lift me."

Daniel gave me the hoist, but when I tried to look into the window, it was curious. Someone or something had painted the inside of the window black.

All Daniel could do was lower me and nod. I returned the gesture and fished the key out of my pocket. I held it out to him. Before he put the key into the small lock near the door handle, we both gazed past the room. There was no exit door or even a staircase up. There was just a white wall.

This meant that if something stampeded us after we opened the door, well, there was truly nowhere for us to go unless we wanted to burp the children from hell.

"Do it," I said.

The key fit perfectly. No surprises there. Two perfect clicks and I heard a spring bounce inside the door handle. Daniel motioned for me to twist the handle, so he could block if blocking became necessary. On a silent prayer, I turned it down in microinches, eventually pushing the door open just a bit. I could smell the fire.

The smell came from a small wood-burning fireplace in the corner. There was more than one creature in this room, and each was sitting in high-backed swivel chairs. One had dark hair; one gray; one no hair. The one with the gray whipped around first, sprang up, and moved to wrap around me.

"Miss Travis," I gasped.

Our beloved admissions guru at the Academy put a weathered finger to her lips. It didn't surprise me that Harold stood next. Finally, it was Howard who just swiveled around and gave us a grand smile. "Maudy, did I tell you, girl?" he said to Miss Travis. "I knew when I first looked at this one that she'd be doing some exploring tonight. If not, I was fully prepared to wake her up and drag her down here."

Harold quietly closed the door.

In many ways, it felt like worlds colliding. The schools here seemed to be their own separate entities, so to see Harold and Miss Travis communing with Howard was like Batman and Superman going on a joy ride and then out for burgers.

Harold spoke quickly, "Dark times are coming here," he told us. "So, yes, to your unspoken question. We know each other and we are working together, which is something you can never tell anyone else—and I mean anyone—including your family or friends."

"This is crazy," Daniel said.

"Not as crazy as a corrupt administration sending you kids on a fool's mission. Even scarier will be what you find when you go back," Miss Travis said. "And the scariest thing of all will be how what you find will be used."

"Maude, we have to get to why we're here tonight. Precious time is wasting," Howard said, moving to a large laptop computer on the only other piece of furniture in the room, which was a white, antique desk. Howard punched several keys. "It's Sunday morning. He usually tries to reach us around four a.m. our time," Howard mumbled. "We needed you to see it, which is why you were invited to sleep here at Frederick Reardon tonight. We knew that it wouldn't raise any eyebrows if we said this was about bonding."

We don't give a rat's ass about bonding," Harold added.

"Harold, really," Miss Travis scolded, and even our tough gate guard meekly looked at his shoes.

"I might have something," said an excited Howard, motioning Daniel and I to come closer to the computer. We did, and Howard actually stood and moved away. "I know he'd want to talk to you," he said. "You'll only have a minute."

The screen in front of me was pure snow. Suddenly, several zigzag lines appeared, morphing quickly into what looked like the inside of a cave. The screen shook as someone tried to right a phone camera on a nearby ledge. He set it down and then was too close to the screen. When he backed up far enough, the words flew out of my mouth.

"Dr. King!"

7.

"Howard, you did it," Dr. King said, a small smile playing on a face that was now heavily bearded. His hair was like this room. Snow white. "Walker. Daniel. You're a sight for very sore eyes," he said and I blinked back tears. "Are you okay? No worse for wear after ITT? When I get back, I'll have a word with the GF. You better believe that I will."

It was the same Dr. King, always putting his students in front of his own needs. I could only imagine how much deeper the pain was for Daniel who was saved when Dr. King fought off the demons in the living realm.

"Sir," Daniel said in a thick, chocked voice. "Is it really you?"

"Are you okay?" I added.

"Existing," he said as the screen broke up into wavy lines.

For what seemed like an eternity, we saw snow again followed by a loud buzz. "Are you there, sir?" Daniel asked. "Sir?"

I heard his voice again before I saw him.

"There isn't much time, son," Dr. King said. "So I'll make this brief. Harold was right. Dark times are coming to our realm. Your new principal waited for my absence to launch a chain of events involving both of you. You must be very careful. He's a ruthless man as is your father, Mr. Reid. I'm sorry to say what you already know."

"I don't have a father," Daniel said with a stone face.

The screen faded again. Dr. King popped back in a few seconds and I wasn't sure how much time was left.

"Where are you?" I asked.

"New York. Nineteen fifty-nine," Dr. King said. "I was in nineteen seventy-nine yesterday."

"How?" I replied.

"Walker, it will become clear once you pass through the next portal. Right now, I don't have long in this place, but let me make one thing abundantly clear to all of you. I've survived this long on sheer will. I figure I can last a little longer."

"Sir, we're coming," I said.

"I know," Dr. King replied, his words faster now. "That's why I needed to talk to you tonight. Because you have the stubborn gene just like I do. I need to remind you—no, make that order you—to actually accomplish the mission in front of you. You're not doing it for them. You're doing it for me. Find The Hiding. If it means never finding me, so be it. What you're searching for will change everything for the living . . . and the dead."

"No," Daniel said, stubbornly. "We will find you."

"Saving me is irrelevant," he reiterated.

Dr. King's face faded in and out, but I could hear him. "There are about five times in your life where you're tested, Miss Callaghan.

Even if you're ninety-six percent wrong most of the time, odds dictate you'll be right at least four percent of the time. I'm banking on your four percent."

A shadow lunged behind Dr. King, and then another. I saw it before he did and my words wouldn't come fast enough. It felt as if I was screaming in slow motion under water. "Sir, move!" I yelled as I heard something else scream.

Tentacle-like fingers stretched and picked the phone up off the ledge.

The screen filled with white snow.

8.

"Go back to bed, children," Miss Travis said, holding back her own tears. "The wall past this room is really a door. Feel for the handle in the bottom left corner, and then use Howard's private elevator. Go to your rooms, rest, and meet on the beach at seven-thirty to go back."

"Howard, thank you for your hospitality. We'll see you soon," Harold said.

It was 4:30 in the morning on the isle of Freaks. I had never been more awake. Daniel and I packed with record speed and then tried to get a little shut-eye, but it was pointless. Around six a.m., I saw a shadow of feet standing outside the door and heard the scrape of an envelope sliding underneath it. Bouncing out of bed, I scooped it up and ripped it open.

It was a note that read: ENJOY YOUR LAST DAYS AND NIGHTS IN THIS REALM. YOUR MISSION BEGINS ON SATURDAY, SEPTEMBER 25, THE AUTUMNAL EQUINOX, AT PROMPTLY 10 A.M. FURTHER INFORMATION WILL BE PROVIDED. THE HIGHER AUTHORITY.

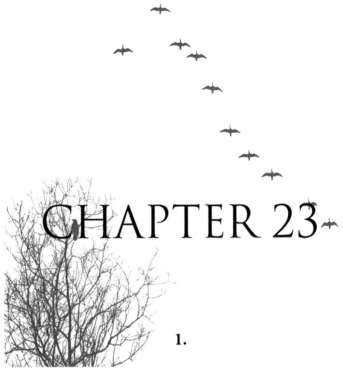

CHAPTER 23

1.

Two weeks passed in a blur of schoolwork and keeping up appearances. It made me sad each time Tosh talked about something we could do in the fall because I knew I wouldn't be there. We had Auggie sign Bobby up for flag football fully knowing that we might never see him play a game.

We didn't speak much about what happened at Freak Island, although occasionally I saw a hopefulness in Daniel. "He's alive," he said on Friday morning, the day before we were scheduled to leave. He had the kind of hope and vigor in his voice that I hadn't yet heard from him about this trip. "He's in New York. We're going to find him."

Pete's ears perked, so we eventually told him about Dr. King and I could see him contemplating. He didn't have time to ask questions because the kids were suddenly racing through the kitchen. Andy and Jenna alternatively helped me make pancakes and asked me about their dresses for tonight. Our send-off would be the big end of summer dance at the Academy.

"Oh, Walker, we've been looking forward to this dance *forever.* You promised to help us get ready," said Andy. "The dresses you helped us pick out from Myrtle's are so perfect. I'm wearing the mango and Jenna looks at least sixteen in the lavender."

It dawned on me in that moment that I never bothered to find a dress for myself, but that was fine. The last thing I really needed to do was go to a school dance. "We have a giant surprise," beamed Jenna, racing into the living room and dragging something out of the foyer closet.

"We got you something because we know you're busy and we've never really had a biggest sister before," Andy said, her gray eyes bursting with excitement, and that trademark black Reid hair piled up in a high pony on top of her head. She looked so cute in her little owl PJs that I nearly lost it.

"Ta-dah!" she said, grandly. "We got three dresses and Jenna took the best parts from each and we made you something spectacular!"

It took both of them to rip off a piece of plastic that was housing the dress. With great flourish, they both now held the most beautiful petal-pink silk strapless gown made with a layered organza skirt festooned with large light-pink roses.

"Do you like it?" Jenna whispered.

I threw down the spatula I was holding and took three steps until I had her in my arms, kissing her forehead. "I don't know what to say," I said. And that much was true. "It's the most beautiful thing ever."

"We know Danny got you a really pretty dress, but you can never have enough princess gowns," said a sheepish Andy.

I opened my arm wider and she joined us. "We love you, Walker," Andy said.

"I love . . . all of you," I said, my bottom lip trembling. Daniel just stood by the kitchen counter, sipping his coffee, smiling in that way where he didn't think anyone was looking.

"I love all of you, too," said Auggie, annoyingly cheerful as he came bouncing in from a back bedroom. He had stayed over since the previous day's training went late into the night. He joined the girls and me in the hug, almost squishing us. "Why are we hugging?" he asked, his own tears threatening to run. Then his attention diverted. "Do I smell pancakes?" he said, still hugging, but with his stomach also on high alert. Bobby was there by now, breaking out the plastic forks and racing him to the table.

2.

We had no choice, but to finally tell them over breakfast. "We have to go back to the living realm again—after the dance. This time, its Principal Dick and the Higher Authority who need us to go on a mission there," Daniel said and the girls looked at each other with a sort of knowing dread. So much for the joy of the last few minutes.

"Pete is going, too," I said. "So is Iz and Bertha."

"I guess you'll have to move to the Academy. It's the smart thing to do," Daniel said. "It's probably the safest thing, too, since you won't have any adult supervision or protection here."

"Protection from what?" Jenna snapped. "Him?"

"Our so-called father?" Andy interjected.

"But Bobby will have to stay with the little kids in a different wing, so we'll never see him. And what about Jake?" said Jenna, who was becoming more like a mini-me in the way she rattled off the questions. "Why can't we stay here alone, the three of us—me, Andy, and Bobby? We can protect Bobby and ourselves. We're not children. At least, I'm not a child."

"Out of the question," Daniel said, omitting the part about daddy dearest wanting to take Bobby only. "What happens if he pulls up in his Mercedes and demands you get into the car?"

"We're not stupid," Jenna said, quietly. "And we know how to run."

"I'm going with you back to life. I know how to do it. You know I do," Bobby said, smacking his lips and drowning his cakes in syrup. "I'm bringing Jake since he has lots and lots of canine friends who can help us. Doberman. Labradoodles. Maybe even wolves. I'll pack my backpack and bring my slingshot."

"Wrong answer," Daniel said.

"Right answer," Bobby argued, stuffing his little face.

"So here's how it will go. I'll stay. The whole time," Auggie said. "You need a semi grown-up and I'm good with kids. I can't cook, but I can order out. Heck, by the time you get back, I'll turn them into a mini orchestra."

"And if there's trouble?" I said.

Auggie wiped the smile off his beautifully round face. "No one is taking those kids anywhere. They'll have to get through me, which isn't an easy route."

There wasn't much discussion.

It was decided.

3.

We walked to the fall dance, the entire Reid family plus the one who never left—Auggie. It was one of those perfect sunsets where the pinks and purples served as a backdrop that looked like we were walking into our very own happily ever after.

"Oh, baby," Daniel, had said when I first twirled around for him an hour before in the privacy of our room.

In that humid summer air, he had danced me down the stairs, out of the house, and onto the front lawn while the kids groaned and the dog danced merrily around us.

Daniel wore black jeans, a white dress shirt, and black tie. His motorcycle boots were the perfect finishing touch. His onyx hair was slicked back off his face, but the dangerous stubble remained. The invite from the Academy did say that it was a formal, and as usual, he followed less than half the rules. That was half as many as he was used to following.

Pete was in a blue suit and we dressed Bobby in little white shorts, a white shirt, and a white jacket. "It itches and I look like a snowman," he cried, but he didn't put up that much of a struggle. "Let's go, let's go, let's go," he cried, racing down the street.

We walked past Perks and Angelina gave us a full-throttle wave from inside. A middle-aged man I had never seen before was outside the local movie theater changing the marquee. It read: HARRY POTTER MARATHON. NEXT SATURDAY'S SPECIAL GUEST SPEAKER: THE ACADEMY'S VISITING PSYCHOLOGY PROFESSOR, ALAN.

"Save you some tickets? I know you've probably seen the movies before—they're timeless, as is Severus," the man said in a beautiful, almost lyrical, English accent. I smiled and shook my head. It made me wistful because I knew that we wouldn't be there.

"We won't be around," I replied, trying not to stare.

"Well, I certainly hope you're going on an adventure, young lady," he said with a smile. "It would be wonderful to think that the future is unknown and sort of surprising."

"Wouldn't it, Mr. . . ." I began.

"Call me Alan," he said. "And please do call on me when you return. I love to hear about adventures."

Despite the fact that I tried not to let my mind go there, I had that sinking feeling that we wouldn't be back. At least not for a long, long time. I knew Daniel felt it to his core. He allowed Myrtle to rush out from her dress shop and not only hug him warmly, but also adjust his tie—maybe for the last time. The old gal with the flaming red hair did a real double take when she saw me. "Jenna! I might have to hire you, you little seamstress, you," she said to the beaming young girl.

My hair was long and flowing in my strapless dress and that wasn't good enough for Vidal, who had kept his salon open late tonight. He was walking down the sidewalk when he saw us. "Walker, darling, you can't possibly . . . no, I won't have it . . . so wrong with that neckline. It will only take a few minutes," said the hair guru.

"I wish I could, but I can't . . . the kids. We're going to the dance," I began as a thrilled Auggie almost shoved me inside the salon where the fine smell of hope and hairspray mixed.

Soon, I was back with a serious updo held into place with a small diamond-looking tiara. "You don't have to bring that back," Vidal insisted. "It's a copy of one that belonged to Rita. Darling, just don't tell anyone it's not real. On you, it looks like diamonds."

"You look like a princess," Auggie gasped.

When my eyes diverted left, I could see Daniel smile from the bench he waited on with the kids. Even in those beat-up black boots, he managed to bow when he got close. "May I?" he asked, taking my hand and folding it in his. "Follow me, Cinderella."

We didn't have to climb the long driveway at the Academy as the teachers had provided a slew of horse-driven carriages to take us the rest of the way. I gasped when I saw Miss Travis in a sleek, black column dress, egg-size diamond earrings hanging from her ears. She had never looked this glamorous before. I had to hug my surrogate grandmother.

"Life is short. Youth is finite. Opportunities for joy are endless. Let's experience joy tonight," she said, giving me a small peck on the cheek.

It took two carriages to bring all of us to the expansive front lawn that was decorated as if we were at a wedding. There were roses in bright pinks, reds, and yellows and overhead lights twinkled merrily above us. A lone violinist played a melodic classical piece as we approached the party.

I whispered into Daniel's ear about Tosh approaching Pete and asking his blazing red face—and the rest of him—to dance. Daniel kissed me tenderly. We talked like lovers and laughed like coconspirators.

I knew I wanted to dance when a tall man in all black took the stage. "I like odd places. Farms. Prisons. But this place, well, it's something else," he said.

"Who are you?" yelled one of the freshman.

"Sometimes I am two people," he said into the mike. "Johnny is the nice one. Cash causes all the trouble. Let's see who wins out tonight."

4.

After the dancing, I went inside the main building to do a little damage control. The first thing I smelled when I walked into the ladies' room was the acrid scent of cigarette smoke coming from the two closed bathroom stalls.

I had no idea who was in there and coughed when the gray smoke clouds floated my way.

There wasn't time to be disgusted. My attention diverted to the four girls primping at the two sinks that had miniscule mirrors above them. They were party crashers standing in dresses that were too low, too short, and just plain skanky.

They knew I was coming. They always knew.

Claire V and Claire C gave each other a knowing look almost daring the other to speak first. V won that one. "Well, look who just walked in," V taunted, pivoting sharply toward me on her mile-high black stilettos. Her red leather skirt was barely past the underwear line and her gold halter left almost nothing to the imagination.

C gave me a slow once-over, her strapless fuchsia dress short and tight.

"Even if you dress her up, she still looks like poor Walker Callaghan," she smirked, allowing her eyes to wander around my beautiful homemade dress.

That one landed. Hard.

Claries A and S migrated to standing in front of the only door. V and C took a small step closer to me. Armed with nothing, I glanced at the only window, which was above the mirrors. Escape wasn't an option.

That's when I heard it. Both bathroom stalls blasted open—metal slamming metal in an epic crash. Stepping away from one porcelain toilet, a tall girl in a white minidress took one last puff on her cigarette, sent it down to the floor, and then used the foot of one of her stilettos to twist it out.

Her friend, in a white leather jumpsuit, took a long drag and blew smoke all the way up to the ceiling.

Demanda was the one who was now without a cigarette.

My eyes widened when she looked at me hard.

V and C scrambled to take possession of the mirrors again as if sink time meant bathroom dominance. They gazed at themselves, but kept an eye on Demanda and her friend Jennifer still standing half in the stall and half out behind them.

"Crashing another one of our Academy dances?" Demanda jeered taking two steps closer to them as she used her long nails to intimidate a few stray hairs.

The Claires preened and puckered. They refused to do one thing: speak.

"The Freak boys not dating hags this season?" Demanda needled. Then she lowered her eyes for a second as if she was about to apologize.

"Sorry, I mean to say old hags. From the look of things, very old hags."

V and C didn't answer, but they didn't move either. Their sisters S and A still commanded the only door. Demanda took another step closer to the mirror, invading some space, while still staring at V's and C's reflections.

Finally, one spoke.

"What the f— are you looking at?" V asked, pointing her mascara wand at Demanda's reflection.

My eyes bounced from V to C to my least-favorite Academy cheerleader. And then the unthinkable happened. Demanda looked at me again—and gave me the slightest of head nods.

"What am I looking at?" she snapped, focused back on V and C. "The answer is simple. Your ugly faces."

By now, Demanda edged her way so close to the sink's counter that with one pronounced hip thrust to the side, she bumped C into the fresh T-shirt dispenser.

Rebounding off the plastic knob, C reached out to grab a clump of Demanda's hair and pulled hard. My hand flew to my mouth when Demanda twisted hard, ripping out a clump and then firing both hands out to each side.

Like some sort of beautiful ninja, Demanda unleashed her three-inch, tomato-red nails, swiftly clawing those pampered talons down the pale sides of both Freak faces.

Shocked by the quick assault and Demanda's obviously blank mind, the Claires scrambled. Pivoting hard on her heels, Demanda rammed a full-throttle, closed-fist punch into V's midsection. C aimed with a fist and missed when Demanda dropped low, a move she no doubt perfected from hours of afterlife Zumba. Bolting up, she sunk a hard knee directly into C's boobs—the ultimate girl assault.

The Freaks didn't have the reset and C shrieked in pain as her strapless bra snapped.

Demanda spun again. She had me on lock.

All of my training went out of my head as I stood like a deer in her headlights.

"Let's go, Walker. Move," she commanded, stepping over C and V who were both slumped on the floor now surrounded by their nearly hysterical sisters.

I didn't need to be told twice. My ass was in overdrive.

Like a trained poodle, I followed on the heels of this former cheerleader's fuchsia stilettos. Jennifer kicked the door open and suddenly we were back in the Academy's plush hallway where Van Gogh's artwork stared down at me while shock continued to set in.

Holy shit.

"Holy shit," I said under my breath. I was still walking.

Holy shit, holy shit, holy shit.

I was still following.

Somewhere between the poetry lab and zoology, Demanda put on the brakes, whipped around, and faced me down. She gave me the second slow once-over of my evening as "why" continued to flash in my eyes.

Only then she answered.

"You may still be a bitch to us," she said, tartly. "But you'll always be *our* bitch. Have a nice night."

With that, Demanda and her minion blasted through the outside doors to go back to the dance and were gone.

My mouth was still open as I numbly navigated my way back to fresh air through those same doors. My first site was Tosh balancing a plate of frosted chocolate brownies and fried chicken.

"Were you just talking to Demanda or am I suffering a cerebral hemorrhage?" she asked.

Only three words applied.

"We weren't just talking. We were on the same side."

"Of what?"

"Savage girl fight," I said.

"Holy shit," Tosh said.

5.

There wasn't time to dwell—although, if a situation ever demanded dwelling, a girlfriend, and a pint of vanilla, this was it. Back to reality at the dance: I was being assaulted from an entirely different front and his aim was uncanny. Walter, in black suit pants and a white shirt, wound up and pinged me in the shoulder with a bunch of wadded-up napkins. I could see Jenna and Andy giggling in their swirling big girl dresses.

Always a prankster, my favorite gym teacher grabbed a chicken wing off Auggie's plate, took a bite, and then gave the wing back. Walter had young Pete, suffering in the only suit he owned, in a chokehold. Then he let go to do a quick lap around the lawn, eventually leapfrogging over all six foot two inches of Daniel.

Daniel and Pete took off running after Walter and I laughed watching them. Eventually, they had the pro where they wanted him. Daniel had his arms, Pete his legs. They carried him near the pond, which was decorated with gorgeous floating candles. Easily, Walter twisted out of their grip and grabbed each by an arm. Daniel and Pete allowed it and Walter stopped short of shoving them in.

As he released them, he wrapped a protective arm around each and reminded them, "I always figured it this way: If I'm going to get hit, why let the guy who's going to hit me get the easiest and best shot? I'd explode into the guy who's trying to take me out. Explode first, ask questions later. Safe travels."

He winked on the last word, released them, and moved on to torment another student.

It occurred to me. Those weren't just frivolous words, but a lesson.

He knew what we were doing. Where we were going. He was one of the few Dr. King had trusted.

Kurt seemed to know, too. In his version of formal—a fresh white tee and black jeans—he walked up to me, smiled, and handed me my phone, only I didn't know it was missing. "I downloaded some of my favorites. You know. For the journey," he said. "Don't look at the titles. Just go with it."

"I don't know if I'm cool enough to have you make me a mix tape," I said with a grin.

"Rather be dead than cool—remember that sweet Walker," he said, winking as he walked away.

He knew.

I tried to divert my focus back to the beauty of this breezy, humid night. All the food was practically spilling off tables for this late-summer feast. Anything you wanted, from sizzling steaks to corn dogs to grilled burgers on large buns, was there for the taking—along with creamy salads, lush fruits, and pecan pie. Auggie, who planned to walk the kids back early, piled his plate high and Bobby was grabbing things off of it.

Leaning against a tree lovingly looped with tiny white lights, Daniel took a pull on a beer.

He was watching. Waiting. Protecting.

If something happened to him . . . well, I couldn't even wrap my mind around it.

We were leaving in the morning and something that Miss Travis said to me a long time ago went through my mind. "They say you end twice," she said wistfully on a rainy day during one of our late afternoon chats. "One time is when you stop breathing and the second time, a bit later on, when somebody who matters most says your name for the very last time."

I stood watching. Then I closed my eyes. When I opened them, Daniel was kneeling down in front of me.

He dug into his pocket nervously, fumbling. Then finally pulled out a small box that he opened slowly because boxes this size didn't work with big fingers.

Inside was the most perfectly round ruby set into a filigreed, antique band in platinum. "I've wanted to give this to you for a long time," he said. "The truth is I found this in the woods the day I met you. I picked it up. Kept it. And I didn't know why. You know I'm not someone who believes in flowers and rings. I don't even know what they mean. And I really don't know what they mean now because I don't have a lot to promise. I have nothing except this beautiful idea that if there is a tomorrow, I want to spend it in one spot, looking at you."

A tear tumbled as he put the ring on my pinky finger.

"I love you," I said. It was the first time I allowed myself to say it.

Then I made my knees buckle to fit myself into his body.

It was our shop teacher, Chuck, who interrupted us. "I'm signing you kids up for sex ed when you get . . ." he said, leaving out the word "back." "Why don't we ground whatever this is—and I don't want to know. Come with me."

When he winked, I knew we had no choice.

Chuck knew. Unlike the others, he was about to do something about it.

6.

"You don't concentrate on risks. You concentrate on results," he said, walking us through the musty-smelling shop class reeking of wood and fresh oil, and then winding us out the back door onto what looked like a dark loading dock. "No risk is too great to prevent the necessary job from getting done," Chuck continued.

It was another moment wrapped in a lesson. Chuck wasn't even subtle about it. He was mysterious as he walked us off that dock into the grass, which didn't really work with low heels. Somewhere in the middle (our favorite place), Chuck stopped walking long enough to duck behind one of the few elm trees in the midst of the nothingness. Then he flipped what looked like a large lever embedded into the wood of one of the trees.

Suddenly, the field was illuminated from the center by giant floodlights. My eyes narrowed to focus on what looked like a small runway. Off in the near distance was something that looked like a tin garage, but it was really an airplane hangar.

Chuck walked us to the hangar, pressed a code into a panel on the tin wall, and a door slid up. Our teacher flipped another light and we were all gazing at what looked like several small vintage planes from World War II.

"I see a beauty with our name on it," Chuck said, lovingly running his hand on the silvery metal of a plane that had the words Aidy's Aces painted in white on the side. Aidy was a redhead painted next to her name, a bombshell in a very low-cut dress.

Darting a look from Daniel to Chuck, I made my role in this perfectly clear. "I'll stay down here. I appreciate the idea of a ride, but I've never been up in a plane before," I said, looking back at Daniel. My tribute to poverty was still something I liked to keep under wraps. The truth was, buying bus tickets to Milwaukee was a splurge for Mom and me.

Daniel didn't even hear me. The man making promises a minute ago was now ashen white. That's when it dawned on me. I was nervous when it came to the unknown like flying, but he died in a plane crash.

"With respect, sir, no way in hell," he told Chuck. "My flying days are over. Never again."

"With respect, let's cut the crap," Chuck retorted. "I should have done this a long time ago with you Dan, but now it needs to be done. New York is a big place. Never know how you'll have to travel. And because of that fact, I want you to confront your last fear before you go."

He darted a look at me. "Yes, Walker, I know. A few of us know. The Higher Authority has their board, and we have another, more secret board amongst the teachers for what's coming," he said under his breath. Then he returned his attention to Daniel.

"Get in my plane. If you want me to say it nicer, I will. Get the hell in my plane, pretty please with sugar on top."

Daniel looked about as immovable as a mountain. Glancing around him, I watched Chuck pull down the silver bird's door.

Inside was an almost empty hull with six seats in back, the pilot and copilot chair up front.

"I have to say I'm with Daniel here, Chuck," I said. "We appreciate your concern, but . . ."

"Get in the damn plane, both of you," he said in a booming voice that made me physically jump.

Then he turned to Daniel and said, "If you can't trust me as your pilot then who can you trust? I'm not your old man trying to grow a pair holding a joystick. I could fly this thing upside down blindfolded in a thunderstorm. Get in. That's an order."

I'm not sure when we joined Chuck's military, but he was so commanding that my legs obeyed and soon I was inside that tin bird. His manhood challenged, Daniel bit out a few choice swear words. Then he followed.

I knew he didn't want me to see the fraction of a second when he closed his eyes.

Maybe it was to pray.

"One more order," Chuck said, lowering his voice and looking back at us before he strapped himself in. "Make it home, kids. Make it home no matter what. Do whatever it takes to make it home. Nothing else matters in life or now except that you make it home." His voice choked on those last words as he clicked his buckle and pressed several buttons. A loud whirl and the plane's engine roared to life.

This was home to Chuck.

"Let's go for a ride," he shouted with glee.

7.

"You want to fly. You have to let go of what's holding you down," Chuck said, focusing on Daniel who was trying to be strong, except I saw his hands shaking.

Our shop teacher's words haunted us as we hunkered down in the hull while Chuck went through his preflight motions. "I got clearance," he announced and I wasn't sure who was the tower here.

Chuck proceeded to taxi down that small runway, the vintage plane whining as it raced for freedom. Our pilot pulled on the throttle and then we were off into the black, starless night sky. Chuck pointed Aidy's nose at a sharp upward angle.

"Yeee-haw!" he yelled.

This time Daniel didn't try to hide it. His face was the color of fresh milk.

"Close your eyes, baby," I said.

"I'm fine," Daniel insisted. His jaw was clenched and I saw beads of sweat forming.

Once I got past my own fears, my pulse settled and I felt giddy and energized. As the jet began to level out, Chuck wasn't satisfied and pulled back on the throttle again. We ascended straight up. "Say one word and I'll put this baby into a roll," he said, unable to sound like an older man. He had the tone of a twelve-year-old boy.

Finally, I looked out the little window into the night sky. A sense of calmness washed over me as I became one with all that blackness.

"We're nearing twenty-thousand feet," Chuck said. "Which brings me to the point of tonight's ride."

I was listening and Daniel's eyes were still half-closed.

"In times of great danger, sometimes you see a light and it gets you through," Chuck said as the plane entered what looked like a giant white cloud. "And other times, like right now, you have to make your own light."

Chuck punched it. The plane blasted through the cloud and our pilot quickly circled around so we could see what he just did. Quite simply, he made a giant hole in the cloud that light was now shining through—thanks to a big ol' harvest moon the color of liquid gold.

"It's called a Skypunch," Chuck said. "All those highfalutin astronauts use the word, but I like it, too. Clouds are cold. When the heat of a plane goes through a cloud, it burns a giant hole. A circle. It allows the light in."

"When it gets real dark, punch it like I just did," he continued. "Make your own Skypunch. Make your own light."

Chuck looked back at us as if he was making a memory.

"That's enough wisdom tonight from an old metal jockey," he said. "Anyway, I gotta land this thing and go back before my wife finds out I snuck away again."

"You don't live here full time, do you?" I asked him.

"Not yet," he said. "But I like to straddle the dimensions."

For a minute, he was silent. But when he spoke, Chuck had our full attention.

"Get out," he said.

Daniel's eyes popped all the way open.

I could see Chuck whip around again. "Do you have a hearing problem, son? *Get out.* Pull that little handle on the door and get out. I told you that my wife is expecting me back. I gotta fly this baby home."

Glancing around the hull, I saw that there was nothing to use.

"But, sir there are no chutes," I stammered.

"You'll be fine. You have the reset. And I'm hovering over a great landing spot. Get out," he said, looking at Daniel whose eyes were now wide open. "Get out now unless Ms. Callaghan, you're a wuss and Mr. Reid, you're just a puss."

I stared at him in disbelief.

"A wuss and a puss," Chuck continued, grabbing the throttle. "I'll go down to fifteen thousand feet. Then that damn door is going to open."

In the end, he gave us no choice. We just had the hope that the reset covered this level of stupidity.

It was the wuss who opened the door and felt that hard rush of night air. I couldn't help but look down. And when I did, the sight took my breath away.

I had never seen a star, ever, during my time here. But now, with my eyes on the ground, I was looking down at what must have been a million of them. There were endless bursts of pure white light emanating from terra firma below. The reflection was so blinding that I could only gaze at it for a second.

When I looked away, my eyes were imprinted with sparkles.

"It's beautiful," I whispered.

Chuck's voice was reverent this time. "We're above them. And by them, Walker, I mean your mom, my wife, and the others who are alive. When you were alive, didn't you ever look up into the night sky, just knowing that you saw someone you loved up there? It's real. They look into the night sky and see us. Tonight, from up here, you can look down at the dead. And see how you shine."

8.

I closed my eyes.

We were now falling into the blackness. Flying free. It was an adrenalin rush powered by a universal bolt.

Me in one word: unlimited.

When I opened my eyes, I saw that my petal-pink skirt was billowing up like a cloud. Letting out a breath, I kept trembling as Daniel held me tight and we plummeted fast as rockets. At one point, we seemed to pause, perhaps swept on a current of warm summer air. Looking down at the stars below, I felt the recognition. Glancing way upward into deep black, the mystery made me ache.

Arms wrapped tight, I looked into Daniel's eyes. We were soaring.

Much faster than I wished, I could see the land below and spied the castle that was the Academy. In the distance, ITT hung off a tall mountain while the waters to Freak Island churned violently.

Our realm was bigger and bolder than I had even imagined, with snowcapped mountains I had yet to see and various other massive structures that remained unknowns. What else was here? And why was it?

Why is it that we don't widen our gazes until we're forced to do so?

Flying together, my legs wrapped hard around him, I spread my arms and threw my head back as the wind kissed my face. When I came back up and tangled my arms around him, Daniel gripped me with his arms and let his legs go, superhero style.

It was a sky ballet with my mind providing the music. The moves were so graceful, delicate, and poetic that my heart felt full. And I finally let go of the past. I loved my mother, but this wasn't our journey anymore—it was mine. Maybe that's what they mean by growing up.

Drifting down, I allowed myself to float, wishing it would never have to end.

It was terrifying and empowering. It was flying and falling. It was loss and love.

As the wind rushed us down, my eyes ascended. Daniel had me pinned in his gaze as the night sky served as our road to everywhere.

"You are my heaven," he said, letting me go.

He knew what I wanted: To be my own pilot.

It turns out Chuck positioned us perfectly. My landing was hard, but cushioned as my backside scraped that frozen waterfall and rode it down to earth like the grandest slide. Daniel was right behind me and together we crashed into the freezing cold water immune from summer's heat.

Water. Air. Earth. Sky.

I didn't matter. I was still drifting in the direction of a soft laugh that became louder. Killing a demon was one thing; conquering one like a fear of flying was far more satisfying.

My boyfriend was now howling out pent-up rage with delight.

It was a deep and delicious sound that made my blood jump. I'm not sure if I swam up to Daniel or he grabbed me, but soon his fingers were curled in my hair, the pins and tiara long since gone. I touched an index finger to his mouth. Gently, he removed it and kissed me with persuasive mastery.

He cupped my face between his hands and went lower.

Clothing became a barrier at best. He unzipped my beautiful dress and flung it onto a rock. The cascading water crashed around us, as suit pants and shirt were recklessly thrown away and floating downriver. The water was ice and my body was fire. The mix made me feel bold and reckless.

He had such a male face and a stare that was unmatched in its intensity. I placed my hands on his strong chest to feel what was inside. He took his hands, cupped my elbows, and plunged both of us deeply underwater. We descended now, a tangle of arms, legs, and longing.

We made love on a soft sandy spot on the river's floor with that early fall moon serving as our candlelight. Silly me. The moon was starting to retreat for the night. As Bob Seger sang, "Ain't it funny how the night moves . . . with autumn closing in."

As for the last bit of brightness, it was Chuck. Making the light.

Punching the sky.

CHAPTER 24

1.

It took us an hour to walk home in what remained of our tattered clothing. Daniel actually found his suit pants on a rock and his boots in the dirt. As carefully as possible, I smoothed out that beautiful pink dress, thankful that the material was so thin that it dried in minutes. What was left of it covered most of me.

So many times on that walk, I felt Daniel turn his head and just look at me as if he was trying to memorize something. When I finally met his gaze, I saw those pools of liquid silver lamenting the fact that time was moving so quickly. In a few hours, the sun would kiss the sky. It would be dawn.

"Wanna grab breakfast?" he asked. His voice was low and my breath caught. He could have been reciting the ingredients from a cereal box and I would have had the same reaction. Gently, he took my face in his hands and said nothing. He said everything.

It wasn't long before Angelina was serving us eggs and toast at

Perks, which apparently was open at this hour. Or maybe she just knew. We dumped too much sugar in our coffee, kissed a bit, and ate our last meal here. I knocked over the OJ glass; he sopped it up with a hundred napkins. Angelina didn't say or ask a thing. It was perfect. It was us.

In that moment, I knew that eternity was overrated. I would trade it for five minutes with him. Perhaps reading my thoughts, he held my hand under the table.

My mind kept replaying our time in that shaking plane with the wind rushing around us. My, oh my, had my existence expanded since I met Daniel. We went skydiving tonight. We were human birds. "You're doing something that makes you feel uncomfortable," Chuck had said. "*That's* living."

That was living.

Why didn't I do more of it when I was alive?

2.

We snuck into the house at four in the morning like our parents were up and waiting. Like there would be repercussions. Of course, that wasn't the case. Instead, we beelined to our bedroom, stripped the remains of our clothing away, and then cuddled in our bed. At first, we cuddled face-to-face, a strong finger tracing over my chin, my nose, the side of my face.

When Daniel was half-asleep, I rolled over and he wrapped his solid arm around me, hauling me in closer. Nothing describes that feeling.

Nothing.

3.

I had willed myself not to drift off, but somehow I let go of the rope and drifted. In my sleep, I heard him before I saw him. His tanned, square-jawed face and long, sun-drenched hair looked like he had just surfed the sunrise. He floated somewhere behind my eyes in that watery time before the night lets go.

"I'm trying to be respectful," Cass said in a low voice like he didn't want to wake anyone, "but there are times when all the trying in the world gives way to what your heart wants." Then he cleared his throat. "This is wrong," he said. "You're in bed with him—and me, because I can't leave you alone. How respectful is that?"

I didn't answer him.

"Walker? Someone needs to get out of this bed," Cass said.

Of course, he was right. And under other circumstances, I might have explored what his persistence could mean. But these weren't other circumstances. I was in love with Daniel and this bed wasn't big enough. Beds are never big enough for three grown people even if one isn't there physically.

I had to dismiss him for good. If I formally dismissed him, he had to go. It was the only thing to do.

"Walker, please," he said, but he didn't beg. Too proud. It was almost as if he was saying it for my own good. "I'm sorry. But I'm not sorry at the same time. I should have told you about my sisters. I was protecting you from thinking about it when you were with them. You would have thought, 'He's their brother? They're related.' My face might have popped in your mind. I have a way of blocking them, but I'm not sure how long it will hold. They're evil. That's why I . . ."

His voice trailed off and something horrible dawned on me.

"The last time they died . . . did you kill them?" I asked. The question had lingered in my mind since our last conversation.

"I didn't save them," he said. "Is that killing someone? I don't know."

"This is none of my business," I said.

"I remain your business," Cass said.

"Cass, you have to go," I said, firmly. "I'm grateful for everything you've done for my mother. More than I can ever say. But I need you to go."

A minute passed.

"Take it back. You can always to take it back," he said, his voice already fading. His image looked like he was slowly disappearing.

I was silent.

"I could use a good yes right now," he said from far away. Cass's head dropped, and when he lifted it, I saw that his face shimmered. It was tears.

"Thank you for everything," I said. "Tell my mother I love her."

"You're betting eternity on the wrong man," he said in the faintest of voices. The last thing I saw was Cass reaching out a hand. "Walker, our destiny is to meet each other again and again. I've waited too long to tell you why. I love . . ."

I opened my eyes wide.

It was morning.

4.

We dressed silently in a room that didn't feel as if it belonged to us anymore. I bashed my leg into the nightstand; Daniel swore when the medicine cabinet slapped him in the face. I felt like a stranger in my own house. Downstairs, we went through the motions of a family breakfast, although no one ate a thing including a despondent Bobby who was fussy and whining while smashing his Lucky Charms into dust.

After, we returned to the room to pack, although there wasn't much room in our silver packs for more than a spare pair of jeans, leggings, a few shirts, and toiletries. It was New York circa . . . we didn't know yet. We'd have to lift some winter coats once we arrived.

I remembered the rules of the living realm. The living could not see us or hear us unless they possessed certain gifts like . . . I wouldn't say his name. If we touched objects like their food, coats, etc., then they became invisible, but were still missed by those who were alive. It was the classic case of I put my keys down and then they disappeared. Blame the ghosts.

The worst of it was that the reset was gone. We could feel pain, hunger, and exhaustion. This delighted the Ka-like demon forces, distorted versions of our former teenage selves, which were lurking. They mostly came out after midnight with the express job of extinguishing us. Why? When we died the good parts of us ascended. Our lesser sides—pain, rage, and jealousy—remained back in the living realm. As young ghosts, we would be forced to deal with never-ending battles.

To that end, I made sure my lucky rabbit's foot was stuffed into the pocket of my pack, which also contained a picture of my parents and a crayon drawing Bobby made me of the entire family. The rest of the pack contained all the medieval weapons we could carry on our backs. Our favorite gym owner made me enough throwing stars to defeat armies of demons. In the pack, he wrote a note: BROADS RULE. WHEN YOU'RE THERE, LOOK UP THE YOUNGER ME—JT. In black leggings and a black shirt, I put on the same gray trench coat from that day in the woods with him. It was mine now.

I wore it as I walked through the house, hugged the dog, and met the others on the front porch. The kids looked sullen and didn't ask many questions while our own personal Mary Poppins paced like he would wear out the boards beneath him. It was still early morning and Auggie was wearing a Bart Simpson tee and long flannel Grinch PJ pants. "I got this. I really do got this," he said, like he was trying to convince himself that he could keep the kids safe during our absence.

In dark jeans, a black tee, and his leather jacket, Daniel hugged the trembling girls, whispering his good-byes to make it private. I bent down to cup Bobby's face in my hands. "You're a liar, Walkie!" he cried. "You're my new mom and now just like her you're gone! I hate you now!"

"You don't really mean it," I said, opening my arms. He pulled away.

Bobby gave the same treatment to his biggest brother. "I'm going to go live in the woods!" he cried. His little red Keds kicked my favorite white planter that was lush with pink and white leftover summer peonies.

"Andy, Jenna," I said, embracing the girls who couldn't even speak. "Sisters forever," I said, gripping them even tighter.

I didn't see the silver Mercedes silently pull up in the driveway. Edward Reid was swift today, grounding out a cigarette on our walk upon his exit from the car. "Just as I expected," he said with disgust. "I knew I'd find some sort of nauseating good-bye scene."

"Enjoy your suicide mission," he said to the three of us. As he approached, stopping again on the front lawn, he addressed me in particular. "I only hope that you survive to see them extinguished," he said pointing to his sons. "My fondest wish is that you return here alone, which would be the worst fate of all."

Jenna took a step forward and then another until she was at the tip of the porch.

"I hate you," she said, looking at her father.

Edward just stared at her blandly. "I never wanted you. Or you." He was pointing to Andy who stepped up next to her sister.

"When it comes to fathers, we never wanted you either," she said, defiantly.

Daniel began to advance, but Pete held him back knowing that Edward would have delighted in sending his oldest to ITT now in the eleventh hour, to worry himself sick, while the rest went on the mission.

"Robert," he shouted to a wide-eyed Bobby. "Get in the damn car."

For a moment, Bobby didn't understand. No one ever called him Robert. "Damn, damn, damn, damn, damn," Bobby began to sing, bending to grab something that he left on the floor. It was his pocket rocket, a small, but high-powered slingshot. He pulled back on the yellow rubber and landed a rock right in the center of his father's chest. "Bang, bang, you're dead again," Bobby said. "I killed a monster."

Of course, Edward was perfectly fine. He brushed off his jacket with disgust and didn't skip a beat. "I've already made the girls wards of the school. Consider yourselves orphans now," Edward said. "Robert, get in the car. I have custody of you as your only parent. Or I can come back in an hour after they're gone to take you."

It was Auggie who barreled down the front steps until he was suddenly towering over Edward.

"You again! Who are you?" Edward hissed.

I knew in that moment why Daniel and Pete hadn't taken care of business. They needed to see what the gentle giant could do.

"Who am I?" Auggie said, calmly. "Well, Mr. Reid, I'm just like every other pissed-off teenager who has some serious issues with authority figures. There's just more of me to be angst-ridden."

"I repeat. Who the f— are you?" Edward said, advancing toward Bobby.

"I'm the bitch who is going to rip off your other arm if you touch these kids," Auggie replied, stepping directly in his way. "Get the hell off our property."

I glanced at Daniel who seemed pleased. By now, Bobby was safely on the roof, a toy sword in one hand, and a little plastic shield in the other.

What diverted my attention was a sound next door in the house where I had lived with my mother. No one had occupied it since we did. Yet, someone in the shadows had turned on the hose and was watering what looked like brand-new red geraniums. It was odd because I never saw anyone move in, let alone plant flowers.

She was outside now, a woman in her early thirties in a long, lovely deep green dress and my mother's white sweater. Stick straight blonde hair fell halfway down her back. Her sky-blue gaze caught mine for a second and I felt safe.

Andy was the next one to notice and she was cougar fast. Bounding off the porch, she took the two stairs like they were made of air. She was next door in a flash, and without a moment's hesitation she threw herself into the woman's open arms.

"Mama!" I heard her cry.

5.

Maureen Reid was almost six feet tall and breathtaking in every way. Strangely calm, she didn't race to her children, but with the self-confidence of royalty slowly made her way the few steps across the lawn. Her unnervingly direct gaze, something she shared with her oldest son, never left her husband's frozen look of horror. Keeping him locked in her gaze, she took Jenna in her arms for a long moment while making some sort of wiggling hand gesture to her oldest sons.

"Mommy?" Bobby said, and I heard him put those Keds in overdrive. He climbed from the roof, slid back into his bedroom, raced down the stairs and flew out the front door. Maureen Reid gracefully bent down, smoothing Bobby's hair back and whispered something in his ear.

"Yeah, I do remember. I really do," Bobby said, his face wreathed in smiles. "Oh, Mommy."

Auggie was still towering over Edward, but one touch from an advancing Maureen made him step back.

Edward spoke first, which I imagined was their usual pattern.

"What do we have here? Are you back from some pig farm in the sky?" he asked. "As your husband, I deserve an explanation. What are you now? What have you become?"

"Empowered," she said, taking a slim finger and putting it on his puny chest.

Harold pulled up at that moment, throwing the Bentley into park. I saw that Iz and Bertha were already in the back, and then, from the front passenger's seat, Miss Elizabeth swung out her famous gams while waving a handful of paperwork. "I'm so happy to report that it's finally settled," she said. "Mrs. Reid naturally has custody of the minor children now because she was their primary caretaker in life." With her shimmering eyes narrowing on Edward she purred, "Someday we might grant you visitation—or not."

"This isn't over," Edward hissed.

His wife now pushed him again with the finger.

She waited for the moment. A woman of few words, she spoke

her mind.

"Go back to hell where you belong," she said.

In the end, Edward went back to his primary relationship, which was with his car. Soon, he was peeling out of the driveway screaming obscenities and promising vengeance.

As always, time was never on our side. We had exactly seven minutes before we were tardy for our mission.

In two giant strides, Daniel was in the middle of the grass embracing his mom who also pulled Pete in tight. I couldn't really hear what they were saying because their words were hushed and fast. Suddenly, I felt like the odd one out. This was their family reunion—this was their family—and there was no need any longer for the stand-in.

Awkwardness seemed to climb up my body like a rash.

There was no point to going back in the house, so I puttered around on the porch, putting toys into a little chest and picking a few of the peonies for the girls to put in the kitchen. Checking my watch, I could see that time was dwindling. Four minutes until we needed to be on the beach, per the instructions of the Higher Authority. I wondered what would happen if we were late? Would we miss the bus back to the living realm?

When I bent over to smooth out the dirt in the flowerpot, I felt a firm hand on the middle of my back.

"I wasn't sure this day would ever come," Daniel said in a thick voice. "Walker, I'd like you to meet my mom."

Sunday school manners.

"Mrs. Reid," I said, extending my hand, which she clasped tightly. "It's so nice to meet you."

What would she think about me living with her son? There was no time to really find out. Three minutes until beach time.

"I know all about you, Walker. It was a long trip here and Mrs. Travis is very thorough when it comes to her files," she began and I tensed. I wondered in that moment what she knew. How much she knew. Her husband seemed to know everything bad about my past. He had already pointed out everything lacking.

My face fell. I didn't want to meet her gaze, so I looked down at my peonies.

She reached low, picked one, and put it in my hair. Then she took her finger and titled my chin upward. "We are our flaws and our damages. That's what makes us human and so lovable," she said, looking deeply into my eyes.

She wasn't done.

Lifting her horse pendant from my neck, she said, "It's where it belongs now."

I don't know why I did it—and maybe I never would. Maybe for a moment I wanted to imagine that she was my mom.

I leaned in and gave her the tiniest peck on her right cheek.

"I know what you've done here for my children—and I can see how my oldest feels about you," she said, smiling. "There are no words."

I turned my face down again.

"I would have really died without your family," I barely said.

"Our family," she said, lifting my chin again and then kissing my cheek. "Family of the heart."

6.

In the backseat of the Bentley, with Harold driving at a breakneck speed to the beach, Daniel couldn't make eye contact with me.

Wouldn't.

I knew he would never allow me to see him cry because in his mind mountains didn't crumble. I felt it before I saw it.

It was the soft plop of a lone tear, hot like it had been warming and waiting a long, long time to release. His tear was filled with years of missing her and only moments of relief.

I put my index finger on top of the tear and absorbed it into my skin.

He had taken on so much of my pain. It seemed only right to love in reverse.

7.

When's the exact moment when summer slips into fall? I could smell the fresh chill of autumn on those sandy shores of our beach. In that rocky and creviced soil, there were still bright, tender young flowers hoping to poke through. My mind flashed to fourth-grade English and Mrs. Ehm reading us a poem from Robert Frost who wrote, "In three words, I can sum up everything I learned about life: It goes on."

Big, strong Harold didn't offer us any speeches or words of wisdom. He pulled the Bentley into the sand and jettisoned out to open the door. Daniel and Pete jumped out, but I moved slower as if leaving this leather cocoon might mark the crossing of an invisible line.

A large hand was thrust into the car and I accepted it. Harold yanked me out and then grabbed me gently by the chin. "You never know, Walker Callaghan, just who you might see in New York City. It's a big ol' place. So save a piece of pecan pie on the other side for your favorite gate guard."

Throwing my arms around him, he caught me. I knew he would.

I didn't realize we were getting an official send-off, yet various members of the Higher Authority greeted us on that sand. They had the look of older souls sending the young off to war: Guilt mixed with sadness and just a touch of envy.

Eddie practically tripped over his brand-new white athletic shoes as he pushed past Bertha, A.E., and Iz, and raced up to me. "I have all the good stuff in my pack. Goldfish. Kit Kats. Twizzlers and Snoballs. I smashed in a dozen Twinkies," he boasted. "I mean, who needs clean pants when you could have quality snacks?"

I don't know why, but I hugged Eddie Wargo.

Mid-embrace, my legs felt like stone.

We were actually doing this.

Our illustrious Principal Dick almost tripped in the sand as he reached for his megaphone. As usual, he had a minion next to him to turn on a tape recorder for the official record.

"As we previously discussed, what we're looking for has been hidden in history. You will have to prove your worth and trustworthiness to those who have been entrusted with The Hiding. If they deem you of the highest caliber, you will receive a clue that will lead you to the next clue. In the end, you will find what you must bring back. There are twenty-seven mortals that were trusted with this secret over the ten different decades you will hunt in. Once you obtain a clue, the entire team will find themselves transported to a new decade for the next search. You only need to convince ten of those entrusted with The Hiding that you're the ones sent for good and not evil. You might run into other hunters of The Hiding who are there for nefarious purposes. Trust no one," he said. "It's imperative that you work as a team until the end when you can work alone. A strong team will ward off evil forces and other hunters. Inevitably, some of you won't return here. If any of your teammates are extinguished, you will not stop to mourn, but continue on your mission."

"One last crucial item," he added. "It is inevitable that your mere presence in the living realm will change certain individual fates. But you can't purposely try to change history in any bigger ways or history will change you."

"We need you to clarify what that means," I demanded.

"Miss Callaghan," he retorted, "how would you like a world where you had never been born?"

Principal Dick cleared his throat and resumed with his last agenda item.

"The student who hands me The Hiding will have their mission wish granted," he said, turning to Daniel. "Perhaps your mission wish is the gravest, Mr. Reid. Upon returning, if you don't personally hand me what I need—if you return at all—you will resume your eternal sentence at ITT."

"Don't give me excuses," Principal Dick concluded to us all. "Just give me results."

Any further words were cut off by a giant splash in the rippling, greenish water. The Mermen had arrived with several small, wooden rafts for our transportation needs. Daniel went first and helped the rest of us get our footing on the small wooden slats. Bertha commanded her own raft with two Mermen, which if the mood weren't so somber would have delighted her.

Our friend Connor swam Daniel and I out to Freak Island, a sad smile playing on his handsome face.

For a moment, as we crossed the choppy water, I closed my eyes.

I had to test this now.

I half expected Cass to come to me, but he didn't.

It was just as well.

8.

At Freak Island, Howard was waiting with two pristine white SUVs that would drive us up to the school—one for him and one for the rest of us.

He caught me watching him toss a perfectly new bar of soap into the sand. "I like to wash four distinct and separate times, using lots of lather each time from individual bars of soap," he said in a low voice. I nodded with respect. "I'm praying for you, girl," he said, handing me a bar of soap for the road.

Howard stayed with us as we walked through the partially desolate and magical lobby of Freak U. There was a smattering of employees and few students around, but they paid no mind to us. Speaking of which . . . the Claires were locked and loaded, packed and ready, sulking and preening on a plush purple velvet couch while Tor was pacing, trying to wear out the sparkling floor beneath him.

All of us packed into the largest service elevator and at the last minute, a small group of students pushed on. They were going to LL for their studies and I couldn't even look at them. How envious I was of a normal school day. Howard pointed for me to push another button. I didn't have to ask. I pushed RR and HH smiled.

"Precious time is wasting," he fretted.

9.

Dark and dank are the only words that described the lowest level of all. The walls were made of filthy white tile and the rest was slathered with black paint the color of tar. I could see Howard recoiling from the dirt, but he stood his ground in this dark hole. In the middle, there were steel tracks that led past my vision point.

It made absolutely no sense.

Who puts a train station on an island?

10.

From miles away came a violent shaking that sounded like rumbling thunder. Something was ripping its way through the darkness and I saw what looked like a large yellow eye barreling toward us.

There was a light at the end of this tunnel.

Just not that light.

This light was a train.

“The Red Eye from the living realm,” HH confirmed.

Darting swiftly toward its final destination, the train choked to a shaking stop where I counted thirty shining cars grinding to a sudden halt. The high-pitched, repulsive sound of screeching metal filled my ears as the silver bird came to a complete stop.

Only two train cars opened.

Numbly, I started walking forward.

“Don’t be heathens. Have a little manners!” scolded the

conductor, a bony man in his seventies wearing a black-and-gray uniform with lettering on his pocket that read: REALM PACIFIC.

"Your classmates have had a long, hard journey," he cried.

Even Bertha backed it up. Then we watched.

What got off that train had me silently wincing because it slithered and slimed, whined and cried, as the recently dead, oddest life forms floated, fretted, and even free-fell onto the platform. One young man looked like he was made of see-through tissue paper. Another bounced high like his flesh was made of rubber. A lovely young girl in dark braids walked off reading. The only thing though? The book was poised at her midsection.

"Existence," I whispered.

"Have some freaking manners. Make room for our new teacher! You're lucky to be the first to welcome him!" the conductor shouted.

He walked off last, running a hand through longish white-blond hair.

"I'm David," he said to no one in particular. Then he threw his hands overhead and twirled around like he was on stage. His chuckle became a full belly laugh. "I always said, 'I don't know where I'm going from here, but I promise it won't be boring.' Turns out, Bowie, you were right."

"All aboard!" roared the conductor.

We boarded the silver car where there were twenty rows of padded black leather seats. I didn't just sit next to Daniel. He spread his legs and I melded myself between them.

"Nothing really ends that's not meant to end," he reminded me. I wrapped my hands around his legs and he dotted the top of my head with his chin. "I love you, Walker," he said, banding his arms tightly around me.

"I love you. Forever," I said, turning to bury my face in his warm neck.

The train whistle screamed. The doors slammed.

Four hard chugs and the train roared back to life. Gathering speed with each microsecond, it burst out of the station and angled upward, causing a blast of pure sunlight to flood the dirty windows.

Tracks rose from the sand and brush as the train pulsed toward the beach. "Stay tight," Daniel whispered as we headed toward the water, thirty tin cans and engine plunging hard into the sea.

The water swallowed us whole and we sank hard and fast. My pulse began to pound and my body jolted when we hit bottom. There was no time for thinking or reasoning. Metal began to rise, grind, and then lock. There were tracks! On the ocean floor!

Bright gold and yellow fish swam wildly next to our window only to be brushed away by human fingers. Whizzing by us were our friends, Connor and his Mermen, hands raised, waving wildly. I put my hand on the train window.

They had one more trick. Underwater, the Mermen lined up and unraveled what looked like a homemade poster: KICK ASS AND DROWN ALL PRISONERS. BE SEEING YOU.

These tracks blasted us straight to our beach, where the train rose out of the water, drops raining down. Jettisoning ahead, I watched as additional tracks lifted in the sand as we were carried forward toward our own woods. As we entered the dense trees, something rather unbelievable happened. The trees took it upon themselves to carry the train from here. The cars each locked into the tree roots growing on the ground. I walked over these roots every single day, but didn't know that they were an intricate maze of tracks leading . . . I wasn't sure where.

At breakneck speed, we were screaming toward the center of my favorite redwood tree, a wide, immovable giant that was certainly hundreds, if not more, years old.

Before we crashed into a million pieces, my eyes fluttered closed. But I forced myself to open them.

I would no longer be a victim of my own fate.

Impact was an unyielding jolt that jacked all of us out of our seats. Bracing for the inevitable explosion, I waited on that filthy train's floor for the fireball that would incinerate us, melting our bones.

We didn't detonate.

The train began to glide like butter on a hot pan. Then the conductor jammed on the brakes and I tumbled forward, bashing into flesh and steel. The pain was searing and to make it worse, I felt claws on top of my numb arm.

"Welcome back to life, bitch," said Claire V. "You're not going to last five minutes."

I've never been much of a back talker, but now I wanted the floodgates to burst. I willed them to blast open. My blood felt like it was on fire.

In the end, I didn't talk at all. I just looked out the window. And I laughed.

11.

In total darkness, the train was still and I felt the air tremble.

The living realm enveloped me, although I wasn't alive and didn't belong here—never would again.

But oh, given just a moment to linger, I could make history repeat itself. I could play the old movies, knowing the plots and twists, embracing the costars, and closing my eyes at the sad parts. I could see that girl with the hope in her eyes. I could reach out and touch my youth.

I could also feel time and how it erases all things. We just leave behind an echo.

Your life is just your place in time.

In the end, there is only one reason to exist in any real way: To embrace the wonder.

"Baby, where are we?" he asked.

"Somewhere in the middle of the infinite," I whispered.

THE END

Acknowledgments

Mary Altbaum, you are a writer's dream. Thank you for being such a genius, nothing slips through the cracks, inspirational, and amazing editor who has made this the journey of a lifetime for me. Are you ready to dig into A3? Wait, just kidding. Let's take a night off!

To Adrijus G. of RockingBookCovers.com, a true visionary visual artist. I said "train" and you came up with another masterpiece cover and killer teasers. Thank you for sharing your immense talents with this series. Each time I get an e-mail from you, it's like Christmas morning and opening a wonderful present.

Once again, thank you Emily Tippetts for your amazing inside design. A special thank you to Tianne Samson and Stacey Tippetts for your beautiful work.

Orian Williams, you are such a creative force. Thank you for all of your love, wisdom, advice, and friendship.

A very special thanks to Vicki Rose for getting the word out. You rock! Thanks Crystal Hernandez for your help each day with social media. Thank you Annie for being a great PA. Big love also to the beautiful bloggers and new online friends I've made during the release of book one. I would love to name all of you, but would be so mad at myself if I left anyone out. You know who you are.

Big love to my amazing friends including Joyce Persico, Sally Kline, Vickie Chachere, and Carrie Healy. Major love to my family including my parents Paul and Renee Pearlman, my brother Gavin

Pearlman, sister-in-law Jill, my niece Wylie, nephews Cade and Reid, and brother-in-law Jack "Uncle Buzzy" Gaber.

Big shout-out to my office administrators, Georgie Doodle and Coltan Shepherd. "Will work for kibble and pets" is their motto.

To my bonus daughter, Sabrina Gaber. You have grown into such a smart, beautiful, accomplished young lady. I'm so proud of you—and not just because you work so hard at school and at dance. But because you're just amazing in every single way. You make each day sparkle for me. Love, your bonus mom.

And finally, to Ron, who owns my heart and keeps it so safe and secure because he's the most loving person on this earth. Thank you for being you. And thank you for being that boy who kissed me at the bottom of the pool when I was seventeen. It's only more beautiful now. Love you more!

COMING SOON:
ASCENDERS: OMORROW (BOOK THREE)
THE CLAIRES

Contact CL at CLGABER@Yahoo.com or
WWW.ASCENDERSSAGA.COM

CPSIA information can be obtained
at www.ICGtesting.com
Printed in the USA
FSOW01n0853290118
43926FS

9 780996 242097